Adeline Dutton Train Whitney

Bonnyborough

Adeline Dutton Train Whitney

Bonnyborough

ISBN/EAN: 9783743305540

Manufactured in Europe, USA, Canada, Australia, Japa

Cover: Foto ©Andreas Hilbeck / pixelio.de

Manufactured and distributed by brebook publishing software (www.brebook.com)

Adeline Dutton Train Whitney

Bonnyborough

BONNYBOROUGH

BY

MRS. A. D. T. WHITNEY

AUTHOR OF "FAITH GARTNEY'S GIRLHOOD," "THE GAYWORTHYS,"
"HITHERTO," THE "REAL FOLKS" SERIES,
"ODD, OR EVEN," ETC., ETC.

BOSTON AND NEW YORK
HOUGHTON, MIFFLIN AND COMPANY
The Riverside Press, Cambridge
1886

The Riverside Press, Cambridge:
Electrotyped and Printed by H. O. Houghton & Co.

CONTENTS.

The Riverside Press, Cambridge:
Electrotyped and Printed by H. O. Houghton & Co.

CONTENTS.

BONNYBOROUGH.

I.

THE SCHOTTS.

"PEACE POLLY."

The congregation stared, and the child screamed, all through the christening.

"No wonder," said the rector's lively little wife to him, when he had got out of his surplice, and was walking along with her homeward in his coat, — "no wonder. 'Peace Polly Schott!' 'Pease porridge hot!' is what it will get to be called. Lucky you did n't have to say the surname!"

"Now, Dora, — Pan-dora, — don't let *that* out of the box!" said the rector. "Other people may n't think of all you do," — which, indeed, they would often have had to be nimble to manage.

"But just think, — if she *should* 'lead the remainder of her life according to this beginning'!"

"*Wifie!*" said the rector. He always said "wifie" when he reproved her, and I am afraid that was not seldom. But he did it under that tender acknowledgment that she was one flesh with himself, even in faults, after all. "You are making pleasantry of the Prayer-Book, now. And remember, too, that this beginning is not the outward, natural one, but the very thing that is to shape and overrule it, — the grace prayed for and promised."

"Oh, I know, dear," said Dora, meekly. "But it *is* funny. And I can't help feeling the grace will all be needed."

So Peace Polly Schott was in the world, and in the church. And both, I may as well say at the outset, grew to be lively in her, as she grew and was trained.

She inherited, perhaps, some curiously balancing or contending characteristics from the same descent through which had come her names. They were the names of her two grandmothers, — Peace Marvin, a sweet old Quakeress, and Polly Schott, the smartest, drivingest, most uncompromising, of housekeepers and family managers. She got her quick perceptions and energies and her hasty tongue from the Schott side; something inward and hidden, that often secretly arraigned and testified against the outer self, from the dear old disciple of the Inner Light.

I have said a good deal about names in many stories I have told; if I live to tell others, I may say a good deal more. For Shakespeare never suggested more deeply than when he put the question, "What's in a name?" I think, myself, there is pretty nearly everything in it; though, as in that other matter he discourses of, we are some of us born and fitted to our appellations, while upon some of us they are thrust, and are either an irony through life, or fit us to themselves by the wonderful power of Name upon the thing or soul that bears it. Why should it not be a power? It is given us solemnly, in the very moment that we are baptized into the Name of the Lord. And the Name of the Lord is his own revelation.

Any way, Peace Polly was the very impersonation of hers, with all its associations. She was born with a rush in her brain, a quick, intense flow of life, and the recognition of life. She was full of idea, of purpose, and she was intense of will in the carrying out of these. There followed, naturally, with one of her temperament, an impetuous rebellion against whatever contradicted, crossed, or thwarted. Things, happenings, doings, — all fell under her sudden indignation, when they jarred, interrupted, contradicted. And inside, all the while, was the " grace " that would not let her be angry comfortably, — a " peace " that spoke itself to her rebukingly in the very midst of her explosions. But nobody knew about this, save herself and the Giver.

Peace Polly was the youngest child of her father, and her mother was the second Mrs. Schott. There had been an interval of eighteen years between the little girl and her half-brother, Lyman. Lyman was tolerably fond of his little sister. He liked, also, to " stir Peace Polly up." He had a quiet, narrow mind, as different from Peace Polly's as calm daylight through a shutter-crack from forked lightning across the sky ; that was what came between them of the two mothers. Lyman saw just what that chink-ray fell upon, — saw it clearly, exclusively, but not an inch on either side of it. Peace Polly's thought illumined all creation to her, for one minute, and was apt to strike somewhere. But it was over — the insight and impulse — as quickly, often. She had many an eager notion, which she raged if opposed in, but which, if left to herself, she might speedily have done with, as a thing exhausted in the inception. She had frequently had enough of it before there was time or opportunity to carry it out in practice.

The nursery rhyme did get fitted to her, and by slow brother Lyman himself. It was apropos of these her brief enthusiasms : —

"Peace Polly 's hot,
Peace Polly 's cold;
Peace Polly 's got a lot
Of plans, but they 've all gone to pot,
Nine days old ! "

And by another application, once, when she had banged away to her own room, and slammed the door, after a wrathful outburst at him, and he coolly followed to write upon the outer panel in pencil, —

> "Peace Polly 's hot;
> Peace, Polly scold!"

These were two of Lyman's exceptional inspirations. He was not ordinarily quick in any sense, and I think these were somewhat careful impromptus elaborated between times.

It is impossible to say that there was nothing in Peace Polly's name to her experience long before she herself was fifteen and Lyman thirty-three.

But Lyman never knew that after the door was slammed in his face that day something gave way in his little sister's heart, and she was down on her knees in the window, with her head upon the sill, and great throbs were seeking their way upward as into the deeps of calm blue that she did not even lift her eyes to, but, like a little publican, clenched her two hands tight across her breast, and sobbed out, purposeless and yet as to Some One, "Oh, I am just hateful, and just as I do hate to be!"

Not knowing, he went on, in a mild, slow, almost mechanical way as it came to be, "stirring up Pease Porridge."

"I wish you'd get married, and go off, and let people be!" Peace Polly said to him, when she was ten and he was twenty-eight.

"Ho, ho!" laughed Lyman.

"Only I pity your wife," added Peace Polly.

"So do I," said Lyman, gravely. "So much that I shall not let her be. You'll grow up, Pease Porridge, and keep house for me when we 're two old folks, — or an old folk and a half. We shan't be exactly old together."

"There 'll have to be two to agree to that," said Peace Polly, in an elderly way.

"Or three, may be. Though it is n't likely," returned Lyman.

Peace Polly looked up with shrewd inquiry.

"What ain't?" she said.

"Number three."

"I know what you mean," said the child. "No; number three *ain't* likely. It 'll be number one, if anything."

"Guess so, too. Would n't advise you to skip him," retorted Lyman, with obscure satire, half suspected by little Peace Polly.

When Lyman went out of the room a few minutes after, she walked straight to the looking-glass, and gazed searchingly and unflinchingly in.

"I ain't pretty, and I ain't good," she said, solemnly honest with herself. "Nobody 'll want to marry me. That 's what he meant. Well, it 's a long time to look forward to, and a good many things may happen," she added, quoting from her child-memory a speech of Mrs. Schott's. And with that she turned away from the glass, and went back to reading "Diamonds and Toads," from which and its companion tales she had got all her present ideas of marriage and seeking in marriage. She could still put herself by into that dim future between now and when so much might happen, and be heart-absorbed in the fates of Blanche and Dorinda.

The first Mrs. Schott had been a zealous, faithful, Puritan woman, a church-member, and conscientious in her family relations, after that devoted and anxious order. Mr. Schott was not a "professor," but he was a very fair, kindly, upright man, according to the light of nature; and nature's light is God's also, that lighteth every man that

cometh into the world, though it be only by his grace that
we find it out to be his light and his living love.

Lyman Schott was, of course, baptized and nurtured
according to his mother's persuasions. He accepted, in
his quiet way, what he had been taught, and in the same
quietness and dependence had submitted himself in due
time to the spiritual processes and helps that he found at
work and offering around him, and took his Christian
name in simple earnest at nineteen. It was not the fault
of his religion that he was of but a limited nature; without it, mere petty earthliness would have left him really
pitiful.

The second Mrs. Schott, Peace Polly's mother, had been
an Episcopalian. Her husband, being no church-member,
adapted his church-going to his wife's, who again, in her
different fashion, was zealous in her faith. And so it was
that the brother and sister held their Christianity under
different forms, and sometimes, as such very different tem-
peraments and characters are liable to do, attributed each
other's incompatibilities and failures to the spiritual quality and motive, when they were quite distinctly of the
flesh and its feebleness. It was odd that the one who
took things in grooves was the non-conformist; that the
other, striking out in all things to test and know for herself, was of the order and succession.

"What you want is to experience religion," Lyman had
said to Peace Polly in some of her tempers.

And she had retorted, "So I am experiencing it. That's
just the trouble. I'm experiencing it all the time. I can't
make it such a short and easy job as you have!"

"If you had a real conviction, Peace Polly" — began
Lyman again, for he felt it his duty; but duty could
not carry the man of slow and reluctant self-utterance
through the sentence. Polly snapped it up.

"I'm under more conviction of sin every day than you ever had in all your life! I know every time I'm ugly, — and you don't!"

It was unrevealed to Peace Polly, in her turn, that Lyman went away silently with that sting, and took it home to himself in a certain dull fashion, which made him quieter and more careful with her for very nearly a week. After that the impression wore down, and habit had its way again.

"Don't you hate people that keep their tempers?" Peace Polly asked of her elder friend, Serena Wyse, into whose bright little kitchen she had run one day with an errand, and paused, as it was her privilege and custom to do, for a bit of neighboring beyond the errand.

Serena was the only person Polly had to neighbor with. There were others not further off, geographically; but Peace Polly used to say she didn't "care to run in, where she wasn't in after she got in." That country phrase of "being in with" people held truth as concerning the intimacy of our tumultuous Peace Polly with calm, considerate Serena Wyse, more than a dozen years her senior.

Miss Serena was down on her knees on the hearth with a dustpan and brush, a heap of sweepings, and a piece of newspaper. She did not answer Peace Polly at once, but finished gathering her dust into the pan, whence she carefully swept it again upon the opened paper, and then proceeded to roll it snugly up therein, making of it a tight little bundle. This she tucked under the sticks that crossed each other tidily from the bright andirons to the clean red bricks below, ready for any future fire-lighting.

Peace Polly was diverted from her subject. "Well! isn't *that* a way!" she exclaimed.

"It's one of my ways," said Serena. "You get rid

of it. It don't fly and scatter and come settlin' back. It's bound to get burned up, some time, and you don't see it waiting. I like things done with, when they are done, specially dirt."

"Serena," said the girl, "don't you wish we could sweep ourselves out so?"

"And take the trash up in dustpans, and bind it in bundles to burn it?" answered Serena, falling into the Scripture word that had said it long before, and that came now, answering of true accord the question.

"Why, that's it!" cried Peace Polly. "That's clearing up, and putting away. Not even hiding in a dusthole; much less putting in your pocket, Don't you hate to have a person 'pocket an affront,' Serena?"

Again Serena did not answer directly. She seemed to follow the first word of her companion, passing over, as unheard, the rest.

"Putting away," she repeated. "Don't everything that comes up just bring some bit of Bible with it, and show it new?" Serena said "niew," with a trace of the peculiar New England voweling; but what does that matter to mention, except that we hear her as she spoke, and so as a living voice? "'He put away our sins by the sacrifice of Himself,'" she quoted, once more involuntarily. "Folks can't put away ever so little an affront without a giving up. Somebody must give up, always, when things fall wrong. I guess that's to *for*-give, — to give for. We couldn't come out of our horridness and give up to Him, till He first come and give up to us. Then it was done. It ain't even in human nature to hold out after that. 'While we were yet sinners,'" the dear little woman went on in a low voice to herself, "'Christ died for us.'"

There was the great, blessed Gospel in a mustard-seed.

Peace Polly was touched. But she had a grievance; she had come to her friend with it, and she could not go away with it as she had come.

"The worst thing that ever happens," she said outright, "is when Lyman begins to keep his temper! It's more awful in the house than a dynamite cartridge!"

"Hush!" the color was up in Miss Serena's face, and her eyes flashed.

Peace Polly stared. Was there dynamite even here, also?

"I beg your pardon, my dear, but I've known Lyman Schott all my days. He's a good man."

"It's his goodness I can't have any patience with," said Peace Polly, her tone lowered. "I wish you had the good of it a while, Serena, — I just do. I'd like to see how you'd make out with it."

"I know his ways, dear," said Serena Wyse. "We all of us have our ways, and most of us have our queers. But he's a good man." And Serena's face stayed rosy, after the rebuking flash had died down. She was very pretty then, with the pink tremble in her cheeks and the blue sparkle in her eyes, although she was over thirty, and nobody was likely, ordinarily, to consider the whether or no of her prettiness.

It came upon Polly, though; and other things in the light of it. She looked at Serena with what people call a blank surprise, — the blankness that intervenes when one sudden idea drives a former out, but is not defined or clear enough to replace it.

"I *wish*" — she began to say, hastily; and then for a wonder fulfilled her name and held her peace, took up the little pitcher of buttermilk she had come for, and went off abruptly.

Serena stood still a moment; then she went and hung

up her dustpan in the corner under the shelf. "It's the child's fashion," she said to herself. "She's got a sight of sobering down to do."

Serena wist not of the face-glow, nor of its lovely tale-telling of a commotion in her life so far off and long ago.

As Peace Polly hurried across the field by the diagonal footpath that gave the short cut from Miss Wyse's kitchen porch to their own, her unsettled trouble tossed itself uppermost again in her mind, and she burst forth, aloud, all alone, —

"If *anybody* only knew! But nobody does — just how it is — to *me* — but me myself!"

One can't be precise with the nominative case, when holding one's self so utterly in the objective with commiseration.

II.

GRANDFATHER SCHOTT built his house double, to accommodate two households of the same family : his own and great-uncle Aaron's. He looked forward to its serving the same purpose for his own two sons, Aaron having no children. But only Joshua, of the two young brothers, survived to occupy it, and to bring there in succession his two wives, as we have seen.

The house was carefully planned and divided to take in the sunshine for its occupants, share and share alike ; though he who can so build a dwelling, or order a family, that no one part ever stands in the light of any other will have achieved what was not even attempted in the solar system, which patiently suffers its eclipses.

The old man fronted it to the south, however ; and the hall, which was both common and separating, as the sea is to the nations, opened through the middle ; a wide parallelogram, — or cubic space, taking in its height, — of really noble size, though plain as a barn as to architectural adornment. The big staircase adorned it inevitably, as a generous smile graces a homely countenance ; it offered easy access and welcome everywhere, like the whole-hearted hospitality of a finely unreserved nature. There were private staircases, smaller, one in each independent wing. These wings were curiously lapped on to the central structure : the easterly one running southward, and the westerly one north, that each might afford in its projection the aspect denied in the apartments joining and opening directly from the hall; so that each inmate had east, south, and west exposures, advantaged yet further by cut-off corners, broadly windowed, at all points except the northerly ones. So scrupulous was the equality that a little corner bay jutted slightly from the west wing at the front, giving on that side a slant bit to the southeast, otherwise lacking. The building, therefore, in its initial plan and chief outline, lay somewhat like a winch, or windlass-handle, along its green level, its west wing running so close upon the quick ascent of a rugged knoll to the north — one of many that gave a real, honest, time-used name to the farmstead and property — that it quite carried out the suggestion of a huge crank set there against it, to draw out of it its treasure, which in good truth poured forth from the shaded rock-face, exactly opposite, across the footpath; namely, the clear water of a mountain spring that found its outlet here into a basin built for it, and supplied the dwellers in absolute untaintedness with one of the two purest things that God has made. The other, the sweet air of piny hills, came down without conduit or hindrance, and swept about them its invisible, waving mantle of life. It was good to live here at The Knolls but that says for itself in the description, already too long, perhaps, for the intended proportions of our story. I was obliged to tell you, though, as the fact of the double home-stead had mainly to do with the ordering of Peace Polly's life, — the thing I hope you begin to care for; it having happened, as you perceive, in this third generation, that Lyman Schott and his half-sister came to be the representatives and successors of the two family sides; the easterly half of the mansion belonging now to the former, and the westerly to Peace Polly.

But Peace Polly's part was mostly left unused; she

kept house for Lyman in the east side, where they had lived on, naturally, together, since their father died; Joshua Schott having chosen, years before, when the whole dwelling became his own through the death of his Uncle Aaron, to continue to abide toward the sunrising, where he had spent his childhood; closing up the other rooms, not needing or consenting to rent them, as he might very readily have done.

Her home inheritance seemed, somehow, like Peace Polly's life, — hers and not hers. It was shut up half the year round.

When the crocuses began to send up their purple and golden lances through the brown beds below the southern windows, and the snowdrops were trembling with their delicate ecstasy of life among the grasses down underneath the old oaks, and the air came in with a blessing, like God's spirit, wherever door or window was unclosed, Peace Polly was used to throw open her domain for its spring airing, to go through all its rooms, dust its handsome old-time furnishings, put white covers on the tables and chests of drawers, even blossoms and pussy-willows in the quaint chimney vases, — cornucopias of blue and white china that matched the tiles around the fireplaces, — and unpin the curtains that had hung all winter in the chintz bags made for them out of yet older draperies. Then she would sit down of a quiet morning with some sewing-work in a southeast window, and play at living in her very own home. Or at twilight, in the first warm evenings, when the frogs were piping, and the woodcock "seek-seek-seek-ing" in his flight above the lower dusks, she would sit in the wide-open west doorway, listening to it all, with the chime of the dropping waters from the hill-face into the brimming basin for accompaniment, and think, with a strange, pathetic fullness of delight and longing all at once, how lovely it all was, and how happy that it was hers, if only she could quite live in it with any real home-presences or uses.

She had had plans, of course; Peace Polly was never without a "notion," as her brother thought. She had proposed an old schoolmate, or a far-off, unknown Western cousin, or even a boarder or two, as summer visitants; but Lyman always quietly answered, "You can do what you like with your own, of course. Rebeccarabby can take care of me; or I can get my meals at the tavern."

If he had said, "I don't like it; I don't want company, and I do want you," Peace Polly would hardly have minded the refusal. It would at least have put a motive and a consciousness of worthy self-denial to her relinquishment. After all, what the girl wanted most restlessly was a *raison d'être;* a theory of her life by which she could give account of herself to herself, by which she could make it out worth while to be.

She was ready to take almost any view of it, and valiantly live it out, could it once present itself in coherent shape, and she recognize herself set in it, as in lawful allotted surrounding, like any sort of person that had a place and character, real, or among those she had read about. She wanted to read some sort, almost any sort, of story of herself. But not to have a story, not to make any picture, any likeness of anything in heaven or earth, to be as a ghost without a body, looking on at life, — this was the strange hardness of it. These were the kind of things she used to say to herself; it seemed to her that she was a mere negative, a being without end, cause, or effect, so far as satisfying purpose, action, or rewarding accomplishment were concerned.

Rebeccarabby, or Rabby, condensed for use from double name of patriarchess and prophetess, could have baked and boiled, darned and swept, for Lyman, undoubtedly; whether she would or no, were Peace Polly withdrawn, might become another question. So that if Peace Polly effected anything essential, it was simply that, by presence and female headship of the house, she kept Rebeccarabby at her post and in her round. All her own housewifery — and she was by no means idle — was but as work of supererogation; her sacrifice but the acceptance of a comfortable home and the saving of her own little income for wider margin in mere personal ways, or for a future benefit. So she thought it looked to Lyman; and so it did; yet when she ventured any suggestion of a different plan, as we have seen, it was, "Oh, yes; I can go to the tavern." Which altogether miserable condition and alternative (Rebeccarabby would have said, not inappositely, "*fraternity*") drove her back to her unrecognized self-immolation, her fifth-wheel circumvolution, and her ache of uncontent.

"It is *company* I want, not visitors; and he does n't see it, nor help it. He's got his mill; all he wants here is his bed made, and his table set, and his newspaper, and the cat. And I may grind my heart out, for my share."

This was what Peace Polly said to herself one April evening, sitting, as I have spoken of her, at the west door. She had not many conversations, you will perceive, in these days; we shall have to depend a good deal, as she did, upon her soliloquies.

"I wonder if I'm turning into a cross old maid? Looks like it. I wonder what crossness really is; whether it's sinning or being sinned against, mostly? Things are crossed — or people — when they go different ways. I don't think it's I that do the crossing always. Anybody can be comfortable and good-natured that has their way laid right along with the grain of the world. But when everything is put athwart, you 're 'thrawn,' you 're 'curst,' — that 's the Scotch and the Shakespeare of it, — and how can you help it?   I 'll just ask Serena Wyse."

As she sat on the broad sill, with her chin in her hands, her elbows on her knees, and her feet on the big, irregular flat doorstone, she did not notice Lyman, coming in his slippers over the carpeted floor of the room behind her.   Behind Lyman walked the cat, also in her slippers. She came up to him as he stopped in the passageway, and rubbed her head against his leg. Lyman stooped down and lifted her up. He held her on his arm and stroked her softly, as he spoke to Peace, startling her out of her deep thinking.

"Did you remember about my thin overcoat?" he asked, not unpleasantly, yet to Peace Polly's ear with the indefinable tone of expectation on the wrong side; namely, that she should not have remembered, especially — so Peace Polly imagined he was thinking — since he found her here in her newly-opened territories, with the pretty evidences of her day's work about her.

"I did," answered Peace Polly, with a short dignity. "I lined the sleeves and faced the collar. It is hanging in the back hall."

"All right," rejoined Lyman. There was no more "thank you" in his words than there had been "I did it with a pleasure, and you 're welcome," in Peace Polly's.

Lyman stood still, and went on stroking the cat. "It 's pretty near tea-time," he said.

Yes, that was the next thing; nothing that in the mean while occupied or interested Peace Polly held any corresponding import or interest for him.

The girl half turned and looked up.

The cat in his arms was an offense to her. She did

not understand, perhaps, that a certain gentleness in his nature that failed to express itself readily to her or any other human being took this roundabout method of making known a mood of mind which she might have accepted, if she could have discerned it under the oblique sign. It was not in Lyman's way to caress, or say soft things, — to people. He could stroke the cat as accompaniment to an ordinary, practical remark, which really carried covertly something of the complacency, if not endearment, with it, over pussy's head; but not every one — certainly not Peace Polly — could take the delicate indirection.

"Nice day, and time o' day, your side of the house," attempted Lyman, again, not quite satisfied, doubtless, with words as they were.

Peace Polly made no answer for a moment. There was this excuse for · her: the cat was an especial offense to-day. Lyman had cosseted her at breakfast, and emptied the cream pitcher into a saucer for her, not discriminating between the two small jugs of cream and milk ; and afterward he had pushed away his second cup of coffee with marked dissatisfaction.

"I don't see why you can't pour out as good a cup the second time as the first," he had said, petulantly.

"Because you poured out all the cream for Zero, before I 'd had one cup," she added, with meek quenching.

"Coffee don't depend on cream," the man said ; wildly, as any woman knows. But then a man hardly ever understands about the cream in his cup, or how it gets there, in whatever sense. "Has n't got any life in it, any way," Lyman went on declaring, "and the last half 's always muddy. Think you might help it, if you tried."

Then he punished her still further by getting up and going off without his second cup, or the last muffin that he had just buttered.

And Peace Polly was "just fool enough," as she said to herself, to *be* punished by his unreasonable self-privation. So she laid up the grievance in her heart, and "mulled over it" all day, against both Lyman and Zero.

Now, in the twilight, the day's work and worries over, — particularly since the assurance that the coat-linings had been duly repaired, — Lyman inclined in his fashion to make amity. He waited even through that minute of silence in which he had been left unanswered.

Then Polly's shoulder turned a little toward him, and her great brown eyes were slowly lifted over it, aslant. There was a pain in them, but it looked to him like sullenness.

"I suppose," she said, "that if I were a cat I might get stroked a little."

Lyman laughed.

"Don't know," he said, tickling Zero's ears. "Fur too full of sparks, perhaps. Dangerous."

There were sparks in the brown eyes, then; and they flashed away from him, and head and shoulder went quickly round, away.

"Pussy hasn't any other way of knowing that you care for her," pursued Lyman, not unpacifically, Polly should have owned.

"Yes, she has !" she retorted: "she's fed, and lodged, and allowed to sit round and rub her paws, if she behaves well; and if she don't, she's scatted. I'm sure she has everything reasonable that anybody has, and the stroking besides ; and I'm lonesomer than any old cat that ever crept off under a woodpile !" she finished with rapid crescendo.

Polly had never quite distinctly said that before. It was as if her heart had burst out of her all at once. Lyman was taken by surprise. The queer, impetuous illustration conveyed to him, perhaps, more of his little sister's real experience than anything else had ever yet done.

Howbeit, he was patient to-night; and he stood still, while Peace Polly's head went down upon her knees, and the grieved and angry sobs broke forth.

She knew that Lyman still stood beside her. She thought she knew that he was "keeping his temper." "You can go away," she cried, "I'm used to it! I never have anybody to go to but old Serena Wyse."

If she had seen Lyman Schott's face then, and the change upon it, as she waywardly and quite insincerely vented all her bitterness upon dear Miss Serena's name, making of her such contemptuous exception, she would not have accused him of any forced placidity. The blood mounted darkly in his cheeks, and his eyes glowed as men's eyes do, where women's only flash.

"Serena Wyse is a good friend," said slow Lyman; and his tone made the girl lift up her head and cease sobbing. "I would n't be treacherous and double-faced, if I were you, Peace Polly!"

He was too displeased to say "Pease Porridge;" and he went away with a force in his tread that was quite unlike the footsteps of his coming. The dynamite cartridge had exploded. Peace Polly knew that Lyman was dreadfully angry. The reaction of remorse that had already set in upon her when she had cried and flung out that reckless last bit of temper was intensified, while it was suddenly petrified by dismay.

And yet, — was n't it queer how those two could flare up about each other!

Peace Polly laughed; and then put down her head, and cried again.

Of course she was ridiculous, and a wicked little ter-

magant, and one of those women that men are tradition-
ally perplexed and tormented with. But after all, if
men — brothers, husbands, *sons-in-law*, the proverbial
sufferers — could just once get inside a woman's real
heart, and feel as she does!

"I want somebody that I can look *way up to!*"
Peace Polly had cried out, times before, to Serena Wyse,
and Serena had answered her: —

"If it is only some human body, you must just look up
to the highest there is in them, for it is all you can get."

But the little things were continually forcing themselves in sight, and Polly was pained and provoked, and
made to feel the littleness and failure in herself, and that
all her sight and contact were just in the region of the
low and disappointing, though she might all the while believe far better in herself and in the only one she had to
love and lean on.

"If people want you to know how pleasant it is up-
stairs, why don't they open the doors and windows, and
ask you up there?" she exclaimed.

III.

"You can do as you like with your own, you know," Lyman repeated to her the next morning, beginning just where he had left off, as if the thought had been with him overnight, and had wrought slowly to some definite decision. "And perhaps it would be well enough for both of us, if you were to try it for a while."

Peace Polly's head went up quickly, and her face lit with surprise.

"Do you mean it *really*, and in good will?" she asked.

"I have n't any ill will," he answered, stiffly. "If you 've had enough of me — and the rest of your friends" —

"Lyman! that 's just it! Why won't you understand? I have n't had half enough of you! You don't let me. You 're off at the mill all day, and you bring home a chip with a lot of figures on it, and sit calculating boards and feet and things, all the evening ; and everything you *do* say to me has some kind of a little m-iserable nick in it! You know I hate nicks! I 'd rather every dish in the house would be broken in a heap!"

Polly came near saying "mean ;" when she made it into "miserable," she was trying to be amiable. Under the circumstances this was the nearest she could come to it. And it was all Greek and tantrums to Lyman Schott.

"I don't see how you 're lonesome, exactly," he said.

"You 've got Rabby here in the house, and " — But he would not mention Miss Serena again.

" Rebeccarabby ! with the manners of a cyclone ! " cried Peace Polly. " Do you suppose I can sit down and take my comfort with her ? " and feeling the storm signals up in her cheeks, and that she herself was very near being tempestuous again, she went off with sudden impulse out of the room ; while the cyclone, with curious coincidence, hurtled in at the very moment through an opposite door.

" Say ! " vociferated Rebeccarabby. " Peace Polly ! Lor', she ain't here, is she ? I was jest goin' to ask if you 'd have dumplin's for dinner ; 'cause th' iz lamb fry, and they goes good after that, you know." And the door slammed on the last syllable, as the whirlwind withdrew herself, and was heard instantly on the other side, effective amongst pots and pans.

" The woman *is* like a hurricane in the house, when you notice it, that 's a fact," said Lyman to himself, picking up his hat and his papers, and a penciled wooden slip such as Polly had reproached him with. " But why don't Polly learn her better ? "

He was off, in his turn, down to his planing-mill.

It seems, really, as if some men — or men, sometimes — regarded their dearest womankind as only of use when they have a blame to fling, or a perplexity they cannot answer. " Why does n't she do this, or prevent that ? " They have no other way of dismissing a difficulty which does not lie in their capacity or province, and before which they are helpless. Nevertheless, precisely because it is in the woman's province, to her thwart or chafing, the man can usually take his hat and escape from it.

Pease Porridge, up in her own room, vigorously bestirring herself in making up the dainty white bed, whose spreadings she pulled in from the open, sunny window where they had grown fresh and warm and sweet as common "laundrying" scarcely makes them, was working off the storm-danger and getting down the signals, bringing her ideas to shape at the same time under the unexpected concession and opportunity.

"I 'll take him at his word, whatever he meant," she said in her mind, which external operative part of her always took a conversational turn with her remoter, inward self. "And he shall see. He thinks I want a house and a summer-time like the Cramhalls'; a lot of half-rate city folks, with wild bangs and water-cart whiskers, racketing about and taking possession, as if they 'd found a deserted village, or a primeval solitude, and we were all nothing but invisible ghosts, or murmuring pines and hemlocks. But there *are* nice people who want pleasant homes, to stay right on in; quiet widow-ladies, with young-girl daughters, may be! and dear, sweet spinster-women, like Miss Thurleigh, who stayed with — There! if I *don't*, just!"

And the white quilt was tucked down, "pincushion smooth," and the pillows placed, and their frilled spreads laid over, even to a half-line, in another minute and a half; and in as much more Peace Polly's hat and jacket were on, and she down the stairs and out at the back door, Rebeccarabby pealing after her through the kitchen window with the dinner question.

"Yes, yes! anything you like; ·anything — but *dumps!*"

Lyman Schott would have given a snip off the end of his little finger to have had as pat a retorting word always at the tip of his tongue when he wanted it; usually he could only keep his temper with a very visible might, and make "nicks."

Peace Polly was gayly out of the dumps and doldrums

now, her spirit sails filling with the breeze of a bright new purpose that carried her straight over, in the very first place, to Serena Wyse.

"It will be better for both of us; for him, as well as for me. He said so. And I 've always known it. And if it *should* happen to come about, in the chances and changes — But I won't think of it now; I must n't have *that* in my face!" she said, as she stepped lightly upon Miss Serena's doorstone. She quite forgot, in the elation of her new project, that it had begun in a disagreement.

Serena Wyse was showering her plants with a whisk-broom. She had a deep window — not a bay, but a chimney recess, all window toward the sun — full of them; and an oilcloth on the floor beneath gave the most delightful liberty for spatters, and glistened, itself, with all its bright tile-colors, in the freshness.

Peace Polly stood still in the doorway. " Oh dear, you never will, I 'm afraid!" she said.

"Never what, — and why not?" asked Serena, turning round.

" What I came brimful of, and because you 're so — wretchedly — cosy and complete right here!" said Peace Polly. " But I 've got sunny windows, too, lots of 'em; and you might do what you liked with the carpets!"

" Dear child! what in the world are you driving at, with the bits in your hands, and the reins between the horse's teeth? " asked Serena, to whom comparisons came naturally, and often oddly.

"At you," returned the girl. "I tell you I 'm full of it. Did n't Mr. Thurleigh want to hire your house on a lease ? "

" Mark Thurleigh? Yes."

" And did n't you say once that if you could move yourself as they move buildings now, slide right along somewhere with your own special particulars all standing about you, like your life on a tray, and be set down easy, you might think of such a thing?"

"I suppose I did, just because I could n't," said Serena.

"Well, then, you can," returned Peace Polly, victoriously. "And you can bring Miss Thurleigh too. That's part of it. And I know Miss Thurleigh wants just that, to live close to her brother's big family, and not in the *mêlée.*"

"My dear Peace Polly! what are you laying out for me? And can't you come a little further in?"

Polly had stood all this while upon the threshold.

"I might, yes. Only that would emphasize the settled-down expression, and I want things to look transitionary to you!"

"They look pretty incomprehensible, as you signify them."

"Serena! would you come and live with me, in my side of the house? Oh, I want you so! But, wait a minute! that's just as true as truth. I love you, and I want you; and yet, I got provoked last night, and told Lyman I had n't anybody to go to — *but* — 'old Serena Wyse'! Now you know. It *would* be double-faced to ask you without telling!"

"Then it's a quarrel again, Pease Porridge?"

"Yes; and no, 't is n't, either. Lyman was mad, — I never saw him real fiery before, — when I said that."

"What for?" As Serena asked that question, she got round between the window and her flower-stand, beginning to sprinkle again. The richly twisted sprays of a trellised ivy, glittering with the shower she gave them, shielded her face from Peace Polly.

"Oh, not that I disparaged *his* company. He blazed

right up about you. You were my — no, *a* good friend,
he said ; and I was treacherous and double-faced."

"To call me *old?*" asked Miss Serena, with a sweet
kind of dwelling upon the word, as if she had learned
already to dwell upon it with a secret gladness. There
was a sudden depth in her voice, also, like the trembling
resonance of a rich note of music. " When to grow old,
in so many things, is to grow safe, and privileged, and
sure? An *old friend,* — why, Polly, a seed-sapling starts
up in a summer, and a hundred things may happen to nip
it off ; but an *old tree!* you must wait years for it, to
have or to be ; but then it 's there, rooted and certain,
and not likely to be transplanted. I ain't a bit afraid of
being old, Peace Polly."

What made her words ripple so like a spring-time
brook ? Peace Polly wondered.

" Then you *will* come and live with me a while ? " she
asked, eagerly, taking the delayed " no " for a good answer.

The real answer came so fore-concluded, so as if nearly
needless, and only transposed by the quite different thing
that had essentially mattered in what had been, that it
shut down Peace Polly's hopes with sheer surprise of simple, indisputable denial.

" Why, no, indeed ! To put you and Lyman apart?
How could you think of it, Peace Polly ? " said Serena
Wyse.

Then Polly surprised and shocked her friend.

She came in, and sat down, without saying a word.
She laid her hands, palms up, into her lap, as if she had
surrendered something out of them, and knew of nothing
else to turn to and take up. Her eyes lowered, and fixed
themselves upon the floor ; her lips drooped sadly at the
corners ; all the light and gladness went out of her face ;

the shadow of what *she* would be when she was old crept over it.

Serena watched her a minute, troubled for her, amazed that she could so have put her heart upon a sudden, wild, most uncertain idea; then she came and stood by her and said gently : —

"Why, child, what is it ? How *can* it be so with you about a thing like this ? "

"I don't believe God means to give me *anything !* " said Peace Polly.

Serena left that word vibrating on the air. It might itself recoil upon the waywardness that dared to utter it. She would not hinder with any small reproof. She went back and finished ordering her plants ; with a little mop she wiped up the water from the pretty oilcloth ; then she came toward Peace Polly again, and said, quietly : —

"Unless you will come upstairs with me, I must say good-by. I 've got a cupboard I 'm going to empty out, this morning. It 's a grand large one, with doors opening away back, fronting the light ; but there 's only odds and ends in it, and there are some of my best treasures I 've been wanting to put in."

Peace Polly was as quick to see as she was to say. She stood up. "If I thought *that* was what it was all for ! " she exclaimed.

"The more room, the fuller we shall be filled. The Lord does n't make space to put in emptiness. Wait and see ; you 're only twenty, and if 't was eighty it would make no difference," said Serena Wyse.

IV.

WHY TO-DAY?

It was to be a day of amazements for Serena, usually so undisturbed in her established quietudes.

In the afternoon, Lyman Schott himself walked in.

He did everything just as if it were a daily doing, let it be never so startling a departure, in the eyes of other people, from his accustomed lines. It became accustomed as soon as he had made up his mind to it. As soon as he had determined, in his deliberate fashion, upon any act, it was to him as a long-foreseen, inevitable procedure, however contradictory to habit, or even to previous clear intention from which such habit might have grown. There are some people who have time, — time being only a relative thing, — during the processes which lead them, mentally or circumstantially, to a new attitude or purpose, to get wonted to it in the acceptance, recognizing it as a lawful sequent to whatever may have gone before, and as an altogether natural link between the past and the to be, sharply as these may appear to contrast with each other. They can by no means so follow the gradations in the reasonings and conclusions of others: to them, results as presented in action are often quite whimsical and irrational; things jumped at, they suppose, without reflection, since the reflections necessary have not passed through the convolutions of their own brains.

Peace Polly would have been as much astonished to see, if she had happened to see it, her undeviating brother, at four in the afternoon, away from his mill and knocking at Miss Serena's great, fan-lighted, seldom-used front door, as he had ever been at any of her own escapades or delirious propositions.

Miss Serena herself, when she heard the knocker sounding its summons away through the closed hall and up the dim old staircase, which led, indeed, to the door of her own room on the one side, but which, with its protracted following of the whole lengths of wall on either hand, and its midway landing crossing the end space between, she had long neglected as a transit, in favor of what she called the "lightning-rod," a steep little corkscrew twisted in the corner of a chimney-side passage, and leading to her kitchen, — when she heard the knock, I say, and glanced from her front window to see Lyman standing upon the stoop, she fairly rubbed her eyes and stared a minute, as in a sudden trance, before she turned and went down quickly, threading hall and old state staircase to and fro, like a slender shuttle rushing across an enormous loom.

In that minute of wonder, she had had a certain Rip Van Winkle experience of bewilderment. Was everything suddenly set back again to a dozen years ago?

Just so Lyman Schott used to come over, when that wide doorway was wont to stand pleasantly open, and the great stairs were the family highway; when the house was full of girls, her sisters and their frequent guests, before deaths and departures had left her, like Lyman and Peace Polly, to the sole use of the dwelling, far too large for her, and the dexterous winding of herself up and down the "lightning-rod," in the busy solitude of her own affairs between her sleeping-room and kitchen. Just so he used to knock, two moderate taps of equal force, like a printed colon; only then he almost always, after that notice of approach, had used to step right inside. Now he waited, as indeed he must, the big bolt within being fast in its place. The house door opening toward the north, Serena had not Peace Polly's inducement to let the early summer-time in by the less frequented way. It was only in the heats of later June, and on, then, through July and August, that it offered comfortable refuge and escape from the southerly blaze, and a shaded daylight for her afternoon occupations, which she would bring into its cool breadth of entrance.

If Serena had not understood Lyman Schott as perfectly as she did, she would not, in that little flight of hers to left and right down the stairway, have so put by her bewilderment, and joined fact to fact across the years, almost as he did, as to receive him so entirely after the fashion of his coming. Pulling aside the heavy bolt with one hand, and turning the handle — not a knob, but a great stirrup-like pendant matching the knocker, that had to be grasped and twisted — with the other, she stood face to face with him in an instant, without the shadow of even a receding surprise, and said, "Good afternoon, Lyman," just as if he had been there twice before that day.

And just as if he belonged there, Lyman walked in, scarcely waiting her showing, turning to the little parlor on the left with the habit of twelve years before.

"You don't make this the family entrance very much now, perhaps," he said.

Serena laughed. "I'm the family, you know. It only needs a 'little hole for the kitten.'"

Lyman did not at once take the chair Serena offered him. He walked across the room to the window that with a deep recessed seat looked out into the old-fashioned flower and fruit garden, and beyond that to his own garden grounds, with the winding footpath grooving the fieldway between. A grassed alley, with hedges of currant on either side, intersected Miss Serena's garden, running straight from opposite this window to where, through a gate in the paling fence at the foot, it struck upon a curving of the outside path.

"There are easy ways enough between your house and mine," said Lyman; "but Pease Porridge seems to make most use of them. I came round from the mill this time by the hill road."

"I 'm glad to see you, Lyman. You 're a busy man in these days. Have you got your new chiselers in for the fine mouldings?"

"Yes. And they 're going to work first-rate. How did you know?"

"Oh, people tell. They all say you 're doing grandly, too. I hope you 're keeping your parallel lines?"

Lyman looked at her in a puzzled way. He had a good deal to do with parallel lines, but it was all by machinery. If they ran at all, of course they ran true. Serena meant something else than this, — he could guess of what sort, perhaps; but the figure perplexed him.

"Don't we live in parallel lines?" Serena asked. "I always think so. I feel as if we walked in the shadow here of the real thing somewhere, — at the selfsame time, I mean. When we *only* walk in the shadow, you know, then it is a vain one, and we disquiet ourselves in vain."

Serena Wyse did not often directly quote a Scripture text; but she was very apt to say something partly mixed with its phrasing, upon which the thing she so spoke threw a wonderful brightness of significance.

"I don't see it all as plain as you do, Serena, but I try to walk according to my light."

Serena did not answer anything to that at once; and in what seemed a sudden way for him, Lyman spoke again without waiting.

"If a talk of ours had ended differently that we had just here about eleven years ago," he said, "I might have been more parallel with you by this time."

"Oh, don't think that!" Serena cried, quickly. "It *must* have been all right. How could it have been different?"

Into the quiet face had sprung a great working, — an awakening, it seemed, of something that had been long lulled asleep; had been carefully kept so, perhaps, by some rocking.

If eleven years ago had been different! Had not Serena, on her side, ever thought of that?

But there had been her mother then, with whom Serena was left all alone. An invalid, exacting, claiming to herself, not knowing what a drain she made, every thought and power of her daughter's; her days filled with changing and querulous wants and fancies, her nights unquiet; the last years of a broken life slowly fretting themselves away in that strange, sad foreignness to all that had been life, temper, character before, so that love and faithfulness have to reach back continually to grasp and hold with determined struggle a memory that alone inspires their service now. This, a mystery that many have lived through, had been the mystery of Serena Wyse's existence then, under whose control at less than twenty-three she so utterly renounced what had before been the growing reality of her own life — its hope so natural that it hardly had the doubt of hope — as to leave Lyman Schott in the belief that it had been no part of her interpretation of their mutual history at all.

Undoubtedly this had been his dull mistake and fault; but to prevent or rectify it would have been to refuse her duty in its thoroughness. No new thing for a woman to do was this that she had done. It may make but a trite

page in a story, yet for each soul that has such renuncia-
tion set for it the pain is fresh and separate, and all its
own.

"How could I even say what would seem to ask him to
wait on for me all those solitary years?" she had demanded
of herself, sometimes, when herself arraigned her.

And then the many years had not been, after all. Her
mother had died in less than two, when Serena was still
but twenty-four; and there had been nine years since in
which Lyman had said no such word again, nor come near
her any more in the old way, though they had been next
neighbors, and had known each other's goings out and
comings in, and Peace Polly had grown up to be Serena
Wyse's friend.

"How could it have been different?" she said.

"I came to-day to ask you if you could make it different now," answered Lyman Schott, his eyes full upon her
face. He was not a man of circumlocutions. He was too
simple, too habitually upon the ordinary, open plane of
things, to be that.

"Why *to-day?*" passed quickly through Serena's thought
as she looked at him. Oh, why to-day? Why, after that
morning talk with his sister? so that she could not help
seeing plainly just how it was; so that through no blessed,
permitted ignorance or mistake she might take, at last, her
own? For Lyman Schott was not a man to come a third
time.

Yes, notwithstanding that there had been, after all,
other hindrance than that of her daughterly duty in those
old days; notwithstanding there had been something else,
she felt, to wait for, and that same thing·might even be
to wait for still, she might yet have risked it, seeing the
word had come to her now, and it was but herself she had
to think of, if it had not been for that coming and asking

of Peace Polly's just before. "All in one day! so plain that the same thing sent them both!"

She answered, after the minute's pause, almost as she had answered Peace Polly: —

"It is something between you and Polly, I 'm afraid, Lyman."

"Something that is n't between us, likely," said Lyman. "She wants to go her way, and why not I go mine? If I can take it, Serena, I think it would be better for us both."

Just that, after all those years! How long had he thought about it; how long had he been quite content with his mill, and his farm, and his sister to keep house, going out and coming in, and hardly ever coming here! How could a woman tell what a man meant, away within himself, when he only did and spoke like this?

That other reason loomed up in the light of these swift askings. Were all things ready for such marriage? Had Lyman even yet overgrown the distance, the difference that had withheld her then; that had made her question whether, once joined in an irrevocable fate with him, she could be so patient and believing, under the little frets or unlikenesses of daily perception, purpose, motive, as she could be standing by? Oh, it was easy to talk to Peace Polly. But in Peace Polly's place — in a closer, more exacting place — could she have done better? She would have "kept her temper," doubtless, but might it not have come to be as Lyman Schott kept his, or his little sister thought he did, — "ferociously"? For Serena, living on her peaceful parallels, knew that she had never tried cross-lines like those, — lines not merely outside and about her, but that must, she knew, run through her heart.

"When once he comes to see things, he 'll be all right," she had always said to herself, "for he 's a good man."

And so she had gone on, loving and hoping confidently for him. But how could she suddenly "make things different" to-day?

And Peace Polly! Oh, that settled it; that was the instant, manifest forbidding that came with the temptation. Yet why need Lyman have come and asked this just *to-day?*

It was as if it were a sending and a sign that she might know it could not be different with them, ever.

"I can't step in between you and Peace Polly, Lyman," she answered, at last.

"That means" — returned Lyman, hastily; for why should that girl, who had a way and might have a life before her of her own, stand between *them?* Only as a pretext, he thought, resentfully.

"It means that we must just keep on being friends, Lyman; it is truest so. But you *will* be friends, won't you, Lyman? I've missed you; may be that is partly why we've grown a little apart, you see. Can't you come back far enough to be 'parallel,' and be content for a while? Everything is but such a little while here," she added, quickly.

She said it all with a most sweet, straightforward, kindly tone and look.

Lyman remembered what Peace Polly so often said about his temper. He did not think or acknowledge that it was temper that he had to keep. If this were affection that Serena Wyse was keeping back from him, it was as easily put down and back he thought.

If he had only cried out as Peace Polly did: "I love you, and I want you!"

But he was not impetuous. Why, then, could he not understand Serena's "keeping back"? He did not; he took his answer; he shook hands kindly with the woman whom he loved, but "in his way," as after all a man only can, and moved to go from her.

"You'll come in sometimes, now you have found the way again, Lyman?" She said the words of invitation just in the fashion common to herself and to the countryside; but she said them wistfully.

"Oh, yes; I'll look in, — when I can," Lyman ruled himself to reply, of like habit; and so he went away. He did not think quick enough to tell her that, though he had found the way, he had found a bolted door at the end of it; that was in his reservation and his tone only, as he added, slowly, the "when I can." It was odd wooing, odd refusal, odd acquiescence, perhaps. In New England, people are not much given to high-wrought climaxes; they dread nothing so much as getting off their proper common-sense lines. The tragic when it occurs is apt to be well covered with the commonplace.

Serena, left alone again, went up to her room that looked over the gardens; then quickly turned, and crossed the hall to the unused easterly spare chamber, and to its farther window, with its closed green blinds. Peering through the slats she saw Lyman, far down, going round by the roadway under the elms and locusts in the direction of his mill again. She dropped suddenly upon her knees beside the window-seat.

"I have done the best I knew. Lord, if I was in a hurry, and did not wait for all Thou hadst to say, if I have made anything wrong to-day, oh, put it right, or make right come of it!"

And so she got up again, leaving it there, where she left everything. He both could and would, she knew; though mistake were piled upon mistake in all their lives. Was it not what He came, and is with us always for, to *judge* the world?

V

MRS. DORA DISCERNS.

AFTER that things so settled down that neither of the principal persons concerned realized that anything had happened except what had happened to themselves. "As you were" seemed to have been a kind of imperative order along the line, and the momentary change of attitude had altered nothing; scarcely interrupted, to be remembered as an interruption.

Lyman thought, as usual, "Polly has got over the new fandiddlum," and letting well enough alone, though he would hardly have admitted the appositeness of the proverb, he made no remark; at least, not until they had run in the old ruts long enough for his doing so to seem a new departure.

Peace Polly subsided like a creature tired of tugging at her chain's length, and let her neck rest in the collar by keeping effortless within her limits. Not altogether as at other such defeated times, either; some words of Serena Wyse's stayed by her, and moved within her; too deep, perhaps, for direct thinking or consciousness, but making a reserve, a resource, put away with but a half understanding, yet with the sense that it might be drawn forth and looked at nearer, — perhaps might put itself forth into some fulfillment somehow.

"He makes no space to fill with emptiness." There was possibility in all the untried years; she had lived but twenty of them. Even when she did not recall or dwell upon the words, the feeling that life was more than the now of it, that there is always something written on unturned leaves, resulted and remained with her. It was the difference between despairing and enduring.

Yet, when any definite thinking came, what after all had arrived, she could but question, to Serena herself, with all her patience of assurance? Peace Polly supposed she would say that she was only thirty-three. Was that the way it was to go on? "Yet if it were eighty it would make no difference." It was hard to rest in that, with three fourths of the desert still before her. The promised land was too far off. And here was fullest food for thinking, only Polly was half afraid of it, and half helpless to see clear; — was it only for some certain " elect," believing as Serena Wyse believed, waiting in the "hope" that only came to such after their unknown, mystical "experience"? There was nobody to answer her these things; at any rate, she must first ask concerning them; and she had a prejudice against "inquiring," though she continually turned to Serena with other, if they were other, interrogations.

Nevertheless, the residuum of comfort lay in her underneath her thinkings or her refusings to think; stored up, according to Swedenborg's great doctrine of " remains." There was no such thing as an emptiness. The world was full, and it moved, though her days rose and set without her feeling any thrill or sweep of their swiftness. She might encounter something, or come into some new place of her life-orbit, — see some new star, or feel the breath of different seasons, — even so, through the very fixedness of the stubborn axis of her fate.

Serena troubled for nothing, save as to whether she had done the right. If she had, all would be, all was already, as right as it could be. If not, even, it would be made right, though by a longer or a harder way. She would not make the way hard for another, if she knew; but had it really been made hard, at all, for Lyman Schott? Was it more to him than an easy, the nearest easy, arrangement of his life? Would he have thought of this that he had asked her, now, except for Peace Polly's restlessness that broke in upon the every-day accustomedness which was life-comfort to him? Did he want more than to establish with as little wrench as possible a new rut and order in which the wheels might run with less jar and resistance, and with no threatening of uncertainty or change, save the uncertainty of life itself, and the great change away from everything by death? Had it not settled itself quite as nearly to his satisfaction, apparently, now that Peace Polly, diverted from her little balk, was drawing quietly in her harness again?

Serena knew more than the other two, since each of the two had come to her, but I doubt if she understood much more clearly than either; and so the two households, so curiously alike in circumstance, each with so much more space than obvious life in it, so much more in possession than in use, went on their wonted, separate, neighboring, near-distant ways.

Meanwhile, outside and about them, though they moved not at all, a little tide of event moved slightly. Visitors and kinsfolk came and went, in other houses, as the summer deepened, and the short weeks of New England holiday opportunity went by. Some strangers were boarding at the Cramhalls'; New York people this year. Lucy Remond was married; she had been engaged so long that it was hardly an event, — or was it, as some said, the more a surprise, as death, long waited for, seems always "sudden at last"? She was nearer forty than thirty; the bridegroom forty-eight. Miss Mallis, the life and

lash of the village, wondered that Mr. Dawney did not
forget, and say "dust to dust, ashes to ashes," when he
married them.

Dr. Blithecome had had one or two ill turns; he
looked badly, people said; he was not an old man, either.
But, if anything happened, what was Bonnyborough to
do without Dr. Blithecome? Everybody in the place
less than twenty-five years old had come into life under
his ministration; how could they get comfortably out of
it without him? A doctor of thirty years' standing holds
the whole community, or it him, in ownership by a kind
of birthright; more than that, by his sole custody of the
keys and combination-signs of all its constitutions. They
dared not be sick, they had no right to be well, without him. This menace through him of their very charters
of existence, this threat of loss and break in the records
by which they held safe tenure, and whose registry was
in his brain, stirred a public anxiety that made the little
occasional news about it not news, — *that* they were fond
of, — but announcement heavy with personal importance
to them; a thing of vital hope or apprehension. Yet it
was news, after all; and there is something even in the
progress of one's own aches or troubles that interests a
strange, independent, inquisitive part of the mind.

And Dr. Farron, with his wife Dora, had come back
to Bonnyborough. This was altogether a new and unexpected happening.

The Rev. Sebastian Farron had been rector at Bonnyborough when our Peace Polly was born: see first page
of the present story. His wife Dora had made her comments, therein rendered, at the occasion of the christening.
After that, Mr. Farron's health had suffered from the climate, and the winter exposures of his scattered parish
work among the wind-scoured hills. Mrs. Dora's brother

had made a place and fortune out on the sweet Pacific slopes; and the clergyman and his wife had removed thither for an indefinite stay. Mr. Farron had busied himself quietly there for a good while in completing a work upon church history and methods, remarkable for its unifying thought and illustration; after the publication of which he had received his degree of preferment, Sacræ Theologiæ Doctor. With the best efforts of his restored vigor, he had then built up a church and mission, which he had now transferred to the charge of a younger clerical brother; and he and his wife both longing for the dear hill country of their earlier life, and the summer joy distincted from the year, like a glowing jewel, by its very setting between the bleaker changes, — the more since Dora's brother had died, leaving his large property equally divided between his wife and sister, there being no surviving children, — they had returned to the home they had built and always owned in Bonnyborough, and to the abundant association and resource for the winter times of the city, only a few hours' travel off.

Their coming back was an event for Peace Polly, though she gave it little thought at first, so certain is it that we rarely know when eventfulness begins for us.

"I told you so!" remarked Mrs. Dora, meekly and enigmatically, as she walked away from church with her husband after a service in which he had taken part, and a sermon they had listened to from the Rev. Richard Innesley, a young deacon at present filling the doctor's former duty, which had passed through a succession of temporary hands since the old Farron days.

"I quite dare say you did, my dear. What was it?"

"About Pease Porridge Hot," returned his wife. "It was right here, at the very corner we have just turned, — how things come back at corners! — that I said to you

after the christening, you know; or, at least, I said *if*
she should 'lead the remainder of her life' — well, you
did n't like me to say it then, and I won't now, but she
has, I can see it in her face. It's been inside, if not
out, and inside's the worst; but how could she help it,
among those behindhand people!"

"Dora, glossary!"

"'Janet! donkeys!'" quoted Mrs. Dora. "Of course
I don't mean *you;* though why 'glossary,' for such a word
as that? It was charitable for benighted, or contracted,
which I did n't like to say; only, oh, those pilgrim-
forefather people that came here to get room to grow!
Do you know, Sebastian, I truly think the Lord meant
just such holding fast of truth as cramps it down and
starves it, when He told the story of the talent in a napkin? That girl looks hungry, Doctor, and — cross.   I
think you ought to see to it."

"You are certainly a person of most remarkable perceptions and suggestions.   Could you tell me how?"

"No; that's what you've got to watch for. If you do,
you 'll see."

"Thank you.   And, Dora, don't be church-proud. I
believe that is worst of all.   It puts uncharity under a
mask, and makes a multiplied, outside self-confidence, instead of a single, personal one that can be detected and
shamed."

"That is excellent," returned Dora.   "And I don't
think that I am.   For it is precisely the thing I am de-
ploring.   When people suppose they have got everything
in heaven and earth packed into their nutshell, they never
take the trouble to pull it out again and use it, but go
along quite satisfied to hold on to the shell.   It was the
way I did with my traveling-satchel all the way from
San Francisco to Denver.   I don't care whether it's puri-

tanical or ecclesiastical. What I say is that it takes an everlasting lifetime to grow to the faith of what we believe in."

"Right, and good. Only you need not say, 'behindhand people.' There are last that shall be first. And 'If I will that some tarry till I come, what is that to thee? See that *thou* tarry not; but follow me.'"

"Your word is the biggest and best, and I have got it," returned the wife. "That is what my impertinences are after, always." And she gave his arm a quick little clinging pressure. "But I did n't mean people, in bodies, though I did lay it back upon pilgrim-fathers; I meant individuals; pared off, and narrowed down; and I was pitying that girl."

It was the third Sunday after the Farrons had been resettled in the old neighborhood; and Mrs. Dora's eyes and ears had been catching up missed chapters. She was now quite as *au courant* to the history of things as if she had sat here all these twelve years reading it.

Peace Polly had not been at church until this third Sunday.

"'People,' in this case," remarked the Doctor, "seems to be a noun of multitude restricted to Lyman Schott."

"*Restricted!* Yes."

"Lyman Schott is a good man."

"Oh, dear! goodness that does n't numerate. A string of ciphers without a value. He is n't this, and he is n't that. But why, in the name of goodness, is n't he t'other? That's what Peace Polly needs. The man has n't grown an inch, I can see that, in these twelve years."

"His planing-mill has grown."

"May be that's the plain reason."

"Oh, if you take to punning!"

"I don't. It punned itself."

" I should like you to see some of the beautiful work he does."

" I should like, first, to see after some of the beautiful work he does n't do."

" Every man's work must be left mostly to himself," said the Doctor.

"Then why can't somebody work upon *him?*" said incorrigible Mrs. Dora. "I tell you, Peace Polly has got the beginning of a peevy-wrinkle at the corners of her mouth!"

VI

MRS. DORA UNDERTAKES.

MRS. FARRON was quite determined to do something for Peace Polly. She took it up, in her own mind, as her direct and instant mission here. But as all missionaries have to find out, the errand cannot be done all on one side. There is a sending of the receiver to receive, also. And for Peace Polly it was not at once a natural thing to do, to draw into an intimacy with a person so differently situated in years, position, culture, command, although she might, and did, appreciate with a modest surprise the kindly approaches and permissions from the higher, elder side.

Impetuous as Polly was to utter herself, when once she had established freedom of speech, it was not in her to rush into a sudden confidence with Mrs. Dora. Nor would that lady, on her part, assume or intrude, for the very reason that she might almost seem to take privilege to catechise. With all her clear-seeing and clear-speaking specialties she had the most exquisite sort of tact, — the tact that really touches and feels, that is not a mere trained and skillful technicality of breeding.

She asked Polly to her house; she kept her to little quiet home teas, or lunches, — considerately sending word, always, to Mr. Schott, through notice to Rebeccarabby, that it was to be so; she gave the girl seeds and shoots of her lovely Californian plants; she brought a new element of life and cheer to her, and this was a great deal; but she asked her no direct questions, and Peace Polly offered no deep confidence. She was a different person, indeed, for the brief whiles that she was with her new friend; it was only out of her old, fretted, crossed, and self-blaming self that her heart-revelations broke forth.

"I think you must need some companionship of your own age," said Mrs. Farron to her one day, having come to recognition of the fact that her own forty-five years and her memory back into the girl's babyhood, while truly making her both girl and woman to sympathize and counsel, might just be, to Peace Polly's apprehension, the distant, different five-and-forty years, as a point arrived at, and the changed — not inclusive — view and experience of life as it affected twenty.

"There is n't anybody of my own age," replied Polly, with the quietest assertion.

Mrs. Farron lifted up her eyes. Here was something, at last. Here was a keen word after her own fashion. She looked at Polly with blank inquiry, though she was quite quick enough to see precisely what was meant.

"Not? Why, is n't Rose Howick, — are n't the Cramhalls, and the Holistons, and Judith Dawney, — anybodies?"

"I was born into a previous generation," said Peace Polly; "and I have n't grown up to it, and I can't get back or forward from it to my own. I think I don't know how to be a girl, and, may be because of missing that, I 'm sure I have n't begun to be a woman."

Well, Mrs. Dora had got it now, certainly! But she did not know exactly what to do with it.

So she waited. She had the uncommon sense to do that. If Peace Polly had any further real word to say, it would not be led forth by a haphazard, misfitting utterance made merely as at her turn in the conversation. Many and many a true-telling has been turned aside in that way. She left the thread unbroken by any such rude, ignorant touch; and she threw the obligation of continuance upon Peace Polly. It is a trick of talk that few master; but Mrs. Farron understood it, and by that one simple fetch had become the repository of more unbosomings and shrifts than even ever the good clergyman her husband.

"And — I 've been uneasy because you could n't suspect it — I 'm so cross, and such a horrid scold. I always thought that grown-up people got over it, and grew mild and polite; so I suppose I 've all my real growing up to do. And yet — I 'm too old for those girls, Mrs. Farron!"

"Are you cross?" asked Mrs. Farron, with just that tone of gentle, unsurprised interest with which she might have said, "You do draw, then?" or, "You are musical?" quite as if the ordinary powers and tendencies of human nature were to be looked for, with but slight variations, in almost anybody.

"I 'm dreadful liable to it, as Rebeccarabby says," returned Peace Polly, smiling. The comfort of not having so shocked or dumbstricken her hearer as to be made to feel wholly out of the limit of her comprehension or countenance positively elated her. It was a kind of absolution.

"Cross people are hardly ever hypocrites," said Mrs. Farron. "Temper generally goes with truth, I think."

"Only truth, clear through, ought to conquer it."

"If you have found that out, you must have 'taken a start,' as they say, to grow."

"Bodily growing does n't ever take a start backward. What you gain stays. If you could only hold on so inside you might have a chance to gain more."

"That 's what the confirmation prayer means; that we

may daily increase in the Holy Spirit more and more, till
we come into the everlasting kingdom."

"I have n't had that said for me," said Peace Polly,
lowly.

Then, indeed, Mrs. Farron was surprised.

" Why, who has been looking after you, my dear?" she
cried.

"I don't know that I have wanted it," replied the girl,
still in her low tone, and evading other answer.

"Wanted looking after!"

"I mean — to do that.   I 've never been ready."

Mrs. Dora looked at Peace Polly very earnestly.

"Should you say, I cannot get ready for the journey,
because I have n't packed my trunk?"   It was odd, like
her, and apt enough.   But Peace Polly was as quick as
she.

"Yes; if I had n't got a single garment made or
mended."

"That's only setting the work back a stage further.
Say, if you please, you won't thread your needle because
the seam is n't sewn."

"I see.   I don't suppose I need try to back out, with
you to get behind me.   But, dear Mrs. Farron, are n't
there a great many people in the church who are nothing
but Prayer-Book Christians?"

" Where did you get that phrase? and what does it mean,
do you think?"

Peace Polly answered the second question.

" Why, taking things cut and dried.   Carrying your religion round by a finger-strap.   Depending upon a church
certificate, somehow, and not taking much upon yourself.
There must be more than just an easy being led, in a gradual, insensible kind of a way."

"Led? Yes," said Mrs. Farron.   " We must be led.

We trust to be. But we shan't be *dragged*. We've got to take every single step ourselves, and choose to take it as it comes. Experience is realizing in one's self what one believes. That can't be done in a minute, though it is always in some minute that everything is begun. I think there *might* be such a thing as a prayer-*meeting* Christian, too. Nobody will ever be a Prayer-Book Christian till they have experienced the Prayer-Book."

While Mrs. Dora had been eagerly saying these rapid sentences, she had not heard the Doctor's step; but he had come along the hall, and stood in the doorway as she finished. His shadow made her turn quickly and flush up. "I beg your pardon. I might have left it to you, perhaps. But I do now," she said.

"You don't leave much," he answered, with a smile and a bend of his deep, kind eyes that she knew by heart. And then, most unprofessionally, he quietly moved away.

"He won't interrupt," said his wife. "He knows it would just make a jumping-off place, and have to be all gone back and over again. But he would be ready, and kind, any time, Peace."

To think she should call her *that*, — alone, as if it really belonged to her! Why, the girl could not remember that anybody had ever stopped at the "Peace" before: the moisture sprang to her shining eyes.

"I'd earn that name, if I could," she said, almost passionately. "But I told you, truly, I am a miserable scold."

"Scolding is not always vituperating. It is often only vigorous explanation," said Mrs. Dora Farron.

Peace Polly had to laugh.

"Temper is truth, and scolding reason!" she exclaimed. "You put it very benevolently."

"It may certainly not be spite, or hate," the elder

woman said. "I know it is sometimes a mere desperate struggle to straighten things ; the manner is a matter of temperament. Anger is pure anguish, which it is the Latin word for, quite frequently. ' Be ye angry, and sin not. Let not the sun go down upon your wrath.' "

" It never does, on mine," said Peace Polly, humbly. " I 'm sorry by that time. Unless," she added, quaintly, recalling that greatest recent quarrel, " things happen at sundown ! But what do you suppose St. Paul, I believe it was, exactly meant by that ? "

" St. Paul, yes ; writing to the Ephesians, who ' could not bear them that were evil.' Not a dispensation till candle-light, assuredly ! " answered Mrs. Dora. " I don't think it was outward daylight he meant at all."

" What is inside daylight, then ? "

" The shining of the Lord's presence," said Mrs. Farron.

And upon that fell a silence ; the talk ended.

VII

ORCHIDS AND TEA-ROSES.

I am glad for Peace Polly, and for the impression Mrs. Farron may make upon those who may read of her, that I had that talk to tell of in the last chapter; that it occurred in legitimate order, before certain other ideas had even entered into that lively lady's head, which, with her promptness of character, she would not long leave unacted on.

I am glad that she began at the right end, or the right depth, with Peace Polly. If she had let the other end, or the surface of things, alone, there might be less remaining to tell, but it might also have been more speedily comfortable for Peace Polly, who has not the passive entertainment of reading her own history.

It would be always well if we worked more with the actual, and its obvious import and duty, in our influencing or helping one another; when we leave that, and the motive and showing involved, to try ordering circumstances, and especially future circumstances, we leave the position of our own power, and take hold of something for which we have no tools, no handling implements; and all parties are subject to wound or loss accordingly.

That word of Peace Polly's, that there was nobody of her own age, wrought with force upon Mrs. Farron's mind. If it was too late for her to be a girl, and she had not come to the full estate of her womanhood, it occurred to the Doctor's wife that there was but one good and natural way to remedy the state of things. It was not good for woman, anyhow, to be alone. That went without saying. It was predicated of man, concerning whom there might be thought to be a doubt, possibly ; but for woman, her very creation answered any such question ; she was not put into the world for the solitude of a day, even. Adam was first formed, then Eve. Mrs. Farron believed in matrimony, in the *holy* estate of it ; and she had good reason. She could invent no outward wish for Peace Polly so satisfying or so setting-right as that she might become some good man's wife.

But where was the good man ?

Serena Wyse would have said that he was safe in the Lord's knowledge and leading, though may be across the world, or years away in time to come. Mrs. Farron would have acknowledged that, but she would no less have looked about her a little, if perchance the Lord might have him in nearer readiness, and even mean her to use her eyes a little. Why might it not be of as much purpose and leading that she herself had been brought back just at this moment, from across the continent, into this new interest ? One need not throw one's self, or one's friends, helpless, on Providence. And right here in Bonnyborough, led also, of course, was the Rev. Richard Innesley. Why should not that do ? Why not be meant, and put into her mind, as part of the good process and working of things ? She asked it in all pleased and hopeful reverence.

It was bad that Peace Polly did not come to church more regularly. It was very bad that she had not yet been confirmed. Mrs. Dora felt that she ought not to plan a bit further, —no, not plan, she was not doing so much as that, but only thinking what might be good to come about, — until she had gone to the Doctor with this most essential matter, and begged him to take it on his mind. For how was anything to be done here, among youthful feminine persons, by Richard Innesley, young himself and very good-looking, and only in his diaconate?

Now it happened that Peace Polly's irregularity at church was greatly owing to this same Rev. Mr. Innesley. The girls all thought him so handsome, — pshaw! — especially in his surplice. She was thrown just enough with her contemporaries to see their follies, and catch the floating rubbish that they sometimes talked. She thought that to say a man looked "sweet" in his sacred garb was the most trashy profanity; and if Peace Polly Schott hated any one thing and revered another, they were trumpery and the solemn faiths that she felt herself to have but barely approached, but that, with the angels, she desired honestly, if she only dared or might, to look into.

Worst of all, she told Serena Wyse, one Sunday, she "caught Mr. Innesley's eye in the Te Deum."

"And if anybody really meant one syllable of it," she said, "they would n't have remembered that they *had* eyes: they would have been seeing from inside them, into the glory of heaven. And one seraph would n't so much as look at another seraph there, though his wings brushed over his face, when they were all singing to the Lord! You need n't laugh; I don't mean that there were any seraphs concerned, and I know very well *I* was n't. Rose Howick sits behind me, and she had just come in."

"I don't know but you are a little mite harsh," Serena answered (she pronounced it a little mite *ha'ash*, but nothing sounded awkward or vulgar from Serena Wyse's lips); "a good many things are unconscious, and a minister in a chancel has the disadvantage of one in a pulpit, with-

out being a grain more human. If he looks at his people
at all, he has to do it sideways, and that always appears
more distracted. And which way were *you* looking, inside
or out ? "

"I was n't *daring* to look inside," said Peace Polly.
" I hardly dare to read those words to myself while they
are singing. Why, only *think* what they say ! "

"I don't know them as you do, but only think what
any words are, sent up to the Lord ; and yet we can't
help wandering thoughts. The best ones can't, I suppose."

" When I wander, I stop ; and there are some things I
don't begin on," said honest Polly ; " but I suppose a
clergyman can't," she allowed somewhat indefinitely. " I
would like to *think* they were up there, though, even if I
could n't get there myself. It ought to be real. It begins
with a 'we,' and it ends with an 'I.' It is n't all left to
the apostles and prophets and martyrs."

And so Peace Polly got a prejudice against Mr. Innesley and stayed away from church, except when some
very earnest need of particular confession or entreaty
moved her, and she went for the comfort of the one ab-
solving prayer, or the one sentence in the Litany ; or on
the days when Dr. Farron preached, or administered the
Communion. She kept her seat for the holy service,
though other non-communicants passed cheerfully out,
after just kneeling to pray that with all those departed
this life in God's faith and fear they might be partakers
of the heavenly kingdom. She could bow her head and
shut her eyes and think, while she heard the soft moving
to and fro, and the low, sweet words of the minister that
came brokenly to her ear as he gave the bread and the
cup, that *these* were "up there" with the blessed company in those moments ; and that while they thronged

with better right about the Master, she might in the very shelter of the crowd, catching some crumb of faith from them, be strengthened to reach her hand to the outermost hem of the garment and gain a grace.

This was as far as she had got in " experiencing her Prayer - Book." And nobody guessed anything. Only Mrs. Farron believed there was more in her refusals than in the conformities of many others ; and the good Doctor, watching for her as one who would fain know and counsel, but would not be in haste with any soul, observed some of these things, and put them alongside his wife's anxious communication that " the child had never even been confirmed."

We have been brought to this closer glimpse of the movement of Peace Polly's mind at this time through mention of what may seem but trivial workings, in comparison, concerning her, and very trivial in contrast to return to; but it is needful that we should return to the things which the present chapter was begun with the intent of setting forth.

Beginning to understand her, and to find so much in her, and even to draw her forth more and more freely in an intercourse which, however timidly entered into on Peace Polly's part, was readily enough accepted and developed by that isolated young person of her own age, as its rare invitation and opening became apparent and assured, Mrs. Farron grew more actively desirous that others, such as she could choose, should discover and appreciate as she had done : the Doctor first, as was his place, for the great good he might do her, as no other could, in the highest things of all ; after him, a long way, may be, for who did not come a long way after her wise and strong Sebastian ? — after him, yet truly on the same good road, and well meet to journey in company with this bright, true, questioning spirit who would so grow toward and with him, the young clergyman, Richard Innesley. For Mrs. Dora knew what Peace Polly could not know, through her prejudice and the hindrance of the girl-nonsense about her, that Mr. Innesley was no feeble, mechanical, lay-figure of a would-be priest, but of much more than ordinary power and promise, and heartily given to his work, though young to it, and possibly — since, as she had reminded Polly, it is life eternal we must have for that — not yet grown to its great measure, or to the full inheritance of all the sainthood that has been on earth, and now is in the light.

If Mrs. Farron were possibly mistaken in undertaking such a matter at all, — and she professed to herself all the while that she did not undertake it, — she was certainly very clever in her moves after she had begun — to play ? Well, to overlook the game.

There was no doubt that Rose Howick was a great deal prettier in a certain way than Peace Polly Schott. And oh, the difference in names ! Although she had told Polly sincerely that hers, sounded to its root-depths, was a most beautiful baptismal gift, since the " Mary," which was bitterness, had the other blessed word put before it, like the sweet branch that grew above the bitter waters in the wilderness, and that all the meaning of life lay in the joined meaning of the two, — she could but own to herself, coming out from this true and hidden to the seeming and palpable plane of affairs, that " Peace Polly " was a disadvantage, and that from the font-side until now she had never blamed the child for resenting and bewailing it.

Rose Howick, tea-rose that she was, justified and illustrated her name like a picture made for it : pure, cream-brown-tinted skin, with flushing colors in cheek and lip, never pronounced or fixed but always palpitating up or away, like sky-flushes in an aurora ; large gray-hazel eyes, with straight, clear brows and shady lashes ; hair that was fair, or brown, or golden, or all three, in differing strands, and not in the commoner way as the light fell on it, so that its soft, thick waves and coils shone and darkened in and out, one day deeper, one day brighter-colored, as she happened to fold or twist them ; the daintiest lines and curves of nose and cheek, and lip and chin, of round young figure and of hands and feet, — there were not many who could be looked at long beside her.

"Looked at in the same day," was the expressive vernacular in which the Bonnyburians were apt to put it. But "looked at!" thought Mrs. Farron ; of course she must be looked at ; therefore let her be there ; and she 's a nice girl, too, though nobody need fash themselves for *her* opportunities ; — let her be there and got used to, or else other people will be elsewhere. There are some who are to be learned, not looked at ; with lovely depths to be searched in them, behind mere eyes and lips. The petal tips are not all the flower with them ; the cups of fragrance, not crowded over with redoubled leafings of corolla-splendor, lie retired like tunneled hearts of lilies, or more curiously recessed as cunning nectaries of orchids. Let the rose be there ; there are always plenty of roses ; there are not many orchises.

Mrs. Farron did not sketch out this figure of argument in form ; it ran vividly across her mental retina, all the same. She made up her mind that Rose and Peace should be made acquaint ; and that Mr. Innesley should be asked in now and then to tea.

Peace came in one day with a look upon her brow as of a tear-cloud folded off on the horizon of her face.

"Ah, Peace!" Mrs. Farron greeted her, "you are come well. I want you."

"I 'm not come well; and I 'm more Polly than Peace, to-day."

"Then I want you all the more, if you want me."

Peace Polly had her work with her, a big bundle of crocheted cobwebbery in a muslin lapbag. It foamed out as she unrolled and tied on the apron, like whip-syllabub; it was a shawl, that Mrs. Farron had showed her the stitch for, and she meant it for Serena Wyse.

"I wanted somebody, and I could n't go to Serena, with this, — I mean the shawl, — and I *must* knit just as fast as ever I can, to keep from scratching. To go to anybody is to be a horrid telltale; and yet, it does n't mount to a tale, to tell. It 's myself, of course; it always is. I 'm all raveled out again. Mrs. Farron, what should you do if Dr. Farron should get up from his breakfast and go off, put out, because there did n't happen to be mustard ready mixed upon the table?"

"I don't know. Unless I gave him all mustard next time."

"Oh, you can jest at scars! And then, if he should come back when everything else was cold, as if it needed a quarter of an hour for that, and say he could n't afford to waste his minutes, if other people could? When there had been a plateful of the brownest, puffiest waffles, that you had made yourself to please him, just coming in, if he had waited? They were like toasted leather when he got them, and he said so! What would you have done?"

"I think I should have looked astonished. Simple surprise is the best rebuke, sometimes."

"It 's too late to be astonished," said Peace Polly. "I can't begin that, now. He would say, 'Oh, that 's the new freak, is it? But it won't make mustard, nor it won't darn socks;' and he 'd pull his foot out of his slipper to show the very only hole that was in a drawerful that I 'd mended up two days before!" Peace Polly had here caught up and linked on, for illustration, a separate grievance; it is but just to say that each successive minute did not furnish one. "I believe he thinks I 'm some sort of machine, and he 's inspector. It 's no matter for the smooth-running; that 's to be demanded, or it 's no machine; it 's his business to find the flaws; if there 's a hitch, a hair's breadth miss, it 's as bad as a broken axle; it means destruction. — I 've tried a great many new freaks, Mrs. Farron," she ended, dolefully, "but they all come round to the same old one. I snap out, at the end. And I tell tales. I shall be just as miserable, by and by, about my talking so to you as about the rest of it. And he never snaps out, or talks me over; he 's just as still; he thinks he 's patient and put-upping! but he puts me in the meanest places! I don't suppose he 'll ever believe in me, or understand me, now."

"I don't suppose," said Mrs. Farron, with serious kindness, "that you can begin all over again with your brother. We can't live over; we have to overlive. The only thing is to let him see what you really mean by your coming to it; by your growing self-control, and your wise ways, gathered up out of your mistakes."

"He would n't knów, — he would n't notice. He would only think he had managed with tremendous wisdom himself not to exasperate me, and yet to break me in so beautifully at last. It *would* be good to rub out the whole slate, and cipher the sum again by a cleverer rule; but I never can with him."

What wonder that Mrs. Farron thought once more, as she was thinking almost daily, and with growing emphasis, that the new place and relation ought to come in this girl's life where she could begin all over afresh, and with some one who would believe, and notice, and understand? It was apparent to her at that moment how life is planned just so, for man and woman, that there should be a break from former link and habit, often from imperfection and mistake, and a clear, clean start for the fulfillment of the best one has grown to even in desire, unhampered by the poorest one has ever happened to be, or to get credit for.

So she spoke from her thought, though not all her thought.

"Life is full of new beginnings," she said, cheerily. "Some change may come, something is sure to come, to close one chapter and begin another. We go on for a long time, thinking things can never be different, and all at once some little turn, or stop, or adding on, and it is suddenly a new story we are in, and even a quite different self. We are trained in episodes. Your new episode will come."

Peace Polly dropped her busy fingers with her needle in the middle of a stitch. She looked up at Mrs. Farron imploringly. "Oh, can't *you* understand me, either?" she asked, with an indescribable pathos. "Don't you see it is that I can't be satisfied until I whole-love my brother; that it is n't the vexes, as they vex *me*, so much as that they make *him* seem small to me, and cheat me of my feeling for him? Don't you see it is n't change I want, until I have lived this right? What good would it do me to go to heaven, even," the girl went on impetuously, "if behind me was a piece of life unlived, a piece of loving that I had n't learned or done? If I have n't loved my brother whom I have seen, how can I love — *any*body that I have never seen?"

Was it heaven, and the home of the Lord, after life ended, that she entirely meant? Mrs. Farron wondered, looking at her face that glowed and yet was pale, and listening in her own moved mind to the echo of the words so high and strange to come, unstudied, straight from so young a heart. She could not tell. "How can I love anybody that I have not seen," "I don't want change until I have lived this right," — was there not in these sentences a foreseeing of a judgment in each following gift and opening, right on from the present instant into eternity, that included all unreadiness and misfulfillment of human relation and possibility, and reached and searched until there came to mind the utterance that might forbid or darken the everlasting joy, " How came this one hither, not wearing the wedding garment? "

Would it be a light or easy thing to anticipate, or to handle chances, for a girl like this, looking so on and through the very heart of things for herself? Could one get beyond or beneath her, in either plan or probing? She began to question what Dr. Farron himself could do with her. Meanwhile, what was to be said? — for something always has to be said, ripe or unripe; a conversation can't drop in the middle, even though all has been spoken and left the subject endless. What was to be said in answer to her at this moment? Perhaps Mrs. Farron did as well as could have been done.

"I think it will be put right, dear," she said. "You want it so, and I am sure God wants it. But there are changes in selfsame things; there are ways of escape and enlarging. I have thought you needed some little outside ones, perhaps, and I dare say your brother needs them too, if he could be got to take them. You people in Bonnyborough pound away too steadily each in one spot; it makes life all pestle and mortar; you don't even look over to find out what each other is grinding. That was what I wanted to see you for. I was going to speak to you about a picnic to Cape Campus."

VIII.

CAPE CAMPUS.

BONNYBOROUGH lies but a brief way back from the sea, utterly inland as it feels to be among its rolling, wooded hills and in the green nooks of its hollows. Over through East Farms to the shore is but a drive of from six to eight miles, as you may strike it. Cape Campus is the farthest point, straight east, and runs out its grand little headland, between two small sand beaches that curve away north and south till bounded by rock bluffs at either end, some half mile on the one hand, only a furlong or so on the other. This last is the pretty little " Brier Cove," scalloping the coast-line with a lovely indentation, on whose landward edges the wild roses fling up gay, hardy heads to the very pebble-line of the highest tide-sweep.

Cape Campus is the broad, rocky spur-foot of a huge ledge. It stands with broken, massive walls of seaworn cliff showing its foundation right and left, and thrusting into the waters that leap unceasingly about its terminal crag a great, fissured, smooth-beaten slope, down which you can go until you may seat yourself close to the very foam-fringe of the up-pouring ocean masses, that rear and plunge and hurl themselves through gully and cranny, everywhere that the mysterious measure of the tide will let, and then slip and crawl and slaver back, like angry and rebuked dumb creatures, to gather force and grandeur again for their alternate change and apotheosis to glorious living personalities of power and splendor.

Across the top, between foundation wall and wall, and behind and above the naze, lies the sweet pasture-field from which it is called " Campus."   Tall grasses, flowered or seeded, wave in the sunlight and the crisp breeze; clumps of the wild rose redden, half the summer through, to such color as the sea-breath only gives; delicate bind-weed hangs its blossoms all over the briery, straggling stems; and dangerous, most beautiful ivy flings itself about wherever it has been spared, and drops its scarfs and streamers of shining green down the gray rock-faces.

Oak-trees grow all about the down that reaches seaward from the highway and the villages; this table-stretch makes space and pause between the swells of land and swells of ocean that, still, and green, and summer-rich on one hand, and clear, cold, opalesque upon the other, roll from east and west toward their meeting.   There are wagon-tracks across, where the farmers come over for their rockweed; but after the hay is cut from these sea-fields, you can drive almost anywhere for two or three miles upon the grass plateau; and you could stop and rest anywhere under the rich tree shades, and enjoy abundantly of sky and earth from horizon to horizon, only that, like the dips of land and the runs of water, once started toward the deep, we human creatures cannot stop, for the spirit that is in us, until we reach the uttermost edge, and come face to face with the vast wonder that is not made up of many, like the gathering and mutual illustration of field and fell, tree, grass, and flower, and the growth and change of them, but is one great, unutterable selfsame glory, majesty, and life.

So it is not a trivial thing to come down here to Cape Campus; though it seemed a fall from what they had been saying just before, when Mrs. Farron spoke to Peace Polly of the picnic.   The outdoor luncheon, though pleasant enough in itself, and sure, in Bonnyborough, to be made up of good things, was a small part; yet since people must eat, and cannot travel a dozen miles and tarry three or four hours without going over a meal, which must therefore be put in baskets and taken along, the whole joy and delight and holiday goes by the name of the material providing.

"Let us all go down and look at the glory of the sea; let us get together in that wonderful presence-chamber, where the airs blow in from the infinite, and will fill us full of new breath of life!"—suppose Mrs. Farron had said that, which was what she meant. Of course, we can suppose no such thing; it was but sane and practical to say, "Let us pack up our eatables, and go and have our dinner at the shore." But everybody understands the commonest speech in the tongue to which he is born.

The Bonnyburians seldom got together in this fashion; when they did, they had a way of doing it with a particular and original wisdom. I don't know who first suggested it, but it came about, and is a good thing to mention and make known. Somebody, on some far back occasion, who had organized a *fête champêtre*, had said, "Now, no heterogeneity! no big panniers, full of everything. One thing only in one basket, and everything in baskets; then our table is set beforehand."

So, at this day, if you go to Bonnyborough, and have the luck to get into a picnic there, you will find it so: a lot of little splint fruit-pails, probably, some small woven willow pottles, even bright pails of tin,— none larger than a two-quart capacity; one holding spicy doughnuts, another crisp and melting sugar cookies, wafer-thin and aromatic with caraway seeds; another sponge-cake, and another cheese,— the first foam, the second cream, how held together nobody could tell; then there would be one of toasted crackers and tongue slices, and one of fine-chopped soft-spread sandwiches; and so on and so on, through such a category of deliciousness as you would scarcely forgive me for setting forth with only printer's ink and paper, —all these tempting little severalties packed, in their turn, by the half dozen, perhaps, in market-hampers for mere carriage, but all ready to serve as single dishes when unladen. No hurry, no confusion, no placing and displacing and replacing, therefore, but the swiftest, simplest tablespreading and the easiest waiting; the easiest picking up, also, when all is over; for it hardly matters which gets which, any more than what is done with the grocer's paper plates from which they have eaten. And every one carries knife and fork and spoon and napkin, either or all, and takes care of them or loses them on personal responsibility. Bonnyborough understands the philosophy of picnicking; it is to be perfectly individual and delightfully congregate, both at once. I dare say this comes of the very thing Mrs. Farron half deplored and reprobated: that they live so individually; are so grained off, as one might say, cohered and rounded in their entities, that no amount of crowding or mixing makes them substantially a mass, or in the least approach fluid; there is visible, palpable space about each atom, and there is palpable atomic law and working. As to that, the thing is largely characteristic of New England; we are individuals here, instead of classes; and it is class that makes mass. Bonnyborough is, but with some peculiar intensity, New English.

Peace Polly had not supposed that Lyman would condescend, or extravagate, to the picnic. He did, however; which was what might have been expected, the unlooked-for being precisely what, in certain circumstances, was to be calculated on from him. Only, the circumstances cer-

tain to himself were apt to be uncertain and unarguable
to all others.

"I don't see why *you* won't go to this, Lyman," Polly
had said to him, and was going on to adduce that Dr.
Farron himself was to be there, and that Dr. Blithecome
had said he should drive down in the afternoon for a salt
whiff and a look at the roses; but Lyman quietly prevented her with "There is no why; I 'm going."

At which, Polly, having started to ride a tilt, was
cleanly unhorsed. She stared amiably, picked herself up,
and remarked, "That 's good of you. I 'm very glad."

There were to be no foreigners at the picnic. Jennie
Cramhall had said, tentatively, that Lou and she could
not both be spared to go unless they took their boarders
with them. But Peace Polly said, "We don't want
strangers. It is our turn not to. It takes too long to get
acquainted. We go to the seashore for a holiday, not to
undertake a new set of social duties. People who join a
picnic ought to be like the baskets, all ready to catch up
and go right along with; and the provision inside them of
a sort to be pretty well counted on beforehand. We 're
sorry to lose either of you, but one of you is worth all your
transients to us." And Peace Polly had Mrs. Farron behind her; therefore so it was. There befell one day of
that summer in Bonnyborough when the city people had
the half-vacated village to themselves, and could not well
get far out of it. Every horse and vehicle of any pre-
tension was drafted for Campus, besides the "rigging"
and pair that carried the straw-riders. The ladies with
country toilets carefully suggestive of metropolitan art
and resource, and the young men with water-cart whiskers and successful British intonations, took their turn at
standing about or sitting on piazzas, to see the equipment
and start-off of the simple, and to stare, as the simple had

been supposed to have stared — only they never did —
at themselves.

By nine o'clock, the main street was as quiet as the
church aisle on a week day, and old Mr. Milleneyer might
have taken his sea-chair nap upon the hayscales. The
very baker's cart had gone round·early to accommodate
the occasion. Pedestrians were independent; Raspberry
Ridge or Dimple Pond or Squarrock Fall might have been
visited, had they not been nearly done to death already,
or seemed so to-day, in comparison with the breezy, briny
holiday-keeping beside the sea; otherwise, the Great Ju-
cundandum was reduced to piazza crochet, backgammon,
the magazines, and the last society-skim of Mr. Swella-
dore's novelettes, or to the eternal love-ten, love-fifteen,
love-all-the-way-up-to-forty, of lawn tennis.

The arrival and alighting of a pleased pleasure-party
upon its ground is a pretty thing to see. It is like· the
lighting of a flock of northward summering birds in a
field new-seeded for their wayside halt. And that, not
because of the mere gain of what the one spot affords, but
for the sense of wings just folded at quick will, of all
heaven open to flee back into, of all choice and privilege
and plenty out of which they take this for the time being,
with a whole world-full waiting for the time to be.

The outdoor wideness, the blue of sky, the shine of
sun, the wave of tree, the smile of grass, replacing the
every day of wall and ceiling and furniture, and mere
door and window outlook, is a great new world into
which life breaks, if only for a day, from the discarded
shell of need and custom. It is a breath of spirit freedom
that dilates every figure, gives spring to every step and
poise, and plays upon every face. It is the first moment
that most glorifies, like all beautiful first moments; because it has in it a wholeness of delight that does not

stop to test detail, and is not touched with any weariness or interruption that must come in the measuring and verifying, item by item, of almost any joy.

Everything was theirs, and everything was untouched, unspoiled. Dresses and tempers were fresh; people all looked pretty. The enchantment of distance was at least speedily within the resource of all, and the outdoor breadth is a wonderful advantager and averager. Even the inevitable, all-surviving white piqués and Roman scarfs scattered themselves pleasantly among the dusky oak shadows, and gave touches of color becoming to the landscape, if not always of best effect in personal concentration. But who wants to be self-concentrate in a general, generous, open-air, all-for-everybody festival? Is it not the very essence of the thing to contribute?

Fresh lawns and ginghams fluttered delicate hems or ruffles among the grassheads around dainty feet, reached by the running breezes in which the grasses nodded; gay-striped tennis suits emblazoned the sea-scoured rocks; Jennie Cramhall had on a pigeon-gray petticoat and a jersey of Burgundy crimson, and was like a tropical cardinal-bird gale-drifted over; among them all, Rose Howick and Peace Polly Schott were the prettiest clothed. There were other garments beside theirs of soft summer woolen,—Mrs. Farron, Miss Serena, and Miss Mallis had them, of one neutrality or another; but these two were just dressed as if no other array could possibly have happened upon either. By hap or forethought, also, all adorning had been left until they had come to the sweet, free fineries of the shore.

Rose Howick's gown was of wool-muslin, in a shade you could not call either brown or olive or green, but a sober-sunny mingling of all three, like the rich duskiness of half-grown leafage that wraps some of her namesake blossoms. She had not been three minutes on her feet before a bunch of glorious sea-daisies was thrust into her belt, and their golden eyes, with the leaning of their stems against the sweet bend of her young figure, seemed looking down with gentle amaze of proud preferment upon their fellows in the grass. Another bunch was cunningly tucked up between crown and brim of the small-peaked hat, innocent till then of all bedizenment save the full-knotted scarf of silk, bronze-tinted shadow-green like the color of the dress.

Peace Polly wore an American-blue bunting, fitted in plaits, and roundly belted in; not so much as a button showing upon it to make it gay, only the crispest of little white crimped ruffles at throat and wrist; but she also had quickly gathered a summer-token of red roses for a breast-knot, and set some thornless tip-sprays with pointed buds of vivid crimson, like young flames from their live stems, against the full coil of her dark-brown hair that showed itself so quietly below the small black-straw bonnet crossed with blue.

Other people had put things on, more or less congruous, that they had before, and had come there in them; these two were of the very day itself, and the day had dressed them.

Once scattered, nothing but dinner or a thunder-shower would draw or drive the crowd of them together again. Like all the rest, — like the very societies above and beneath, — we have therefore but to choose and follow our own group.

Shells and weeds in Brier Cove drew a rambling party quickly together; a net, racquets, and balls had been smuggled down, and kept a few inveterates, who might as well have been in any common field or orchard, upon the oak-tree down, near where the horses and wagons had been picketed. There were two or three sketchers posted here and there with pads and pencils, or blocks and paints ; and some who had come for the mere sake of wind, and wave, and sun, and all the beautiful rush of vital gladness from the free hemisphere they shaped and filled, had left as much of earth invisible behind them as they could get away from, and on far-out reaches of the Campus Cliff had found low, seaward nooks, where they could lean against some sun-warmed break or slope of granite, and sit quiet for the lovely turmoil to beat close up and about them with heaving, sweeping, shattering changes of gorgeous color and grand volume, and swift outpour and gathering back, in mass and crest, and hollow and spread, and tiny, truant, half-lost runs and dribbles of the gloriously wasteful water, that flung itself everywhere in seeming of sheer wantonness, yet only in that perfect liberty of a mighty law in whose hold not a drop could really get astray or stay beyond, to fail of rendering again its little measure to the vast bulk that up and down the jagged continent-line still keeps, from tide to tide, the awful sea-brim even.

The group we want is down here, upon the white forefoot of Campus Crag.

Each side the water-rush booms up into deep fissure and inlet or along slow rock-incline, pushing with every pulse a little on or over, making swift, long thrusts where some narrow scoop or level matches the tide-gain, or tossing fretted spume, beat after beat, across some tiny rockhead bravely holding up, by ever less and less of its unsmothered height, against the urgent onset, until at last one smooth, complacent wave pours easy triumph clean athwart, and makes a clear, round water-knoll above the vanished crown.

"It gains, and gains, and at last gives up itself, and

goes back beaten. The sea is disappointing, after all," said Peace Polly. "I always long so to see it do a little more."

"Don't we long that for everything?" asked Serena Wyse. "Even when a frightful wind blows, or a great fire rages, even when we are afraid or sorry, is n't there a strange wish underneath to see how a little more would seem?"

"I remember I felt that in the great September gale," said Mrs. Farron. "A whole orchard of little trees lay flat between my window and the road, and a great larch had fallen beside the gate. I stood and looked, and said, Oh, how tremendous! but all the time I was so in the wild spirit of the thing that it was as if I myself were the tempest, struggling with the elms that bent themselves over double, but would *not* go down. I felt as if I could not let them off until they did. I always want more in an aurora, and I never saw enough shooting-stars, though I was up and out all night in the meteor rain of '65. And the only earthquake I was ever in was such a mild shake, and so quickly over, that it was really a defrauding that it did not come again and let us know better what it could be like."

"*Wifie!*" came Dr. Farron's voice from behind them, in one of the water-lulls which alone let them hear easily each other's speech. He had but caught the earthquake sentence.

"That always means," said Mrs. Dora, "'I 'm one with you, but we 're both wrong.' Yes, dear," she called back to him. "It 's very bold, but it 's bold truth. We *don't* like to come to limits, until it is a clear question of bodily danger. Then the desire shifts sides, of course. The mind has its own little vehicle to take care of, and is n't free for cosmic revel. Aside from that, we just want everything to happen! I truly can't sometimes see" — but the little lady's voice took a changed tone with the last five words, and she left her say unfinished.

Mr. Innesley was closer than the Doctor had been, a little below the group of ladies, and the soft land wind blew down his way. He had heard all quite plainly.

"You can't see what, Mrs. Farron?" he asked.

"How God refrains his utmost," she replied, with awe.

Dr. Farron had come round beside the young clergyman, and had gathered understanding of the thing in thought. "He does not," he said. "His utmost is the balance; his will on *all* the sides."

"Ah, yes; and that keeps our wills down. We are the poor things that can only feel one side, — our own," said Mrs. Dora.

"Is *that* all our wanting, I wonder? Because we don't know the other that our want gives way to?"

Those words came half voluntarily from Peace Polly.

"That's all our *passion*," said Dr. Farron. "Our *wanting* is something that waits quieter and surer. It is on God's side."

"Who is Wholeness, having neither parts nor passions," said the young deacon, discerning a wonderful meaning suddenly in something nearly meaningless whim before.

"Only com-passion; the divine difference from the human," answered Dr. Farron.

"But the com-passion enters in, feels with, seems therefore to allow," returned Mr. Innesley.

"Passion is the suffering of the waiting!" cried Peace Polly, not half knowing the fullness of what she said.

"It seems to me we are going very deep," said Rose Howick, in her sweet way. "Passion is temper, impatience, hurry to have, that sort of one-sidedness, is n't it? And the other side, that might keep us straight, is calmness, fairness, a quiet, lovely way, — the 'virtue and the praise'? It might stop us just to think how little graceful it is to be in a passion."

"Graceful? But it might be grand!" broke forth Peace Polly.

"About little petty things?"

"No; that is what I would like to be able to save up from, without growing too amiable for the other. Not because of the gracefulness, though; it would make me furious not to be able to go deeper than that!"

"I thought we were only considering a safe balance," said Rose Howick, pleasantly.

"And a very poor stick may sometimes help us small acrobats to keep that," said Mr. Innesley, smiling upon pretty Rose, who had towed the conversation back to shoaler water, certainly.

None the less, what Peace Polly had said, and the outrightness of it, remained in his mind, the beginning of a very fresh interest. Real individuals were wonderfully attractive to Mr. Innesley. He found them tolerably rare.

"We have n't got out of *our* limits," said Dr. Farron, "or found or said any very new thing. We began with Job, about the reservings and bindings of creation, and we have come round to the blessed antidotes of St. Paul. Perhaps now we had better go up the cliff again, and see what some of our contemporary fellow-creatures are about."

IX.

THORNS.

MISS MALLIS was up there; she had got hold of Lyman Schott and Mr. Dawney the minister, and was half amusing, half shocking, and wholly astonishing them, after her way, with sharp, audacious speeches that had, nevertheless, to do her full justice, as often as not some fair foundation of sense and sagacity as well as mere smartness. Judith and Ruth Dawney, Jenny and Benny Cramhall, and the Holistons, Dianthe and Sarah and Quincy Adams, had followed along, sure of some game or diversion where Miss Mallis was; and the party was settling itself along the " Lounge Rocks " upon the southerly reach of the cliff, where the rounded or slanting outcrops were cushioned, between their frequent splits and at their turf-bound edges, with the short, elastic sea-grass that grew up over and seemed to bed in the old, bleached, snaggy stones, quite concealing the fact of its own shallow concretion and the unity of the vast, age-worn mass whose mountain roots were somewhere away below all reach or measurement, between the ocean undercalm and the everlasting fires.

The merrymakers sat down comfortably among the crown pinnacles of the sea-alp, nor dreamed how really high they were, nor what a piling and upheaving there had had to be of old to build this basin-rim against whose lip the torrents were rolled up, and where, at the surface of the mights and wonders, they should find ready, careless resting-place, in the shine of a sweet summer morning.

Miss Mallis wanted them all to play a game, a conversational one, while they sat there and rested before dinner. Miss Mallis was good at these little tournaments of mental quickness and telling repartee. "People must have something," was her argument, "and I do what I can. It's as good as lawn tennis, any way. And that leaves me out in the cold, you see, for it only counts up to forty."

"Mr. Schott," she said, "you must shake the sawdust and shavings all off your feet, and the buzz of the steam plane and chisels out of your brain, to-day. And I won't have Mr. Dawney thinking up his sermon for next Sunday. Sufficient unto the — wise is a word, you know."

She managed the shift of her allusion without any actual light quoting. Not even the minister could find room for reproof or check; his half-startled look at her hung fire with eyelids raised midway. She delighted in half-startling serious people, and then leaving them there *sine causâ*. But to help Mr. Dawney's eyelids down with dignity she did point over to the opposite cliff.

"The water is almost up to the Wolf's Hole," she said. "Some folks call it the Devil's Den; but that is so worn out, you know. There's always a Devil's Den, and a Spouting Horn, and a Pulpit Rock, at every shore place, and in every wild, bouldery pasture; that's the pulpit, there, swarming with boys, as pulpits mostly are, right directly over the De— Den. Seems to me it might do more good if 't was planted square down in the face of it, — don't you think so, Mr. Dawney? Why, there is n't a calmer, more unconscious place on all Campus than that sunny Pulpit Rock. The highest spray never touches it; it does n't know what the sea-beat is; but down there, the waves go tearing in and out of the Wolf's Hole every three-quarters tide, with an uproar of more than a thousand-preacher power. It 's always done it, and it always will."

"I thought sermons had been interdicted," said Mr. Dawney, with his quiet smile, yet looking as though the carelessly flung word had touched some tender loyalty in him, quick always to truth's countersign, however rendered.

"Oh, no," returned Miss Mallis; "only the taking thought for them for three to-morrows ahead. You can't hinder the sermons in the stones, of course, nor an old hen's lay cackle. There may turn out to be sermons in my game, too," she went on, as the other party approached them up the slope. "It will all be according to the players; and here are Dr. Farron and Mr. Innesley. Really, I don't see how we are to escape with so much clergy."

She made room for them, and invited them to seats, as she spoke. It happened that Dr. Farron took a place beside her. Rose and Peace Polly passed a little aside and back, and Mrs. Farron and Miss Serena came between. Lyman Schott was near by, in front, on an outpushing projection; it was a point of possible danger to a less heedful person, which I think was why he had occupied it. The few boys who were about looked hatreds and vengeances at him accordingly.

"We 're just going to play 'Thoughts,'" said Miss Mallis, begging the acquiescence; "and there are two ways, you know. Shall it be Hap-hazard, or Abstract-and-Tangible?"

"We could n't venture to answer Hap-hazard, of course," said Mrs. Farron. "Suppose you explain your Abstract-and-Tangible, and the difference?"

"One is conundrums, and the other is correspondence," returned Miss Mallis, oracularly. "One way you think anything and say anything, and then find out why; the other you only think of abstracts, and you compare with substantive facts. For instance, Dr. Farron, I think of something intangible. What is it like, tangible?"

"Like that little boat on the beach down there," replied the Doctor.

"Well, I thought of Theology!"

"I might say, perhaps, that it had been lugged in, as it often is," rejoined the Doctor, dryly.

"*You* 're not stranded, any way!" said the lady, in a laughing half whisper.

"Did you mean me to be? But now I 've got a thought. Miss Serena, what is it like, in the concrete?"

"Like sticking-plaster."

"Beauty; why?"

"Best sort won't rub off," Miss Serena answered, with quiet quickness, which a general laugh applauded.

Lyman Schott looked round from his perch, and caught her eye. It was but a homely bit of aptness, scarcely wit, but it served for a little pleased exchange between them. That it did so might have told them something that was but waiting under contradiction.

Miss Serena spoke across to him. "What is my thought like, Mr. Schott?"

He had not counted on this. "Oh, a broken bone," he answered, at most desperate random, taking the suggestion, perhaps, from the opportunities of the place.

"I thought of Plenty."

"Well," said Lyman, recovering his slow sobriety, "when a man 's got that he don't want any more, does he?"—which drew a shout; then came a pause.

"But *you* must think," said Miss Mallis, as mistress of ceremonies; "it 's your turn. Something fine and philosophical, now."

"Very well, ma'am.   Likeness?"

"Like my thumb."

"Common sense," declared Lyman.

"I might say I 've got considerable of it," said Miss Mallis, holding up contemplatively a generously proportioned member, "but I won't.   If I had n't got it of my own, I could n't borrow any; there!"

"Mr. Dawney, I 've thought again.   Compare, please."

"This bit of driftwood."   He held a piece curiously moulded and veined like a leaf-shaped fungus.   Mrs. Farron had shown it to him; she had picked it up, and was treasuring it for a bracket.

"Worldly wisdom.   I thought I 'd take an opposite this time; why is it like that?"

"I must transfer the question with the property.   Mrs. Farron can tell us, probably."

"Oh," said Mrs. Dora, accepting the scrap of wreckage and the commission with instant, undemurring tact, "it is very smooth, very polished, bears the marks of long experience, comes in with the tide in a comfortable sort of way; but it is rotten and worthless, really, and gets left high and dry at last.   Mr. Innesley, what thing is Mr. Dawney's present thought like; for I suppose he is to give it to me to pass on?"

"Like this wild rose," said Mr. Innesley.

Good Mr. Dawney was already at least three to-morrows beyond or above the game again. Mrs. Farron would have supplied the thought herself, and left him so; but Miss Mallis poked the minister's shoulder softly with her parasol.

"Your thought, Mr. Dawney, please.   Mrs. Farron wants it, and we 're all waiting.   I 'm sure you have one."

The serene old face turned round toward her from the sunlit ocean.

"Yes, — Peace," he said, not without gentle satire.

Miss Mallis and Mrs. Farron looked amused, and instantly, on both faces, the amusement deepened with a further perception of application and consequence, of which the good pastor was most profoundly innocent.

Mrs. Farron wondered what Mr. Innesley would make of it, and reflected that it was none of her plot or doing, all in the flash of time in which she drew back to give the word.

"The Peace that passeth — comprehension," whispered Miss Mallis, all aglee, and nodding over toward Peace Polly, who, not following the turns of the game, and leaving Mr. Innesley to draw off Rose Howick into pleasant interludes of talk, was gazing away after something beyond her horizon, quite as abstractedly as any third-to-morrow preacher of them all.

Mrs. Farron breathed a sibilant rebuke through the edges of her teeth. "Sh!" she said. It was not the soft contraction of a "hush!" so much as the first indignant sound of a scarcely repressed "shame!" But Miss Mallis went on whispering her little laugh, and wondering, with eyes all but audible with fun, what the Rev. Richard would do now.

"Mr. Innesley, why is Peace like a wild rose?"

The clear voice shot through a sudden silence, and everybody heard.

Peace Polly, with the roses on her bosom shining and breathing up into her face, started and flushed like them, catching the whole question without previous noting of its parts.

Mr. Innesley turned the stem of his brier-blossom gently in his fingers, regarding it thoughtfully.

"Because," he said, "if a man would gain it, he must brave the thorns!"

That was irresistible. Miss Mallis laughed aloud. A queer little smile played and quenched itself upon Mrs. Farron's face. Lyman Schott lifted his eyebrows and cleared his throat, and sent a look, that was curiously amused and concerned at once, toward his sister. A smile and rustle went round ; other than these indications there was only that extinguished silence that implies a putting-out of something or somebody in a social circle.

It did not last longer than to begin to be felt. Mrs. Farron spoke out : —

"I should have said" — the words came clearly and significantly — "that there was a rare thing to be perfected on earth, and so it was set, for safety of its own growth, *among* the thorns!"

Peace Polly had turned her face toward the sea again; that was all Mrs. Farron could be sure of as she spoke; but by some *rapport* she felt the hurried heart-beat, and even the hot moisture ready to spring behind the proudly leveled eyelids.

A big, shining tin dish-pan, hung to a tree on the oak-down, and rung in good imitation of a Japanese gong, sounded across to them with shivering resonance, and they began, with some alacrity, to move. Luncheon was ready, and the game was over, certainly.

"That was too bad!" said Jenny Cramhall, coming down with the Dawney girls.

"Or too good," said Quincy Adams Holiston, who had memories of a snub or two, when he had needed them, from Peace Polly.

"For shame, Quin!" said Sarah. For the young minister was close by, with Rose Howick and the rector's lady.

"What did I say, dear Mrs. Farron," besought Mr. Innesley, "that was funny, or amiss? And why were you indignant? I thought I made the very tritest sort of answer."

Peace Polly herself came up with the group. She had only lingered to pick up a shawl that belonged to Mrs. Farron. She would have scorned to palpably take time.

Her head was up with a kind of honest, wild-rose dignity. She might be conscious of her thorns; she might have to wear them in open-air confession; but she knew her own heart-mystery of hidden, waiting, possible sweetness, too.

Her brother and Serena Wyse were behind; but she took no refuge with them. She stepped straight forward among the speakers in that frank-flushing pride that sat upon her well.

"It was I that made it funny, Mr. Innesley," she said, with simplest directness; "but it was not amiss. My name is Peace, and I have a very bad temper."

They all heard; she was quite willing.

Benny Cramhall, on the outside edge of the company, threw up his hat. "Bully for you, Pease Porridge! You 've got the dead wood on 'em this time!" he exclaimed.

The girls looked at each other with quick color in their faces, and there was a drift of the little concourse closer toward Peace Polly. Quin Holiston snickered feebly, kept aside, and got left out.

Peace Polly moved on quietly alone, without another word. But Mr. Innesley hastened beside her.

"My dear Miss Schott!" he said. "You may have a *quick* temper, possibly, — most people have who are sensitive to this world's misadjustments; but it is very evidently not a bad one!"

"Thank you, Mr. Innesley. You are very kind." And then Peace Polly slightly checked her steps, and turned, to slip her arm in Miss Serena Wyse's, and so went down the hill.

6

X

PULPIT ROCK.

" I don't know how you feel about that little sister of
yours, Lyman," said Miss Serena.   " But if I was her
brother, I should be proud of her."

" If you were her brother, you 'd be a man," said Lyman Schott.   " And a man would rather be comfortable
with a woman than proud of her.   She 's got good stuff in
her, I know, if she would n't turn it wrongside out."

" A woman turns a good thing wrongside out sometimes to save the rubs," Serena answered.

" If you can take her part like that, I don't see
why " — but Lyman checked himself.

Serena knew what he meant.   She could not, therefore, ask, " You don't see what ? "   The color came, and
she smiled.   " I 'm where I can take both parts," she said.

Peace Polly had eaten her luncheon, and had walked
off toward the south cliff.   It was quiet and solitary, all the
way to Pulpit Rock.   The boys had gone away up shore :
some of them to the bathing places on the longer beach ;
some of them had been lucky enough to be by when fisher-
man Doughty came down to his boat, and had got taken
in with him for a trip round to his lobster pots.

Peace Polly felt like being alone a while.   All along
the way she took, the bayberry and brier-bushes, with
the full-flowered bindweed and the rich-matted ivies, made
a screenwork of tangled beauty, behind which she moved
in a safe, still cover.   And out at the end, she knew the

way, as well as the boys, by the narrow side-ledge path and
the curious foot-bridge of lodged stones across the Wolf's
Hole gully, to the free, lofty outlook that she might have
in full possession, since only a young, sure foot could gain
it, and she did not know of a Bonnyborough girl except
herself who cared to take its *mauvais pas.*

It happened, however, that some one else, with sufficiently young muscles and steady head, had been inspired
with the same thought, and had just preceded her so as
to be kept well out of her sight in the windings of the
bushy pathway. At the descent from the wild green of
the high shrubbery to the bare ledge-side, she overtook
the Rev. Richard Innesley, standing, hat in hand, the
shifted breeze, coming in now salt and strong from seaward, blowing his hair back as he faced the beautiful
grandeur of the open water, and his whole attitude expressive of an eager, full-drawn, satisfied inhaling of delight.

Peace Polly was not silly enough to turn round and
run; she would not go further, however. Mr. Innesley
would pass on presently, perhaps; then she could retrace
her steps, or stay here for a while. She sat down where
she was, upon a little verge from which she must next
have made a slight jump to a lower terrace of the irregular rock, and waited.

For a minute or two, each was as much alone as if the
other had not been there, for Polly was partly shielded
by a jut, behind which she just leaned sufficiently not to
see her neighbor, and Mr. Innesley still faced the sea.
By the queer magnetism, however, which a person under
even the slightest cognizance is subject to and so compelled into response, the gentleman, as he replaced his
hat to move onward, was drawn to turn partly round and
look back.

A sea-blue skirt and a pair of stout little boots crossed over each other at the ankle were revealed to him beyond the projection, and at the very instant Peace Polly's parasol slipped off her lap, and shot gently down the causeway.

A short " ah ! " was surprised from Peace Polly's lips, and the parasol landed at Mr. Innesley's feet. Of course he picked it up, and brought it to her. " It is you ! " he said.

" Yes. I did not know there was any one here at all," she answered. " I was going " — but she stopped her self-committal of further intent.

" Beyond this ? " he asked. " Is it possible, for you ? "

" Oh, quite possible ; I have often been ; but I did not say — I mean, I had not decided, now."

" If you would decide, now you are here, if you are sure it is quite safe for you, you might pilot me, for I was in doubt of the best path, myself."

" There is only one," said Peace Polly, who had naturally risen to her feet. " I will show you, if you wish."

If the young clergyman supposed she was likely to make any small fuss about it, he had quite mistaken his young lady. He could see very well that he had unconsciously stopped her in her plan ; he could guess, also, as was perfectly true, that at this very moment she was ready to break her parasol in bits with vexation for the trick it had played her, but which some girls would have been quite capable of playing for themselves ; yet she accepted the situation with that kind of quietness that ignores all crisis, where demur would at once have been significant, simply saying, as she moved by him, " I had better go first, perhaps ; and after this I could not pass."

Below and beyond them, all along the south front of the promontory, was a confusion of heaped and projecting masses, among which, from one to another, might be some feasible way to the extremity; but that reached, where was the ascent to the dominating Pulpit Rock which overtopped all else along the shore, and raised its front serene far above the changes and the charges of the tides?

Peace Polly led her companion by a turn he had not even noticed, where a bolder jut than that by which she had been sitting overshaded a little shelf ending apparently in nothing, but which when stepped upon revealed just breadth enough beyond to enable them to round the crag quite safely. Then they found themselves in a crosswise split or gully of the cliff, along whose side ran a path, a mere ledge-line in comparison of the vast surfaces about it, yet for the most of its extent fully three feet wide, and with holding-place along the way by the roughnesses and fissures of the precipice above.

Notwithstanding the rational safety, Mr. Innesley was conscious of an inward shiver which he would not have felt for himself, as he saw the light figure before him move securely on and on, here and there dropping easily to a lower level, as the downward breaks occurred in a continually descending trend, at last pausing, like a bird alert for flight, upon an edge where there seemed again an end in nothing.

As he came close, she faced round upon him with a smile, and once more stepped down. The ledge-path turned here, and ran back beneath the upper one about half as far, still descending. Here it ended, at the blind extremity of the narrow inlet, near whose wall, but separate from it by some feet of vacancy, hung a broken, wedged-in mass of rock between the two sides of the deep crevasse.

At this strange foot-bridge Peace Polly stopped again,

and again looked round. Mr. Innesley stood still, of necessity, a little at her left.

"Do you feel afraid?" she asked, with the same smile as before, seeing something in his face that seemed to justify the slight mischief of both smile and question.

"A little, for you," he answered. "I suppose I need not. But I should never have asked you to show me the way, if I had thought the way was this."

"Don't you like it? Listen!"

A great booming surge was rushing up the Wolf's Hole; one of those torrents that one watches for at a wild sea-gorge, coming at intervals, — ninth-waves, they say, — with all the accumulation of a grand swell that began far out, and marched in slowly, royally, stretching to right and left and gathering in the lesser pulses, never pluming its full crest till just upon the shore, and then at last tumbling its heap and roar and fury full against some outmost breakwater; its tremendous volume searching, forcing a tumultuous way into cave and cranny, choking them full, and with vast recoil from everywhere far underneath and out of sight, bursting and shattering and leaping forth again in fume and spray at every outlet, making the rocks to shout with mad reverberation, and to stand smothered for the magnificent instant in the white smoke of watery wrath.

The Wolf's Hole was in the easterly side-face of the Pulpit ledge toward Campus Cliff, both promontories bearing southward, as so many fringing capes along the shore do bear either north or south, as if the great ocean-beat upon them turned them this way or that, refolding the shore. Its tortuous upward excavation tunneled the crag and opened through upon the gully spanned at its head by the Boulder Bridge. Beyond the bridge, on the Pulpit crag itself, another ascending ledge-path gave access to the grand outwork.

The heavy waves at highest tides which poured clear through the hole met the uprunning floods in the gully, and the shock of their encounter sent up white columns in the narrow cleft whose spray sometimes shot over the footways, while the inward drive of water penetrated further or retreated sooner, and rose to more or less of measured height against the ledges, according to the happening of wind forces and the current ruling of the tides.

The huge breaker that came thundering in with mighty salute as the young clergyman and Peace Polly stood there, dividing through the tunnel and around the crag, and reuniting in the chasm to rear its spouting, vapory pillar just beyond them, and fling its salt fret in their faces, poured up the channel with a sweep that touched the undermost stones of the bridge itself, and left them dripping as it receded.

In the lull that followed, before another wave came in, Mr. Innesley questioned Peace Polly once more.

"Are you sure about the tide?" he asked. "Does it never sweep this pass?"

"Oh, no. That was an extra wave. The tide is beginning to go out."

As she spoke she set her foot upon the bridge, and was across it in a moment. Mr. Innesley could but follow. The climb upon the other side was sharper than the one they had come down, but the roughened rock had natural flags and steps, and fewer breaks and pitches. They were presently upon a top, higher, more stupendous, than any other up or down for miles, broad, sunlit, safe, sloping upward slightly toward the front, ending there with a curiously formed parapet, like a great horseshoe, which rose and rounded outward, its heel ends lowering to a level with the general surface.

"This is the Pulpit," said Peace Polly, as they reached

it, "though I think it ought rather to be called the Chariot."

"It is like an ancient war-car, certainly," said Mr. Innesley. "But what an out-gaze!"

He made a breath between the syllables; "outlook" was a feeble word to denote that which made the orbit of the eye feel vast, encircling vastness.

"I will leave you here, shall I?" said Peace Polly, quietly. "You will like to stay a while."

Mr. Innesley turned, surprised.

"You to go back alone! Did not you come to enjoy it too?" he asked, quickly.

"I might have. But it did n't matter. You came to be by yourself, I think."

"And you, as well," he said, with some curious amusement in his voice. "We have interrupted each other; had n't we better make the best of it?"

"The place is big enough," answered Peace Polly, with composure. "I need n't bother you, of course."

Mr. Innesley stepped toward her, down out of the Pulpit.

"I hardly know if you have forgiven me, Miss Peace, though you told me I was kind," he said.

Peace Polly flashed her eyes up at him.

"Did you suppose I was minding that?" she cried. "You must think I am thorny!" and with that she laughed. People were so queer in their ingenious misunderstandings. "I had forgotten that you said it, I believe," Peace Polly went on. "But I had not forgotten the thing itself. I am reminded of it too often. I have enough to do with that. You *were* kind."

"I might well be," returned Mr. Innesley, smiling, "if Shakspeare is right about the wondrous working of a fellow-feeling. I have a most impatient, treacherous temper of my own."

Peace Polly did not say a word to that, at first; the look in her face straight into his spoke for her. Then the fresh laugh broke gently again.

"It would be a dreadful thing, then, if we two should quarrel," she said, and held out her hand.

Mr. Innesley met it with his own as frankly, and laughed as simply as she. "There is no safeguard against war," he said, "like the most dangerous munitions on both sides."

For the moment, at any rate, they understood each other.

Peace Polly did not care to sound the sympathies further; a general amity sufficed. She turned toward the broad flash and leap of waters that stretched away beyond them to the pale horizon line. "How the white-caps are tossing up!" she exclaimed.

"Yes; there is evidently a great roll coming in from mid-ocean, from some storm centre whose wave-circles are just reaching us."

"It is so different from the morning," said Peace Polly. "The whole sea was just a fine little shimmer, then, of blue wrinkles and sun-sparkles; now see how the peaks are lifting up and bursting into white feathers at their tops; closer and closer, like plumed heads of soldiers. It is like an army gathering."

"Does n't look like retreat, does it, whatever the almanac may say? Look how they crowd and head on, from as far as you can see."

"They always do head on, though the whole ocean is pulled the other way underneath them. Hear that rumble in the Wolf's Hole; that does n't sound like backing out. Yet it is backing, all the time."

"Not much, yet. The high-line over there gets covered still, every two or three waves. I don't know when it can have been slack-water. I wonder if anybody ever really catches the precise minute of the turn."

"I suppose so.   How many things we don't know, that we always thought we did, when we come to the point of a clear statement!"

"Are n't you rather too near the edge, Miss Schott? The wind is strong."

"Not too much ,for me as yet.   But I 'm going away, Mr. Innesley, over toward the other side, where there 's a lee shelter I know of.   The Pulpit is nice, too, when you sit down behind it."

"You mean that for me, then?   And you won't give up your bit of solitude?"

"Nor take away yours," returned Peace Polly, with that frank smile of hers that made her directest speech a thing neither discourteous nor a challenge of contradiction. It had in it so much of the " you know as well as I do " that no one would offer a palpable pretense of disclaimer. "I shall not stay here to chatter," she said, and moved to go.

"Are you sure you won't chatter, in spite of yourself, in this breeze?   It is not like the land wind of the morning, any more than the sea is like its sea.   The upper deep is getting mighty, too."

"I shall be below the break of it; and I have this, too," said Peace Polly, slipping from her arm some soft thing that hung there by two armholes: a knitted sleeveless jacket of wool, dark blue like her dress.   She drew it on, and buttoned it as she spoke.   " You are not half so well protected, Mr. Innesley."

"Oh, I shall do.   If this east wind brings up a regular sea-turn, we shall hardly make much longer stay; and out there it looks like it."   He pointed to the southeast, where a creeping haze was showing along the horizon edge.

"When you have had enough, I shall be ready," answered Peace Polly.

Mr. Innesley had his hand in an inner breast-pocket.

"May I show you something I have happened to think of?" he asked, as he opened a wallet-memorandum, and took out a small folded paper. "Our words a few minutes ago made me remember it. I wrote it down from memory, from a thing I heard read or quoted, once. I have had it by me a long time. It is not the whole extract, but the lines of it that meant me, and so stayed by me."

"Will they mean me?" asked Peace Polly, with her quaint unreserve that refused shy consciousness, and was her cleverest barricade.

"You will know," Mr. Innesley answered, putting it in her hand. They had walked along together down and across to the middle of the cliff. They were about to separate here, Mr. Innesley raising his hat, of habit, at parting with a lady, though for such brief space and time. He replaced it with some care, for the sea wind was urgent. At this moment they caught sight of a group opposite, on Campus. Two or three handkerchiefs were waved quickly at them, and an arm was lifted with a sweep that Peace Polly did not understand, the arm being that of her brother Lyman, not ordinarily demonstrative.

"What are they cheering for?" she asked her companion. But she pulled her own handkerchief from her little side pocket, and gave it a half-toss, as if to say, "Hardly worth while; there is nothing extraordinary; but we 'll be civil;" and Mr. Innesley once more lifted his hat, for his share of response. Then these two took their unperturbed ways, and were presently hidden to the party on the other headland; the one by the rise of rock behind which he passed upward to the Pulpit again, and the other by a lesser, corresponding ridge which ran from the central open in which they had paused down to a most comfortable embracing angle with the rampart which reared upward from the gully. Between these was the lee shelter Polly had spoken of, — three sides protected, the fourth open southwesterly toward the calmest quarter of both sky and sea. Even in the present upper-firmament tide-sweep, the air came to her with fended force; she forgot the rush of it upon the crown, the possible sea-turn, and the descent on the ledge-path around the precipice.

Several things were surging a little in her mind; the impulse of them had sent her here, and kept her quiet, outwardly, while they tossed and drifted within.

If Mr. Innesley imagined that she could be glad of this encounter with him, and their little half-wild expedition together, as some girls would have been, — and would have let him see it too, fast enough, however demurely they might fancy their silly satisfaction hid, — he should only perceive clearly from her how utterly the whole thing was a contretemps which she was merely "making the best of."

And those girls! She wished she did not know so well what they would be thinking, seeing her off here with their cynosure, their "bright particular," as Dianthe Holiston with feeblest folly called him! — as if she had sought, or wanted, or was pleased, or would make the most of it!

She was glad they had all seen her go a different way from him. The cliff was big enough, as she had told the man. She had come round to this part of it mainly for that reason, the likelihood that she might be noticed so to have taken her own way.

And why were they waving at her so senselessly? Lyman, too; perhaps he meant disapproval, ordering back! In the face of all that crowd, with Mr. Innesley to see it also, would he have dared to mean or signify that? The blood rushed up into her temples as she thought of it.

She would act for herself; she would account to nobody; *nobody* should suppose, or impute, or spy, or prognosticate. She had never liked Mr. Innesley; she was not going to begin to like him now; they should all see that. If she were thrown on a desert island with him, it need n't even make them neighborly — after they got off!

Her little clinched fist rapped nervously the knee it rested on, as her thoughts ran thus; she felt in her palm the edges and corners of the paper she was crushing. She opened her hand and released it, smoothing it carefully; what would he think of her if she could n't handle a bit of paper like a lady? She cared that much, for herself, not for him in particular.

This was what she read, written in a strong, positive hand, that had yet gentle flows and turns in it : —

> "Give me joy, give me joy, O my friends ;
>   For once in my life has a day
> Passed over my head and out of my sight,
>   And my soul has nought to unsay.
> No querulous word to the fair little child
>   Who drew me from study to play ;
> No fretful reply to the hundred and one
>   Who question me, gravely and gay ;
> No word to the beggar I fain would take back,
>   No word to the debtor at bay ;
> No angry retorts to those who misjudge,
>   And desire not a nay, but a yea :
> No word, though I know I remember them all,
>   Which I would, if I could, e'er unsay.
> Give me joy, give me joy, O my friends,
>   For the patience that lasted all day ! "

She drew a long breath as she ended the reading. " I must have them to keep," she said, and searched her pockets, though she knew she had no bit of writing material in them. A little rubber pencil hung to her watch-chain, however; she spread her handkerchief upon a stone, and wrote the lines upon it. She would not for anything have asked Mr. Innesley to let her have them. She would just return the paper, and say nothing. Had he not virtually given them to her? She might fairly write them from memory, if she pleased, as he had done; but she preferred the surer, immediate way. She rolled the handkerchief small, and thrust it down into her pocket, which she fastened with a pin.

After that, she sat still; she forgot place and circumstance for a while, in a new wrestle with herself. Had she ever lived one whole day like that? Or if, through the quietness of her surroundings, the word had not always been provoked, had there ever been heart-patience all day long? Had there been that abundance of content and loving-kindness out of which she might have spoken at any moment, and been sure to speak without sin? Even with inanimate things, whose total depravity somebody once wrote of so cleverly, had she always kept that miserable temper of hers that could not bear a crossing? If her thread knotted unreasonably often, did she forbear to break it with a twitch? If her scissors made a point of slipping away, and nothing would do for them but that she must rise and scatter work and other implements, and give a shaking to herself and everything about her, did she not give it with a good — or evil — will too often? And what of the bitter little spoken apostrophes, sometimes, as if to a personal intent that thwarted her? As when that same misbehaving thread went out of its way, one day, to run around and hold on to, with vicious loop, every button and corner; and the very ring on her finger, instead of meekly following the way of the needle's eye, did she not ask it, with the irony of intense affront, if it had not better try to go and get snarled up with the door-scraper? And what was all this, in kind, but the very being angry with her brother without a cause which, when it mounted to that sin, had brought her consciously to danger of the judgment? Whom verily was she angry with, when these things happened? Might it not be with Some One who was disciplining her with little lessons, in the great laws He binds himself in all his work by, and which we irritably resent when our maladroitness fails to adjust itself to their wise and gentle hindrances?

One thing suggesting another, she brought up her days and ways to account and sentence after this manner; one thing revealing another, she recognized the word of command that comes, the task that is set, in the daily little befallings; the small things that try us if we will be faithful, before the higher things are sent, over which we may have rule to our reward; the life that might be, growing from each accepted and obeyed word proceeding from the mouth of love. "A good man's *steps* are ordered by the Lord," she remembered; and the tender sentence of the divine reproach, "Could ye not watch with me one hour?"

And yet she knew that she should go home and take a new, clean day and spoil it again, more or less, to-morrow.

"One *might* do it, — I can think how one might do it. But whom have I to give me joy? Where are the 'friends,' I wonder?"

She said the last half dozen words aloud, starting to her feet.

"All Saints, I think," said Mr. Innesley's voice beside her.

"You had n't any right to hear!" cried Peace Polly, angrily. But as she turned upon him to say it, he saw that her eyes were bright with tears.

"I know it. I beg your pardon. I came to tell you that the mist is rolling in from sea; we ought to go."

Peace Polly marched up to the middle plateau of the cliff without a word; then she turned suddenly and faced Mr. Innesley. "I am ashamed," she said; "and you were kind."

She held out the paper to him with the words; he took it; it was the second time to-day she had told him he was kind.

The sun-gleams out of the cloudiness of the girl's nature — or was the nature only a fair, heavenly one, easily clouded? — touched him keenly. They were truth itself. Where truth is, the love of which it is born cannot be far off, or utterly separate.

Peace Polly interested the young minister greatly. He did not think that she perplexed him at all.

XI

SUNSHINE IS SUNSHINE.

LYMAN SCHOTT walked down into the Brier Cove with the woman he had twice asked to be his wife, and should never ask again.

That point having come to be so definitely settled, — the door finally bolted, and acquiesced in so, — he found himself quietly, and to a certain extent comfortably, taking out a new lease of friendship.

He should never ask any other woman; that was a foregone conclusion in his steadfast, one-purposed mind. He did not even take the trouble to think of that. But he did think that Serena Wyse would not be likely to marry anybody, since she would not marry him. There was not the same kind of despair in the disappointment that there had been eleven years ago.

Serena, on her part, gave the matter pretty much the same relative consideration. So, tacitly, they agreed that they were rather more to each other than before; mutually preventing and securing all hindrance and help to a franker if a remoter belonging.

Was friendship the remoter, though? This was the woman's question, — she who had said with such a lift in her voice, "To grow old is to grow safe, and privileged, and sure."

Eleven years ago, whatever Serena might have done or reasoned, Lyman Schott could not have resolved or submitted as he thought he was doing now. Then, notwithstanding his matter-of-fact, undemonstrative nature, he had been in the full earnest of a man's life-purpose and desire. To lose then seemed to lose everything. His very singleness and slowness made the denial a more absolute and final thing. He put it away, as he did all else, beneath that still, dull exterior, and went on with the things that remained. But he could not go to the Wyse-Place any more. That old intimacy was broken, and there never came a time when it could begin again, without signifying less or more than was differently true in him, from time to time, in the course of years that changed him very gradually, though only as the years have bounded power to change. Alteration is another and a deeper thing.

Now, the whole subject having been renewed, sensibly and dispassionately, — so, or equivalent to that, he reflected within himself,— and having been forever laid aside, there might be neither pain nor mistake in a neighboring which he inwardly confessed he was right glad to claim and use again, in the modified and calmer fashion of his eight-and-thirty years; compatibly, too, with the preoccupation of practical interest and industry to which he had transferred that part of a man's life-impulse and enjoyment — and it is with years a growing part — which can find satisfaction in material concerns and successes. He had become more and more the Lyman Schott of the big lumber business and planing-mill; that which would have been the Lyman Schott of home and affection was put in abeyance. Yet there remained in him enough of his possible self from which he had drifted aside, to grasp even now at even this, — a late friendliness that had been once refused as cheap, because it could not become more.

He had grown satisfied in his half-living; he had shut up that side of his nature as he did his house, and lived in what he could. And however we may wish or attempt to deny, it is true of us human beings that, whether it be a lung or a love, there is a capacity for adapting ourselves to what is left after a lesion, or to the next best; so that the loss that leaves us heart-broken and wishful to die, dropping gradually back into the past of our history, leaves us again, more terribly bereft, perhaps, content in that which has become our life because it had to do so, and oblivious of the pain we would in some moments be thankful to call back, only to prove to ourselves that it, and something of ourselves with it, is not dead within us. Whether dead, or waiting only, as they say the blessed wait in rest of Paradise, depends on the quality and motive of the life we take up in its replacement.

Serena Wyse had read all this in Lyman Schott; she had been sorry and afraid for him, seeing him more and more absorbed in, and apparently narrowing to, his saws and planes, and chisels and boards, and the mere increase of the profits they could bring him in.

She would not have married him like this, though it were the last time of asking, — the last time of any possible holding out her hand to take a gift of any joy. Unless it were a true joy, a true, whole asking and giving, she would have none of it. She would not let him utterly wrong and ruin himself with that last mistake, of living upon a half, a deteriorated, a superseded affection.

But that he wanted friendship once more with her, this made her hopeful for him, and glad like a girl, though she had that morning found the first white thread in her abundant, pretty hair.

"Roses are roses, after all!" she cried, as they loitered down the blossomy slope together.

"And sunshine is sunshine. A holiday is good once in a while, Serena."

"And how the tide is coming in! — or the waves,

rather; for it's past the full. It is even quite boisterous in the cove. There's a great sea running for such calm weather," Serena answered. It was answer, though they seemed but to itemize to each other things quite distinct and irrelevant to anything but the mere pleasantness of an outside bit of the great world to-day.

"It's not high tide till one, and there's a new moon," said Lyman, who was always sure of the practical side of a thing. "The wind is in from sea, too, now; the surf is splendid."

"Why, Polly thought the turn was at twelve and a quarter. She looked in the almanac, she said."

Lyman put his hand in his inner coat pocket.

"Wrong column, I guess," he answered; and opened a little diary compendium of all ordinary information. "Full sea, *morning*, — just changed, you see, — twelve hours, fifteen minutes; that's just after midnight. Evening, one, nought."

"Why, Lyman!" Serena cried. "She has gone round to the Pulpit. I saw her, all alone, walking over the Brier Ridge. And there she is now, on the tip-top, with somebody else. Where did she pick him up? The minister!"

"Then they'll both be caught by the tide, unless we can hurry them back. It must be up the gully by now. What's the child thinking of?"

"She says it never swamps the Boulder Bridge."

"Much she knows," was all Lyman's answer; and he turned abruptly to retrace his steps up the cove and around to Campus again. It was of no use to follow the way of the others; it was longer, by a great deal. There was now not a minute to lose. To reach the height of Campus Cliff and signal across was his instant intent. Serena Wyse, slight and spry, turned as swiftly as he, and kept on after him.

They came into the midst of a lively group, through which the two sped, much like an engine and tender.

"What's up now?" called Quin Holiston; and the girls stopped their chatter to see. Presently, catching the point of the situation, their waving handkerchiefs at once dilated and confused the telegraphy which the others were endeavoring to make concise and forcible.

"No use," said Lyman, when the obtuse pair returned the salute and moved on their separate ways in the *dégagé* manner already related. "They'll have an hour extra to spend there, at least; that's all. And in a fog, too, if that bank means the usual thing." With that he turned as quickly as he had come, and started down the hill.

Serena hastened after him. "Here, take this," she said, piling a soft gray shawl into his arms. "And this," pulling something out of her pocket.

Serena was old maid enough already to have provided a little bottle of ginger cordial against emergencies.

Lyman Schott did not stop to thank her.

He reached the midway point of the ledge-path descending from the ridge, alongside of a tumultuous, deafening plunge of water that hurled past and beneath him up the little gorge, scrolled itself under and around the Boulder Bridge, reared and rebounded against the blind end of the gully, and poured back over the crossing-stones with a combing, foamy sweep.

Lyman Schott sat down where he was, with his back against the cliff, and waited. He picked up a loose stone, rolled it in the gray shawl, whose ends he twisted tightly together into the folds, making a close bundle.

"I wonder if that fellow ever played catcher at base?" he said to himself.

XII.

THE hazardous point of the descent for Peace Polly and Mr. Innesley was the turn at the brink and brow of the height at the westerly corner. Fortunately the path did not skirt the very edge, but began within it, and made its first drop into a comparative rest and shelter in one of the broad, broken angles of the cliff-side. Here the pressure of the wind — something to beware of in venturing upon the margin above — was suddenly, after a moment's wrestle there, escaped; and the space gave sufficient opportunity for safe pause.

As they left the plateau and moved cautiously downward, watching for advantage of a lull in which to double the exposed point and attempt the first stage of actual descent, Mr. Innesley took a tight grasp of Peace Polly's arm with his right hand, his left arm next her waiting for other service.

"Now!" he said, as the slight abatement fell; and without a word of notice or apology he threw the strength of that left arm closely around her shoulders, and, leaning backward himself against the push of the wind, held her forcibly in like manner.

The instant they had gained the top of the deep step to the ledge-shelf he sat down upon it, bearing her with him to that safer, if less dignified, position.

"Turn round and hold fast by me," he said; and bracing his foot against a knob he let her down, with a careful creep, to the security of the lee nook. Directly, he was beside her.

Words had to be few and strong-voiced against that chorus of wind and water. On her part there were none.

"I must leave you here and reconnoitre," he said. "Keep perfectly still."

The command, as well as utterance, was strong. Peace Polly could not help herself. It was the desert-island part of the story, now. She was not bound to be a bit better acquainted with him after they got off. She comforted herself inwardly with that.

Mr. Innesley proceeded down the ledge. Half-way, as Lyman Schott had been on his side, he was stopped. The roar and smother of water came driving in, towered up and burst, and went slowly weltering down again; but it kept its barrier level over the narrow, broken pass. There was clearly no crossing now; the imperial pageant and splendor had the right of way.

Lyman Schott stood up opposite. As the fume and spray scattered, the clergyman saw him, but no shout of warning, advice, or explanation was possible. Lyman held up his gray bundle at arms' length. He gave it an interrogative movement, as if to toss it; Mr. Innesley held forth his arms and hands in answer. The big, soft, weighted ball made a clean parabola across the chasm, and was caught "plumb." Then Mr. Innesley drew forth his watch and held it up, describing with one finger an exaggerated round of the dial, and making with his hand a questioning gesture.

Lyman Schott indicated a full, deliberate circle in like manner. They would have to wait an hour. Mr. Innesley understood.

He went back to Peace Polly, opened out the shawl,

and wrapped her in it. " Your brother is over there," he told her; " he says it will be an hour."   While he spoke the dun veil of the mist, a solid sea-fog, came spilling over the scarp and closed them in.

" It is not long often," Mr. Innesley said, when the noise of a boisterous wave had again just retreated. Shut close into the rocky embrasure, they had the sound of their speech to themselves, concentrated and kept from the scatter of the wind as in a bowl. " It is the meeting of the land-breeze with the sudden current from the sea," he went on to explain; " as soon as either prevails we shall have clear sunshine again, or else a thinning of the fog as it spreads in."

" I know," Peace Polly answered. " Don't mind me; I 've been a goose."

She gathered herself into the deepest angle of the rock, bent her bonnet lower over her face, and set herself to counting the great waves. " There will be about sixty of them," she said; " at any rate we can find out."

She did not mean to be a bit more entertaining than that.

Mr. Innesley asked her if she were cold; to which she replied, " Not at all. This rock has been baked all day. It will hold like a foot-stone on a sleigh-ride."

But everybody knows what a sea-turn is on our Atlantic coast; how in ten minutes that which had been baked and sweltering is chilled with shuddering cold; and the heavy vapor, like an upper ocean, pouring around and over them, swathed them in its darkening volume, until even the glory of the close breaker was dimmed and merged; and only one great, blind envelopment, and one hollow, thunderous din complemented each other in air and sea, and fused the elements together.

It was awkward, tedious, uncomfortable; but, provided

the fog should lift, there was no inevitable danger. They were caught by the tide, indeed; but ignominiously, where the tide could not possibly reach them. The path might be slippery with wet, and the bridge would be a bad step, certainly, but the worst that was likely to happen was that they might take cold.

"Lyman has the worst of it, waiting over there, not knowing how we can manage," said Peace Polly; and the thought of her brother patiently biding as near her as he could, to see her through and out of her folly, brought him closer to her in reality, across the fog and chasm, than he had been for many a day in the matter-of-course, apparent nearness at home.

If the fog did *not* lift, however? If a thorough, staying, easterly storm of days was beginning? There was this to think of, and it did not make the matter that was immediately before them — their landward passage across the gully, down and up these narrow ledges, and over the wave-washed bridge of stones — a thing to felicitate themselves upon.

Peace Polly saw it all: that it was simply a foolish dilemma, in the one view; in the other, a pretty serious risk to which she perceived she had subjected her companion and herself; and Lyman had it to worry over all alone. She felt very tender and sorry about that; for the rest, it was nothing to talk or to complain of. So she sat there absolutely still, wrapping a corner of the gray shawl about her head and across her mouth, "to keep from swallowing the fog-bank whole," she said, in half apology, as she so shut herself up.

Mr. Innesley, left, perhaps on purpose, to a like quietude, found himself wondering if any other girl in the same circumstances would have behaved precisely so.

After about five minutes he ventured a remark.

"You are showing pluck, I think, Miss Peace," he said.

"Am I?" she answered from behind the meshes of the knitted wool. "It is n't very different, then, from feeling myself extremely small. I was imagining just then that we were in the Deluge."

"The last two?"

That was a slight blunder. Peace Polly hurried to say something.

"No, Lyman is over there. Do you think there *were* just any small particular number of last ones; or only eight last ones in one particular place, to begin a particular history over again?"

"Do you mean that seriously?"

"Well, I really thought of it; I don't know that I mean anything seriously."

"I think that what we chiefly have to do with is the particular history that has come down to us, and that we are in the line of. If there were any other last ones at that time, the Lord seems to have put them asunder for a while from the one unbroken story He was telling in the earth."

All that was not said without a break from the interruption of the water rush; but the full tide.was hushed a little by its own fullness; the hungry echoes of hollow and channel were muffled by their repletion. The sea hung upon the turn; the mysterious pause was on it, as if it listened to the "Thus far." Only the great impetus of its long heaving and surging westward still rolled up the breakers, that knew submissively the time of their going down.

"I think, too," said Mr. Innesley again, "that most especially of all we have to do with the very bit of the history He is making with us, and what it is saying to us, any hour."

"Then what is it saying to us this minute?" asked Peace Polly, impulsively. If she had been in the very least like those other girls, she would never have put the question. If she had been, on the other hand, very much like the most of them, she might have put it for whatever personal leading it might prove. I do not think Mr. Innesley would have answered one of them as he did her.

"It was saying to me," he replied, "a very old, beautiful word, 'A Man shall be a hiding-place from the wind, and a covert from the tempest.' It was singing a hymn to me, too. I shall never join in 'Rock of Ages' again without remembering this place."

"I beg your pardon," said Peace Polly.

He supposed — and she supposed he would — that she was confessing herself of her own lightness of asking. So she was; but she was also remembering her accusation of this man's wandering glances in the Te Deum. Was he showing himself such a one as could have trifled so?

But why was she always to be begging pardon of him? It vexed her; she would not do it any more. What could anything she had thought matter to him? And of her, and her levity or otherwise, he might think as he liked.

Lyman was out there, waiting in the fog, alone.

Fret and tumult — something like fear and danger — were between her and him, separating them. Would it always be so? And did he care? Should she ever get across it all, and would he be glad of her if she could come to him?

The deep movement of this girl's life was not in any dream or desire at present for a new thing in it; its centre was her brother; or perhaps its centre was a vacancy where she felt her brother ought to be; and its effort was to coincide the two. And so its course was an ellipse, eccentric enough; sometimes near and sometimes far away from its occupied focus. Would any force or adaptation ever reduce its wayward curves to a pure circle? With all her petulances there was a strange, persistent patience in her that waited for that. Should she not learn to be a true sister, first, whatever else there might be to learn and to find beautiful hereafter? This was the bit of history that God was making with her now. There was a thoroughness in her that would not skip a line unread to reach however pleasanter a place beyond.

Mr. Innesley's words had touched and roused all this. There was not the beginning of any little personal excitement that it should be this young clergyman who said them to her alone, and here; she would not have permitted that in herself for a moment.

It may be a sufficiently unusual bit of human nature that I am telling you of; but it is not an impossible one, nor above the human, for it was Peace Polly Schott's.

She leaned back against the rock; she turned her head toward it, touching cheek and temple to it as a thing to rest heart and thought against. Was this strength of God, this upbearing might of his that He has put into mere things, put there as a word, a reality? Was it his living might, for our living need, that our bodies might be safe in, might have, this wonderful comfort we call "rest"? And was power so placed for the physical dependence that the immaterial might know, in the essential correspondence, that it was also there; that underneath the spirit of the human, just as actually, are the everlasting arms of the divine?

She did not think it out metaphysically; she only discerned its contingence, tenderly, marvelingly, during those instants in which she rested her face against the rock, and felt her whole self calm-sheltered in the cleft of it.

Just for those moments she could seem to gather up her whole being and experience — that which had been and which was to be — into some strong keeping and sure hiding; as if she lay in the very might of a thought that knew and meant and included it all. She would have to go out of this place, mind and body; scatter herself again, as it were, into detail, probation, failure; live the thought out, point by point, gaining or missing, or half touching, — not knowing it in its wholeness; but something revealed to her, if only dimly in a glimpse, that a whole it was, and should be, and that One who did know held it in his hand, in his intent and heart.

What Mr. Innesley was thinking at the same time I do not know; but they talked very little more. A question now and then as to her comfort, and her answer; . a mention of the time at intervals, not restless or impatient with either; a quiet endurance and acceptance of the circumstance, — these were all that seemed to occur to or to concern them. Perhaps Peace Polly's silence after what he had said about the bit of history of the minute was to the young man an apparent reversion to her first resolve "not to be in his way." If so, he allowed her to oblige him after her own notion, and fell in with it as he fell in with all the rest.

Very gradually, the water swept back and back, with every plunge remitting something of its grasp and energy; a half hour passed, as half hours do in waiting, at once slowly, and with a strange slipping off, and ending while we are yet saying, How slow!

A second half hour was gone, yet more to their surprise, when Mr. Innesley showed his watch to his companion, and bade her once more keep quiet as she was while he went down the pathway.

He found the crossing clear; the great rebounds no

longer flooded it; the water ran beneath the hanging bridge, and the inclining footways were open to it upon either hand, though wet with the long wash, and slippery here and there with clinging weeds, and full of little un-drained pools between the stones.

Lyman Schott stood watching where he had stood an hour before.

A few minutes later, Peace Polly was led down by Mr. Innesley, who would go first and have his own way this time, and Lyman stood to meet them at the landward end of the boulder crossing.

"Give her your hand first; hand her to me," he called out; and the minister passed her carefully beyond him on to the yet dripping stones, and held her fast on his part till Lyman could reach and draw her to himself on the other brink.

"You're well out of that scrape," was all her brother said to Peace Polly. But she knew that his putting it so, instead of asking her sharply how she ever came to be in it, was a wording that meant some answer to her question, — Would he be glad if she came back?

The fog was scattering already; the way was free up the Brier Cliff side, and in not many minutes more they were at the top again, among the ivies shiny-wet, and the roses lifting ruddier heads from their sea-bath.

Down the wild shrub-path came Serena Wyse to meet them. The first thing she did was to make them all three drink of the ginger cordial, which Lyman had thrust into a pocket and forgotten. Then she kissed Polly, and told her that the fog had begun to drive people off, but that the livery van and Dr. Farron's carriage were still waiting.

"All those girls!" thought Peace Polly; and she fell behind as they crossed the pasture, and took her brother's arm.

Serena, for reasons of her own, as natural, walked forward with Mr. Innesley.

"Tired, Polly?" Lyman put the arm about his sister as he spoke. She wriggled out of it, but kept close, and slipped her own within it again. "Not like all that, Ly. But you are real good to me. I was such a goose."

"You came tolerably near not ever being a goose again," he said. "If you'd been enough of one to have got wings, you'd have been better off."

"I was beautifully off, as it was, if it had n't been for bothering you all so," returned Peace Polly, with a small toss, remembering the real wonderful good of it, and taking refuge in something of her old waywardness, to cover deeper things.

And at that little signal of the withdrawal of the flag of truce, Lyman took up his tease again.

It was partly just out of his very gladness and relief — though it did not so occur to Polly — that he said what he did say next.

"I did n't think you were such a greedy chicken, Polly. To grab the one best crumb, and run away with it to Pulpit Rock!"

It did not tease precisely in the way he had expected, — if he expected at all. She drew her arm from his, and suddenly made a little distance between them.

"I don't see why," she said, in a low, restrained tone, "when you have just been a little good to me, you should go right and spoil it all!"

"I have n't spoiled anything, Polly. You did run away with the parson, you know. I was only thinking of all the other chickens."

Still it was but a side graze that the thrust gave. It missed the point direct, but somehow seemed to rasp sharply.

"I know very well, of course, you don't really mean a word of *that*," the girl said, in the same slow, hurt way. "The thing that makes me despise it is that you can care to pretend you do. I would a great deal rather not despise, if you would let me, Lyman!"

"Take care of that ivy bush!" Lyman reached out and caught her toward him, away from the dangerous wreaths and streamers she was almost touching. "There's *real* sting in that," he said. "It's hard for a tender skin to steer clear in this world."

Peace Polly walked behind him. "I think it's hard," she said, rather as if to herself, "that two people can't keep alongside of each other for fear of the stings."

"They can," answered Lyman, with utter good humor, over his shoulder; "it only depends, I guess, on which two, — and where."

"It ought to be you and I, right here, this minute ; and at home, every day. Or else what are we made brother and sister for ? "

To that Lyman only said with some philosophy, "May be we should jog along more comfortably not to notice so exactly about keeping step."

"But I *should* like, Polly," he resumed, not irrelevantly, as they came into a broader spread of the pathway, and he dropped abreast with her again, — "I *should* like to know how you managed the parson ! Did n't you have any falling out in that hour and a half, with him?"

"Yes ; two that he knew of, and two or three more that he did n't," said Peace Polly, composedly.

Lyman laughed relishingly. Certainly, he had this excuse, that there was always something in Pease Porridge well worth the stirring up.

Miss Serena turned round and came back to them.

"I forgot to tell you, Lyman, that we took a liberty

with you while you were away. Mrs. Dawney gave out with one of her headaches, — I knew she'd have it, riding sideways in that van, — and they were afraid of the chill for her, too. So by our urging, Mr. Dawney took your horse and buggy, and drove her home; and they left their places in the van for you and Polly."

"All right," said Lyman, who was a kind parishioner, and kept his equipage habitually almost as much at the minister's service as at his own. "I told him he might have it to come down with, if he chose."

Peace Polly was not equally resigned. Miss Serena was of the rector's party, with Mr. Innesley, in Dr. Farron's carryall; there were "all those girls" and their chatter to be faced in the van. She resolved to keep close to Lyman, at all events. But Lyman put her in, and then went back to gather up somebody's baskets, and her resolution was defeated. She was penned in by the laughing rush, so that she could not even get out again, as she tried to do; and in the merry tumult, before she had the protection of his presence again, they assailed her with their not scrupulous remarks.

"Well! Peace Polly Schott! you did steal a march, did n't you?"

"How came you to go off there with the minister?" Dianthe Holiston asked her that, with manifest awaiting of an answer.

Peace Polly looked up at her quite calmly. "I found him on the ledge," she said. "He did n't know the way, and was a little frightened, so I helped him over."

A shout of laughter pealed around her, as she sat grave, immovable.

"Oh, Peace Polly! do tell us what he talked about! It is n't fair to keep it all yourself."

This was Ruth Dawney, who had to get her share of

Mr. Innesley by hearsay, through being inexorably bound to the other congregation and ministry.

"He did n't talk. He wanted to be let alone. He said we had interrupted each other, but we must make the best of it. I told him the rock was big enough, and we went two separate ways."

"You must have had a gorgeous time!" said Sarah Holiston, with irony.

"I did; and the waves did," returned Peace Polly, with neither smile nor frown.

Then Lyman came in, and the van started with a great lurch and bounce that shook them all down into their seats.

It was not much wonder that Peace Polly had told Mrs. Farron there was not anybody of her own age.

Rose Howick sat in the forward corner of the van; she had quietly made her way there early, before the rescue party with the tide-bound stragglers had come up.

The great white daisies hung with limp heads from her bosom, and she had not spoken a word.

Nobody believed a syllable that Peace Polly had said; but neither did they know a bit the more what to believe.

"Pease Porridge, all over!" said Dianthe Holiston. "The hottest thing there is, and the stone-coldest. And both when you can't account for it!"

XIII.

PEACE POLLY would have cut a finger off, — at least, have tied her fingers up to keep them out of mischief, — I think, before she would have written a diary of her life. Introspective as she was, — yes, because she was genuinely introspective, — she would never have been so upon paper. She was particular about her toilet, about the arrangement of her hair and collar and ruffles; she stood honestly facing the looking-glass till the last pin and hairpin secured the orderly and fitting result. She was anxious to look well, for she could rest in no imperfections, but this done, she would never have attitudinized before the mirror for an instant; herself being adjusted, she simply went away and was herself. In like manner, she would have arranged and harmonized her whole nature, — thought, affection, mood, purpose, impulse, — so that all should have been shaped, turned, composed, brought into a fair, strong unison of character, could she have done with it what she would, as with moral pins and hairpins; there should have been smoothness and grace for dishevelment, roughness, uncertainty; but to have "made a note of it" from day to day, to have contemplated her own presentment, or measured her growth like that of a child that is penciled from time to time against the wall, would have been contemptible to her. And for mere happenings, what were they to keep account of? They kept account of themselves in what became of her, or they were of no significance at all.

Nevertheless, in a certain impersonal way, guarded from all obviousness of actual experience, she had, a few times in her life, written down something truly of such experience, that she wanted to keep; something that had occurred, or said itself, or shaped itself to her in a way that moved her, and of which she would not lose the first strong vividness. Now it was seemingly as a copy, among "extracts," in a little book; again, it might appear an original effort, but quite fictitious and imaginary. She would have no automanifests biding a possible discovery, even by herself, at a later and a wiser day. I think she was more afraid of that than of the finding out by other people.

It came to pass that the day after the pleasure party upon Campus she had something to write down. The great sea had spoken to her, the might of the rock had been a living thing; these had encompassed her and held her close, while at the same time she had been very busy with questions and self-judgments that made need for mighty signs and answers from without herself, and which the sea and rock had only met with types, as indeed they only were. Outside her own outer self were these, of the same mere matter; what or Who would speak from a like grandeur and fullness and suffering to that of her which was within, behind her living, that which was of the unseen reality itself, and which only an unseen Supreme could reply to on the true plane? Something in her behind the poor faultiness which was all she could put forth from depths that yearned with the groaning of creation for that which should be, demanded the intent and promise that were behind sea and breakers, sky and winds, sun and scorching, earth and dumb, terrible, unyielding force.

She did not analyze or understand that which moved

her; if she had, the dream might not have come to her. The whole was in the region of the unshaped, and so it shaped itself in that first might and wonder which the real takes when it descends into the phenomenal. For it was a vision which she had that night that she wrote down and kept by her, if haply at some great coming day it should interpret itself. It read, in the little manuscript scroll she made of it, like a pure flight of fancy.

A SLEEP-WAKING.

Out on a wide, high moor. A wide, high sky, blue and clear, rearing a huge round over it, and sloping down to a horizon that seemed the hemisphere of some planet a great deal vaster than our earth. Hills and hills, like sleeping green waves of a wonderful ocean, struck to sleep when at their noblest height. Stillness, solitude, as if the world itself, whatever it were, had been so struck asleep. Not a sign of habitation, or of humanity; only a great, beautiful Place.

Beautiful things growing, trees, shrubs, blossoming grasses, all sweet and wild and wavy in the stillness where no hand or foot seemed ever to have come. A smell of gardens, as if somewhere near were beds of lilies and rose-thickets, turfs of mignonette and violets, tangles of honeysuckle, and long, sweet rows of pinks, their breath meeting the aroma of ferns and pines and clover and wild thyme. There was a world of odor, as well as of sight and space.

I was all alone there, and I did not know the way. There was no way, no *where;* it was untraversed, unoccupied, homeless; a deep of beauty with no sail in sight.

There was life all about me, but no person. I felt as if lost in a delightsome mere existence, with no purpose or outcome to it. It was lovely to be there, but I was

alone; there was nothing to abide for; I must go, I had
the sense of pilgrimage upon me; it must be that I was
upon a journey, and I did not know the way.

Suddenly, I was not alone. A tall, grand, gracious
figure stood beside me. Whether man or woman I did
not know, it was so noble-sweet, so mighty-gentle. It
towered above me so, and so smiled down upon me.

No more could I say whether the simple-stately dress
it wore were royal robe or workday garment. It seemed
like either, and like both.

The feeling upon me was that it was a man; the gar-
dener, or carer for those garden spaces that I could not
see, but that I thought must stretch beside these moor-
lands that were so swept and filled with their near fra-
grances.

I asked him if he could tell me the way, and he came
and walked beside me.

Then he showed me something that he was holding in
his hand. It was like a flower, but it was like a live
creature also; there was a pulsing motion in every petal;
the color palpitated, and it lifted and swayed and swung
upon its stem, as if with a kind of rapture that struggled
to lift it out of its bounded nature; as if it might already
take wing and spring away, but for something lovelier
than the mere grasp that kept it to the hand that held it.

The man began to tell me about it; but he was so high,
so great, he was away above me so, although beside and
close to me, that I could not easily either see or hear. He
seemed to know that; and presently with very gentle
touch he put upon me the hand nearest me, and lifted
me, I could not tell how, to his shoulder. Not upon it,
like a child, but beside, at shoulder height, where I
seemed to cling and rest. It was as if he had simply
gathered another sort of flower; and I knew that I was

gathered to a strength and tender wisdom that it was sweet and safe to rest on, and that would surely make all right for me.

My head lay upon his neck; I saw the flower in his hand, below my eyes, right by his heart; and somehow heart and eyes seemed to flow the wonderful life into it, as he looked at it, and talked to me, telling me such marvels of it! I cannot recollect a word about it now, but it must have been a key, a text, to some heavenly knowledge, for my whole spirit received the life and gladness as I listened.

So we walked, — I mean he bore me by his side, — and he talked. Then he left speaking of the flower, which instantly quieted its throbbing, swaying motion, and was as if it had folded itself to sleep; and he told me of other things, a story of some human life, and I listened as if my very own heart were in it.

After a while, somebody else came up and walked beside us. This person also was half vague to me : once it seemed Serena, then Lyman; then some one different from either, but quite as naturally there ; some one — that was all I knew or cared — who, belonging with me, was led with me in the great presence and companionship that overbore, while it gave reality and joy to all. Nothing surprised me; I did not question any longer how we were to get home, or how far away from home we might be, or in what manner we had come; it was only as if all that was around us had spread forth and manifested itself because of one actuating verity, and that mere *place* was nothing and had never been.

Serena — I will say Serena, for I believed at first that it was she — wondered, I thought, to see me lifted to the man's shoulder, but she did not ask how or why it was; and we kept on, all together, in such great content!

By and by we reached the brow of a great, sudden slope, a hill-bank, but of a vast breadth and incline, like no hill that I had known of or imagined. It was more like the side of a green world; for there was no farther horizon visible to us as we stood there than the sky above, below, and all around. It was a gradual, verdant, mighty precipice; not sheer descent, a bank as I have said, but a precipice to such as we.

I seemed to have been put down from the man's shoulder, and to be standing upon my own feet; and as we all three looked from the brink, he stepped or sprang — though his motion was too grand for that word — over the steep edge, and with gentle, swift descent through the air along the declivity swept down and alighted without shock, as one might pass rapidly down an easy stair; and he looked back, smiling, from the foot.

His smile seemed to command. "Follow me," it said.

"Oh, we cannot do that!" exclaimed my fellow-pilgrim, who was now uncertain to me, and held me back, as I was following without thought, except that he was there, and waited. I remember a surprise in me that it was a going down, and not a climbing up, to which he had led us, and which we perceived a harder thing than an ascent might be.

Then we two simple ones moved along a little at one side; and as we moved, we found that the hill trended more gently eastward; and presently we were at a place where the depth did not look so terrible, and at the foot the man still stood, smiling, having companied us all along, from where he had gone down the harder way. So we gave ourselves to the leap, for he beckoned us; and we came down softly and safely, and the grand man was beside us again, and walked with us, telling us more and more wonderful things, so that we listened delighted, as if we were being fed in our minds and hearts with delicate, satisfying food. But nothing of all that he told us comes back to me now; only that beautiful sense of it, and the satisfying; the words of it are the lost part of a dream. I feel, nevertheless, as if it were saved away in me somewhere, and that it would strengthen and comfort me again whenever I am at the place for it.

At last we reached some end or edge in the wide moorland way, and he stopped, and pointed us to a path that he said was ours now, and bade us good-by. I put my arms up to him like a child to its father, and he bent to me and I kissed him on the face. And in that instant the face, and the look of it, the kiss given me again, the tender holding of the arms about me, seemed like those of a woman; and it was as a great, glorious woman that I saw my friend, as I said good-by.

But I cried out, "Oh, where could I find or hear from you again? Where do you live? For I do not know the place, or the way to it. Could I ever send a letter?" Then there was given me what I think was a picture, that looked beautiful as I took it from the hand, but which I hardly stopped to see, I was so earnest to know of the Person; and like all the rest, it has faded out from me. I reached the paper sheet back again, and said, "Oh, write your name on it, — on the back of the picture, — as we give pictures to each other on dearly beautiful days in the year!" for it seemed to me like a Christmas and an Easter and a Whitsun time all together; only more than any of those days can be as we keep them in the small earth.

The grand, beautiful Person took the sheet, and wrote upon it. I could see strange, noble characters formed upon it as the hand moved. They seemed like an old text of an unknown language; and they grew and formed until they themselves made a picture, all over the reversed side of the sheet.   When it was given back to me, it was a lovely house that was drawn upon it, all made of language, outlined in sentences, as the hand had written it; a fair, most pleasant plan, different from any house I had ever seen; and some reminder said within me, one thing after the other, as if drawn through my memory by links: " The ' house of life,' — the ' house of life; ' 'man liveth by every word that proceedeth from the mouth of God; ' ' I will abide in thy house; ' 'except the Lord build the house, they labor in vain that build it; ' 'we have a house not made with hands, eternal in the heavens.'   'In my father's house are many mansions; I go to prepare a place for you.' "

Besides the picture, with its wonderful word-draught, there was left in my hand another sheet, with some printed record on it.   For the Person was gone, and I saw the grand face and form no more.

I turned to the friend left by me; it was not Lyman nor Serena now, but it did not seem to matter; it was some one representative of near human fellowship to which I must needs turn with that which the other had left with me, and I showed the printed record.   I folded my house of life and hid it in my bosom; and the printed sheet was full of names.

And one name stood out in glowing letters that throbbed like the colors of the living flower; it seemed above all the rest, but it was put in the midst.   It was the name I wanted; though I cannot read it now in the memory of my dream.

Every name had a place written against it, as of a dwelling-place; but the Name had only, in those shining, living letters, — THE COUNTRY.

XIV.

"Dora!" called Dr. Farron, coming in the side hall-way.

"Well!" answered Mrs. Dora, from the depths of her store-closet, which ran in under the stairs.

"C. P. is in town."

"Well!" answered Mrs. Dora again, very brightly. The monosyllable that may mean query, or impatience, or the ironical reverse of its natural definition, always came from her with the tone of its original intent, — an "all well!" response to whatever hail. "We shall have him here, then."

I like you to observe Mrs. Farron's delicate self-reve-lations in her small points of diction. It was not "we *must*," or "we will," have the guest, but "we shall;" of course, and of happy opportunity. If she had not meant just that, it would, instinctively, with her, have been the "will." The "must" would be rarely forced from her.

"Certainly. He is coming to dinner."

"And to stay? And where is Mrs. C. P.?"

"In the city, shopping, and seamstressing, and shutting up the house. Partly packed for Europe, he says. Sails in July. Takes the children abroad for schools."

"Lovely! how nice that will be — for them all!"

"Wifie!"

"What did I say?" She came forth with a tin scoop in one hand and a dish of sugar in the other, all sweetness and innocent inquiry, her eyebrows up in an infantile arch.

"Implied that when some people were well off other people might be better off."

"Oh, Adam! how quick you bit the apple! I never said it; and you never said they were n't all going!"

"C. P. is n't, then. And whoever bites, you always manage to leave the core on my hands. Have we got a good dinner?"

"We're getting it. Only cream soup, and chops. But I can have a lobster salad."

"Ah! that will be nice, — for you. What shall we others do, simultaneously?"

"Contemn‑plate. As the fox did the grapes, you know," retorted Mrs. Dora.

The Doctor gazed at her, and made a funny little groan.

"I never realized before what a horrible bad spell the poor fellow had of it," he said, slowly.

Mrs. Dora in return lifted up her soft, wide-open eyes at him, as if he were talking Sanscrit; then meekly shook her small head and gave it up.

"I wish he would spend his summer in Bonnyborough," she remarked, with easy return to the previous question.

"That is what Dr. Blithecome wants," replied the Doctor.

"Oh! *would n't* that be — just exactly right?" she exclaimed, with a quick delight in her first words, and a change of look and tone as she paused, and added the last three quietly. "It is just like dear Dr. Blithecome to think of that," she said. "He knows *we* could n't forecast for ourselves. After all," she resumed briskly, making a snatch at her mischief again, without successfully catching it up, "unless Mrs. C. P. stayed in Europe — But dear me, Sebastian! you must n't keep me a minute longer from my snow pudding!"

She left him with that, and ran away with her sugar dish into the kitchen.

But Sebastian had seen the sudden watershine in her eye put out the laugh and the sparkle. When that happened, — when she could no longer keep her powder dry, — there was never anything for Mrs. Dora but to run away.

There was lobster salad for all three, and the snow pudding, with its clear fruit *glacé*, was delightful.

They were sitting over their dessert of big Sharpless strawberries, when Mrs. Dora began training her gun carefully toward her object, with little gradual shifts and slides of talk, and sightings by quick glances between the same. C. P. would make, as she had said to the Rev. Sebastian, such a capital Central Point, *sae-pe*, for little social arrangements.

"If you take to it in Latin!" the Doctor had cried, despairingly.

It is time to say that the gentleman in question, now occupying the third side of the table at their strictly home dinner, was Dr. Fuller, medicus and savant, whom the world — conventional — was beginning to know, because he was beginning to know, beyond their commonness into their wonders, a few common little bits of the world natural, that holds to the naked eye its middling shows of things between the infinites of large and little. Dr. Fuller and his microscope were powers in the urgent science-movement of the day, that sends down into the farthest secret depths of minute cause its artesian tube of search and question, till it touches and draws from the very life-springs of matter some clear drops of the truth that is one and everlasting.

And it needs explanation, on our lively lady's behalf, that nobody in Bonnyborough, or any other of his accidental sojourns, and very few in his more fixed abiding places, ever knew any more of the doctor's name than so much as Mrs. Dora made wit of in her unwittingness,— the name under which his few but remarkable essays had been published, and which he signed invariably to all private or business writing, " C. P. Fuller."

Mrs. Farron was not sure, at this day, that her doctor did not know more than he pretended of that concerning which she pretended persistent curiosity ; she declared he kept his friend's initial letters for Capital Punishment to her inquisitiveness.

"Whatever it is, it was his father's before him," said the Doctor ; "and C. P. senior was always C. P., though his name was great in his day on bills of exchange, and the style and firm of C. P. Fuller & Co., as far as it went, was indubitable as Baring Brothers. How many people know, I wonder, the full baptismals of the Barings ? or of our Harpers, even ? When you think of it, it is n't so exceptional."

"Not at all," Mrs. Dora had acquiesced, indifferently. "I dare say he was christened C. P. Perhaps the only place where it must have ever come out was the College Register. Only there, there was a ' muss ' or a ' miss ' to it that would muddle it comfortably in with all the rest, and never be noticed any more."

" Precisely so," said the Doctor, laughing ; at which moment Mrs. Dora made up her shrewd mind that Sebastian knew all about it, and from exactly that very source.

" But it makes it rather absurd for Mrs. C. P., does n't it ?" she said, linking the name with gentle legato into identity with the title of the Father of Waters.

"Then you have n't hunted out all the bacteria and the polly-poddies and things, even in Bonnyborough ? You can still find fresh fields and pastures new ?" she asked of the naturalist, as they sat with coffee after their fruit.

"Still find!" he ejaculated. "My dear lady, when I have exhausted an inch bit of this earth anywhere, it will be time to look for a new planet."

Mrs. Farron gave a little sigh of very relieved satisfaction. "That is so comfortable to be sure of," she said. "And it would be so nice for us if you would only pick out your inch here, and set seriously about it."

Dr. Fuller smiled.

"I might," he said, "if anybody would bear the infliction of my nets and bottles and bits of bog in wash-basins. The inch of the world, where I begin to pick it to pieces, becomes a considerable area of chaos."

"Come here," said Mrs. Dora.

"I am too fond of you," returned the doctor, shaking his head.

"You mean I am too fond of my housekeeping," said the alert lady. "And that is a reflection upon my other virtues, to say nothing of my friendship."

"Not that. I must be where the bog, as a rival or an arrival, would not matter. And I know it would matter here. It would be matter totally out of place. I must be independent; not bound to be agreeable or polite, in return for an exquisite hospitality."

"Why, you are in earnest. Then there is a possibility that the fens and creeks of Bonnyborough may keep you within reach of us, in your off—I mean, your back again —hours?"

"Dr. Blithecome is asking about board for me. I would not go there, either. The doctor needs all his wife's and daughter's care, and both are partial invalids."

"Why, I *am* so glad! Not about the Blithecomes, dear souls! there is always one side of everything to be sorry about. How long will Mrs. Fuller probably remain abroad? Will she return after she has placed the boys?"

"I really do not know," returned Dr. Fuller, placidly.

Dr. Farron asked "*Pan-Dora*" for some more cream. And she always knew that that meant, gently, "shut up!" So she left the subject, with a comical meek glance across the table, and a crushed little dropping of the shoulders that only Sebastian saw; and she urged Dr. Fuller to take another tiny mug of coffee.

Evidently, there was more yet concerning the friendly scientist that Dr. Farron knew and did not mean to talk about. And if he did not mean, confessional secrets would not have been more inaccessible to wifely invasion, supposing their holders ever to have been left to that supreme test and torture. Dora Farron never applied it. "'All things come, in time, to her who patiently waits,'" she said to herself. And she had a way of waiting with the lamp of her best and most wide-awake intelligence well trimmed and burning.

"Have n't you got something lovely, just out of the mud, to show me?" she asked of Dr. Fuller.

"Yes, I have a *Volvox globator*," he replied.

"That will do. That sounds velvety and volatile and swift and voiceful."

"It has two of your qualities; but it is more like lace than velvet, and its voice is for Fineears only. Then I have a *Stephanosphœra pluvialis.*"

"My dear doctor! that is altogether too much for any one pair of ears, or eyes either. Should you mind my calling in a little assistance?"

"I shall mind nothing but my microscope, — and my object."

Mrs. Farron turned to her little davenport, as they left the table, and minded her object; writing and twisting three little notes asking three people to tea by and by, and to a peep into an inside universe.

Dr. Fuller walked over to a long bookcase that wainscoted one side of the room. Upon its top were pieces of quaint and beautiful china. He stood examining an old Wedgwood pitcher.

"I like this room of yours so much, Mrs. Farron," he said. "You mix the needs of life so beautifully. I detest a room that is for nothing but eating; and one that is only for leather and paper and printer's ink gets cupboardy and musty in a hardly less undesirable way."

"That book-shelf sideboard is my hieroglyph," answered Mrs. Farron. "I invented that to stand for 'entertainment here for man and beast'!"

"Choice signs on both parts, and choicely fulfilled," said the doctor, stooping a little to peer in among some rich old octavos.

"There 's a pile of your own science away down there on the folio shelf," said Mrs. Farron, coming over. "In the right place, at the bottom of things."

"You are a wonderful woman for right places."

"Not much merit among inanimate things. If I could carry out my ambitions with living creatures " —

"Ah, then indeed!" quoth the learned man, as one who had learned that difficulty also.

Two hours later, the young deacon walked in. Peace Polly, in a fresh, sweet dress of white mull, and Rose Howick, carrying the bloom and grace of her pretty face and head above cool puffs and frills of a pale-green summer tissue, were already in the little airy nook Mrs. Farron called her drawing-room. In the summer it was just the merest nook-shelter between three broad, low veranda-balconies, vine-hung and breeze-swept; in the winter, wide-paned windows closing off cold and taking in space and prettiness, the room was a central snuggery between open fire and open sunshine.

Mr. Innesley had been bidden, in his little note, to drop in and see something pretty. The young girls had been told that Mrs. Farron had something interesting here tonight.

Dr. Fuller was in the library, — tea and dining room also, as we have seen, — adjusting carefully his plates and lenses, and examining critically certain muddy-looking little vials at a window-table, with his back to the door. The visitors saw him as they passed on to the drawing-room, but he never moved at the sound of their young voices in bright greetings, or Mrs. Farron's animated welcomes.

"Is *that* the object of interest?" Rose whispered, with a little nod toward the broad, bending shoulders.

"That," Mrs. Farron answered quietly enough, but with no special caution against overhearing by the intensely preoccupied person under observation, "is a medium; the first of two media, I should say, through which we shall be put in relation, by and by, with another world. The object — is in the vasty deep, — or was; subject to his summons and control. He is busy with his incantations at this moment. We can be comfortably commonplace for a while in the drawing-room. That is," she added, with a sudden little tone of half-dismay, glancing out through the veranda at the sound of a crunching footstep — "Well! here is Miss Mallis." There was the cadence of the inevitable in her closing inflection.

But in five minutes Miss Mallis had begun to render herself entertaining. She was one of those experiences which we have a habit of dreading, on general principles, in their known possibilities, before they arrive; but which often, when they have become facts accomplished, and turn out better for the time than we had expected, we begin first to tolerate, and presently to enjoy. In this she was not unlike a steamboat trip or a summer thunder-shower.

Of course all the news of Bonnyborough was in Miss Mallis's pocket, and came forth with the first easy little waft of her small fan, which she drew thence when she had sat down.

She was very funny in a description of a steeple-chase that had been gotten up last year by a sporting club in Broadhills, where some of the riders had summer places, and that had swept through the edge of Bonnyborough. There was talk, she said, of another now.

"They had the ground all carefully surveyed before-hand," she declared; "fences taken down, or lowered nicely, to suit their jumps; little flags at the brook cross-ings to show where it was safe; and everything made comfortable. Why, I could have ridden it myself. I'm not sure they did n't put down feather beds wherever it was a little risky; and then they came in with such glory at the end, at the gray-church hill, where the ladies and the car-riages were all waiting, and the winner got a pair of spurs! I hope he'll dare to use them this season. I believe Farmer Rylands cut a lane through his silo corn, and they kept the road as if it had been the way of the ten com-mandments. Don't you think we ought to feel splendidly Anglo-Saxon when we have that sort of thing done right up to the notch, here in the heart and front of Yankee land? It's enough to make us apologize for Bunker Hill, and begin all over again with all the British institutions! Just think what we've missed by taking up in such a hurry with stars and stripes and Hail Columbia! It's like mar-rying before you know any better, and shutting the door against all your future advantages and contingencies."

It was at this point that the young clergyman had come; happening in the wake of Miss Mallis quite as if there were equal extemporaneousness in the occurring of the two. That covered Mrs. Farron's intentions very neatly. She felt benignant, and had half a mind to ask Miss Mallis to stay to tea.

"They say poor Dr. Blithecome has had another of his ill turns," Miss Mallis remarked, after the little stir of Mr. Innesley's entrance ceased. "He's out to-day; but there is n't a minute's certainty of him, I do suppose. Well, things keep happening; seems to me they never did keep happening so fast; and — well, I don't know, I 'm sure, how Bonnyborough is to get on without him, whenever it does come to that. I hope he has a good insurance: he can't have laid up much, they 've lived so generously. And he just gave away half his practice. I should n't wonder if there were n't fifty families he ever sent in a bill to."

Mrs. Farron wavered in her secret benignity. Her friends, she thought, were not put through their most searching experiences, or given the grace of their highest righteousness, to keep Miss Mallis's conversational cruse and barrel full.

"I suppose his own bills have always come in regularly," she remarked, bringing the subject to a point where she could add, sweetly, on her own part, "But we need n't meddle where we cannot make, need we, Miss Mallis?" and so quenched the lady's fire on that side.

"Professor Fuller has come. And they do say the doctor sent for him. I think I like a doctor who is n't a professor of anything else, don't you?"

"Not even of religion?" asked Mrs. Farron, still most innocently.

Miss Mallis laughed. She was bright enough; she appreciated and enjoyed Mrs. Farron's little turns of war. She brought up another battery.

"Did anybody ever see *Mrs.* Fuller?" she inquired.

"I believe she is a myth. She is always somewhere else. Now, I hear, she is going to Europe. Dr. Fuller went last year, alone."

"Partly to arrange for her, perhaps. She is to take her boys to Vevay."

"And then travel with a party through Switzerland and the Tyrol, and spend the winter in Rome. A friend of mine heard that mentioned in Broadhills by some one who knew about the other people who are going."

"A long genealogy to a bit of news, Miss Mallis," said Dr. Farron, who had come in a moment before. "One hardly ever gets the two ends, or sides, at once, to anything in this world."

"You don't of the world itself, Dr. Farron. Unless you flatten it all out to make geography of it. And how you are to get at two sides when they are people, and keep themselves hemispheres apart! Well, it 's the usual thing, — not congenial, I suppose," she added, easily, to Mrs. Farron. "Though I don't see how anybody *could* be congenial, in this case, exactly, unless it was a pollywog. There! I 've just thought what those two letters mean! Collector — or Colporteur — of — Po— "

A tall handsome figure stood in the doorway. Miss Mallis was on her feet before she was aware.

"Come in, Dr. Fuller," said Mrs. Dora. "Won't you sit down again, Miss Mallis? We 're a party of polly-wogs to-night, and Professor Fuller is to preside."

"No, indeed. I should only trouble the waters," returned Miss Mallis, with great presence of mind ; and retreated in order, hoping articulately to herself, as she went down the walk, that the professor had heard nothing more than the joke about the pollywogs.

Mrs. Farron was but human. It was that little trespass upon her own domain of special pleasantries that she found it hardest to forgive at last.

XV.

Dr. Fuller moved gently back from the table where he had sat oblivious, as he had promised, of all but his microscope and his object, until the two, and the bright light upon them from a carefully reflected double-burner, were perfectly adjusted to each other as he wished.

"Now," he said, with a tone as if he had Paradise to throw open to the Peris, — "there is the *Volvox!*"

"You would n't believe it was anything that he could have brought home in this, would you?" asked Mrs. Farron, touching a little homœopathic vial that lay now upon its side, "or have picked up with this," showing a hair-loop set in a fibre of tapering stem. "Would n't you suppose we were going to see at least the moons and rings of Saturn, or Jupiter, the great *Volvox?* Come, Rose, and look through the nether telescope."

Rose looked, waited a moment, and then gave a sudden cry. "Why, it *is* a little live world!" she said. "What makes it whirl so?"

"You have said," answered the professor. "Life."

"And inside there are more worlds! One, two, three, four, six, beautiful tiny green planets!"

"Plants," said Dr. Fuller.

"Then they are just alike, when they begin," said Rose. "Mr. Innesley, do come and see!"

"Miss Peace, first," said the young minister.

But Peace Polly, with silent expectation widening her

eyes, drew back. "Not yet," she said, under her breath. Then Mr. Innesley put his eyes to the instrument.

"Marvelous!" he exclaimed. "Why, there are hundreds of little green dots like beads at the crossings of a fine network that runs all through, or over, the large crystal. And the inside planets, as Miss Rose calls them, — are these the dots grown larger?"

"Extremely likely," answered the professor. "They will develop and fill up, until the containing sphere bursts at last, and the new ones float off to produce the same increase in their turn."

"But they are not the finished plants?"

"Hard to say when or where anything is finished. They are spore-cells, — life-seeds. They have yet to seek their conditions."

Peace Polly quietly moved to Mr. Innesley's vacated place at the microscope. She said to herself, "Whatever I see, I won't exclaim. It seems to me it is a thing to keep silence over."

And that she did; gazing and gazing, with awe-struck eyes, into what looked to her a very secret place of creation, the first moving of organic particles away down in the deep of the invisible beginnings. The crystal globe whirled and floated, in a kind of remote ecstasy of its own unknown and wonderful life to be. It seemed to say, in every motion, "I am begun, I am begun! and to begin is to be sure of becoming! I shall become something! I am meant to be! I am alive!" Or it was — and her second feeling was this rather — the far-down inception of a Thought that stirred mere unconscious matter with the joy of its own high distant purpose. "The Spirit of God moved upon the face of the waters," she remembered; and she drew a deep breath, and came back with a half-dazed look into the little world of the bright library, and the waiting friends, and the moment of her own present existence, — æons beyond, was it, what she had just amazedly beheld?

"How was it, Miss Schott?" asked the professor, coming to her presently; for he had noticed her face, and would willingly learn what was in her mind behind the look.

"I don't know," she answered; "I have hardly got back here, yet, — from *that*. I think it is the way it was in Genesis." And then she smiled, not meaning certainly to say any more to this strange wise man.

"A genesis continually going on," he said; so that she did not know from his word how he might even regard the Bible Genesis. Perhaps she was hardly conscious of the inquiry her eyes sent to his in her silence.

"It seemed to you 'the way it was;' what way?" he urged her. And somehow she could not help but answer.

"When God had the first thought of it," she said, simply; "when He made every plant and herb *before they grew.*"

Dr. Fuller was silent an instant, still looking at her. Then he said, merely, "I have something else to show you," and went back to his table, which Mrs. Farron and the Doctor were just leaving.

"Come away," said Mrs. Dora; "he 'll be busy ever so long, as likely as not, catching and fixing another piece of chaos."

Rose Howick and Mr. Innesley moved after her, and they were presently chatting all together upon the veranda. Peace Polly slipped into the nearest seat and waited.

It was not what Mrs. Farron had meant, but she could not help it now; and before she could plausibly accomplish any change they were all called back again.

"I have been particularly fortunate," said Dr. Fuller. "Caught it in the first drop."

"What is it this time?"

"*Stephanosphæra.* Come, Miss Schott, it is your turn first."

Peace Polly went to the table and seated herself in the chair Dr. Fuller rose from and offered her. She leaned forward, put her eyes to the lens-tubes, and saw again, as she thought, "way down into creation."

A clear, floating globe, trembling, whirling in a watery space. Translucent, beautiful; a little germ - world; a mere invisible atom, she knew, to the naked eye. Alive, with the throbbing life of all worlds; one of myriad myriads, unknown except by this marvelous revelation; tender and frail as an air-bubble, — perfect and firm as a silver planet in a summer sky; the same Force forming and holding both. Within its glassy circumference other smaller globes also floating, whirling, instinct with the beginning of being; these of a fair, vivid green, with little nerve-fibres stretching forth delicate lines, two to every one, and grasping, as for anchorage, the inner surface of the pellucid shell. How could such beauty, such pure transparency, such tender color, come of mere seeming scum or slime or weedy film clouding clear water?

Suddenly — what was that? Peace Polly started, almost to the disarranging of the instrument.

"It has burst through," she cried, "one of the little green things, — and gone away!"

"I wondered if that might happen for you," said the professor. "I was watching for it. That was a spore-birth; the escape of a seed - vessel, as from a fruited flower."

Peace Polly turned round and looked at him; her face had become pale with strange excitement. Something stirred her memory with a quick thrill of recognition ; she had seen, or dreamed, something like that before. A live, breathing, spirit - moved flower. In that instant, her vision, that after-sleep had obliterated, came back to her for the first time, as if she had but just awaked from it, and began to unroll its sweet recorded impressions, to recall its presence ; began to be lovely and warm again at her heart. But no one knew, or could guess. She hid away her treasure instantly, like something given secretly into her hold, to be all unfolded at some other time ; she spoke to Dr. Fuller about what he had been showing her.

"Is the world all like that?" she asked, "all full of great spaces where there seems nothing, and powers like the powers of heaven?"

Her voice was low and distant like the voice of a sleep-walker. Only Dr. Fuller heard the words. The others were talking of something else while they waited.

"There is power like that in all the earth," he answered, almost as low, "down to the universes of the molecules, in which the atoms are like constellations, and every atom, may be, in some way as a world."

Peace Polly moved away to let Rose Howick see ; and the wonder and the wondering went on. One after another the new little cells escaped through the clear circumference of their crystal envelope, and rushed away out of the field of the glass.

Each observer made in turn some characteristic remark.

"It is exquisite !" said Mr. Innesley, "and all this is only — a protophyte ! A long way up from that to the ' Rose Enthroned,' Miss Howick," he added, with a smile.

The girl was a little embarrassed, not understanding

his allusion, or how far up in creation he meant to reach his measure of comparison.

"You know Miss Larcom's lovely poem?" he made a little haste to say, interrogatively; for Richard Innesley was always and quite a gentleman.

"No; what is the 'Rose Enthroned,' if you please?" she asked him, recovering her poise and color.

He repeated quietly, but with real feeling of their inspiration, the lines: —

> "And life works through the growing quietness,
>   To bring some darling mystery into form;
> Beauty her fairest Possible would dress
>   In colors pure and warm.
>
> "Within the depths of palpitating seas
>   A tender tint — anon a line of grace,
> Some lovely thought from its dull atom frees,
>   The coming joy to trace; —
>
> . . . .
>
> "At last a morning comes of sunshine still,
>   When not a dewdrop trembles on the grass,
> When all winds sleep, and every pool and rill
>   Is like a burnished glass
>
> "Where a long-looked-for guest might lean to gaze;
>   When Day on Earth rests royally, — a crown
> Of molten glory, flashing diamond rays,
>   From heaven let lightly down.
>
> "In golden silence, breathless all things stand;
>   What answer waits this questioning repose?
> A sudden gush of light and odors bland,
>   And lo, — the Rose! the Rose!"

"Oh, is that all?" asked Rose Howick softly. "Isn't there any more of it?" It was very sweet, her quite forgetfulness of her own flower-name. Mr. Innesley went on, smiling upon her as he did so: —

> "What fiery fields of Chaos must be won,
>   What battling Titans rear themselves a tomb,
> What births and resurrections greet the sun,
>   Before the Rose can bloom!"

If he had not meant subtile flattery before, it was hard to miss the honest, admiring application now, as the rose-like face looked up to him, listening. But he finished gravely, after that instant's pause, what took the thought, even so prompted, far on beyond the little compliment or suggestion of a moment : —

> " And of some wonder blossom yet we dream
> Whereof the time that is infolds the seed.
> Some flower of light, to which the Rose shall seem
> A fair and fragile weed."

Mrs. Farron had been very quiet at her watch of the water-marvel. The gentle sound of Mr. Innesley's recital was all that broke upon the stillness that covered, surely, many thoughts in the different minds. If we could see a *moment*, and the human souls standing in it, as we see a water-drop in a microscope !

But an instant after the verses were ended, Mrs. Dora's sprightliest voice set talk to a sudden new key.

" And what becomes of them, after all, professor ? Aro they ever anything more than ' stuff-in-a-sphere ' ? " she asked.

A quick chorus of amused laughter broke up, as she had intended, the solemnity. " Who can say ? " answered the professor. " They go to their place, and that becomes of them which they are making for. They are on their way, doubtless, to the Rose, or the day of it."

" And what are they all, — this whole tribe of protos ? For I always like to know family names and connections when I make acquaintance."

" These are *Algæ*, Mrs. Farron ; low forms of plant life, though not, strictly speaking, protophytes, since there is a long step between these and the very lowest that we know. There are, indeed, infinitely more varieties below visibil-ity than are developed above into what we call the vegetable creation. There is kingdom beside kingdom; way down below all, the innumerable host of the bacteria."

"There! I told them so. I said it was another world, but that precisely defines which. What a good thing a composite language is! We had 'exterior' and 'interior,' and 'anterior' and 'posterior,' and 'superior' and 'inferior,' and now we have '*back-terior*' for this world behind all. Nothing else would have described it."

Afterward, Dr. Farron asked his wife if she had not been " just a little too " —

" Frivolous ? " suggested Dora.

" Well, — for the subject ? "

" My dear Sebastian," she said, "in the face of such things the scientifically ignorant must either talk top-froth or the depths. I saw that girl's face, — Polly's, — and I knew that I must keep a buoy afloat, if it were only a pun, or she never would come up again. How tremendously she takes everything ! "

" And how tremendous everything is ! " returned the Doctor.

" That 's where the frivolous mission comes in. There has to be a bob wherever there 's a sinker. Did you hear what she said in the first place about thoughts ? "

" Yes. It was a fresh putting of the Psalm - words, ' How wonderful are thy thoughts unto me, O God ! How great is the sum of them ! ' "

" She is a strange girl. Have you ever spoken to her about confirmation ? "

" No. Perhaps some day she may come to me. There are spiritual processes I do not dare to meddle with. You would not have me try to hurry one of those little life-globes out of its firmament ? "

" No. It is too beautiful to watch it just where it is."

"And it is sure of its own time," said the Doctor. "Life may be let alone. It is dying we have to struggle with."

"But if she only knew! I think sometimes her 'environment' looks so stagnant to her that she does not discern what life is working in it. She might take more courage if her own self could be shown to her a little."

"She is under God's microscope," said Dr. Farron.

XVI.

PEACE POLLY sat in the pleasant open hall by the hill-side door. She was trying to paint wild roses. She had made sketch after sketch of flowers in different degrees of openness, different attitudes of bright heads, — up-looking, down-looking, straight-facing, turned shyly half aside. There were as many moods and expressions of them as of so many human creatures. One or two she had tinted carefully, and brought to a certain finish; but with the last precise lines and shades they had been, to her thinking, finished utterly as to any success. The idea was so elusive. It hinted itself well in first outlines, then it got obliterated in detail. She had thrown them all aside, one after another, in all stages of their progress and of her discouragement. They were pushed together upon her little table, sheet upon sheet; a pile of pretty refuse, from which peeped here and there broken suggestions of beautiful things that it certainly seemed possible to pick out and save.

She was in despair, at last, over what she called a "blind rose." In the others, the mere dotting in of the little golden-raying stamens gave character and resemblance of itself. This, she said to herself, looked "like an old, wilted penwiper." The upper petals in the original were so dropped forward over the yellow centre, as the flower leaned from the water-glass, that the sign was hidden which should have said, "This is a Rose." She

wanted to have drawn it so that it should not have needed
a sign, and she had found it impossible. What had such
a sweet, peculiar grace in the real bloom was confusion
and effacement in the copy.

Lyman came in at the open door, and stopped beside
her to see what she was doing. He turned over the stray,
unfinished sheets. "What are all these?" he asked.
"Blights, or worm-nips?"

"Things that never were," Peace Polly answered.
"Failures."

"All spoiled?" he asked, kindly enough. "May be
they would n't be, if you only kept on. There 's a bad
time with almost everything; you have to worry past it,
and then, likely as not, you come out right. Why not finish somehow, and bring out as right as you can? They 're
all roses, I can see that; so there must be something of a
rose in every one. I 'd work 'em up."

"No, you would n't," answered Polly, gloomily.

"You don't know. I 'm not apt to leave things. My
mother's rule was never to begin and not finish. It would
be a good plan for you to go by, I think."

"Why do you always skip over *my* mother? I can't
be expected to take after yours," retorted Peace Polly.

"And why should she or you be so much patienter than
God?" she said again, turning upon him suddenly, after
the pause in which Lyman had replied nothing.

"Patienter than God!" Lyman repeated, slowly, with
amazed emphasis. "What makes you dare to say that,
Peace Polly?"

"Is n't that what you believe *He* does with us? Does n't
He spoil ever so many of us and throw us away, to one
that He finishes and makes all right?"

Lyman was not prepared for such a bolt of doctrine
hurled square in his face. There was something wrong

about it, he knew; with just about as much reminder of orthodoxy as of rose-likeness in the failed roses. He could not deny it a certain recognition, and he could not risk repudiation of anything that might be fairly deducible from the Westminster Catechism. The thing had never been put to him in that shape before.

Perhaps that was why a certain light fell upon it that he had never looked for before.

For he answered Polly presently, after a slow thought of a minute, during which she sat with her elbows upon the table and her forehead leaned upon her fingers locked across it, looking down upon her blind rose : —

"We 've got a will and a hand in that matter ourselves, Polly. We have the choosing and the keeping on. If we 've a mind to be saved He 'll begin with us; and He won't be done with us until we 're done with Him. That 's what we 're human souls for, and not " —

"Plant-spores!" Polly ended for him, eagerly, clutching at the new thought which instantly completed and illustrated itself to her. And then the girl's fingers relaxed, and her face was lifted from them. She turned round and looked up at her brother.

"Why, that 's the best thing you ever said to me!" she told him.

Doubtless Lyman began to fear he had compromised dangerously.

"I don't know," he said, slowly; "I dare say I 've left out something." So he had. He had skipped all the Everlasting Decrees without thinking.

"I don't understand spores, and I can't talk theology. I came to talk to you about something else. I hope you won't be provoked. I 've engaged a boarder."

"A boarder!" Peace Polly exclaimed, the idea striking her from the other side in a reverse way, and as if it had never before been mentioned between them.

"Yes.   That is, you 've got the refusal of him."

"Him!" ejaculated Polly again.

"Yes.   Is n't that just what you 've always wanted?"

Now there is n't anything much more exasperating than to be taken by surprise, in a way you never meant, by a thing you have forgotten you ever did want, or have ceased to want, and then told that you have got precisely your heart's desire.

Peace Polly whirled round upon her chair and faced Lyman.

"When is 'him' coming? and which side of the house am I to take? or am I to go away altogether?   And who is '*him,*' if you please?"

The supreme scorn and derision of the "him" cannot be put into print, even with the aid of the italics and bad grammar.

"I told you you could refuse," said Lyman, calmly.

"I can't refuse a man till I know who he is!" remarked Polly, with a clear, emulating calmness; as clear bitter, however, as camomile tea.

Lyman passed her without an answer, and walked to the front entrance, where a comer suddenly stood upon the threshold.

"Good morning, professor," said Lyman, comfortably.

Peace Polly rose to her feet galvanized, and stood there like Lot's wife, only not so pale.   All the color that she had not put into her spoiled roses was up in her face.

"Polly, you know Dr. Fuller?"

Was it only imperturbability, real and serene, or was it the still intensity of triumph? and how much had Dr. Fuller heard?

She had never yet solved that first question; the enigma

of Lyman's temperament was beyond her.   And nobody was likely to answer for her the second.

But Polly had also the advantage of her temperament. After that first instant's shock she walked bravely forward.

"We were quarreling, — my brother and I.   At least, I was. I wonder if it could possibly have been about you ? "

So far with the magnificence of conscious candor. Then a distinct recollection tingled through her of the last few words which were possibly all the professor had caught. And of these, naturalist as he was, he could not have constructed the entire subject. They were a fragment that might suggest a quite different fact of history. And her present apparent absurd application — Polly was a splendid, fiery rose again, but she stood her ground.

" Do not trouble yourself, dear Miss Schott," said the professor, with the most beautiful ready politeness.   " I shall not feel personally slighted if you refuse me. You have known me such a very little while."

Then all Peace Polly's chagrin and dismay shook themselves clear, and rushed away on the wings of a full, pleased laugh. She held out her hand to Dr. Fuller. She recollected, also, at the instant, that the man had a wife. She laughed again.

" If you are the boarder, you may come," she said. "Only, I don't believe you will, now. I generally get my punishments as I go along."

" You will this time," said the professor. " For I am certainly coming."

And so that most unexpected matter found its settlement at once.

Only, what ever had possessed Lyman Schott ? Peace Polly asked herself that question. She would not by any means ask Lyman.

We naturally wonder about it, too; and we, whose business it is to read between the lines, can ask Lyman.

The truth was, Lyman was one of those persons who do not, all their lives long, get over an infantile sort of objection to strangers. He wanted to know a person before being introduced. And as that disposition works on in a life along with other maturings, it matures for itself in this way. Out of its own fashion of doing, its own reach of knowing, is always strangerhood. It cannot give and take; there is no exchange or barter in its theory of social intercourse. If it has only plain corn and potatoes of its own to deal with, it can by no means establish relations with the man who offers milk and honey, or with him who can paint him a picture, or sell him out of a grand, wonderful conservatory of exotic cultures a night-blooming cereus, or a century-plant, or a great date-palm. It can have nothing to do with aught but corn and potatoes in return for its own simple cereals and esculents. A singular philosophy of a commerce of the spheres!

Moreover, distance, absence, a coming from an unknown, far-off experience, even a little elderhood, made a barrier against any near approach; Lyman Schott held himself instinctively aloof from any human nature which he suspected of being rooted deeper or wider, or to have sprung from any different conditions of soil or climate from his own. Yet, with the sweetest inconsistency, he could have sat down serenely with Solomon himself in all his glory and wisdom, if he had ever seen him familiarly in jacket and trousers, or whatever the Oriental urchin wore instead of those, or had thumbed the same old scrolls of learning with him before their beards were grown.

The sole reason why it was a tolerable thing to him to meet this Dr. C. P. Fuller, of recent brilliant fame, was that he had known him, some three years younger than himself, a simple schoolboy at Wendover Academy. He had helped him do his first examples in algebra. He remembered that, although he had pretty nearly forgotten his own algebra altogether. He had actually forgotten also, alas for Bonnyborough! what the mystical "C. P." stood for. They had always called little Fuller "Scipio" at school.

Besides, it was good, simple-hearted old Dr. Blithecome who had asked Lyman if they could possibly take his friend in at The Knolls. Professor Fuller was Dr. Blithecome's intimate *young* friend. There was nothing terrible in him or his achievements to the doctor, and there was nothing formidable about the doctor to Lyman Schott. Things which are equal to the same thing are equal to one another.

Lyman thought he should rather like to have "little Fuller" at The Knolls, and show him his farm and his planing-mill, and help him get bugs and weeds and pond-scum. That his work and delight and knowledge lay among these minute and insignificant things brought him somehow comfortably down to where a plain man need not be abashed with him. If his tool had been the telescope instead of the microscope, then indeed I think Lyman would have shrunk. He would not have assumed the ambition of even such indirect intimacy with Arcturus and the Pleiades.

Beside all else, there was Peace Polly, who wanted to have a boarder. Now she might try. Lyman counted on a little quiet amusement in seeing how she would succeed.

"I could n't even make a new beginning with a *boarder!*" Peace Polly said to Serena Wyse, when she told her all about it, half laughing, half tremulous. "It

makes me think of that dreadful verse, ' No place for repentance.'   But I guess I 'd rather be honest, after all.
I 'm glad he saw a bit of me as I am, and I 'd. as lief Lyman would n't think I was just turning over a new leaf
for this microscope man.   I 've no doubt I shall be bad
just a little while longer.   But I *have* got help, Serena,"
she added, with a sweet, swift seriousness.   "I 've had
things come to me ; I 've had a glimpse — Jacob saw
the ladder, you know, when he was way down at the foot
of it, all discouraged and worn out, running away from
his sins, — and running into them again, too ; for he was
just half-way between the two sets of them.   Why do
you suppose he had the vision then ? "

"Just because he was right there," said Miss Serena.
"He had got through with one piece of his story, and was
going to begin another.   When he came back from that,
he had a different dream.   The first one showed him
something ; he only looked at it.   The second one tried
him ; he had something given him to do in that.   There
was where he first really got the better of himself, and
made his new beginning."

"He got the better, yes ; but he came off halt."

"It is better for a man to go into life halt than to go
whole into the burning," said Miss Serena.

"I wonder what part of my story I am going to begin," said Peace Polly.

"Does it make any matter ? " asked Serena, with a
smile.   "It was after that very first vision, the glimpse,
that the Lord said to Jacob, 'I will not leave thee till I
have done that which I have spoken to thee of.'"

A brightness flashed over Peace Polly's face.   "Now I
have had it said to me," she said.   "I wonder what it
means."

But she did not tell Miss Serena of the dream which
had been her Jacob's ladder.

XVII.

"Miss Peace!" called the professor, from the little parlor on Peace Polly's side of the house, which they had given him for a study.

Peace Polly stopped at the open door which she was passing.

"I have something here which I think you would like to see. A rusty leaf."

"Thank you. With your long eyes, of course?" and the young girl stepped in.

The tall slanting tubes of the powerful microscope sloped in the full light of the west window down to — what? A bit of curled, blasted, unsightly leaf, apparently; really, as Peace Polly was sure beforehand, to some gate of glory into that under, beautiful infinity that stretches among the atoms as the upper spaces stretch among the stars.

Dr. Fuller looked at her as she came forward, eagerly; a fine flush upon her face, a clear shine in her eyes, the stir and gladness of a new expectation in a new realm just opened to her. For her part, she scarcely thought of the professor; of herself she thought not at all. She went and stood there as a spirit called to behold and learn a word; to receive therein an errand or an empire; as Uriel might have gone and stood within the sun. Everything to this child-woman was so significant, so "tremendous." For "tremendous" only means, after all, something to tremble — to thrill — at; and these things thrilled her; their great meanings stirred a great possibility of apprehension and reception in her.

There was nothing about her of the average girl; in her impulses or failures she would always rise or fall far beyond that. So she seemed to this man, who had never come across just such a woman before; who had been tired and disappointed, it must be told, with such women as life had brought him nearest to. He had had no mother for thirty years.

To Peace Polly he was but a half-elderly, all-absorbed scientist, a man with a little severe touch in the lines of his face, and a fleck of silver on the temples, that may come early in these days of intensified thought and accelerated labor. Beside all which, even to an average girl, there would have been a prophylactic against consciousness or sentiment; he had, somewhere, of however little account to him it might appear to be, a wife. The fact of this littleness of account bore against him in Peace Polly's first impression.

Here were two persons, therefore, with whom she had all at once been thrown in a way to arouse a certain sympathy on somewhat unusual grounds; for each of whom she had also conceived at the outset a slight distinct antagonism. Was nothing ever to approach her in all her life but after this fashion, with an exception? or was it her way of taking exception, so over-readily with all, — with even herself, and to begin with?

But the rusty leaf. There it lay, under the light, a blighted, refuse thing; through the miracle - working glasses Peace Polly saw a flower-patch of most exquisite soft bells, of a buff-amber color, transparent, delicate, holding up their little clustered cups, in each of which lay treasure of round, tiny, heaped-up seeds, its bountiful intrusted riches of life.

"There we begin with the semblance of a plant," said Dr. Fuller.

"But they *are* plants, with most lovely flowers; what else?" said Peace Polly.

"Nothing else; not quite that; only spore-bearers."

"Dear, little, meek, glorious things!" said Peace Polly, softly to herself.

Somehow, with Dr. Fuller's words, had come involuntarily to her the refrain of the hymn, "Only an armor-bearer."

Only treasure-bearers, these were, away out of human recognition, in invisibility; but they bore their charge safe for the great Lord of the treasury.

"Are n't the ferns spore-bearers, too?" she asked.

"Yes. They are of the same natural kingdom only, beautiful as they are."

"Not more beautiful than these, when you see these," said Peace Polly. "Now I know why the fern-seed gave invisibility. And it seems to me"— She stopped on the verge of a thoughtful saying which her second impulse withheld.

"What does it seem to you, please, Miss Peace?" asked the professor.

"The kind of invisibility that does not see itself," Peace answered; as she always did answer when not to reply would be to make the matter of her own saying more important than she ever cared to do.

Then he showed her some diatoms, — wonderful little shells of dead and gone spore-bearers, — fairy filigrees, like little canoes, or long, lace-like pods, formed of silex, Dr. Fuller told her, and forming in their turn, in the slow deposit of ages, great foundations on which cities have been built. Peace Polly thought of the " battling Titans." These were the Titans of the little. Another sort were in every pretty shape of vases, baskets, censers, flasks, the tiniest things conceivable in form, even under the microscope, yet all perfect and lovely in each mesh and line and intersection, and of shapes the furthest like of which, out of big, tangible material, only the fairest art has ever approached in construction.

After that, some spicules of " glass sponge," crystallized fibres in crosses, stars, lances, anchors; and last of all, some mould-particles which showed like a little field of spirit-daisies.

When she lifted herself up and turned around to go away, " I feel like a mastodon," she said. " When I was a little child, somebody told me that every step I took I crushed a million little living things. I know better now. My step could not get near enough to crush them. They are quite safe in their infini-tesi-mality."

The professor smiled to hear her gradually arrive at the formation of the big derivative, which she wrought carefully into utterance as the only word to use, though she must needs make it as she went along.

" You will come again, Miss Peace? " he said. " I have many things that I could show you."

That saying brought up another to her. It was the saying of the Lord himself, who is the word of all this wonderful creation. And the sentence with which He followed it, speaking it of spiritual things, truly, yet how true it was also in the signs, the parables hidden in the foundations of the world! " Ye cannot bear them now."

" I have had as much as I could take to-day," said Peace Polly; and went away with a sweet shadow on her face, the dropping of the shining eagerness into the stillness of a satisfied delight. Professor Fuller noted that also. The girl herself was beginning to be a study to him.

If she were any more so than to herself, he might indeed have realized that a new science was before him; something beyond lenses and tests, or even records of observation. For no human being is to be classed or judged, arbitrarily, as being of this or that definite character, like a polyp or a mollusk; nay, it is often quite as hard to say where the true progressive connection lies, or the step is made, from one order to another; it is kingdom beside kingdom, truly, and even in the very individual.

And that brings me to what I had been thinking of before, and was shortly about to say, and with which I may as well begin another chapter.

XVIII.

CROSS LIGHTS.

Human nature is a very complex thing, a truism safely asserted of the race, and leading to not much of anything in particular statements; but when I tell you, for instance, as I find I need to do, that the Rev. Richard Innesley was of a very complex character, you not unreasonably expect explanation in some detail, and some sort of reconciling key to declared contrarieties. This threatens a long analysis. Do not be concerned; I shall hardly presume to make it, abstractly; if the story does not do it in any degree, it is my failure in telling the story. I am not fond of vivisection; let the live thing render its own revelation of living; find out from the dead thing, if you can, what it had to live with, and why it had to die.

There is this to say: that to pronounce a nature complex is not of necessity to decide it great, or the higher toward perfection, but rather the contrary; for, once arrived in the scale of life at the human, we have come to where advance means or involves an ascending reduction. The unit of mere existence must develop into manifoldness, refine and complement itself to complexity, the more and more as the revealing order rises; but by and by arrives the point where the refractions begin to converge again; the rays run inward; the differenced attributes join and merge toward singleness; the noblest is the simplest; the Infinite is One.

Richard Innesley was not farther on than many of us

in this long fulfillment; there were contradictions in him; he knew them, even bitterly, himself.

He believed, and he revered; he did not handle holy things with carelessly profane hands; he examined himself, as it fell to him to exhort others to do; he would gladly have had his soul in white, arrayed for the true priesthood. But he was particular too about the set of his surplice, and aware that his handsome, round, white throat became the clerical collar well. He did know, sometimes, even in the Te Deum, what was happening below the chancel. How could he help catching the gleam when Rose Howick's light summer dress and white ribbons came fluttering and shining through the dusky aisle and into the third pew in front?

What was she asking, as she knelt there, for her young, fresh life?

"O Lord, save thy people, and bless thine heritage. Govern them, and lift them up forever!"

He chanted the words, remembering that elsewhere it is, "feed them," and that either way the meaning is of the instant ordering and providing that are for the blessed and continual lifting up out of all "partiality and hypocrisy" into truth and entireness, into the numbering with the saints, and the walking before God in the land of the living, which is the glory everlasting.

"Day by day we magnify thee."

"Vouchsafe" — pledge us surely — "to keep us this day without sin."

His heart was in the prayer that is only another wording of "deliver us from evil: because thine is the continual glory of all Thou wilt make of us, of all Thou wilt show thy power in us to be."

Yet Peace Polly had been right, and he had not got altogether away from earth, while leading his people's ascriptions up to the very gate and glory of heaven.

Out of the pulpit, as in it, there were the lesser and the larger side of him; the natural and the spiritual man. Why not, since they were in St. Paul also, and fought out their everlasting battle in his converted, consecrated life? We accept without blame or wonder that grand, general confession; what we blame and wonder at are the small, special illustrations of the same in people at our side to-day.

Peace Polly wondered if the young clergyman had meant all those things he had to say, at all, when she saw him, after church was over, walk up the shady street with Rose and her mother, chatting blithely with them by the way. How could the minister from the altar come down so straightway among the common places and speeches, the common social encounters and exchanges, even to seek and to be briskly pleased with them, like any other man who had only " been to " church, and got done with it?

Yet the words that he had said to her, that day upon the rock among the breakers! And of course he had to come down into the street and to go home, as he had had to come down off the great ocean cliff, and leave the splendor and the speech of the sea behind him, for a time. He could not soar off overhead, or disappear until another Sunday! She was unreasonable, of course; but she wished things held together better. She wished it had not been, so evidently, because Rose Howick was the prettiest girl in Bonnyborough. She had not the least bit of acrimony toward Rose, however. She thought it might be a very disillusionizing thing to become a clergyman's wife. Yet it was natural enough for a clergyman to have a wife, as it was for him to come down from his pulpit into the street and to walk home to dinner.

She caught herself wishing, in one of these captious soliloquies, that things might be lifted up forever, or else, once for all, be comfortably let down to mere every-day.

Meanwhile, Mr. Innesley had not forgotten, on his part, the afternoon upon the rocks, or the proud, clear, self-judging spirit he had caught a glimpse of there. I think he rather carefully tried and compared Miss Rose in these days by some half-acknowledged standard, to see if haply there might not be as much beyond mere beauty, of some fair strength, in her. I suspect him of having said to himself once, looking into her pretty, smiling face, and seeing there only the smilingness, that, though the confession of an unruly temper was a brave and noble thing, the possession of a sunniness that needed no such avowal might, for the comfort of human relations, be quite possibly a better still.

At the same time, he had got in the way, since Dr. Fuller had been there, of coming a good deal to the old Schott mansion.

With the lesser and the larger of him, he began to be divided in his mind. Which, however, was the really lesser and which the larger may have been question within question, such as waits, in most lives, final proof.

Moreover, I do not mean to say that it was but the division in his mind as concerning his acquaintance with these two young girls which was at this time influencing his movements. He had but just begun to be aware of that; hardly so much as aware, even; there had but just begun to be anything of the sort that he should gradually become aware of. It was in him, but he had not directly looked at it.

There was another complexity which his intercourse with the professor, and especially in the company, as often happened, of Peace Polly as a third, just now touched upon. And of this again, in its full import, he was not yet openly self-suspicious.

I have said that Richard Innesley believed. He did, devoutly, that there was a glorious thing given into the world to be believed. He could as little have imagined a world without the Christian revelation in it as without himself in it. It was here; how otherwise could he have it to think of? How otherwise could there be question or dispute of it? He had not put himself here; he had not always been here; but to think of the whole creation without himself anywhere in it, — he could not so discharge himself of the very foundation of his thought. Neither could he put Christ, as the central fact of it, out of the world.

But was He right here, *in* his world, the world of every-day? Was there as little need to talk about it, to prove it, as to assert the sun in the heavens?

What were all these new facts and theories that were springing up, these clouds of heaven in which the Son of man did not seem to be? What were the indubitable reconciling answers, on the science side of the Lord's word, that made the word a whole, and showed it to be in his Son from the beginning? He would indeed have had a conclusive argument to all this; something that he could say to himself, to others, irrefutably. He searched for some Star in the East that should move triumphant among these very clouds, and go before all wisdom, all question, all slow, entangling research, until it should stand clear and central right over where the manifest Presence lies.

He was in peril of the stumbling-block of all reverent materialism; the demand that that way we shall touch God.

The agnosticism of the day was so sublimely knowing; it stopped, in such grand humility, so short! If it could but be pursued on its own pathway, a little further!

Unless, indeed, so seeking, he might himself get led the further back!

He would fain learn what Dr. Fuller had come to, as regarded faith.

The professor came to church, sometimes; Mr. Innesley had not yet seen him at the Communion Table.

The young minister could not ask him questions, even lead to them in talk, as other men might; that would be to seem to catechise, in virtue of his office, yet in its minority. He was too modest to do that. It was here that a third person, a bright woman, young, learning of life, eager to know and to reconcile knowledges, came happily in. The visits at The Knolls would have been but poor opportunities, but for Peace Polly.

Peace Polly, all unwitting, was gathering on either hand, comparing, making such conclusions as she could.

She was very careful, at the same time somewhat whimsical, in her way with the young clergyman. She was mindful of her decision that the beginning of their acquaintance involved no special continuance of it; she therefore eluded all specialty. The pretty distance she kept up, as if whatever ground they met on, whatever common subjects might chance to interest them, left them quite as separate as they began with them, as individual as the same wave leaves two round pebbles on the shore that may be rolled side by side by one impulse and far apart again by the next, was not the least of her attractions to Richard Innesley. She would have been ferocious with herself if she had known it; but no policy of the most finished coquette could have been surer or finer to such end of attracting. He had to begin all over again with her, from some fresh, accidental starting-place, every time. It was always an interesting uncertainty in his mind at what point he should find or take up acquaintance with her, next. He was divided, again, between the interest of this and the comfortableness of always finding the

11

bright, sweet readiness, not forward, but allowing duly the pleasant advance of growing intimacy, that he had with Rose Howick.

Peace Polly's gatherings and appropriations from her life in these days were far more impersonal. Persons contributed to them; that was pretty nearly all.

XIX.

ONE day, just before the young clergyman dropped in, there had been a little breeze in the house.

Peace Polly had been very lovely lately. She was happy in new thoughts; she was not thrown back upon herself; there was a new element in the life at the old homestead, and she was taking it in, as the very element she had lacked. Assimilating it, she was growing; she was thriving as a plant set out from winter housing into warm spring air. Or she was like a human creature let out from a long, cramped winter between brick walls into freedom and broadening sunshine; permitted to make a new summer abiding among great hills and pleasant fields.

She had had a latch-key given her to let herself in to a very House Beautiful, — to the chambers of grand, underlying, significant truth; from these the lofty ways and stairs led up to the fair higher rooms, with their windows wide open to the morning and the midday and the evening light. Only the place was vast, and one might wander long; might be stopped by many a blind turn; might stand questioning at a closed door, often. It was they who questioned least, perhaps, but who just saw the shining above them and followed the light gladly, without trying to understand all the intricate plan, or map the passage-ways, who got furthest up and saw widest both within and abroad.

Now and then she stopped and looked at herself in this wise : —

"Did it take all this to pacify me? to put my temper and my restlessness away out of sight, and keep me safely occupied, like a fractious child? I am seeming quite amiable now, even to myself; but it is only because I am kept pleased. I am not a bit better than I was before. Lyman lets me alone more; ought I to want him to let me alone? And don't I let him alone a great deal more than a good sister ought? Have I just got rid of him, living right here in his house, and gone off worlds away from him, contentedly, in my real inside living? And does n't it seem to him just as I thought it would, that I am behaving well now, like that same fractious child, only because there is company?"

When these things came into her mind, she felt like any outburst, that should show she would not put on a piece of made-up character, a kind of good gown for an occasion; should honestly reveal her as she knew herself to be, to these new friends, who, she perceived quite intelligently, were already thinking a best of her that was only her transitory and conditional best.

There were, indeed, the untrained child and the sweet, high-souled woman in her; they were on her every-day and Sabbath sides, — the earth side and the heavenly. There is a divine hypocrisy in some natures that reaches continually one way to the very, absolute best, and the other way has continually to reproach itself as false, because all of it has not yet grown up to the fair, celestial level. I do not think these were the kind of hypocrites whom the Lord scourged with his rebuke.

The breeze arose after this fashion.

Peace Polly and Serena Wyse were comfortably busy in the cool, open hall. Serena had come over in the early afternoon, with a "society quilt" — if the reader chances to know what that thing is — in a big bag; it was in patches as yet, separate artistic efforts in calico, of some five-and-twenty women : stars and stripes, and hexagon and suns ; here and there a more modern touch in a piece of brilliant " crazy-work," or an " applied " design. These five-and-twenty women were the sewing-circle, of which Serena Wyse was the devoted president. She had all these stars and stripes and individual ambitions to regulate and harmonize into a whole, with the most careful distribution of positions, according to the best spirit of a pure public service ; to find place for everybody's work that should well agree with its neighbors', and put nobody in a side row or a corner, ignominiously ; in fact, put everybody in the middle. She had brought it to Peace Polly for her help with the problem and in the tacking it together.

The two women were cheerful over it. Women who like each other are happy with a piece of industry between them ; and every woman is happy with her work well laid out before her for some few straight-going hours. Her occupation is so apt ordinarily to consist chiefly in interruptions.

The house was very bright and cool and still ; shady-bright, with the leaf and branch shields waving before the open doors. Rebeccarabby had done clashing her cymbals of tin and sheet-iron ; everything was clean, you may be confident, and put away in place, in her territory ; and she herself was in her afternoon repose up-stairs, which alone accounted for the pleasant hush, unbroken by any distant tramp or ring.

Lyman had gone to East Bend to-day, to see a builder ; the professor went out shortly after dinner with case and net, collecting. The women chattered unconstrainedly over their big table on which the patches were spread, placing and altering them, and mixing up their calico perplexities and reliefs with any other talk that came. The lengthening shadows grew cooler, and the freckles of sunlight between the white-oak boughs ran dancing further in upon the floor through the garden doorway, as the rays shot more level from the west.

"Why, it must be five o'clock!" said Peace Polly, suddenly, as a bounce down the kitchen stairway proclaimed the descent of Rabby from her dreams, and the resonant rasp of table-legs across a bare floor followed, betokening her instant vigorous onset upon the next domestic duty, the getting of things together for the preparing of the day's last meal.

"Rabby's tumble and rush are as sure to time as the stroke of the hour; if the clock stopped I should set it by her." At that instant, the hammer behind the dial fell; five clear notes counted themselves forth from the tall old case on the landing.

"We are to have something good for tea, I am sure; she does n't drag the table to the front unless something very precise is to be handled. It will be blueberry cake, I think."

Serena was folding her quilt. She knew Peace Polly expected her to stay; she was thinking whether she had better. She never made any little false preliminaries; she never said, "I must be going," when she only meant "if you don't ask me to stay any longer," and was prepared to yield to the expected invitation. She wondered quietly within herself whether Lyman would be back in time.

"Have you seen my red memorandum book?" was heard, in an annoyed voice, from over the stairs.

"Why, where did he come from?—Yes, it was on your mantel yesterday," called Peace Polly back.

"Where is it now?" There was something more

vexing in the strained moderation of the tone — in its absolute assumption that the person addressed was accountable, and was simply to be dealt with in a forced patience — than would have been in an explosion of ordinary irritability.

"In your other coat pocket," answered Peace Polly, coolly. It was an assumption in her turn, and a sarcasm; but Lyman took it literally.

"I don't see why you should meddle with it," he said; but he went and looked, and evidently found it, for there was silence for a minute or two after that.

Then he called again. "Where's my two-foot rule? and my *pencil!*" accumulated grievance and an according righteous resentment intensified in his voice.

"What is the reason," asked Peace Polly, cheerfully and deliberately, — it might seem in soliloquy, — Serena hoped so, — to the listener above, "that men, some men, never can endure the losing or mislaying of their least little bits of property? The exasperation seems to be in inverse ratio to the square of the value. They can go through really terrible things, a fire or a failure or a shipwreck; but if it is an inch of lead-pencil that is lost, ah!" The long breath she drew and let go was the very abandonment of sheer despair at further expression.

Serena shook her head reprovingly; at this instant the professor stood in his doorway. It really seemed as if he had an apparitional knack with doorways at exciting junctures. Lyman, looking from the opposite baluster above, whence he could see only the professor, naturally thought that it was with him Peace Polly was making ridicule of his misfortune.

Serena felt relief. She did not care, or quite know how, to make her presence known; but Dr. Fuller was obvious; he ought to do as well.

Lyman spoke again. " I should like to have you answer me," he said, with bitter self-control. " I suppose you have cleared them all up while you were about it."

Peace Polly was as cool as a fresh water-cress, — with the same bite inside. As yet, she had not lost outward temper in the least, for she undoubtedly had quite the best of it.

" You might look in the left-hand secretary drawer," she answered ; " or, perhaps I put *those* two little things in the trousers pocket ! "

It was perfectly evident to the two spectators that she was still playing with his small injustice, tracking his own probable disposals with her calm suggestions. Lyman took everything persistently down to the very ground of the letter. There was silence again, except for his footsteps to and fro, and hasty openings of drawer and wardrobe.

" The best way another time," he said at last, taking the trouble to come and say it as for the sake of a certain condonation, " will be for you to leave my things for me to put away myself."

This was irresistible. As he turned away again overhead, Peace Polly's laugh broke forth. But for that all might have been well; at least the rest might not have happened. The laugh sounded somewhat exaggerated; for in truth there was something a little out of control in it, and it might quite easily have been tears. Undoubtedly Lyman felt its mockery, literal as he was; it was hardly possible to fail of translating that. And Professor Fuller was down there, as he knew, and doubtless laughing also.

There was this mistake : the professor was not there now, nor laughing. He had smiled, but a grave look had followed, that Peace Polly caught and felt the smiting of, although, and because, it was quite gentle and unmeant; and he had turned again within his room. Very likely he would have closed his door, but for the rebuke which that might seem.

Miss Serena laid her folded quilt within the bag. "Good-by," she said softly, and slipped toward the hill-side door.

"Oh, you'll stay?" Peace Polly just managed the three words.

"Not this time, dear; I could not stay to-night. It is Susannah's night for her prayer-meeting, — too," she added, on the door-step, whither Peace Polly followed her. She was so honest, she had to put on that "too," which told all the rest of it. Susannah could have locked the house and gone to meeting well enough. But here Lyman had been laughed at. Serena would not have him know she knew it, much more think she had taken part, even though at the moment he had deserved it. Lyman Schott was a good man; and she was where she could take part both ways.

Peace Polly walked back without a word to the front of the hall. She stood shamed; she had shown up her brother in his fault. Not his fault so much, either, as his deficiency.

And then Lyman came down-stairs with a high look, wearing a clean starched seersucker sack conspicuously torn at the elbow, with the flap of the rent stiffened back.

Peace Polly turned round upon him. She took vengeance upon herself now by showing out her own fault relentlessly. She had been so fine, so superior, in her calmness and her derision!

"You look like an injured half-angel," she said; " one wing just sprouted, — and blighted. Where did you get that coat?"

"On the basket."

"That was the mending-basket. There is another in your bureau. You have come down with that on to mortify me."

"I did not suppose the mending-basket would be standing round till Friday. It was n't ever so in my mother's time."

"I wish that your mother's time had lasted till this day; and that there never had been question of my mother or me!" and Peace Polly fled up-stairs.

"Pease porridge hot!" said the big brother, as the professor came out of his room again toward him. "The little girl has a temper; but she gets over it as quick as it gets over her. And that's allowing considerable."

"Is n't there something somewhere about causing the little ones to offend?" asked Dr. Fuller. "If I were you, I would remember where she is tender to touch. If it were a lame foot or a finger, you would."

Lyman looked at his friend, surprised. It was a quite new idea. "I never thought of that before," he said, simply.

Undoubtedly, Lyman Schott's self-control, exasperating as he might make it, sprang from a true intent of righteousness. If he could see another thing that was quite as much his duty to do he would do it.

I think it appears in this story that we have not to concern ourselves with a single person who is either saint or sinner. Even Miss Serena, — well, we will leave that to the penetration of the reader. He will take pleasurable credit to himself in the discovery of the least palpable thing, perhaps, in the whole chronicle.

Lyman went through the rooms and up the other stairs, changed his coat, and, coming down, took up his hat and went straight out of the east door across the garden to the Wyse house.

"I want you to come over and see Polly, and take tea," he said. "I've been vexing her again, and you can smooth her down, — comfort her up, I mean," he added, with that peculiar smile of his that now and then showed forth the whole real sweetness of the man.

"I ·don't believe I'd better come, right away," answered Serena, with her staid gentleness; "by and by, may be, in the cool of the evening, when you 're all out round the fore door. And, Lyman, why won't you remember about the 'little ones,' and the 'millstone'? You could n't bear that about your neck; it would hurt your heart, I know."

Lyman was silent; it was strange to have that said twice to him. It was strange to have Serena troubled for a hurt to his heart. She had hardly treated him as if he had one, he thought. Nobody had been very near to him all these years, on any ground like that. He did not think anybody had cared very much what became of that part of him, since he was a little boy, and had the mother to go to whom Peace Polly could not bear to have mentioned. He forgot to consider how he had been most apt to mention her.

"My mother died twenty-six years ago to-day, Serena."

"Why don't you go home and tell Peace Polly that?" Serena asked, quickly.

"How can I ?" asked the man, with the ingenuousness of a boy. "I 've just been twitting her about my mother's mending-basket. I don't mean to be ugly, Serena, but she bristles up so easy, it leads me on; and then — well, she don't always toe the mark exactly, in the good old times-ey way. She was n't much to blame this time, though. I suppose I might have let her alone, only I was bothered."

"And when a man is bothered, he must turn round and bother somebody else ? " Serena asked him.

"Well, he's apt to," acknowledged Lyman. "Things get passed round, in this world."

"The trouble is they don't get passed round whole," Serena said to that. "If all that was in our minds and all that was in theirs"—Serena let her grammar take care of itself in her earnestness after the thought—"was clear and plain both ways, folks *could n't* differ as they do."

"I don't see but they'd be pretty much run together into one, in that case."

"Yes, they would. That's what's to come. 'That they, Father, may be one.' Lyman, we don't give each other but the merest little piece, the crustiest little corner, where we ought to give the whole fair slice. Go right home and tell Peace Polly what you've been telling me. She'll know a bit about you, then; it's time."

"Good night, then," said Lyman, laughing a little, and looking happy. "It's well for a man to have a conscience outside of him,—if he could only be plumb sure of it's being alongside when he wanted it!" Serena did not pretend not to understand.

"I'd be a pretty poor dependence for a conscience, Lyman, beyond myself; but I'm right here alongside, any way, and you know I take an interest, always."

Polly had her cry out; she had nobody to go to, or thought so. Then she bathed her eyes and smoothed her hair, and went down-stairs again. It was not a particularly pleasant thing to do, but it was one of those things that in the vicissitudes of human history have often to be done. If we could throw ourselves away, like broken china, every time we think we have spoiled ourselves and all our story, the backyards of creation would be full of the pitiful flinders of us. We can't do that; and it is n't done for us; not even when we crumble down into the grave, I do believe. At any rate, in this life we have to keep on among our fellows, with all our cracks and flaws and rim-nips turned inside, perhaps, as well as we can manage or fellow-kindliness can wink at, but there, all the same, every one, and open to remembrance if not to instant inspection.

It had come now; Dr. Fuller could be under no further hallucination about her; he had seen her in the old gown that had seemed to have got worn out and to be done with; he need not think of her at her company best any more. She did not find herself very much more comfortable for that, however. Was it the same thing that had happened to Cinderella in the fairy tale? Was that what she had run away and sat down again in the ashes for?

It was when she came down in this mood that she met Mr. Innesley, just come in.

Of course she greeted him courteously; it seemed to her that at this hypocrisy of amiability Dr. Fuller, the enlightened, sitting by, must instantly cry out. Instead of that, he told them both, in a manner just as usual, that he had some very good specimens of bacteria to show them.

Peace Polly turned her eyes, yet cloudy with their recent tempest, straight upon him, almost reproachfully.

"Don't you think there have been almost specimens enough for to-day?" she asked him, with a cold gravity. For the pride and dignity of her manner, it might have been he, and not herself, to whom she was administering the haughty little rebuke.

"I think we have not had enough, or of the right sort, to draw conclusions from. Though I suspect you have been willing some very one-sided ones should be made."

"I don't want you to conclude that anything is different from what it really is," returned Peace Polly, still calm and lofty.

"And so —? Miss Peace, there is a little plant called Honesty which is very lovely to examine."

" Under the microscope ? "

" Yes, that also ; but it does not need a microscope. It has a wonderful delicate transparency. It is one of the *Cruciferæ*, the cross-bearers."

" Does it explode ? " asked Peace Polly, scornfully.

She was not going to forgive herself, or accept the consolation of a flattering comparison.

But she wondered within herself if her new friend really did see so far into her as that : that she had let herself be horrid chiefly because he had been there, and because she had let Lyman seem as horrid as he would.

At this moment Lyman came back. He greeted the young clergyman, who moved to meet him. Peace Polly was standing just beside the open door as he passed in. She slipped out upon the porch.

Dr. Fuller joined her, quietly.

" Would you like it better that I should say all I might ? " he asked. " I don't want *you* to conclude any half truth from me."

" Say on," said Peace Polly. " I shall feel better."

" Then, you were angry ; but anybody might be that. It cannot always be helped, at the moment. But we ought to be careful to hinder ourselves from the thing that is worse, — contempt."

That was being very true, indeed !

He did not say she had been guilty of it ; he only told her of the thing that might be worse.

The three condemnations ran swiftly through her mind.

To be angry with the brother without a cause ; to say unto the brother, Raca ; to say, Thou fool ! The judgment, the council, hell-fire !

Did he mean all that ? And he had talked to her of the honesty-plant ! There was something like a horror in the girl's eyes as they met his, that made him hasty to say, — and he laid a quick, gentle touch upon her arm, but withdrew it as quickly, —

"Understand me. When we are most anxious to find all we want, most troubled that we seem to miss of it, — then we must take care that we look for what there *is*, although it should turn out to be something different. It would be worse to miss of that. It is the narrow demand for just one sort of admirableness that betrays us into disdain."

Peace Polly drew the breath that had been arrested.

"Anxious," and "troubled," — because she wanted, and missed. That was the fairer understanding of her, she truly felt. She thanked him in her heart for so reading her. No, God's goodness forbid, she did not despise her brother yet !

"I don't think," she said slowly, "that I expect any particular sort of admirableness, in myself or anybody else; but what I never can have patience with is smallness. It hurts me. Little vexes are a great deal worse, I think, in people, or in things, than big tribulations. I could put up with a real, worth-while injury, or bear a loss, — of a possession, I mean; but to be blamed or misunderstood about a trifle, or to miss my thimble just when I want to sew a glove-finger, — Dr. Fuller, those are the terrible things ! " And there she laughed, slightly, shortly. She forgot what her illustration argued of common human frailty and excuse; or to apply it to men, and their lost lead - pencils. The thing she felt and meant was, that she could not bear a smallness in a man ; in Lyman, her brother.

Dr. Fuller might have perceived his opportunity ; if he did, he did not use it.

"You are ready for the battle, but you cannot stand the drill ? " he said, putting the question with a smile.

Peace Polly threw up her face with a flash in it. " Has that kind of drill anything to do with the battle ? " she demanded.

" As a philosopher, I should say that no development of conquering fitness came about except through little innumerable struggles with the smallest and nearest obstacles and needs."

He was very careful to be philosophical!

" Do you suppose that it is set, that it is meant so ? " asked Peace Polly.

" I see it so," answered the scientist; " all the way up. What intent there may be runs all through."

It sounded a cold way of saying it. Did this man believe, or only see ? Peace Polly wondered. Yet somehow the word shot straighter home for its feather-tip of natural fact than if it had been weighted with a solemn, inherited assertion.

Did he lead her up with the thing he saw, toward the thing it fitted to, that she had been taught long before ?

" What intent there may be runs all through." If God meant anything for her at the last, He was surely meaning a way to it through these beginnings. They were as pot-hooks and trammels, that should join by and by in lettering, to form his word, his sentence, of her creation. Was that it ? Something like that gleamed in upon her mind.

At any rate, Dr. Fuller had led her away from that which was unbearable to think of to something which had a hope in it.

And then he said, " But you do not do yourself justice about the small things. The small things of the microscope " —

" Oh, those are grand! " cried Peace Polly. " That they should be so far down out of sight, and yet have such life in them ! That is their glory ! "

"Q. E. D.," said Dr. Fuller, quietly. "Come in now, and let me show you the bacteria."

Polly had not meant to let herself have any pleasure like that, to-night. She was too out of order to look in peace down into that wonder of order; to stand before that depth of revelation. It was like an altar which she might not, unshriven, profane.

Now, it was as if some voice had offered absolution.

But then there came another utterance to her from within.

She looked up, with a gentle humbleness in her face that she knew not of. "Presently," she said. "I must go first and speak to Lyman."

"First be reconciled to thy brother." It was not Dr. Fuller who said that.

Lyman at the same moment came out, looking for her.

"Pease Porridge," he said, "I'll tell you how I happened to be thinking of my mother. It is twenty-six years to-day since she died. She was a young woman, only thirty; and I was a boy. I remember her so well, and all her ways."

Just a simple telling of himself, as Serena Wyse had counseled; no word of either apology or fresh reproof. What made Lyman so different all at once? was Peace Polly's first wondering thought.

And then, "Only six years older there than I am here!" she said within herself. "And only ten years more of this life behind that than I have had already!" Somehow she had always thought of Lyman's mother as an old, old-fashioned woman.

This brought her near; into sudden relation and presence with herself. "And that is the way you have been doing for my boy!" She felt as if this were said to her.

Lyman had had no woman to be tender over him for

such a long, long while. If he had realized a little more
that not a child-sister, but a woman, had been growing by
his side! But she would not think of that now; it had
been his mistake. What, then, had been hers?

He had told her once the love-name his mother had
made for him, when he was a little bit of a fellow. She
had used to call him her little Mannie. Who had cared
so for her grown man, since?

Peace Polly's own mother, too: sixteen years ago she
died; she was yet in her heaven - girlhood, — younger
than herself here. What might these three, they and she,
be to each other at this moment? What ought they?

There rushed into her mind Mr. Innesley's answer to
her question, "Who are the friends?" "All Saints."

Had she been earning love and praise from these?

All these things followed one another in a single mental
thrill, a single heart-throb.

"Oh, Lyman!" she turned around and cried. "I am
so sorry! You have n't anybody but me, and I 've been
horrid!"

She stretched her hands to him, and the tears that
started sounded in her voice.

Lyman did not like to be pathetic. "Well, well!" he
said, half impatiently, "we can't either of us be each
other's mother, I suppose; but may be we can brother
and sister a little better. You must n't mind all my
kinks and hard knots. Something else ties 'em up first,
and then I bring 'em along to you. Who else is there?"

But he took one of Peace Polly's hands, and elder-
brotherly walked with her back along the front stoop to
the open door. There, in the light, she slipped away
from him, and met Mr. Innesley. In her mind those
last words lingered, "Who else is there?"

It was privilege, then, after a sort, to take Lyman's

little snubs; to be the only one for him to bring hard knots to. Well, she would try to look at it that way, next time; and perhaps, after a while, he might bring something else to her. She was glad, at any rate, of the one little glimpse into Lyman's shut-up mind; and that, looking in there, she had found such a sweet and human thing as his long-loving memory of his mother.

"He may tell me of her mending-days, and her linen-chest, and her countings-up, and her darnings, just as much as ever he likes, after this!" she cried inwardly to that Polly of her that the Peace had such sharp work to keep down.

It was thoroughly and especially comfortable, also, that Professor Fuller, wise and friendly, was upon no possible false basis with her any more, but had seen her once as bad as she could be.

"Now I can be as good as I have a mind," retorted Polly upon Peace.

XX.

ATOMS AND OWLS.

IT was deep in the gloaming when Serena Wyse came quietly in with her knitting-work that she could do in the dark, and was there among them without an arrival, like the shadows.

They were all in the big old hall, sitting around just within the "fore door," as she had said. Mr. Innesley was beside Peace Polly. When Rebeccarabby presently brought in the lighted lamp, and put it in its hanging frame, Lyman drew near the table under it, and watched Dr. Fuller, who began to arrange his microscope.

Serena could not tell how matters might be. Lyman was quiet, as always; Peace Polly spoke easily, but not volubly, with the clergyman.

"This is nothing very beautiful, to unscientific eyes, that I am going to show you now," said the professor, peering into his tubes, and delicately touching his object with some minute instrument. "It is curious, as one of the smallest things that can be seen. It measures, I mean the individual, about half a thousandth of a millimetre."

"How much is that in inches?" asked Miss Serena, simply. "I mean," she added, laughing, "how much of an inch?"

"A little less than a fifty-thousandth," replied the professor.

"Why, who measures them, and what with?" inquired Serena, coolly sensible, as far as she could see, like the Yankee woman that she was.

"Anybody who can catch and hold them; and with means proportioned to all else required in observing them. Did you ever see the Ten Commandments engraved on the space of a pin's point? I will show you that, presently. That may exemplify. Now, Miss Wyse, here are some living things a thousand times less than a pin's point."

"How do you know they are alive?" she asked him, as she bent to the instrument, and discerned, among some flecks of cloudy film, a group of tiniest clear globules, single, connected in pairs, and again others in chains and spirals, like strung beads. All moving, swimming swiftly, spinning, darting; the slender threads or chains waving and creeping.

"By their motion; by their separations and joinings. They are busy with life; they are, or hold, first atoms of life; every one of these, at a certain stage, divides in two, those into two again, and so the life multiplies."

"Atoms of life," said Miss Serena. "Then you have got at life, at last?"

"At its earliest reachable manifestations," replied the professor. "These cells are not life; but life is in them."

"Oh!" said Miss Serena. "Then you are not one of those wise men whose Bible begins ' In the beginning the atoms made heaven and earth' ? "

Dr. Fuller looked up at her. "What is a Bible?" he asked.

"A book of truth," answered Serena.

"I am afraid *my* Bible does begin with the atoms," said the doctor. "They are the smallest elementary parts that I can spell. Doubtless there are other Bibles. *The Bible* should include all the rest."

Who could tell, from this man's word or manner, where or on what his faith stood fast, or stopped?

Mr. Innesley regarded him attentively. "How would a book of Genesis go on that should begin as Miss Serena has quoted?" he asked.

"Suppose Miss Serena should go on and try?" said Dr. Fuller.

Serena looked at the two, from one to the other. "Are you in earnest?" she asked.

"Why not? I have never framed a chapter of creation. Let us see whether it would go on."

"I suppose it would have to say," said Miss Serena, slowly, "'In the beginning the atoms made the heavens and the earth.'"

"'The earth was without form and void; and the atoms moved about in it.'"

"'And the atoms wanted light; and they moved more and more, and rubbed against each other, and there was light.' Oh, what have I said! What am I coming to?" cried Miss Serena, in sudden consternation.

"Go on," said Dr. Fuller, gravely. "That is just what would have to follow from the beginning. What would be next?"

"Oh, Dr. Fuller! there was nothing but the atoms; there was nobody there to see that it was good! The Bible would have to stop right there! Every verse after that begins 'and God saw,' 'and God called,' 'and God said!' You can't have any Bible without God in it!"

Dr. Fuller smiled, and said not a word. He turned to his instrument, and began to work carefully at it again.

Peace Polly and the others had forgotten, in listening to the strange talk over them, to look at these first bacteria at all. The professor had now placed a small drop of another sort upon his object-class.

"This," he said, is larger, and of a slightly higher order of development. The others were of the dividing order; they grow by cutting themselves in two. In these, we come to the budding process; they are more like true plants in that. One cell grows out upon another, and so they heap themselves in masses. This is the way your yeast makes itself. This *is* a drop of yeast, Miss Peace, that I begged out of your kitchen. Your help-woman there was very rebellious at my taking so little. 'It would n't riz nothing,' she said."

"Nothing but questions, I suppose," returned Peace, obeying the doctor's motion and crossing to the table. "I should like to know," she said, presently, after she had observed the pretty foam-balls that clustered or branched, like bright little tree-boughs or umbels of flowers, in the speck of fluid, — "I should like to know why the different kinds work exactly opposite ways, turning their backs upon each other, as it were. It is like creation working up and down, each side of a dividing line."

Dr. Fuller answered her as concisely and as strictly within scientific definition as was possible; watching her, as he did so, much as if she were an object from which he had logically to expect some curious or beautiful development.

"We have not come to the actual dividing line yet," he said. "These give us a hint of higher growth, but they are still mere infusoria. The great distinction is between the unorganized and the organized vegetations; those which live upon organisms by their decomposition and those which organize themselves by appropriating from inorganic substances."

Peace Polly followed him with keen attention.

"Is it all a battle, then?" she said quickly. "Are there really reverse orders of life-atoms? Is it life of death, and life of life?" she finished earnestly.

"It is the equilibrium in which the globe exists. Life

would be impossible upon it, if it were not for the destroyers."

"And they never can take their turn at anything else!" said Peace Polly, turning away from the microscope. "It is the same old puzzle."

"I do not understand your development theory, your evolution," said Mr. Innesley, following Peace Polly's lead, and coming into the discussion as somehow on her side.

"Is it mine?" asked Dr. Fuller.

"I don't know. I should be glad to. I think you told us that it was 'kingdom beside kingdom,' irrevocably; that by no means these beginnings ever grew to the higher forms; that a bacterium never works up, itself, it only makes the way, toward the rose?"

"I don't know what it does. It fulfills its office right here. So far, it is in the preparing of conditions, the keeping of equilibriums, as I just remarked."

"And there is nothing among all these lives to indicate that any life can be different, can go on farther than to some such blind end?"

"Nothing."

"Then where is the evolution?"

"In each species, I suppose, toward its perfection."

"By 'selection,' and by mastery?"

"It looks so."

"You see, then, a certain assurance beyond the present, in all creations?"

"I see just one thing: that every kind of creature gets all that it is made capable, by any patient continuance, of seeking for."

"Ah!" said the minister, quickly, with drawn breath. "'Glory, honor, immortality, eternal life.' You mean that!"

"I may at least remember that men have become, or

been made, as you choose to put it, capable of desiring, of living for, that."

"And of asking to be 'lifted up forever,'" put in Peace Polly, softly.

The professor glanced kindly at her.

"I can think of no better use to put life to than such hope and effort," he said; "and I can conceive of no purpose for it which can be carried out without such desire and self-urging. If we are to be immortal, it must come, at least on our part, in that way."

"'Work out your own salvation,'" quoted the clergyman. "Yes."

Miss Serena wondered that he stopped there. It was really simply because the professor's enunciation brought to mind as identical with it the saying of St. Paul. And at this moment Mr. Innesley himself was looking, or endeavoring to look, merely from the science side.

Miss Serena could not help finishing. "'Knowing,'" she repeated, very quietly, but with clear emphasis, "'that it is God who worketh in you to will and to do according to his good pleasure.'"

Dr. Fuller was either disinclined to pursue the topic further, or he thought it rested well with that word. Perhaps it was only that he noted, being in the habit of noting everything, that Lyman had been silent, and as it were alone among them all, for some little time. He left his table, and came round to where Lyman had partly withdrawn himself, into the shadowed angle by the house door.

"You have taken that contract at East Bend?" he asked.

"Yes," Lyman answered. "It is a heavy job, and a nice one." He spoke as if the matter were already occupying his mind, and a little anxiously.

"A good deal of that fine antique moulding?" asked the professor, again. "The close-grooved and crenelated cornicing that you showed me?"

"Yes. All in expensive lumber, too. I don't quite know whether I have n't taken it too low."

"I hope not."

"I don't think I can lose. But I may n't make as good a concern of it as I ought to. There 's a lot of nice panel work, and mitering, besides; and the frames and arches are in special sizes and measurements. Everything is odd and special, I think, these days. You want new machinery, or at least everything new-set, for every separate job."

"And very skilled workmen, I suppose."

"Yes. The skilled workmen, or the skilled overseer, is the very mischief!"

"Your man, Morgan, seems very capable."

"He 's too capable. I don't like the fellow, and I can't do without him; not yet awhile."

"Ah!" The monosyllable was all the professor could have to say to that. The two gentlemen were now alone. The others had gone out at the cliff-side, to drink the cool water of the spring from a shell which Peace Polly had had hung to the rock by a long, light chain.

Presently Lyman said again, "I like a man to be shrewd and wide awake. Morgan knows that, and he thinks that 's pretty near all, with me. He only knows one side of me. It takes something of a sameness to make an understanding. Morgan 's cunning, and I don't want that. He makes a slippery suggestion now and again. He 'd like to get a share in the business, but he works the wrong way for it. He 's got a little capital that he could put in, if I needed it, but he 's too sharp."

It seemed to relieve Lyman to say these things to somebody outside, who could have no relation to the things themselves.

" I should think," said Dr. Fuller, " that a good partner might be a good thing for you. You have too much to carry, all in your own mind."

" I presume likely," returned Lyman, in his New England fashion of speech. " But somehow I don't seem made for other folks, in anything. I guess I shall have to work it out on my own hook, to the end of the chapter."

Dr. Fuller did not reply to that, at once, or directly. When he spoke, he said : —

" Meanwhile, you are not afraid of any of your own interests in this man Morgan's hands ? "

" No, not exactly. And yet I sometimes feel as if the fellow had two strings to his bow, and would n't much mind which he pulled, as soon as he could clearly calculate his chances. I don't *know*," he added slowly, — " it ain't easy to come at in our mixed business, — but I *have* wondered, a few times, whether or no he had n't been overshipping, to some people of his own we deal with."

At this moment the three came in again at the farther door.

Mr. Innesley walked forward to the two gentlemen, who pushed their chairs a little apart, and faced themselves differently, so as to include in their group a third seat, which offered itself naturally to the visitor.

The latter could but take it, with some casual remark. The two women lingered together. Seeing all well disposed for the moment, Peace Polly drew Serena suddenly by the arm. " Come back," she said, " down the garden. I want to get some cardinal flowers by the brook, and to see the little screech-owls."

" And leave Mr. Innesley ? " Miss Serena whispered, in her old-fashioned politeness.

" Oh, **he** won't go till ten o'clock.   He 'll be looking at spores again, or arguing about them.   I want you.   He comes to see Dr. Fuller."

Miss Serena doubted, but went.

The way led down beneath the cliff front across the garden space and orchard, into the edge of a strip of brook-meadow at the west side.   Here the quick, narrow watercourse rushed down toward the road, and crossed it underneath a little bridge, all but washing, on its way, the feet of the old twisted apple-trees.

It was pleasant in the rising moonlight that glimmered down through the boughs and touched the tops of the leaps and ripples of running water. There was the smell of damp, sweet growths, and of the green, grassy, fruity orchard.

The elder - blooms, lingering in these shady places, poured their rich scent also into the wide-mingled summer night-breath of the earth.

An evening bird broke forth with a late, clear song.

Then all was still again, and then came the cry of a bittern from the river-swamps low down toward the sea. The wailing hoot of the owl had not yet sounded : that strange, pathetic outcry, contrasting with happy bird-notes of the fairer-feathered creatures; that lament which some-body has translated " oh-o-o-o-o, that I never had been bo-o-o-o-rn ! " but which may only be, as Peace Polly understood it, " ' oh-o-oh who-o-o-o would ever want to be an ow-ow-ow-ow-owl ! "

When Peace Polly was cheerful and content, — and at twenty, such whens must be in the larger proportion of life, after all, — she delighted in the brookside orchard din-gle, in the daytime : then the quail ran whistling through the corn a little way off, and the killdeer called out of the clover ; humming-birds flashed among the old boughs, and up on the oak knolls the woodpecker tapped and chuckled, while every now and then all other notes were silenced to make way for the delicious solo·warble of a brown thrasher in the wood-edge.

Flower and bird life rioted together in this gracious nook, where upland, meadow, and sedge, cool waters and sunshine, woodland and pasture-opens, all lay so near, and so mingled and lapsed one into another. Violets and wild roses followed each other, the white dazzle of the arrowhead and the red blaze of the cardinal proclaimed the midsummer, and golden-rod and aster and the scarlet lances of the sumach brought up the royal pageant of the autumn crowning of the year.

But when her day had in any sort been a hard one, or life and the world looked especially mysterious, and put strange, contradictory questions to her; when her "screech-owl" feeling and mood came uppermost, and she half wanted to cry out, " O-o-o-oh ! would n't I like to be somebody else if I co-ou-ou-ou-ld ! " then she would wander down in the late twilight, and lose herself in the soft glooms, and hear the night-rush of the water, and the night-voices of all waking creatures, and feel that she had got away into the edge of some different existence, into some little other-world of her very, single, secret own, in which she could moan or be soothed, as it pleased her.

In truth, it was Peace Polly's very own; the world of her discovery and occupation. She alone, except Miss Serena, whom she sometimes, as now, brought with her, knew its loveliness of life and growth, and felt, away into her heart, the rare pulses of its scents and sounds. To the farm people it was only the brook-hollow, in which they seldom had anything to do; to the few strangers who had ever strolled there, it was but a pretty bit of a long walk across from the village to Squarrock Fall, which, fortunately for Polly, was out of distance for any ordinary pe-

destrians, and was commonly visited by wagon parties taking the road around by the Long Ledges.

"You can't see the cardinal flowers," said Serena, as
they came down into the shadows.

"If I could n't I could find them. I know just where
they are ; and the spikes will show fast enough against the
white sheets of arrowhead. I want some to-night."

They kept on upon the dry slope of the orchard, skirt-
ing the brook edge and its wet, spreading border.

"There ! " said Peace Polly, pointing. Above the small
grasses of the sedgy hussocks, shooting from among the
shimmering patches of the sagittaria, were the tall, lithe
stems and flower-tips of the cardinal, that in bright light
would burn with vivid color like spears of flame. "There
they are for the picking. They can wait. I want to talk
a little with you, Serena."

They had come far toward the end of the orchard, —
almost to the low, old wall that divided it from the wide
turf-side of the country road, but broke off at each margin
of the brook toward which the turf-way sloped, cut by the
tracks of wheels where people drove their tired teams
through the water.

"Here 's the dear old saddle-horse ! " cried Polly, stopping at a bent apple-tree which a lifetime ago had taken
that curious horizontal creep in mid-growth, which is
the delight of rustic little folk, and of tender association
often with the trysting times of their later years.

"You 've lifted me up on this, Serena, when I could n't
jump to it myself. When you were the good, big girl, so
kind to the little fractious one. I come here with my frac-
tiousness now by myself. I 've saddled many a bother on
the rough pony-back, and ridden off many a cross fit under
the cool old branches."

The two women sat down on the tree-trunk together.

There was no need for a jump now. Peace Polly wondered if it had really always been as near the ground.

The little screech-owl uttered its long-drawn, melancholy whoop.

"O-o-o-oh, who-o-o-o made me to be nothing but an ow-ow-ow-ow-owl?"

"Oh, who did?" cried Polly.

"Why, the little screech-owl," answered Serena, not at all understanding her.

"That is exactly what I supposed, and that is the worst of it," returned Peace Polly. "And yet the owl would like, I dare say, to be a yellow warbler or a bobolink."

"What *do* you mean?" asked Serena, as she often had to ask Peace Polly.

"The screech-owl wants to know 'who-o made her to be nothing but an o-owl'!" said Peace Polly, with ludicrous imitation. Serena laughed.

"I don't believe she knows a bit of difference," she said.

"Then what is that how-ow-owl for?" asked Peace Polly, when the long, weird note had just been repeated.

"For us, may be. We can feel the voices; the birds can only make them. Polly, there is just exactly this difference. The Lord has got *us* where He can speak to us and tell us things, — of ourselves and Him. We are not apes, nor owls, nor spores, any more, whatever we have been. And He says to us, 'Fear not, little flock; it is your Father's good pleasure' — that very good pleasure, according to which He makes us to will and do — 'to give you the kingdom.' The whole of it! 'All things that the Father hath are mine; therefore I said, He shall take of mine, and shall show it unto you.'"

I think Mr. Richard Innesley may be pardoned for what I am about to tell of him. At this moment he had reached the low wall of the orchard, which he had crossed by an upper path from the front that struck the road at a point but little further back than the brookside footway, near whose end Serena and Peace Polly were sitting.

He had been something discomfited by their sudden disappearance, and conversation had not sprung up with much ready purpose between the three men thus left to themselves with a preceding talk interrupted. Rebecca-rabby had crossed the rear of the hall on some vigorous errand to pantry or store-room, and Lyman had turned and asked where his sister was.

"I see her 'n' Miss S'reeny go off down the otchard, whatever 't was fer. 'T wa'n't Bald'in apples, ner Roxb'ry russets; that 's all I know."

And then Mr. Innesley had bethought himself of some sermon-writing, and had taken leave — by an orchard path also.

The close lap and gurgle of the water and the second cry of the owl had covered his approaching steps, almost noiseless, any way, from the attention of the women. He had reached the little breakdown in the wall that had been made for crossing, and had paused there, catching the shine of white garments under the old apple-tree, just in time to hear Miss Serena's words spoken in her clear, calm voice. When the preacher was so preached to, who can blame him severely for stopping to hear more?

Richard Innesley sat deliberately down in the chasm of the old wall and listened.

"But the between-places," said Peace Polly, "that no creature can skip over to become the next? Are n't there just such between-places for us? and shall we ever get over them? I shall never be you, Serena."

"Nor I any saint, or different sinner, that ever lived. We shall each be our particular own selves. God has 'called us by our name,' but we shall live our whole names out; we shall be what you said, — 'lifted up forever.'"

"I suppose there might be a glorified owl, even," said Peace Polly. "And that it might be a majestic creature, — when its howl gets answered, and it learns a new song."

"Ah, the 'new song'! It's all saved up to come out in that," Serena said, joyfully. "And in the between-places," she went on, following her first thought, "it must always be as it was in the beginning. God was there, all the way through, seeing that it was good."

"Between the evenings and the mornings," thought the audience by the wall. "We are always in the evening of some day, perhaps, beyond which the morning of the next is waiting."

Peace Polly was struck with a new idea. "See here," said she. "Somebody says that man is a microcosm, — a little world. Don't you believe we've got the whole history in us, somehow? — cells and spores, and ferns and roses, and bats and owls, birds of prey and singing-birds, wild beasts and gentle ones, and little children and grown souls?" Polly ran on rapidly with her words, as her own thought climbed in an instant the scale of creation.

"Something of all is in us, I do suppose," said Serena. "Or else we should n't be so as to feel the natures and the wants, or hear the voices. I guess, Polly, it's all wrapped up in one nutshell. We're in a world of choosing and beating, — or getting beat. Every step of the way we're letting something get the upper hand, to be the biggest part of us, whether it's the bats and owls, or the singing-birds, or the little children of us, or the growing angels. Yes, I guess that's it. In a certain way, we're all of it. And God made us so, that we might 'have dominion.' There is n't

13

anything in the world that is n't somehow human, because
it was the human of God that made the world.   And then
He gathered it all up into us in his own complete image, so
as we might learn it, and rule it and use it, as He does.
Why, *that*, written out from the first chapter to the last,
is just *Bible*, — Genesis and Jew-history, and Gospel and
Revelation, all, ain't it ? "

"Look, Serena ! There they are, the whole lovely little
family of them ! "

The moonlight struck through an open space full upon
a dead, bare branch, not ten feet distant from them in their
straight line of vision up the orchard side.   Thereon sat,
softly huddled, a group of gray, fluffy-feathered things,
with great heads and wise, shining eyes.   They were the
young brood, now grown and fledged, that Peace Polly
had known and watched since they were white and
downy.

"Lovely ? " repeated Serena, surprised at Polly for the
word.

"Yes, owl-lovely ; what more can they be ? " replied
Peace Polly, whimsically.   "They 're beautifully queer,
anyhow.   I suppose I should n't care for a person, or a
world, that had n't some oddity about it."

"Oh-ho-ho ! it 's a brave thing, after all, to be an ow-
ow-owl ! " cried the old bird, far up overhead.   Or so
Polly the next instant rendered it, with the funniest trem-
olo upon the long, last note, like a triumph getting the
better of a whimper.

Mr. Innesley laughed out, and came quickly forward.
There was a certain ring in his laugh as of relief from
a passing perplexity, and the buoyancy of some freshly
strengthened hope ; the same thing that had been in
Peace Polly's owl-call, without its inimitable little touch
of absurdity.

"Miss Serena," he said then, earnestly, "I was on my way home to write my sermon, and as I went I have received it. I must thank you as the messenger."

"They are all messages, Mr. Innesley," answered Serena, quietly; "we can't any of us get one except we know the language."

"Miss Peace," the young man began, and then made a second's pause, holding out his hand for a good-night, "I shall never hear that sound again as a hoot. You have turned it into a hallelujah." Then he said the good-night, stepped lightly over the low wall to the roadside, and went off.

"Was n't that a cool way to get a sermon?" quoth Peace Polly. But in her heart she liked his honest word, and felt in a nearer fellowship and understanding with him than before.

When Lyman went up to his room that night, he found his candle lighted, and a bunch of cardinal flowers glowing in the shine of it on the table beneath his mother's picture.

The next Sunday, — the eighth after Trinity, it happened, — Mr. Innesley declared for his text the Collect for the day, and the eighth chapter of Romans, from which was taken the Epistle.

The earthly and the heavenly order, and the "never-failing Providence;" the earnest expectation of the creature; God's reason and hope in the passing subjection; the deliverance from the law and bondage; the Sonship; the manifestation; the glorious liberty of the children of God; the mind of the Spirit, that helps, and breathes intercessions for us all through our limitations and infirmities and ignorance, according to the blessed final intent and will of God. The foreknowledge, the calling, the justification, or setting right of all; the glorification, the giving of the one only Son, and with Him the giving of all things; the love of Christ; the conquering in Him; the great Persuasion, in the face of all that is, or has been, or may be, that nothing of all the things that appear or are, "Neither death, nor life, nor angels, nor principalities, nor powers, nor things present, nor things to come, nor height, nor depth, nor any other creature, shall be able to separate us from the love of God, which is in Christ Jesus our Lord."

Peace Polly listened, her whole soul glowing and rising with the theme and the glorious linked sentences of it. Had all this come of the few words of Miss Serena and the night-cry of a bird? It had surely gone through a mind and soul grandly open to wonderful receptions; the message had been heard in a language that only a heaven - touched spirit could know. Was this Richard Innesley, whom she had half held cheap because she could not always see that his face shone when he came down out of the mount, and because he walked and talked pleasantly with pretty, winning, gracious Rose Howick?

"Where did you get that sermon, Innesley?" asked Dr. Farron, in the robing-room.

"From St. Paul, with the help of a wise woman."

Dr. Farron was not so much the wiser for that answer, as his Dora would certainly have been.

Miss Serena had gone to her own church, and had not heard this delivery of her message at all.

XXI.

EVERY WORD.

Up to this time Peace Polly had pretty carefully remembered her intention not to be any the more neighborly with Mr. Innesley because of their having been cast away together for an hour on Pulpit Rock; she scrupulously dated their real acquaintance later, and let it go no whit further in appearance, or by any tacit reference, than their subsequent intercourse accounted for. She never by any means reverted to the incident; she kept warily aloof from any word that might otherwise have grown out of previous words that had been spoken there. It struck even Mr. Innesley himself as curious, the utter expunging of that page, apparently, from their brief mutual story. Perhaps this curious fact was an added stimulus to his certainly growing interest in the peculiar girl.

After the bit of honest eavesdropping in the orchard glen, and the sermon of the Sunday, Peace Polly felt and demeaned herself with a decided difference.

Here had been something not at all of her seeking or suffering, in which she was not even the prominent person, which, with its following, had really begun something between them aside from circumstance. It was the first positive step that had been made.

Peace Polly may have thought, as I believe I have said somewhere back, that she would like to live a story; but it would assuredly not have been a story of mere outside happenings. Even in a book she was impatient of such.

Her own story, if it began at all, would begin like a live spring, somewhere away down underground.

It meant a great deal more to her, after hearing that eighth of Romans sermon, that Mr. Innesley seemed to care to come here so much, and that he so often deserted the professor to make a third with Miss Serena and herself.

Peace Polly was not a girl who would drift on through a growing intimacy with a man to the day of a declaration or the day of a disappointment, without ever discerning what might, in the ordinary course of human affairs, happen to either of them. It was not a thing to chatter and laugh and speculate about, — least of all, to try for; but she knew that it was happening every day where young men and young women were thrown pleasantly together; and she had outgrown, partially, at any rate, the positiveness of her childish conviction that she was n't pretty, and she was n't good, and nobody would ever want to marry her.

But she would by no means have such a befalling a thing of circumstance any more than — churchwoman as she was — she could take up her religion by its circumstance. Little encounters, surface or chance words, social opportunities, the becoming accidents of dress and fortuitous favoring juxtapositions, — she despised them all. She was a kind of Atalanta maiden, who would have been most likely to run the other way when any seeking of her began, and give the suitor a hard chase through retreats, and contrarieties of character-showing, and willful distance-making between them. If she threw an apple, it would be Atalanta-fashion, to stop the man with a folly, and hinder him with a mere distraction. And as to outside observation, it seemed probable that any looking on or prophesying, anything of a romance to be read of other eyes as it went along, would utterly overthrow an otherwise possible result. Mr. Innesley, if he were inclined to fall in love with Peace Polly, would have it very much against him that her winning of him would be the winning of a day against a somewhat general rivalry. To enter the lists, — to have it said or thought that she had carried off a prize, — Peace Polly would have hated and resisted that concomitant or its idea with an absolute rage, and to a self-renouncing struggle.

Nevertheless, she was beginning to like the man behind his agreeable every-day presentment, to reverence the minister behind the clerical dignity of his surplice.

She was beginning to look up to him; if he continued to rise, or sustained himself at the altitude at which she saw him just now, she would find her own stipulation fulfilled, — would find she could "look way up to him." Respect and reason would need be the foundation of any love with Peace Polly; she knew that of herself; she held herself of will, almost, to such conditions; she knew so well what it would be to her to make a dream and find it emptiness. She thought — for even Peace Polly did think sometimes of the possibility — that, should she ever be in love, it would be only for sufficient cause, well proven; that she had not been all this while taking exception to her present life, and half refusing it, for want of a satisfying *raison d'être*, to drift helplessly into a new one only because a chance little wind or current filled her sails or caressed her that way. She thought she should not only know, but be deliberately consenting, before she should fall in love.

But many people have watched with careful intent, without ever being able to catch themselves in the act of dropping asleep.

As for Mr. Innesley, he was recognizing more and more

the high, strong points of character in this girl; was learning to interpret — and this, in a reflex way, is an especial force of fascination in a friendship — her difficult ones, and altogether was finding her to be the most suggestive and stimulating young woman he had ever met.

It is not to be supposed that, as filling the duty of her clergyman, and looking forward to the full cure of the gathered souls among whom she was numbered in his parish, he had left unnoticed the open facts of her religious life. Of course he knew that she was not a confirmed member of her church. He felt in duty bound — or at least that he soon should be — to do something about that, but it came in strangely with his natural interest in her as a young woman.

He approached the matter one day with Dr. Farron.

"Ought I to say anything?" he asked the old rector.

"I think you may as well let it alone, for the present," the elder clergyman replied. And Mr. Innesley took that to mean until after his own priestly ordination. He was to go away for this in the end of August. The bishop was to be in Bonnyborough in September; then there would be a confirmation, for which Dr. Farron was preparing a class.

Rose Howick had been brought forward at the usual age. She had taken upon herself the promises of her baptism, had renounced duly all the pomps and vanities, and was sweetly and innocently blooming along her adding years, shedding a pleasantness about her which was neither vain nor pompous, though her pleased consciousness of it may not have been high-saintly, either. Her happy temperament was not troubled by deep question or searching self-judgment.

I know very well that scarcely one man in ten, in Mr. Innesley's place, would not have preferred, out and out, a girl like Rose Howick, ready-made as it were, and lovely, to a struggling, contradictory, incomplete human creature like Peace Polly. And the other nine men need not have been as mere tailors, either. I think it speaks a great deal for Richard Innesley that he was drawn so strongly, as he now realized himself to be, toward The Knolls, for Peace Polly's sake, who dwelt there.

Dr. Fuller did not occupy himself quite so much in these days with Peace Polly. Whether it was that he withdrew a little as the younger man's interest — which might be likely to grow to something different from his own and of a ranking claim — so evidently increased, or whether he were now becoming more absorbed with his new anthropological specimen, to wit, her quiet, and to a casual observation inferior, brother, or whether there were any secret sense of danger that a good man would steer clear of or a wise man would escape, it was certain that he invited less of her attention to his own work, and put himself less often in her way; and that when the friendly little circle gathered about the fore door of an evening he was apt, unless busy in his own room, or talking half apart with Lyman, to stroll away up the hillside, to get a breath of the high airs, and the glory of the solitudes of the bare ridges under the great night sky throbbing with suns.

Once or twice Lyman walked away with him; and it seemed that, whereas there was a slight depression and preoccupation noticeable frequently in the mill-master when he sat with the rest in the leisure of evening, he came back from his walks and talks with the professor with a refreshed and assured aspect, like a man who had found some welcome alternative to the pressure and monotony of cares and interests warping and straining him all one way.

Peace Polly noticed this; she noticed everything about

her brother; it was as if her eyes were opening now to many things. Her old limited life was widening, even in that which had cramped it; or was it only that, like the blind man, she had discerned thus far nothing but the mere vegetative life which she had thought was all, but that a touch had come upon her beginning to reveal more clearly what she had said to herself was no more than a man as a tree walking?

If Dr. Fuller did not directly approach or address her quite so much, he was not the less alert to her movement, her expression, her recognition of that which was passing, and which he himself was gradually bringing about. He could not if he would, perhaps, divest himself of his habit of close scrutiny of all things.

He saw when her face lit up, as he and Lyman came in together; he caught the glance, half question, half satisfaction, which sought them as they sat aside, so evidently interested with each other. It was dawning upon Peace Polly — and Dr. Fuller knew it, perhaps he meant it — that there were some things in dull Lyman that everybody did not find so dull. He read the surprise and pride of it that flushed her softly now and then, and as keenly detected the little fall of the eyelid and the sighing outbreath that came of a sudden inward asking, "Why can he not be like that to me, or I to him?"

Something made her feel very grateful to Dr. Fuller. It was as if, instead of soothing, or strengthening, or solacing, or diverting her, as one who had an inevitable thing to bear, he were taking away the thing that had troubled her, or showing it, indirectly, to be quite different from what she had believed. She did not suppose, of course, that he could be conscious of this; none the less, she looked upon him thankfully; her heart beat secretly towards him as to one who brought her healing.

Not for an instant was there betrayal of any jealousy or sense of slight, in that Lyman was gaining the friendship that had begun for her, and that she, a little bit, was losing or missing as in consequence; if there were a touch of such a pain, it was that a stranger was gaining Lyman as she herself had never known how to do. All this, under the lens of his high life-reading power, the curious professor saw.

At the same time with all this, there was evidence that Lyman was either worried, or was working too hard. Miss Serena told him, using the word that New England people always apply to over-workers, whether for state or trade or housewifery, that he was "too ambitious."

"Money is n't everything," she said.

"Money stands for a good deal," Lyman answered.

Serena's brow contracted gently; this was a flaw she thought she had always perceived in Lyman; and it had given her sorrow, always. She feared that gain of the world which threatens the losing of the soul. She trembled, sometimes, for the "parallel lines" she had admonished him of. With Peace Polly, it had been one of the things she had thought small in him; it kept him down to a mean level, she thought, as a man. She did not worry so much about his soul; there must be a full man, first, to have a soul.

Peace Polly and the professor were both by when Lyman said that about money. It touched an old, aching nerve with the girl.

"Lyman reverences a quarter of a dollar," she said, laughing; but there was an echo of the old bitterness in the speech.

"And so I ought," answered Lyman. "A quarter of a dollar stands, or used to, for a man's struggle and labor for a quarter of a day. Money means manhood; it 's what a man has got to show for being a man, for what he has done in the world. I should n't like to lose my certificate, Polly."

Peace Polly threw up her head with the flash of herself in her face that she had a way of ; as if suddenly the best of her were appealed to and came forth at call. I cannot otherwise describe the lighting up and response of her look.

"If you mean it that way!" she exclaimed, with a kind of joyfulness.

"Your brother means a great many things in a noble way of his own," said the professor, quietly.

Lyman looked from one to the other in a slight bewilderment. He had not known that he had said a noble thing at all.

Peace Polly put her hand upon his arm. "I beg your pardon, Lyman," she said. That was another way she had, as we have seen before, — her begging pardon. The word came instinctively whenever she retracted a secret injustice. It was only very lately that she had begun to have the way with Lyman.

Lyman laughed, not unpleased, but still puzzled. "You are queer people, I think ; I 'm not up to all your ins and outs," he said.

Miss Serena took up the previous question.

"There are other things," she said, "that mean manhood, too. That was what I told you ; money is n't everything. And a man has n't a right to waste his strength for it. What it stands for may be wanted in some other ways."

Persistent as she seemed, however, she smiled in speaking ; and a little happy relief sounded in her voice. Lyman felt himself exonerated from something, though the acquittal was as perplexing to him as the implication.

"I am only a man," he answered Serena, — "a workingman; with a workingman's way of looking at things."

Serena did not say to him as she had said about him, "You are a *good* man, Lyman;" but the look was in her face that had been with those words, and Lyman himself had not caught sight of just such a look in her before. Perhaps that was what moved him to go on.

"May be you don't see what I mean," he said. "A man must have used his strength, or his capacity, for something besides money, or he would n't have got it. It 's the token. What would you have a man do with his strength, if not his piece of the world's work, Serena?"

"I would have him just remember to make a heave-offering of it; then there would n't be any danger," Serena remarked, strangely and simply.

"A heave-offering?" Lyman repeated, with surprised interrogation.

"Yes. There was the wave-breast, you know, and the heave-shoulder. Don't they compare to the heart and the strength in the commandment? Ain't everything that we have in our hearts, or that 's good to them, like the sweet, rich food of fine flour and oil, and the fat of the breast, to be lifted up first of all, before we take it to ourselves; and ain't the strength of a man's shoulder to be heaved for the Lord? I guess that 's what it all means, in the sign of it." And Serena took up the knitting-work again, that she had let fall with her hands for a minute into her lap, and set her fresh needle quietly.

"That 's like Rebeccarabby," said Peace Polly, after the mere instant in which nobody answered. "She 's pious just as she 's everything else; it's all heave-offering with her. She told me the other day, when I went into the kitchen, 'I 'm going to iron to God, to-day, Peace

Polly!' and the iron was smoking hot, and it came down upon a big, heavy, damp sheet with a whang and a steam!"

Peace Polly lifted up a great glass bowl she had been filling with water-lilies, and carried it over into the best room and put it upon the round table in the middle. The air was all sweet in a moment with the breath of them; the fragrance hung behind her in the wide old hall, and followed her like the trail of a cloud.

The professor, who had been standing in his doorway, came across.

"Each in her own way," he said, smiling, and bending down to smell the lilies close to their hearts. "Miss Wyse mades wonderful interpretations of the old words. Did it ever occur to you, Miss Peace, that she might have interpreted all living more fully to your brother?" He asked it in a low tone, regarding her across the table as he raised his face from the sweet heap of flowers.

Peace Polly returned the look intently. "Lately," she said, "I have thought there must have been, some time, some mistake."

"Ah, the mis-takings, and the mis-leavings!" said the professor, leaning again toward the lilies, and touching the smooth, pink-olive sheath-petal of one most exquisitely half open. "And all the ignorant beginning, when we can only lay up things for late wisdom to repent of! I don't mean in marriage only; human life seems all like that, except by some blessed sort of accident here and there. I have such a great respect for your brother, Miss Peace!" he concluded, with a breath and movement as if casting off the other thought, and replacing it with something that might be replied to.

He was looking straight in her face again. Did he mean it half for rebuke? she wondered. He had seen that she had failed that way, toward Lyman. Could he discover that she had failed to her own pain, and that such rebuke carried a sudden gladness in its very sting?

It was in her face for him to see, at any rate.

"I think, Dr. Fuller, that you have done nothing but show me beautiful things that I could not have seen for myself," she said.

His eyes lit deeply as he kept them upon hers. "I would like to show you all beautiful things," he answered. "You receive them very absolutely."

And then, as if recalling himself, he turned from her and her flowers, and left the room with a composed and casual air, as he had come in.

"There is something odd, and a little secret, about C. P., besides his name," thought Peace Polly, with a purposeness she used sometimes in her thoughts with herself, as in conversation with others. Was it, in like manner, to check with nonsense a little too much earnest; to turn with a sauciness what she did not care, or dare, to follow directly to full understanding? In herself, as in others, she was perceiving, all at once, a drift and presentiment curiously intensifying in a daily going on that had heretofore been so commonplace and unmeaning.

Not the least significant thing was that she was growing a little afraid — unwilling, at any rate — to stop and investigate. And yet there was one point about Dr. Fuller — and it was not his initials — that she could not reconcile, and that she would have liked to have clearly explained. She could not speak to Lyman about it; he would wonder why she cared; certainly not to other people, for she contemptuously detested gossip, and a guest was sacred. But such as he showed himself to be, and marvelously and generously as he divined others, how was this one thing possible with him?

She had said she must whole-love her brother before she could be content. It was beginning to be needful to her to whole-reverence this friend.

The little talk just repeated had happened in the morning. Serena and her knitting-work had come over for that pleasantness which women who live busily, yet easily, so much enjoy between the day's early housewifery and the dinner hour. Lyman had come up from his mill for something that he needed, and had let his horse wait at the door an unusual five minutes, while he fell into the bit of conversation, standing, sorting some papers, at the stair-foot. When Peace Polly emerged from her parlor again, he was gone, and the professor's door was closed.

It was in the afternoon that, sitting alone by the hill-doorway, she heard Dr. Fuller's step approaching her through the hall, and his voice, in quite the old way with which he had begun with her, asking her to come and see something new through the microscope. Perhaps the acknowledgment of the morning had been so very pleasant to him that he could not resist offering her this one more beautiful thing to see; or the rarity of the opportunity was upon his kindly conscience. He might possibly have waited till there were others also to enjoy; or waiting might have involved a loss. That he had to settle within himself. However it was, there was no doubt of the pleasure with which he accosted her, finding her there by herself in the stillness, or the delight which answered in look and step as she rose and came to meet him.

He put the glass upon the hall-table; he rarely asked her now into his room. It required a few moments to readjust his object, a small thing with a little water about it, set in a glass-hollow beneath the instrument. Small as it was, it was largely beyond the field of the glasses.

But it was a whole, he told her, and must not be separated.

"It is a bit of living sponge," he said. "A friend has sent me some specimens from an aquarium in which he cultivates 'objects.' Now you shall see the little water-volcanoes. Or, wait a moment. I will show you first the whole island, in a bird's-eye view."

He withdrew the glass receptacle from beneath the microscope, and brought a large lens of strong but not microscopic power, which he gave into her hand. "Look through that first."

"Yes," she said: "it is a little island, in a real little sea of glass. It is all cones and peaks, like little ant-hills."

"Exactly. Now you shall see some of those cones in operation." He put the whole back in position, under the microscope. Gazing through, Peace Polly beheld, to her enchantment, a wonderful life and action. Two or three of the little cones were in full eruption, sending up jets of finest water-particles from their minute points, the thread-like columns breaking and falling, in prettiest fountain showers, down into the intervening hollows again.

Dr. Fuller waited for what she might say to it. If she had known how curiously he expected that first word of hers after a wonder, she would have disappointed him, of course, through the mere consciousness. He was most careful not to question, or seem to await anything. While she still looked, he busied himself with some slight movements and handlings about the table.

It came at last. "Oh, Dr. Fuller, life is n't long enough!"

"That is one reason I cannot help thinking we shall have more of it," answered the professor.

"But what a satisfying, even as we go along!" said

Peace Polly, looking up with a long-drawn breath. "Just to know it is all there, and that there is no end to it! One might almost live on these things."

"Does n't the good book say we live on 'every word'?" asked Dr. Fuller, with that kind of outside air and question with which he always put such suggestions. He never spoke *ex cathedra*, but always as reminding other people of that which from their established standpoint might be seen and said. He held a lens to everything. Then people might just use their own eyes. It was so he had shown Peace Polly her brother. The girl felt his way, and the peculiar force and efficiency of it, but she had not yet wholly found him out.

"'Every,'" repeated Polly; "that means all the little prepositions and conjunctions, disjunctive ones and all, as well as the substantial facts, and the being and doing and suffering. It means the ifs and the ands and the buts, and the things that are hung on or separated by them. Interruptions, and interjections, and all sorts of parentheses. Other people's words, their facts and prepositions, the contrary notions and — oh, dear! all the interrogation points!"

"I suppose St. Paul's charity takes it all in; all this human etymology and syntax," said Dr. Fuller.

"How did you mean to spell that last word?" asked Peace Polly, quickly.

The doctor thought a second, and laughed. "Well, yes, in this sort of grammar, it might as well be with an 'i,'" he answered her.

There was a very diverted admiration in his eyes. There was depth in this girl's nonsense; real insight, always, under her word-cleverness.

Meanwhile, there rushed through Peace Polly's mind the lately aroused question. What had he to do, this professor, charming as he was with his deep wisdom and his gentle, strong ways, with that great charity of St. Paul's, and the other things from the holy New Testament, that he reverted to so tangently, so easily? What was it about the every word of his own life, or how as to long breaks, omissions, phrases understood or misunderstood? He had become so much her friend, he had made her so rely upon his truth, his sureness, that she had a claim to know how sure, how true, he was, all through; or if there were — she would not say a falsehood, but an incoherency, anywhere. He was a great deal older and better than she, and yet she felt compelled to sit in judgment upon him in this matter.

"I think it is more often a worry with women, this every word," she said, "than with you men. Our charity, or good-temper, or something, has to cover such a conflicting multitude of little demands. Now, with you, all those give up to one great thing, that you can be left in peace with: there's Lyman with his mill; and you have your science. It seems as if in every-day getting along the whole swarm of interruptions was turned over to women, that they might simply keep them out of the way of men. I suppose that may be why men can hardly bear them at all. You seem to have a different right about engrossments. And a man's engrossment is so often a woman's desolation. I wonder" — and there she stopped, but her eyes searched him.

The doctor looked at her with a curious, frank, waiting amusement.

"You wonder what?" he asked, when she did not speak any further.

"Something impertinent, I am afraid," answered Peace Polly, turning away. "But it was pertinent, too, to my puzzle." She would not accuse herself of impertinence without this bit of justification.

"Then it cannot be impertinent to me. I am quite ready, with any results of longer experiment, to help you, Miss Peace."

"Well, it was n't so bad as you may think if I don't say it. I wondered how Mrs. — how your wife managed about the engrossment. I was thinking what the mill is to me, and whether even this — might be quite satisfying, always, on the other side."

She put it very directly, now she had dared to put it at all. It was almost as if she had said, "Have you let this take you away from her, as Lyman's boards and mouldings and figures on chips have taken him so much away from me? And is that what she is tired of, and has gone off from? Is that what it comes to, in the long run, in the home, that after all ought to be the most beautiful thing? Have you searched into the life of sponges and spores, and let a woman's — that depended on you — go on, or starve, as it might happen?"

The amusement played slightly, even yet, on the professor's face. It was mingled with a little perplexity, a kindliness certainly, and something more that Peace Polly could not read.

"My wife," he said slowly, — "well, if she were here, perhaps she might say that she was interested, too."

"I dare say she would," returned Peace Polly, continuing to regard him with eyes of which she knew not the keen inquiry, "for a pleasure spared to her out of it, as you spare to me. But this is a kind of holiday time, and I have leisure. She must have a great many of those other things, those little teasing words that we women do have to spell out, work that you have nothing to do with, till it is done, and then — you just expect to find it so, don't you?"

"I suppose she naturally would ; may be I should n't

always know how much, till it was done, as you say; I dare say we men don't realize that. But while men and women are busy, each in their own way, is n't it, or ought n't it to be, — I don't say it is, in any particular case, — a making ready of results, to share each with the other? Life is divided, that it *may* be one."

"You talk in the potential mood," said Peace Polly. "We have to live in the indicative."

If he did baffle her with his mays and oughts and woulds, she left him quite as disconcerted with her quick detection and possible conclusions.

Did she think he had spoken in a mean way, with his potentials, of a woman whom he ought to honor? Then he must even leave it so.

Peace Polly went and sat down in the hillside door, out of sight, in the corner hidden by the great staircase. She had left a basket of pretty work upon her light stand there, when Dr. Fuller had called her, some bright little scarlet and buff tea-doylies to whose fringed edges she was whipping a selvage. She took the basket down beside her upon the sill, and picked up thimble and needle again, some mental process accompanying her quick stitches like the whipping in of thoughts that might else have raveled. Underneath a certain determination not to think any more, the ripple of cogitation that she would not recognize still moved.

After some minutes, the busy fingers dropped upon her lap with the work in them. She made some absent, useless little stabs with her needle in the linen, looking off the while where the clear water fell, bobble, bobble, dickle, dockle, plop, plop!

"C. P.," she said, softly, to herself. "Certainly Peculiar, and a Complete Puzzle." She laughed a little as softly as she had whispered the syllables. Then she went on, mentally, —

"But Mrs. C. P. must be more so yet. What does *she* want to go to Europe for!"

As the words clearly came up to her, emphasis and all, she started from the saying of them, as one starts bodily from a dream, threw back her work upon her basket, and walked away with a severe dignity, as if leaving some one who had spoken unbecomingly unanswered.

She went and stood by the little rustic tree-trough full of ferns and water-plants that she had cherished and petted beneath the trickle of the always dropping water.

Things would not let her alone this afternoon. While she lingered there, half vexed and ashamed with herself, and half happy with the beautiful fresh, growing things, Rebeccarabby's shout came across to her.

"Here's the—parson, coming up the grass-walk to the fore door, Peace Polly!"

Of course she could be heard both ways; when could Rebeccarabby not? Peace Polly was only glad and grateful that she had not said, as apparently she had caught herself back from saying,—"the dough parson." It was what, understanding him to be but a minister in the raw, she had taken it upon herself to entitle him in her private remarks. To check Rebeccarabby in her private remarks would have been something too much like applying a positive force to keep down nitro-glycerine. She was safest let alone.

Peace Polly stood still where she was.

"She's out there, ter Horib!" pealed forth Rebeccarabby. "That's what I call it; 't allers puts me in mind of wher Moses smut the rock."

Peace Polly heard Mr. Innesley's slight, well-bred laugh in reply, and his footsteps coming over the smooth-varnished floor. She waited, and let him come all the way through; then she turned with a smile. She affected nothing, either way; she was always quietly pleased, now, to see Mr. Innesley.

The professor, in his room, took down his straw hat from behind the door, and walked forth at his long window, and down the orchard. It is as well to say here as anywhere that, except in the usual encounters of the household, Peace Polly saw no more of him after this for two or three days.

And those days gave her several things to think of.

XXII.

ALONG THE RIVERSIDE.

"Mrs. Farron has sent me for you," said Mr. Innesley. "She told me to say that you had not taken tea with her for ten days, and that she should neither eat nor drink until you came."

"Is that an irrevocable vow?" asked Peace Polly.

"She meant it to be understood so."

"Go back and tell her I 've company, and a headache, and I 've twisted my ankle, and it will have to be ten days more." Peace Polly said this with the utmost gravity.

"Ah, but none of that is true, Miss Peace!"

Peace Polly opened her eyes wide at him.

"Mr. Innesley! It is three times as true as the other, which I wonder you undertook to tell me. I 've you here, at this moment; and my head does ache — this warm day — enough to mention; and " — She swept back with her hand the hem of her dress, and showed one little foot atiptoe behind the heel of the other.

The graceful bit of foolishness was all the more bewitching that she was apt to be so intensely earnest, and that there was not the smallest tinge of coquetry in her action; she was thinking only of her retort. It was always very plain that Peace Polly meant but one thing at a time; she was aefauld, as the Scotch say it.

"I do not know how I shall dare go back without you," said Mr. Innesley, as grave as she.

"Oh, then, if you are afraid! I suppose I must help you out of it, — again." She did not say that last word aloud; she laughed, gently, instead. "But you must let me go round by the mill, to tell my brother."

Now the walk round by the mill, taking the meadow path from across the road, and following the river bank a little way, then coming up into the street again through a wild, sweet green lane, was not only longer, but greatly more enticing, and a way they were likely to have very quietly to themselves. If Peace Polly had any arrear thought about it, it was that the staring, commenting village folk need not be encountered. She did not care to have it reckoned how often she even went to the old rectory to take tea. And the lane way would bring them up from behind, through the shady rectory orchard and garden.

A while back, Peace Polly would have left word merely with Rebeccarabby. Mr. Innesley shrewdly refrained from the reminder of the headache and the hot day, to say nothing of the palpable little fraud of the distorted ankle, and assented with alacrity to the longer, pleasanter round.

So Peace Polly put on a little close-tilted straw hat with a silvery scarf-cloud gathered lightly about it, and they went off down the long grass-walk from the front between the maples, and across the dusty highway into the green meadow.

Professor Fuller saw them from the pasture-knoll beyond the brook. He stood still a moment, looking after them as they strolled side by side along the winding track that was at once cartway and double footpath.

"I suppose that must go on," he said to himself; and the cloud that contracted his brow betrayed a furrow as of some habitual pain.

"But what right have I to hope otherwise?" he demanded of himself sternly. He struck the stick he carried sharply into the crisp turf, turned, and walked on, over the ridge of upland, out of sight upon the other side.

Peace Polly and the minister found the sun warm in the open meadow, but the air came fresh from the river, and the ground under their feet was cool; it was far better than by the dusty road. They came down upon a shingly margin which sloped up from the waterside between thickets of alder and bittersweet on the field side and button-bushes on the other, that stood in the river-edge and were all full of blossom and song; the round balls of their flowers, bristling with their long out-thrust pistils, showing pale-colored among the thick leafage, and the close coverts of the branches hiding away countless blackbirds' nests. Here it was shaded and lovely; the river rush and ripple met and swept by them as they walked up toward the mill landing and the dam.

"I think it must be pleasant to have one's daily work by a riverside," said Mr. Innesley.

"The riverside is pleasant," said Peace Polly. "But wait till you get into the whiz and whir of the saws and planes. You can't bring work, of any active sort, you can't even bring common living, into the real pleasantness of natural places. You displace it the minute you come. It's no use to try to eat your cake, and have it too."

"Still all this quiet and sweetness is close by," said the minister. "It is good to know that. We have to take most of our good in that way; eat our needful bit of cake, and be glad there is more, or different, for a different kind of hunger. The closer we can keep to the life we don't have to make meat of, and the oftener we can escape into it, the better. I am very thankful to get a country home at last."

" And I have had it always, and have sometimes not been thankful at all! " said Peace Polly.

It was not in the least an ordinary young lady answer; none of Peace Polly's were particular to be that.

" You are not impatient of it ? "

" Not for itself. But I have sometimes felt shut away, — to very few things and people. It has been different lately."

" It has been different to me lately," said Mr. Innesley. " I came here a stranger; and one cannot do without friends."

" Not even the blackbirds can do that," said Peace Polly, blithely. " Look at that flock of them. They have been marauding somewhere; and they have come back to call together more marauders."

A cloud of the handsome creatures in their black satin coats with scarlet epaulets came hovering down, fluttering, chucking, chattering, about the round hedge-tops of the water-shrubbery, out from which rustled and rushed a home crowd to meet them; and sailing and circling with a great sound of small strong wings churning the air, the whole multitude of them swept jubilantly away, far across the river, to where full cornfields shook their green banners in the breeze like another army standing fast to challenge them.

" It is good to live in a still place if you have wings," moralized Peace Polly.

" I 'm afraid human beings were hardly to be trusted with them, or they would have been provided," said the minister.

" They have almost contrived them," said Peace Polly, perhaps catching willingly the chance to turn the channel of talk a little. " Do you suppose we shall ever have the real 'wings of the morning'? King David must have got a glimpse very far down history and invention to say that."

" 'The wings of the morning,' " repeated Mr. Innesley. " Why, that would mean to skim over the meridians actually with the sun. I don't think it ever occurred so to me before. We do pass over a great deal as mere poetry of phrásing that is really a wonderful putting of fact or possibility. Miss Peace, you are always suggesting something to me."

" Am I?" laughed Peace Polly, lightly. " Let me suggest now, then, that we go up this bank while we can. We shall be against the bluff presently, and among the lumber-heaps."

And with that, and a moment's climb, which occupied their breath and kept them apart as they went up where each could best choose footing, they were at the mill.

XXIII.

HARD KNOTS AND SLIPS.

THEY went in at the upper door of the mill building from the bluff side, and came into the great roaring, whirling moulding-room. Below, upon the floor entered from the riverside, were the saws and coarser planes, with the hoisting machinery and platforms taking up all one end. Beneath the whole were the engines, and the water-wheel in its deep sluiceway of solid mason-work.

Fizz-z-z! z-z-r-r-r! whackle, whackle, — brattle, brattle! It was of no use to speak here; one could only look. Long, swaying strips of board were being fed across frames and rollers, smitten and scored as they passed by the vertical and horizontal chisel-blades, the chips and shavings flying every way as from explosives; the plain, unornamented pine or other wood slipping continually from the finished end, no longer plain, but bended, banded, reeded, grooved, even crenelated, for lovely cornicings of ceiling or dado. There were piles of finished pieces ready for sending off; there were also heaps and heaps of fragments.

While Peace Polly and Mr. Innesley stood and watched the workmen tending a long chiseling frame, a door opened from a farther corner, and Lyman Schott came down the room. He smiled to see his sister; she did not often come to the mill. He gave courteous greeting to her companion. Peace Polly beckoned to her brother to come out at the great side door by which she had entered. She could not tell her errand in the dazing din within.

"I'm going to Mrs. Farron's," she said, "if you don't mind. It will all be right at home without me, I guess."

"I'm going over to East Bend," said Lyman. "I sha'n't be back till late in the evening." Nine o'clock, by the way, was very late in Bonnyborough. "I don't suppose that will matter. C. P. does n't mind; or perhaps he 'll take the drive with me. Any way, I 'm going up to the house first. I 'll tell Rabby to look after him, if he won't. Mr. Innesley, I wish I had time to show you over the mill."

"Thank you; I should be sorry that I have n't time myself, if you were at leisure. I 'll come down again some day, if you 'll allow. It is an interesting place."

"When you get at-tumulted," said Peace Polly. "I never have. And Lyman puts in a new craze every year. Well, good-night, Lyman. There are early sweet apples baked; you 'll have them for your supper when you get home."

Lyman looked after them as they walked along the little sandy table of the bluff to the foot of the green lane.

"I wonder if she means to marry the minister," quoth he.

What the minister meant he did not trouble to wonder; it was so very likely he would mean whatever Peace Polly would let him. Lyman had gotten over, if he ever had it, his doubt about Number One, or even Three. Seeing Polly with other people, he had begun to appreciate at second-hand, as brothers sometimes have to do, her peculiar charm. He would not so much have wondered, now, at the three of them, had there been three in Bonnyborough, all coming forward as one man, without separate numbering. He remembered another old nursery rhyme: The three brethren out of Spain that came to court my sister Jane.

He did not know the quotation about single spies and battalions ; but he had a misgiving that when things began to happen they might keep on, and that a lively history might follow, unless Peace Polly were easier suited in matrimony than in most matters. He half hoped, to escape repetitions and complications, that Number One might be successful. "I don't suppose, in that case, she need go farther off, either, than her side of the house," he got so far as to say to himself.

The "either" was significant. .

Peace Polly and Mr. Innesley were half-way up the lane. Its lovely hedgerows of barberry and bayberry, glossy catbrier, and tossing clematis and creeper, nearly met in places overhead, and again widened out or were broken so as to give fair glimpses of sweet-framed country pictures. At this midway point, they paused on one of those rounding heights that occur everywhere in this region, and which here made the crest-line of the pretty climb, to look either way from its vantage, seeing over against them, townwards, the roofs and chimneys and porches of the village street showing pleasantly from between or against the billowy crowns and bosoms of rich shrubbery and old trees, and the other way, farther off, across the gleam of river and the stretch of meadow and the far sea-flats, a horizon twinkle which was the shining of the great ocean line.

"It seems to me your Bonnyborough is simply the loveliest place in the world," said Mr. Innesley, taking off his hat to feel the breeze that crept lightly up from seaward.

" One might like to make the comparison and find it out for one's self," said Peace Polly. "I 've said that before, to-day, have n't I ?"

" Something like it. Miss Peace, the working of things

in this world is sometimes like the work we saw in your brother's mill. For a while — for half a lifetime, may be — all is flat, unscored, uncharacterized. Then suddenly we are put under the wheels and chisels, and everything is wrought out at once; something beautiful turns out that we had not dreamed of, and the meaning and purpose come to light, swiftly, in a few crowded days or minutes."

"Or else we go to chips," said Peace Polly. "There are quantities of failures, and broken bits, — hard knots in the lumber, you know, or slips of the grain. You saw them piled up there, knee-deep. That is all kindling stuff."

Perhaps she felt the hurry of the wheels, and that some stroke impended over her, that she put forth this little feminine averting twist. It is a way women have, even when the possible shaping of their lives has begun to look beautiful to them.

If it were likely that Peace Polly would be taken by surprise by what might come next, she could be scarcely more so than Mr. Innesley. He spoke truth when he said that forces had a way of concentrating into sudden fate, or the revelation of it. I am sure he could hardly have analyzed — so why should we make the attempt? — the course and culminating, during this little walk, of feeling and decision that impelled him now. However that might be, the impulse seized him, not as a caprice or a temptation to one blind rush that should overbear uncertainty and settle all, to be acquiesced in then as the best or at least the irrevocable, but as the summing into clear conviction, and the sweeping off with power, all that had been either drawing or hindering him before. At this moment his whole mind and heart filled themselves with the desire and purpose toward whose avowal he pressed on. The woman stood beside him whom to have beside him all his life would be beauty, joy, stimulus, to all that was good or might be great in him. Yet the woman was not wholly good or great, herself; he knew her needs; but she was growing with such a sure and vital force!

There are moments in life like moves at chess; when it may be this game or that with us, and either may seem, in its after course, as if it were the right and the only one that we could have taken. All other combinations form accordingly; compensating opportunities befall, and ripening judgments avail; the end may not be losing for us; and yet there was a strange alternative that by and by we have almost or quite forgotten, that would have made it all another story. How many other stories, truly, any one of us might have lived is only known to the Thought that holds in itself all the infinite potential variations of number, form, and fate.

Mr. Innesley made answer first as to that refuse, — the hard knots, the slips, the shavings.

"There is a casting off in everything," he said, "that the true form may come. I think that should be the courage of living."

It was good for him that he said that; that he met her thought with a reply, instead of urging his own question. Peace Polly stood silent, but the light came into her face that sprang there with any turning upon her of a vision of the best.

"I think," said Mr. Innesley, after a moment, "that Bonnyborough has really resolved itself for me into one point, — your home, — your companionship there, Miss Peace."

He did not venture upon the "yourself," which would fain have finished his sentence.

15

The girl started inwardly, though to all observation she remained in utmost quiet. It was as when one hears a sudden sound in the night that may be an alarm, and with an instinct of caution petrifies one's self to the non-moving of an eyelid, until a clearer perception may come of what it is, or what is to be done. It may be but the motionlessness of an instant, but for the first instant it is that.

Peace Polly was not ready for him to say more.

"Our home has been pleasanter than usual this summer," she said, easily, but feeling her way with every word. "I am glad you have happened to share the enjoyment. It has been very good for us to have Professor Fuller there."

It was a great deal cooler and quieter than he cared for; but he was in earnest; he was not to be dropped so, as with a chance remark.

"Miss Peace, that is not all of it; it is — you must know " —

His hesitation upon the word ruined his opportunity. And yet it was as well for him that he did not make the rush. If Peace Polly could not have stopped him for that time, she might have stopped him finally.

"Thank you; you are very kind," she said, rapidly, now. ("Oh, dear; I'm always telling him he's kind!") she parenthesized with herself as swiftly. "Don't you think we ought to go on? Mrs. Farron will be expecting us. And there," she added, with relief that she could not keep out of her voice, "comes Rose!"

Peace Polly had turned herself a little, imperceptibly, while Mr. Innesley had gone on speaking. She saw, as he did not, still facing down the lane, the flutter of a girl's garment moving slowly toward them under the thick shade up beyond. She knew Rose Howick's step, and the delicate pink frills above the feet.

Nothing could have more effectually silenced Mr. Innesley. There was no longer a doubt, he thought, in his mind; and he knew Rose Howick could have naught against him; they had but been to each other as each might be to a score of others; yet the approach of no one would have so utterly postponed his speaking.

The two moved on up the green ascent, together. Of course, in a moment more, they met Rose Howick. "I was going down to the mill," she said, "to beg some scraps of pretty moulding for my brackets."

Her tone was a little languid, and Peace Polly thought she was a trifle pale. "Lyman is n't there," she said; "there are only the men, and that old Morgan. Come back with us; I 'll go with you another time. Mr. Innesley came for me to take tea with Mrs. Farron, and I 've dragged him all the way around to let Lyman know."

Rose Howick thought that Peace Polly had not always used so carefully to consider Lyman, and she imputed all the difference to the companionship of Mr. Innesley; in which we know that she was much mistaken. The pretty Rose was learning part of her life-lesson now; but she only folded her sweet petals a little closer over her own heart, and hid the thing that hurt her there.

At the end of the rectory orchard, they all paused. "Come through this way, won't you?" said Peace Polly. "I 'm sure Mrs. Farron is always delighted when you come. You must have deserted her, or she would n't have sent all the way for me."

But Rose shook her head, and bade them a gentle good-by. "My mother wants me to-night," she said, as a child might, and turned away. It was as near as she could come to being proud and cold.

The pink gleam of her muslin draperies flitted across the leaf-latticed intervals of the shrubbery as she kept on her way, and the others followed the inside orchard path. Somehow these two were very silent.

Richard Innesley wondered what sort of consciousness or mistake might be between the young girls; there was something that he would not care to have Peace Polly think, and there was a smite of generous pain lest he might, after all, have been in fault regarding Rose. He was one of those men who are hardly vain enough to be readily conscious or evasive of such fault; but then if he had been thus vain, the consciousness would not have been conscience. It is these kind, pleasant, simply complacent ones, enjoying as they go along, and hardly supposing that their conclusions can be paramount to any but themselves, — certainly not before they are concluded, — who may graciously break a heart or two.

Mrs. Farron was altogether too wise a woman to give so much as an alternate eyelid flash to one and the other of her young guests when they came in; but she knew, without the stirring of an eyelash, that the position of affairs was altered, ever so little; that some breath had touched to a delicate poise what had been before on the mere safe basis of every day. Of course she had known — and all her kindly forecastings had been built upon the fact — that any day this change of equilibrium might come. She had given it opportunity. Well, that was all that she had done. She was too nice, too fine, too tactful, to put forth curious or impatient finger now. She fell back into the last place, which few tacticians know the precise moment to do, and let that work which had begun to work. She gave fate her own head, and in a delicate, impalpable manner followed the lead of almost as imperceptible indications of will or un-will on the part of the two — and especially, with *esprit de corps*, on the part of the woman — who had the weird to dree.

Peace Polly lingered in the veranda; Mrs. Farron perceived that. So, although the evening was likely to fall a little cool, and the room inside was pleasant with the low, bright light let in between the curtains pushed widely back, and a new book of quaintly lovely illustrations in fine water-color — "My Lady's Casket," of symbolic ornament and triflery — was on the table, where a soft porcelain lamp might presently be lighted, she stopped out there with them, and left her little device of graceful appositeness to take its after chance.

She did not even leave them once, though her hand-maiden came half-way through the hall with the little nod and beckon that housekeepers know, but said quite frankly, to the considerable discomfiture of the worthy feminine Balderstone, "Yes, Fidelia; two more plates and cups, and the daisy set and the blue doylies."

Peace Polly watched the road; and when Lyman's chestnut pacer came ambling along, she caught the sound and the glimpse of shaking, creamy mane, and ran down the garden walk to the gate. Lyman was alone.

"Oh, Ly!" she cried. "Stop here for me, please, when you come back. I forgot."

"All right. C. P. won't be left by himself, after all, Polly. Doctor Blithecome has sent for him."

"Oh! Is he worse again? He has been so well lately ! "

"I'm afraid so. I'm afraid that matter will have to be decided soon."

Peace Polly went slowly back to the veranda. "Dr. Blithecome is ill," she said. "He has sent for Dr. Fuller." And at that they were all very shocked and sorry.

But it was provided that the young minister's escort should not be needed for seeing Peace Polly home.

All that Mrs. Farron noted ; it had not escaped Lyman, either ; each in each one's own way interpreting it, knowing Peace Polly, her perpendicularities and her whimsies, and that these might mean anything, but most assuredly did mean something.

Peace Polly would like to play Logomachy. She turned the brilliantly exquisite leaves of the "Casket" with but a half sense of its charmingness and significance, and when Mr. Innesley came near gave over the book to him, to whom it was an utter blank. So Mrs. Farron got out the box of letters and cleared the table, and even called the Doctor, whom Peace Polly sweetly suggested, and they made 'sin' into 'saint' and 'strain,' and 'constraint' and 'consternation'; and 'hope' into 'pother'; and 'life' into 'lifted' and 'trifled,' and 'filtered' and 'reinflated'; and 'far' into 'fare, safer, falser, refusal'; and 'rest' into 'tries,' and 'strive,' and 'restive'; and wit got bewitched, and a word was a sword; and then Peace Polly turned that into 'drowsy,' and Lyman's buggy was heard at the gate, — earlier than had been expected, for the man at East Bend had been away from home, — and the little party was broken up.

Mrs. Farron walked about and put out the lamps.

"Did n't get a new chapter into that little romance to-night?" said the Doctor, wickedly. "Well, chapters or sermons, they won't always be written when they are bidden, Dora."

Mrs. Dora reached to a high burner in the hall as they passed up-stairs. With her head very lofty as she did so, she said over her shoulder to her spouse, —

"Unconscious cerebration, Sebastian. You know your sermons wait for that sometimes. Why should n't there be other unconscious working to allow for, too? If I were you, I 'd go to sleep and not think about it. I shall."

XXIV.

THERE are two motives from either of which a girl may put off a man, turning aside the question which, once fairly uttered, may not be put aside. She may do it to spare him the refusal which she is already certain she would have to give. This evasion, often as it is resorted to in novels, and possibly in real life, is utterly futile. A man who can be either hurt or blessed by a woman's word will take nothing short of that clear word in the end. And Peace Polly was not the woman to expect he should, or to make her own mere temporary escape in such way. She acted from the other reason. The instant it flashed upon her what he would ask, she demanded time to search herself for her answer. Upon her impulse she would have said *no*. She was by no means conquered, to the yielding all her absolute determination not to like overmuch the man who had charmed so easily the young womankind of Bonnyborough, — to the stoop of the conquering that would have that detestable village *éclat*. She put back her impulse, defeating his ; because she would first be sure there was no hidden corner in her where a possibility of happiness should so be crushed into a reality of pain. There was nothing especially generous in this, except that truth is always the most generous thing. If she had for him what he wanted, — and she could only know by this possibility or impossibility within herself, — she would give him that which was honestly his, all Bonnyborough and its small honors and envies, or malices and misjudgments, to the contrary nevertheless. She would have to look at herself to find this out.

Moreover, a woman like Peace Polly will have no mere impulse from a man. She will have that deliberate, masterful, whole purpose with which only an absolute wholeness of love in a full-souled capacity of loving brings itself unmistakably to the demanding of its sentence from one who holds its life or death — no, not that, for it must be alive beyond the possibility of dying, — but its earthly fulfillment or denial in her sole power. No half-ripe passion, sunned only on one side, for her. It must be full-grown, full-sweet. Some intuition told her it had been too soon for that to-night.

Yet if it were coming, when it came what should she say?

She rode home with Lyman, thinking all the way; so busily that she did not notice how very silent Lyman was himself.

It had been different lately. Was it all to go back again to the old sameness, the old contraction, or was something to come of the temporary changes that should make a difference and a betterment always? The way in which Peace Polly should decide the pending question might be the answering of this. But was this the only hesitancy, the chief argument? If so, the answer was already apparent.

Something had made Peace Polly happier; had made her feel as though the old troubles could not ever trouble her again so much. She found a new strength in herself, a new sentiment toward Lyman. Something had helped her to understand a little, to respect more, her brother. Home life was pleasanter; she was pleasanter in her own moods. Was all this to vanish like a fairy glamour when the summer should be over, the professor gone, she and Lyman left alone again, and the dull winter coming? when — but that 'when' was the if of the whole matter — she had sent Mr. Innesley away with a denial, and so stopped short and spoiled her friendship with him? Could she give up the friendship, and what it might have grown to, all at once?

What would it have grown to? Why had she not been left to find out? It is a hard thing between man and woman that the one must speak more or less at a venture, and the other, at whatever instant the asking may come, must answer for all the days of her life. Say yes, — or else forever after hold her peace!

Peace Polly knew one thing: she could not bear to lose; but could she accept more? She wished that friends would just stay friends awhile.

She had just begun to be glad — a little bit proud — of Lyman; then all these good things, these fresh companionships, had added themselves. Or, was this way of putting it a transposition? Which had come first?

She knew another thing: she would not leave Lyman now, until she had been more to him; until the reproach of years had been worn off her conscience by some lasting and repeating of new kindlinesses. But here was something that need not take her away; that might bring more to Lyman instead of depriving him. She had always known she could be better to him if some third element of life could be introduced. It had begun to be so already, with a mere little social enlargement for them both; just as she had always said. It was in her hold and choice now to make this sure, and more; or to throw it away, to shut off the new opening of the future for herself, to set all things back as they had been in the time before, when she had told Serena, desperately, that she did not believe God meant to give her anything.

Her own side of the old house! That came into her
mind as it did into Lyman's. That she should open it,
and let affection, and cherishing, and daily happy minis-
tries, and pretty cares, and sweet appreciations, in! That
it should be hers, alive with a home history, a kingdom of
which she should be the queen! If a man — or a woman
of masculine mental altitude — should happen to read
this book, he need not criticise; only a woman knows
how much this home-reigning is to a woman, and how
close the hope of it lies to her early ideal of love.

She thought if she had been let alone a little while, it
might have come; she was growing to like Mr. Innesley,
and to believe in him, so much. Her self-inspection was
very like, indeed, — but she did not know it so, — that
aforesaid wide-awake kind of watching to see if one is
going to fall asleep.

In the midst of the watching, it may come, no doubt;
there is from that instant, however, no question or watching any longer. There will be nothing but the beautiful,
vivid dream. And one may be startled from it, and
prevented, by too soon or solicitous querying of its approach.

There was something away back behind her questioning
that she did not reach, or analyze; a certain sense that
some calm or safety, otherwise endangered, or open to
risk, which she dared not meet, depended upon her action. Peace Polly knew enough of herself — she did not
ask or guess how recently the knowledge might have come
— to be sure that something in her might be terribly intense if ever it should be roused; some pain of thwart-
ing, that might be only to be evaded by a quiet fore-
ordering, a prevention, a preoccupation in some settled,
determined, accepted tranquillity. And she thought she
knew that of the world which told her that the alternative

— the satisfying of that in her which was so deep, so supreme, that it could be so thwarted and so suffer — was not in any human, natural likelihood.

"For people's stories are half told before they can have grown to that," she said to herself in a vague way, thinking what love might come to be, yes, what it ought to be. "I hardly think they ever find each other in time. Or perhaps it is ordered that they begin so young that they may begin low down, and grow to it together."

She had time to think these things well over in those next few days. Nothing of all her usual interests and occupations hindered her. Everybody about her was all at once especially and individually absorbed in some way. The close little friendly circle was disintegrated. Each one had some new circumstance, apparently, to meet. It seemed as if the little summer-history had suddenly come to a crisis in all its points.

Lyman went once or twice to East Bend. He looked tired, and was silent. "I think Lyman seems worried," said Serena Wyse.

"He has too much to do," said Peace Polly. "But there is no use in telling him so."

Mr. Innesley was away for a brief visit to his family. He had told them that evening at Mrs. Farron's that he should be. His mother expected him, he said, this once more before he entered upon the rectorship, and made his fixed home here. It was settled that after receiving his orders he should be instituted over the parish in Bonnyborough.

He had come to The Knolls before leaving, but Peace Polly was at Serena Wyse's. Her window looked well up and down the road, and commanded the grass-walk from the low gate. It was very easy to be off up the diagonal field-path and behind the Wyse-Place hedge, while any comer was approaching at the front. Few persons got in at The Knolls except when its young mistress was quite ready and pleased to receive them. Rebeccarabby knew very well what devolved upon her, when she caught from her kitchen-bedroom window of an afternoon the sudden flit of light raiment along the green slope. It was to take her at least three minutes to answer the fall of the ancient knocker at the fore door; and she usually came down the long hall with her knitting-work still clicking in her fingers. Whoever saw from the threshold this easy advance understood beforehand her leisurely, sole possession of the premises.

"She's stepped out somewers," she announced midway to Mr. Innesley, with the simple reference of the pronoun. "An' 't ain't more 'n problymatikell she'll be in agin." The statement closed without a word of limitation. Noah's dove could not have found less excuse for lingering upon the uncertain waters than Mr. Innesley here. He was disappointed, but not quenched. It had happened before; it was the way of the house. When Peace Polly "stepped out," the place was void; the great mansion was a lifeless waste; Rebeccarabby was but as an owl of the desert, a pelican of the wilderness, emphasizing the solitude.

Mr. Innesley could but turn away with a polite regret; early the next morning he had to leave Bonnyborough.

Peace Polly could not explain, even to herself, why she ran away from him so childishly. It was childish, absurd, useless, she admitted in her own mind; but it was an instinct.

She analyzed that also; she said if she had hated him, — and she thought she should almost hate a man who wanted to marry her, if she did not like him, — she should have stayed quietly, and told him so, or a polite equivalent.

Mr. Innesley was good; he was fine in nature; she

had found him out to be even something great. He was "kind," and she "begged his pardon."

That was precisely the attitude of her mind toward him when this farther question had loomed upon her. It was a little too soon ; was that all?

Undoubtedly many a germinating growth has death dealt to it in a too curious inquisition. Peace Polly might be right to hide her heart and run away with it, for a little time.

He was a good man ; that was what Serena Wyse had said of Lyman. But Serena had never married Lyman. Was she waiting also, all her life through, for something to which she could altogether give herself? And would that ever come in Lyman? Was that the way people had to do, or marry on possibilities?

Ideals. She had heard of them ; the word had not had much force to her till now. Now she knew it was what people waited for, or went without.

She sent a rapid reconnoissance all through her present world, — the world of persons and characters she had contact with. Where was there one who filled the demand she knew she should make sooner or later, or find her life a fragment, thrown away, perhaps? And after all, what right had she to make such high demand? She waived that last question, or met it with the half-conscious answer, the right of need. She *must* have some things, claim or no claim.

It took hardly as many seconds as there were individuals to pass in review all the marriageable or impossible-to-marry young manhood of Bonnyborough. She swept them all aside as one, as utterly aside already from any question. There was no hero, no ideal, among them. Marriage might develop, — very well, let some of those girls, who were none of them of her own age, try the experiment.

She thought over the married people. Where was the life-idyl that she would have thought it happy to have lived? Where was the man whose wife was the woman, like a Lady Grandison, to be the worshiped of the world for having found and won the sole and peerless knight and gentleman? (Not that she would have wanted Sir Charles, either!)

There was Dr. Farron. She began with him. She reverenced him; she was fond of him in a daughterly way, or what would have been so with a little more of intimacy and of the fatherly kindness he had always ready for her. He was a high, pure, gentle, scholarly, saintly man. But she could never have been Mrs. Dora, and have had him to say, "Wifie!" to her!

There was Dr. Blithecome, another fatherly friend, whom she had known ever since she was born. Now he was going to die, and she was very sorry. But that life Mrs. Blithecome had lived, with just the dear, prosy, comfortable, comforting old physician jogging to and fro, never quite her own; mending his worn trousers that the everlasting jogging in the old buggy frayed out so in the larger parts, and always finding the right shirt-cuff broken-edged with the rubbing of the driving-hand ; mixing up "simple syrup" for his medicaments, and making out his bills from his confused day-book, full of crosses and interrogations that meant foregoing, certain loss, or kindly intent of reduction. She did not think that forty years ago she would have cared to rival her for whom the years were laid out like that.

At last here was Dr. Fuller. She came round to him slowly, as with her last thought held behind her, and here her judgments paused, silent. Perhaps she had better not count him in. He was so different. He was neither young nor old. His "story was half told," as she had said. He was not at the beginning point, neither had he proved it all. And his wife had gone away from him to Europe! She wondered why she felt so angry with Mrs. C. P., when the woman came thus into her recollection. She would not ask herself if there might be another C. P. in the world, since here was this one, or what such a person might be to herself if they could find each other — young.

She put him away, unjudged; he was quite different. She did not care to think him over now. But those two letters of his name stood illuminated in her alphabet. She would so like to know what they meant. She could n't help thinking of them, he was so often called C. P.; and then, from Mrs. Farron's " Confucius Plato," " Charles Pretender," " Christian Potentate," " Chief Police," to Miss Mallis's ' Collector of Pollywogs," there were so many plays upon possible interpretations. It was like Logomachy; it ran in your head, with all sorts of variations. For all that, if anybody could have told her, she would not have listened. She liked to have Dr. Fuller explain himself; or not, if he chose. Name or history, she would have pried into neither. But if Dr. Fuller, by any chance, could ever bestow a voluntary confidence upon her! She could think of nothing more beautiful than to be placed so high as that in his friendship.

After all, did she want anything better in this world than beautiful friendship? If friends would stay friends; but you can hold to nobody. They will go off; they will get married; they cannot belong to you, except for better, for worse. Which reflection brought her back almost to her starting-point: that so they are to be taken first, and proved afterward. Was it not put into the very marriage service?

In one of these moods, her dream came suddenly back to her.

Was there but one great Friendship, in which all others live? Is the ideal only, and forever, filled in that? Does that hold all manhood and all womanhood, making them one in itself? Leading, and protecting, and perfecting them; lifting up, that it may set side by side, and little by little show and give them all things? Were there myriad little names, little abiding-places, put each for each, in some tender ordering; none central, none complete or supreme, only sharing, imaging; giving in partial, lesser ways some expression, some reminder, of that which was only full in Him, the Lord? "Ye are complete in Him," she remembered. Was this the interpretation of her dream, and had the time come in her life for her to read it?

Whatever happened, should she not always have the Mighty One? Yes, if she belonged; and that brought up other questions.

Truly, life was deepening all at once for her. And it was not that she was weak or inconsistent, this straight, true, positive, sometimes impetuous girl, that it looked uncertain. It is shallowness that decides instantly; that always thinks it knows what it is about. And whatever Peace Polly was, she was not shallow.

XXV.

MRS. DORA'S BALCONY.

DR. BLITHECOME had had several motives in persuading Dr. Fuller to come this summer to Bonnyborough. He had great faith in the younger man, so much younger than himself, yet fast settling into middle age, and still not following regularly his profession. The elder physician did not think that this was good. He believed in direct work among his fellow-men, as well as in the knowledges that are to advance them and meet more and more their practical needs. He would have these followed, but he would have them put in practice as they went along. And he was persuaded that it would be better for C. P. himself to come more in daily contact, to have his sympathies kept more fully in play, with those around him, and in a widening sphere. Beside which, he knew that, however strongly or for whatever interval he might himself rally to his work, his days were but briefly numbered. He wanted this man, whom he believed in, to lean upon in the last days when his own skill would not help him, and he would gladly induce him to take up the labor that he was laying down. He would do this service to his own old people, whom he loved and was going to leave.

And C. P. had come, thinking that perhaps his old friend was right, and that it might turn out according to his plan. He had quite understood all the thought and desire of the beloved old doctor for him, as well as for Bonnyborough and himself.

And then he had found his way into the home at The Knolls, and now, like Peace Polly, he was faltering before his decision.

Why should he not? The duty, the consideration, that had lain upon him elsewhere had been removed, at any rate for the time. And when its claim should return upon him, possibly the two might be reconciled. He would willingly plant a home and form associations for his boys where life might be so clean and safe and simple; even if they came to it half spoiled, as he had half dreaded, with this experiment abroad; even if it were only home to them, as might be, for a portion of the year. Perhaps he would have them a little to himself, in this division of dwelling-places. It had looked like a fair and reasonable hope and motive.

But now, something that he could not have foreseen had made a hardness and a doubt for him. Now, in a way that he had never looked for it, a struggle had come. Why must this also be added, at last? Had there not been enough before? Was not blank, was not negative, enough, without this real and positive pain?

So he talked with himself now, upon his solitary drives that he took for Dr. Blithecome, facing it, admitting that it had come.

He had not had much work to do, thus far, in Bonnyborough; there had been little sickness, and Dr. Blithecome had been well. He had accompanied the old physician — of whom one of his patients had said that he would rather see his horse at the gate than have any other doctor come in and prescribe — occasionally in his rounds, and held gig-consultations with him on some more important or interesting cases; he had sometimes gone into the sick-rooms, and he had had a bell hung in his own chamber, that could be rung from the west porch, out of hearing of the family, and had taken some sudden night cases which Dr. Blithecome felt obliged to refuse : but all this had been the merest introduction. His work was now to begin. How far it should go on was the point he must determine.

He could not turn his back upon Bonnyborough now, for any reason whatsoever. He must stay and see his dear friend through. That might be a duty of days, or weeks, or months. C. P. was curiously perplexed. He could have laughed at it, but for a spasm that caught him at the heart.

Could he stay and bear it all ? Would it be any worse here than elsewhere ? Would not the fact remain the same, that thing that he must put from him, the "might have been" that now could never be ?

For he had seen it now, the central denial, the certain sentence of his life. Whatever freedom might come to him henceforth, this would never come again. In the midst of his trouble he found a place for thankfulness. He was glad that he had not known this beforehand, years before, when he might therefore have acted differently. There was this mystery in the untold story : he was glad he had not acted differently. And now, he had to be glad, also, that there was nobody else to be the less happy on his account. He was satisfied that the story had remained untold, and that there could not possibly, with anybody else, be a hard mistake.

He would like to be quite sure of this last thing, that somebody else, by a superseding experience, was altogether beyond the question, beyond all possible concern in anything that accident might bring ; he thought that would show itself soon ; in that case, it would only matter to himself. What difference, then, if he gave up, and endured a little more ?

It occurred to him, one day, that Mrs. Farron might help him. He wanted another eye, another conscience, to look at his position with him. He could not trouble Dr. Blithecome. Dr. Farron? Well, it was a woman he wanted, after all. A woman would understand best about another woman. And Mrs. Farron was bright, and wide awake, and kind; and nothing, he thought, escaped her. Mrs. Farron had been at the best point for seeing all. She would know, or guess shrewdly, what he might otherwise have to wait for. And he had not time to wait.

So one of these days, he walked over, in mid-afternoon, the time of Dr. Farron's daily nap, to the rectory, and asked Mrs. Farron if she could give him a quiet half hour.

Mrs. Farron took him through the little drawing-room, and up a twisted staircase balustered with wild-vine stems, that led from the veranda corner to a balcony above, latticed and shielded with swinging tapestries of woodbine and Japanese ivies. Here were low chairs, and her little work and book table. Down below, now, she was not at home. She had given orders against admissions. She was altogether at Dr. Fuller's service for that quiet half hour. She saw plainly that he had come to tell her something; Mrs. Dora was used to people coming to her to tell her things.

I am not going to repeat to you what he said to her. He surprised her utterly; he overset all her schemes and theories and wishes; he made her at last start almost to her feet, and cry out, with her hands held up clenched before her with rigid elbows, as if they were manacled things, —

"And I can do nothing, nothing! I have tied my own hands! What a fool I have been!" With this wonderful admission for Mrs. Dora, she sank down limp into her chair.

"My dear lady," said the professor, "you forget that nobody can do anything. All remains precisely as it was before. The same obligations bind me, the same circumstances restrict. It is only that some things cannot always continue unexplained, and there would still be that left which could never be explained. And in the mean time, unless I could stay here under a hopeless certainty, I had better not try to stay here at all!" At which grim paradox crowning his enigma, C. P. himself was constrained to smile.

"There could be ever so much done, and circumstances alter; we are in a changing world. The very possibility would be based on different circumstances, if you would not be — luciferously — proud! If I had only thought that Providence had this in store! I'll never meddle with Providence again. Oh, I could do twenty things! And I am a traitress this minute, and can do nothing!" Into this incoherence Mrs. Dora relapsed and wandered, her head quite lost for the minute with the shock.

It was half nonsense; deep feeling took refuge in half nonsense with Mrs. Dora. She quieted herself presently, and said gently, —

"Stay, Dr. Fuller. You have an errand and a work here. You cannot leave it now. Providence does unravel things for us, when we most perversely tangle them; that's the rough-hewn ends, and we've Shakspeare besides the Bible on our side. Wait and see. Fortunately the other thing has gone beyond my help or hindrance. I can sit still, *if* I can! Don't you see it all rests with the child herself?"

"Ah, yes, but you still ignore the afterward!"

"Let the afterward take care of itself. Stay here; I tell you so, and I'm a wise woman, especially when I'm just convinced I've been a fool! Don't try to plan, or look ahead. Do the duty nearest to you. Stay with your friend, and decide nothing more."

To her husband, that night, Mrs. Dora said suddenly, "C. P. is a Cunning Patriarch. He's been as wise here in Bonnyborough as Abraham was among the Philistines, and almost as wicked. If you'd told me before, you'd have saved me lots of trouble."

Dr. Farron lifted up his eyes. "Which you need not have taken, probably, in any case, my dear," he replied, on general principles. "But what is the particular difficulty now?"

"I couldn't begin to tell you, and you couldn't begin to understand. It has got to work itself out. It's everybody, and I'm afraid somebody has got to be hurt. How should you feel, Sebastian, if you had put a log of wood on a railroad track, and saw the train coming?"

"As if I had better take it off again, even if I got smashed myself, in doing it."

"Ah, but it isn't a log, after all. It's another train, sent full tilt down the same track. It will have to stop itself, — I can do nothing, and I am afraid I have done it all! everybody is smashed!" The little lady laughed, and then burst into tears.

"Nobody has ever done *all* of anything," said the good Sebastian, laying his hand softly on her head.

"I know," she answered, between sobs and smiles. "I take a great deal too much upon myself, sometimes."

"Especially when you take to self-blame?"

- "No," returned Dora, stoutly. "I won't steal comfort that way. Sebastian, say the 'never-failing Providence' prayer, and the one about the 'abundance of mercy,' and 'the things whereof our conscience is afraid.'"

XXVI.

BEFORE the persons concerned concluded anything, the usual thing happened. While they were musing, a little fire burned, and ran through the village, amusing that, undoubtedly. A breath took word, and became a thing that was said, repeated, until everybody was saying, or said to be saying it. For the particular property of this kind of word is that it is nobody's property or owning, but that each one has heard that somebody else has asserted it. It was one of those words that nobody authorized could have spoken; it bred itself in the air. It did not set off, full-grown at once: it floated as a germ; it took to itself indistinct shape, and wiggled, as a faint interrogation-point; it got transposed and wafted along; it found its element; its slight wiggle of a question-mark dropped off in its development; the tadpole became a frog, and sat up and croaked. If this natural analogy be not correct in all particulars, I cannot help it; I only do as the scientists, giving simply that which I have observed, not claiming a perfect theory.

The word was that the new rector to-be was jilting Rose Howick, and that Peace Polly Schott "could have him any day;" that he had "as good as asked her."

That does not sound graceful or refined; it is, indeed, very obviously vulgar. But I am telling you of a slimy frog; and that is the way a slimy frog hopped and croaked in the marsh-levels of Bonnyborough society.

And any society may be at a marsh-level for a moment, when it drops to talking snakes and toads instead of diamonds and pearls. And a reptile is a reptile, though it be shaped in jewels.

This "they say" was a reptile that might fatally have hurt three persons; and it certainly did hurt one.

It is noticeable that there is usually in any neighborhood where such germ-stuff gets astir, some individual who, if not altogether responsible, is yet pretty sure to be a fountain-head of information; to know just what they say, and how long they have been saying it; who appears to be the nucleus of the nebula, but who, when you approach closely, resolves herself — it is ordinarily, I fear, *her* self — into the minutest innocent hazy particles of vague idea, or the recipient of such, of which the centre is nowhere. There are only a good many of them, and converging, as it were, about her.

In Bonnyborough, this person was Miss Mallis.

Now, really, there was not more malice, spelt as the common noun, and I think hardly so much, in Miss Mercuria than in other people, notwithstanding her significant patronymic. She could not help what she inherited, of name or nature, and evidently she was a "born gossip;" and of perfect gossiphood malice is undoubtedly a large element; but notwithstanding the undeniable entail of Mallis proper in her family, she seemed in her heredity to have received but this other complement of the gossip character, the newsiness and relish for small knowledge, particularly the first sharp guess at anything, with also a certain shrewdness and brightness that can make the guess supply unfinished links, and put the whole with cleverness, and which cannot resist a keen venture or a capital joke.

So, naturally, everybody who heard anything pungent

or pregnant turned in thought or reference to Miss Mallis. She, if anybody, could tell what it all meant. She, if anybody, so felt the victims of report, was to blame for the currency. At any rate, she could do more than anybody to stop it, if she chose. This, perhaps, was rather hard upon Miss Mallis.

When this particular lively batrachian utterance reached Rose Howick's ears, — and here is another mystery like to the lost link of creation, namely, who it is that repeats the croak to the person most painfully interested, — it struck hard on her poor little heart.

"Do they say that of me?" she said, with a betraying thrill in her tone that might have gone even to the heart of a frog; though she put on a brave face for the moment, and made believe to laugh. "I suppose he will jilt us all, when he makes up his mind for one. A man has a right to be generally agreeable until he does that, has n't he? And I'm sure he never made his mind up for me!"

They thought she took it very well. That clever little touch about their all being jilted, as if no particular admiration had fallen to her share, went far to pacify the envious.

"Rose Howick is no fool," said Mrs. Farron, when they told her of it. That might have meant that she had been equal to this especial emergency, or that she was not so weak as that there should be any emergency at all.

But the trouble weighed secretly with Rose, that she should be so talked about; she tried to persuade herself that that was all.

"Peace Polly would hate it as much as I," she thought. "I wonder if they have dared to say anything to her!" and then it occurred to her that it would be a comfort if they two could understand one another about it. She did not put it to herself that by understanding with Peace Polly she might learn at once, perhaps, how the truth lay, and take all her misery at a draught, or throw it away entirely. She was not miserable at all, she insisted, except that people should say such things. "I have not deserved it!" she cried in her heart. And indeed, the sweet, pure Rose, that had never even nodded her fair head with a coquetry, had not deserved it. She had only bloomed and been delightful. That somebody had found her so as he passed by, was that a strange, new thing? But somehow it had not seemed to be just in passing by.

"Peace Polly is a brave, true girl. I will go and see her." And so one warm, still morning she walked in at The Knolls.

XXVII.

PEACE POLLY'S SKIRMISHES.

PEACE POLLY was in the large, light pantry, papering jars and glasses of blackberry jam. She sat before the broad table-shelf on a high red stool, with a gingham bib-apron on, the tip of one little foot resting upon the edge of a wooden chair half pushed under the shelf. With the other heel upon the rung of her " housekeeper's throne," she rose and reached, when necessary, to right and left among her tumblers and preserves, taking down the empty glasses, and ranging in rich, sparkling order those she filled and covered. She sang a little as she worked, but there was a slight preoccupation in the song, which ceased now and then in mid-measure, and then began again where it had left off, or at some *da capo*, as might happen.

To her Rebeccarabby ushered in Rose Howick without ceremony, pushing wide open the door that led in from the hall. Another stood pleasantly thrown back between the pantry shelves into the cool, clean, shaded kitchen, where the breakfast fire had gone out long ago.

" Here's comp'ny fer ye, Peace Polly! I'm goin' up ter fix the ell bedroom fer Aunt Pamely Chirke. She'll be here Monday. — 'T 'll dew her good ter talk young a little," Rabby said to herself, confidingly, as she went off. "She's awful sober sence all them 'tall an' wise an' rev'rund heads' hez been r'arin' raound. An' Lyman, he's iz dull latterly 'z an old cheese-knife. 'T ain't good fer Peace Polly, 'n never wuz. Fust it riled her all up,

an' now it's meachin' her all down. Seems ter me the
Lord's kinder goin' ter 'xtremes with her. I s'pose He
knows, but I wish 't He'd see fit ter try a middlin' course
awhile. She's gitt'n most too chassened down to be
nat'rul."

The rumble of her soliloquy came back down the ell
stairway, but she had fortunately shut the door after her
at the foot.

Peace Polly slipped off her elevation, and bade Rose
pleasant welcome. She fetched a chair from the hall, and
placed it for her. "If you don't mind my housewifery?"
she said.

"Oh, I like it. It means something. Peace Polly, it
is so still and nice out here! I'm so tired of the village
street and a front garden, and the neighbors and the
passing and the talk! The Knolls is just lovely, and
you're always strong and real. I believe in you, Peace
Polly."

"Thank you, Rose. I'm not so sweet as you, but I
don't make believe — any more than you do," she added,
lest the other words might sound ambiguous.

"You can live to yourself out here," Rose began again,
but stopped. "No, I don't suppose people can live to
themselves, or die to themselves, anywhere. It doesn't
seem so."

"It wasn't meant so, was it?"

"I don't mean that way. Peace Polly, do you know
the things they are saying about us?"

Peace Polly looked at her companion. She saw that
she was pale, and that the corners of the pretty mouth
quivered and drooped.

"You're tired, Rose," she told her, "with your long
walk. You don't look strong lately. See here, you must
have a little bit of lunch before you say another word."

She took down a tall, slender jelly-glass, whose contents shone ruby clear as she held it to the light. Out of a corner of the pantry she brought forward an ice-pitcher; poured the cold water into one of her prettiest tumblers from a narrow shelf at the china-end of the double-serving closet, where the delicate glass stood in glittering rows; dropped in some spoonfuls of the congealed fruit-juice, and added a sip of raspberry vinegar and a lump of sugar; stirred these together till the liquid was clear and bright, and set it beside Rose. Then from a huge stone jar she produced thin, crackling caraway cakes, and piled them upon a plate of porcelain wreathed with pale pink roses. "Just on purpose for you, and just like you," she said, caressingly.

Peace Polly did not often caress, even by a word, and the other young girl felt it. The tears started and trembled in the deep, soft gray eyes.

Peace Polly noted it. All she said was, "Take the shrub, Rose; it will do you good. And eat the cookies."

"Cookies! Those ambrosial things cookies!"

"They're cooked, any way," said Peace Polly, lightly. "They did n't rain down. They are n't manna."

Rose nibbled. The dainty cakes beguiled her; they tasted good in spite of trouble. She drank the cool currant-water, and was refreshed. But it was only to say the say she came for. She pushed back the pretty plate carefully. The movement was somehow like putting away the prettiness of roses that were not really for her, after all.

"Peace Polly," she said, "it may be true of you — this story that they tell. I 'm sure I 'm very glad — for you — if it is. But it 's different for me. It 's *cruel!* And it 's a *shame* that they should say it of Mr. Innesley! He *never* flirted with me — never! So how could I be " —

She could not say the ugly word.

The quiver of the lip, the great, pleading pain in the eyes, the paleness changing to a hot flush, the pause, — all said enough.

Peace Polly swung round softly on her stool, reaching out two kind hands. She put them on Rose Howick's shoulders. She looked at her as a strong elder woman might have looked. "Tell me the whole, Rose," she said.

Rebeccarabby would hardly have called this "talking young." Up-stairs she was wondering already that she did not hear "them gaels laugh out *like* gaels." "Seems ter me the world's turned gray," she said. "It's gitt'n t' be the' ain't no healthy nonsense in it!"

"Tell me what they say about me," said Peace Polly. And she let her hands fall away from Rose's shoulders as softly as they had touched them; but she kept her eyes, full and strong and steady, on Rose's eyes.

If Rose had known what was pulsing through Peace Polly's thought as she so looked at her!

"Could I care like that, though they said a dozen men had jilted me? Should I grow pale, and would the tears and flushes come, if another girl — if Rose Howick — were going, possibly, to marry — anybody? Not this man, — not Mr. Innesley, surely. I could give him to Rose to-morrow, to make her happy. I do not love him, and she does!"

All this was plain as in day-glare, before that sad, sweet, troubled face; in hearing of that wrathful-tender voice.

And something all the while, unwhispered even in thought, unlooked at, told Peace Polly what such a trouble, such an indignant pain, might be. Only, in her case, she knew it would not be so meek, so gentle. She would have been raging, even if silent; she would have been silent, because she was so raging, — against herself and the whole mean, bitter world.   Her own cheek flushed, and her own eye kindled, as she felt this, and would not think about it.

Rose thought she was guessing and growing angry. She was half afraid that it might be with her.

"Tell me," said Peace Polly, firmly.

"They say," said Rose, "that you are going to marry Mr. Innesley. No, that you *can* marry him, if you choose; that he has asked you.   And I am sure they can have no right.   Why *will* they meddle with people so ? "

"Rose," said Peace Polly, deliberately, "look at me."

The girls' eyes met.   Maidenhood — pained, insulted, haughty, sorry — stood in them, each to each.

"They will, because they were never girls. They have been nothing all their lives but old maids, — in dread or in reality; and because they have forgotten that they were ever women.   And listen, Rose! I am *not* going to marry Mr. Innesley, and he has not asked me."

The swift relief, the rapturous glow, the shining and softening in the still gazing eyes, — did these again tell any story that Peace Polly knew? Could anything ever happen, anything be contradicted, or explained, or undone, that would make her feel and look like that ?

"I do not want to know," she answered herself.   "But until there is something that *could* make me feel like that, there can be no word with me of marriage."

"Now, dear," she said to Rose, "we will go away and talk of something else."

And so they did.   They went away into the garden; they drank fresh water from the rock-spring; they wandered down to the brookside, and Rose got her hands full of lovely ferns and the last cardinal blossoms, and as they came back again broke off the first sweet day-lilies from beside the grass-walk at the front.

How the day had changed for both! Peace Polly was clear, now, what she was to do. She was nearly happy that she had not this to do that had seemed perhaps to be set for her. "Friends are best," she said again to herself. "And the world is God's world, and all the nobleness in it is for those who can find and feel it."

Her musing, between the common, pleasant, girlish sentences she said to Rose, lifted itself inwardly with the memory of that chant of prayer, "Make me to be numbered with thy saints, in glory everlasting."

Another sentence of the book she was to " experience," unrolling suddenly all life and its secret from its wonderful syllables! If only that! To be numbered with " the blessed company " ! One might forget any separate, selfish wish or claim, in that oneness with all light and joy; that dwelling with all great, true spirits in the atmosphere, — the moving, living realities of God, — his very outshows of Himself in every new and beautiful amazement to them, — the Glory Everlasting!

Some little, little glimpses, — one near approach to one who knew and reverenced and dwelt in them, — a little kindness of sympathy and recognition between herself and him, — only a friendship, and may be merely for a time, — had had power to open up all this, to so content her. In these moments, she thought it had been, could be, absolute content. She could even let it go, and wait till somehow more of it, or more like it, or more, even, than it had ever yet been, should come again to her, since it had been begun, and it had made her feel so sure.

She did not ask then whether it could have been coming to her with that yet unspoken word of Mr. Innesley's; whether they two might not begin low down and grow to all height together. Something had interposed that had changed all that; had thrown a sudden light upon it, making it strange that it had ever been a question, as even yesterday it had been. Rose Howick's tears and blushes, her full, anxious heart so guilelessly betrayed, had put it quite away as something belonging elsewhere, — that she knew by the very token could not possibly belong to herself. Nothing had ever happened that could have made her feel as Rose felt now.

It mattered not that it would not have been with her either tears, or blushes, or self-revelation. Whatever it would have been with her would not have been, as this was with Rose Howick, for Richard Innesley. She knew that now. There was something in her as yet unawakened : oh, yes, quite unawakened ! There was no question of it now, for any one. Oh, friends were best !

The recollection and significance of her dream swept over her. She had been lifted to the height of a man's shoulder ; she had seen lovely, marvelous things. And somehow, it was all the gift and the will of the King of the Great Country.

"I believe, — I believe," she said to herself, exultingly, "in the Lord and Giver of life, and in the Communion of Saints ! "

All this while she walked and talked, simply, sweetly, with Rose Howick, of any common little surrounding things.

Rose thought she had never found her so simple-sweet before.

When Rose said that she would go, Peace Polly told her she would walk down the street with her. " They may as well see that we understand each other," she said.

Rose smiled. " Oh, that was what I did want so," she answered.

Peace Polly stopped and said good-by at Miss Mallis's white front door.

"Are you going in *there?*" Rose asked her, with a little shudder. And then Peace Polly knew that she was quite right in going.

Miss Mallis knew by Peace Polly's face what she had come for. There was an errand in it; one that made no little ordinary preface, but showed there in a quiet determination; waiting only to pass by the ordinary formulæ of reception. These met only the answer of dignified inclination and measured thanks.

"I have come to you, Miss Mallis, because you usually know everything."

This was said with the coolest gentleness. There was no onslaught; it was an orderly advance.

Miss Mallis put on instantly, as she was capable, a coolness to match. Underneath that was fun, utterly good-humored. From her altitude of years and experience, she looked down on Peace Polly's little fume as simply a thing to amuse herself with. There was nothing bad in Miss Mallis; she was only as impertinent and as much at home with everything in which she had no real business as a house-fly. She nodded to Peace Polly's remark as half accepting its attribution, but lifted her eyebrows in slight counteracting deprecation.

"Possibly you expect a little too much, Peace Polly."

The name, with its every-day comfortable assumption, saved the distance of the speech from offense-defensiveness; and then Miss Mallis waited easily, at guard.

"It has come round to me," said Peace Polly, without a feature-movement except such as was necessary for speech, "that 'they say,' here in Bonnyborough, where they say everything, that I will, or can if I will, marry Mr. Innesley."

"They do say so," answered Miss Mallis, 'at parade.' Inwardly, she commented, "Does n't look like a girl in that position, I 'm free to confess."

"Say-soes have to be singular before they are plural," remarked Peace Polly.

Here was a thrust; but Miss Mallis fenced well.

"Well, why do you come to me about it? I'm not the most singular person in Bonnyborough."

"You are most in the possessive case."

Miss Mallis laughed. "Of news, and the facts of the news? Well, perhaps I am, usually, — except, of course, the parties in question."

"People should n't be in question!" said Peace Polly, indignantly.

"Should n't they? Then they should n't be alive."

"Miss Mallis, you can stop this talk."

"Excuse me; I don't think anything but events can."

"There won't be any events, if everybody meddles." That was off guard, but Peace Polly was thinking of Rose. She thoroughly puzzled Miss Mallis, however.

"What would you like?" she demanded, in genuine earnest. "That I should go about saying, 'The minister does n't want Peace Polly, after all; if she thinks he does, she 's over-Schott herself'?"

"If you like. It would be better than the other. At any rate, he would n't suppose I had started that. And if you thought I wanted the minister, the other would be the surest way of spoiling my chance." She said it as coolly as if she were talking over somebody else.

"I don't believe in my heart you do!" said Miss Mallis; "you 're too calm and collected about it. But that does n't prove you can't, And the story runs that way, I think you said?"

"Miss Mallis, see here." Peace Polly, by a sudden inspiration, changed her ground. It was great generalship. On the very battlefield she discerned points which had not been taken into account, and adapted her manœuvres to them. "If I say something that I ask you not to repeat or to hint at, I do not believe you will."

"Your good opinion is invaluable to me, little Peace; and I think you are so far justified in it."

Peace Polly was as good as a charade, Miss Mallis was thinking.

"Suppose some one else, here or elsewhere, did care?"

"Now, Peace Polly, fight fair, either with or against me. What do you put in 'elsewhere' for? The minister is n't elsewhere?"

"He is, at this very moment. But I will fight fair. I put it in because — I 'm a *girl*, Miss Mallis; and I can be proud for another girl!"

Miss Mallis looked at her with the very best of herself showing in the look. "I like that," she answered. "Well, we 'll name no names, and we 'll let the place alone. So you don't mean to have the minister? He may go to — Greenland for an Eskimo — for all you?"

"Miss Mallis, he has never come for me at all; and I don't believe he ever will. Since you will think me over in that way, you may have the plain truth. It can only hurt everybody to have such things said. If you please, you will stop them." And Peace Polly stood up to go.

"Is that an order, or an allowance again of my wonderful capacity?" Miss Mallis rose also.

"It is, — whichever you like best. I think I have a right to speak." Miss Mallis moved with her toward the door.

"Now, Peace Polly, look here; I like this of you. I think it 's fine. You have n't madded me a bit. I 'm all on your side. It 's better fun than the other. You act up to what you 've said, and I 'll undertake Bonnyborough. They say everything here, as you observed; one thing as quick as the other, so it is something. People must talk, as they must eat ; and they don't ever object to a second or third course, when they 've had about enough of the first. If everybody came up to the scratch like you, there would n't be half so much scratching. And after all," she added, as she opened the white door, " I 'd full rather it *would* be — the Eskimo — that they say has been left out in the cold — if only " —

But Peace Polly was swiftly beyond reach of her " if only."

This was on a Saturday. Late that evening Mr. Innesley arrived, and was in his place in the chancel on Sunday, as had been expected.

Peace Polly walked over to the Presbyterian church with Lyman and Serena. She did not mean to run away from Mr. Innesley again, but she meant to see him, when she should do so, of a purpose, and not casually. So she went to-day and listened to Mr. Dawney.

Miss Mallis stopped Mrs. Howick on the stone steps, when service was over, and drew her into the porch again. Rose would have passed on, but Miss Mallis caught her back. " I want you, my dear, presently," she said.

But she made her business with Rose's mother long enough to keep them all till Mr. Innesley had come down the aisle. Everybody greeted him, but he never stayed long for any. Mrs. Howick held out her hand as he came near. That was no more than usual and unavoidable; and Mrs. Howick had not heard the gossip that had hurt Rose.

" Rose, my dear ! " she said, remindingly. Rose turned, obedient, lifting up the prettiest possible flushed, sweet face. " We are glad to see you back, Mr. Innesley," she said, with the gentle sort of dignity a flower might have, bent backward by a breath upon its stalk.

Miss Mallis and Rose, the minister and Mrs. Howick, left the porch together. Mr. Howick, who was a warden, came out a moment later. The group moved slowly up the village street, under its colonnade of elms. Miss Mallis was first at her own door. She slipped from Rose's side, who somehow forgot to notice.

"Good-by," she said, loud and clear, so that one or two heads among the little stream of people turned to look. Mrs. Howick, pausing to return the word, was joined by her husband. Mr. Innesley walked forward with Rose, who, recollecting herself, had nodded back to Miss Mallis, and kept on. And all the little stream of people that came up behind could see.

At the next corner, the Presbyterian congregation was coming down. The Schotts and Miss Serena turned and went up just far enough ahead to be out of reach except by determined effort. It happened precisely as Miss Mercuria had foreseen and planned.

The Dawneys and the Holistons and the Cramhalls fell in together between, amicably mingling the different denominational currents. Heads turned, and eyes glanced, either way.

"Well, that's funny!" said Dianthe Holiston. "I thought all that was over with."

"How could he help it?" demanded Jenny Cramhall.

"Peace Polly Schott can help anything she has a mind to."

"And she has n't a mind to be talked about. That's all. Peace Polly 's deep."

"I believe it 's all great nonsense," said Ruth Dawney. "Miss Mallis don't give in to it. She just said, '*per-adventure!*' to me last night, in such a brimful way, with her eyebrows up. That meant, 'You 'll all know better by and by.'"

"Miss Mallis hedges," said Dianthe, who visited at Broadhills, had seen the races, and had betted gloves, and delighted in a little knowing slanginess. "She means to come out right either way."

"She 'll take her eyebrows down in time to come out with an 'I told you so,' if there 's any likehood," said Roxy, the eldest of the Cramhall "girls," whose only title to the classification was in the circumstance of younger sisters, and the convenience of mentioning the family in the aggregate. "There is n't a much safer Old Prob than Merky Mallis, — you may rely on that."

Roxy could not, for the life of her, refrain from saying "Merky Mallis," though it betrayed and reminded of the fact of ancient school-fellowship. It made great impression on the younger girls, who had not known the sharp, spry spinster so, and were a good deal afraid of her.

It may be said that for the next few days, at least, Bonnyborough was wavering. Of a consequence, lively, but uncomfortable; like a fish on a hook, for example.

Mr. Innesley did not quite thoroughly enjoy his walk with Rose, though he could scarcely have told why. It was not clear to his mind that it was because she was an impediment, by any means; he would not so much have minded, if it had been Miss Mallis herself; then, indeed, he might have been pretty honestly sure that he would rather have had other company, which was the state of mind he knew he ought to have been in. It was a little too pleasant to have Rose smile up at him, out of the first restraint and shyness that he was slightly puzzled with, but that his kind words soon broke through; and if with the puzzle there came a beguiling wish to know the reason of the gentle withdrawal, there was certainly something rather of his conscience than his will that made him put it by.

Richard Innesley was just a little puzzled with himself.

His full intent, he thought his full desire, was toward
Peace Polly; but the little overstrain he felt·with her,
the very utmost of him that so recognized her, was curiously let down into something a wee bit restful, a sense
of mere Adam-happiness more simply paradisiacal, beside
this delicious, tender, womanly little Eve. He had not
reached the tenderness of Peace Polly. If that were for
him, indeed, or for any man, his whole reason and understanding told him it might be something deeper, richer,
rarer, than is given ordinarily to any common Adam.

He had set out for the apples of Hesperides; he need
not be blamed if he found himself less than a Hercules,
who could support the whole vault of heaven with un-
wearied shoulders as a service for them.

Such a thought as that never occurred to him, however;
there was only an unbending, of whose repose he had just
the consciousness to make him turn away from it with a
jealousness of quick integrity. He was no flirt; he was
no man with double meaning; he was only not a Hercules.
He might surely wish that Peace Polly, when they came
to know each other well, when they had reached the ease
of sure affection, might sometimes be a little sweetly
commonplace with him.

On the afternoon of Monday, he went over to The Knolls.

Peace Polly was sitting on the doorsill, a basket of
colored yarns beside her, a rug-strip that she was dili-
gently knitting in some new fashion, with tufts and twine,
hanging across her lap as she worked upon it. A basket
chair was on the broad stone step, unoccupied. This was
as things were apt to be in that pleasant fore doorway;
but it was curiously ready for the minister and his errand;
as well preconsidered, perhaps, as the outlook from the
bay-window overhead and the run up the field-path had
been that last time of his coming. It was all far too ready
for any hopes he might have come with now.

As he let the gate fall to behind him, Peace Polly rose up. She dropped her trailing strip and ball back upon her cushion, and came down the walk to meet him. That was pleasant, but there was not a trace of shyness in it; it occurred to him that he would rather she had been a little shy.

Peace Polly was all alone. Lyman was at the mill, of course. Rebeccarabby was in the kitchen regions, absorbed in expectation and in last items of preparation — which would always last till the final minute — for the arrival of Mrs. Pamela Chirke. Dr. Fuller was away, as he was constantly now, on duty with and for Dr. Blithecome.

Mr. Innesley took the basket chair which Peace Polly offered him. The girl herself quietly resumed her work.

"I am very glad to find you," the minister began.

"I am almost always to be found," returned Peace Polly, with a smile.

A finch in the great linden-tree over their heads filled a little pause with a half-song.

"Summer and singing are not quite over," said Mr. Innesley, glancing up where the flutter of wings and leaves revealed the little presence.

"No. And the flockings and flights are to come. I think they are about the prettiest part of the bird-year," said Peace Polly.

"Only they are the end, like autumn leaves," said Mr. Innesley. "Or that is our fashion of speech about it. We make great mistakes about the ends."

"We make great mistakes about many things, I suppose," said Peace Polly, picking up and throwing down two or three knots of yarn before she found the right one. "And so — a good deal of life — has to be — raveling." She suited the action to the word, pulling out a row of knitting, and beginning carefully to pick up her stitches again.

"Miss Peace," said the young man, "when I went away, it was an interruption."

"Going away is always an interruption. That's one of our ends," said Peace Polly, with cheerful coolness, patting out the worsted-work upon her knee, and contemplating with satisfaction the change of effect in it.

"Now I am back again," persisted Mr. Innesley, with quite as much self-possession, "I have come to ask you what I then had in my mind."

Peace Polly was sorely tempted to twist his words, and to retort, "How can I possibly tell you, Mr. Innesley?" but she refrained. She had need of better caution. Under her coolness and her pretended half abstraction with her work, she was as watchful, as still, as that very bird in the tree would be at a human movement toward it, a hand reached out upon it.

"I think you must have perceived — you have had time to think since then," Mr. Innesley was going on; but this was the outstretch of the hand for which the bird had been on guard.

Her wings fluttered in his face; she escaped him suddenly, to perch further off. "Mr. Innesley, I suppose it may be about the Confirmation. You have been with us a good deal, as you said that day, and I know it is n't only just these pleasant things; you think you must remind me; but please don't ask me *any* questions; I'm not ready yet; when I've thought a little more, I may ask you, or Dr. Farron."

Her conscience smote her, indeed, for using this as a fend; but what could she do? He was her clergyman, — only that; she must put it all on that ground, and make it stay there. She must make good her own words, "He has not asked me, and he never will." For Rose Howick's sake, for his own sake, he should not do this, which would be a mistake; which he would not like to tell to Rose; which he could not, with self-respect, remember.

And it was not solely a fend, either; it was an argument, only she could not let the subject go far enough to bring it in as argument. She would remind him beforehand that it was the thing rightly to come first; how could she properly become a minister's wife without it? He must not, she said waywardly to herself, think to press her with all the services at once!

Mr. Innesley was taken absolutely by surprise. Was it sincerely possible that she had understood him so?

But whether she spoke in utter innocence, or whatever she meant, — escape for herself or him, — he could not take it that way, now. He could not withdraw, under cover of such pretense, what he had honestly been about to say. She might refuse him; very well, she had a right to do it now. He was too much of a man not to keep on.

"It was quite another matter, Miss Peace. One that concerns you and myself, — myself deeply, coming to know you as I have."

Certainly Peace Polly was inspired; so swiftly rushed into her mind the expedients of elusion.

"Oh, Mr. Innesley!" A quick, natural blush came to her reinforcement, as she plunged into the subject. "Then *you* have heard that story, too! It is too bad. Don't mind, though, for me, please. If it meant anything, I should have cared; if they had talked of anything I had the least consciousness of, you know! If they had said anything about Lyman and me, for instance; things I often *am* ashamed and sorry for, — I could n't have borne *that* gossip. I dare say they do, but I hope I shall never hear it. I should kill somebody! — It is very good of you to think of me. A man can't care for himself so much, though it is a shame, — because he can make his wishes known if he has any, or he can prove the contrary by saying nothing. But it *is* hard on us girls, sometimes,

Mr. Innesley! And I have been very sorry, for I know *she* has felt badly."

And there at last Peace Polly stopped, or rushed back into herself, rather, as she had rushed forth so reckless of all but the desperate necessity that she had taken into her own hand, alone. She stood, safe, within the citadel of her reserve and absolute maidenliness again, all glowing red and palpitating from her sortie; her eyes shining with the excitement of the daring, but steady, very steady, fixed resolutely upon his. If she had paused before, had quailed, had hesitated, she would have been covered with confusion; she would have failed.

But she had not failed. She had stopped him, now. She had not waited to choose words, or to contrive impressions; she had let them take care of themselves; she had done well. Did he not notice that little touch of difference between her own "not minding" and the "feeling badly" of some one else?

She had shown it all plainly enough; she had declared in words that no "story about him and her could touch anything in her consciousness." If he wanted a refusal, he had got it now, and might take it and go away with it and be content. And yet he had not asked her anything. I think Peace Polly had conducted her skirmish well, if on somewhat an unusual method. She had conquered, yet no one had been defeated. There was no need now of a pitched battle.

Mr. Innesley looked at her with a certain admiration. He found, thanks to her showing, that he could admire, approve, like warmly, and go no further, and be an honester man; perhaps some day a happier one, for this that she had done.

"I have been very sorry for her, she has felt badly." Was this dear little Rose?

"Have they been saying such things about us all, Miss Peace?" he asked. And Peace did not consider, or choose to see, that they were shifting ground, that she was taking the frank-friendly part she had attributed to him, but went on to give him full enlightenment.

"They have given you — and taken you away — and given you again," she said. And then the absurdity of the whole thing struck upon her excitement, and she laughed.

Mr. Innesley did not laugh. He put out his hand, and Peace Polly gave him hers.

"I suppose I have to thank you for more than I can see now," he said. "You have understood me better than I have understood myself. Peace! you are a very noble woman."

Peace thought, and with reason, that there was something noble also in him. Should she ever find more, at her own service, than this that she had let go so easily? The restless heart-pulse prompted the transient asking, but the deep heart itself in her sung in a still gladness.

Standing there hand in hand, Rebeccarabby burst out on them from the hall behind.

"She's comin', Peace Polly! there's the stage!" And rumbling and tetering up the side drive beyond the garden paling came the unwieldy vehicle, its big wheels scattering the gravel, and its straps and canvas flapping as it swung.

Mr. Innesley took his leave.

At the same moment Dr. Fuller opened the low gate at the road front and came slowly up the grass-walk.

XXVIII

GOOD WISHES.

" He likes me because I say what I think, and have ideas enough to be 'suggestive.' But he will love Rose Howick just because she is lovely. I don't think he is a man who can live on liking, or high-esteeming ; but I dare say he supposed he ought to. He is interested in the making of me, out of a kind of strong, rough material, very crossway ; Rose is cut out already, by the right threads, and smoothly fitted to a gracious, proper pattern. Not but that she 'll grow fitter and prettier the longer she belongs to anybody ; well-made things, of good stuff, always do, even till they grow old and wear out ; but she won't need to be made over into any better fashion. — He 'll wake up to that now, — or give up to it, — and it will all come right. Heigh-ho ! " It was a soft little sigh, but it can't be printed any softer ; it has to be as you breathe it.

Dr. Fuller had been into his own room, and had come out into the hall again.   He looked tired and grave.

"I am afraid Dr. Blithecome is worse," said Peace Polly, noticing this suddenly.

" On the contrary, he is more comfortable. But there is nothing to count upon, any more than before."

" You have had a hard day, Dr. Fuller."

" Not very."   And there fell a silence. Peace Polly had settled to her cushion again, and taken up her knitting.   Presently she would go out and give courteous welcome to Rebeccarabby's kinswoman. The two were now up in the ell-bedrooms, whence proceeded sounds as of dragging trunks, or shifting furniture, like small shocks of earthquake. Rebeccarabby's tread and her voluminous voice resounded like elemental rush and explosion. "When the tornado has passed by," thought Peace Polly, "I can venture." That was as usual with things and occasions in which Rebeccarabby took violent precedence.

Dr. Fuller drew a chair to the large hall table, and turned over the papers and mail of the day.

Peace Polly looked at him furtively. "He is n't troubled, and he is n't tired; what is the matter with him?" she wondered.

"Would you like an early cup of tea? Did you miss your dinner?"

"Oh, no, I dined with Mrs. Blithecome, thank you."

Peace Polly glanced again, and caught an expression resting upon herself which she could not quite understand. She put down her work, got up, and walked over opposite to him.

"Have I done, or not done, anything that I should n't or should? Are you vexed with me, Dr. Fuller?"

"Vexed with you! How should I be?" The first words were almost tender; the latter sounded impatient.

"I don't know. You seem — you have been — a little different. I am sorry I asked," said Peace Polly, her words proudly apologetic.

"My dear Miss Peace! you have nothing but my highest regard, my very true, good wishes."

What did he mean with a set speech like that?

"Why, Dr. Fuller!" she cried, in a mixture of fun and feeling. "People say that when anybody is going a journey, or into business, or to get married; when they may break their necks, or their fortunes, or their hearts.

What danger am I in of either? Why do you wish me such solemn good wishes?"

She stood over against him, her hands folded before her on the table, an arm's length of distance between them. His hand, against which he had slightly leaned his cheek, while with the other he had turned the reading matter before him, left its place, was reached across, and laid gently upon her two. His head lifted, and his eyes looked into hers.

" I do not wish against danger; I hope for all best possibilities to be fulfilled. I was premature, perhaps; I have no right, — you must pardon me. I will wait your pleasure; my good wishes are always ready."

The color came up in Peace Polly's face, so hot that tears rushed and filled her eyelids; the fun, if it had been such, was gone; her breath came quickly; her eyes, even under their tears, glittered.

" My pleasure is now," she said, proudly, passionately. " Dr. Fuller, you are mistaken. There is nothing to wish me well about. I have no particular happiness whatever."

How beautiful the sorrowful storm was in her face! She stood an instant, absolutely forgetful of his fingers still resting upon her own, intent only upon his face, to see if he took the truth from her. Then suddenly, she drew both hands from his hold, dashed them across her eyes, and smiled like a rainbow.

" I have no *un*-happiness, either!" she exclaimed. " Don't mistake the other way. And forgive me, for I thank you, all the same."

While he still watched the swift-changing, full-fraught features, the face turned from him, and she went away.

What was it she had seen in his? At that last assurance, what kind of gladness swept from brow to mouth, what smile broke forth ?   She did not wait to understand ; she went away wondering, and remembering.

Dr. Fuller carried some papers into his study.   It was a good while before he looked at any of them.

By and by, alone as he sat, a low exclamation escaped his lips.   He had a Boston newspaper open in his hands. This was the notice upon which his eyes had fallen : —

"In this city, 15th instant, Cecilia, widow of the late Elijah Gray Winterhouse, 74 years."

He read it slowly, thrice over ; then he put the paper down.

"It can make no difference," he said.   "Cecilia never has heard a word from her aunt since she was married."

At that, the tea-bell rang : tea-bells have no deference ; they break in on anything.

18

XXIX.

MRS. PAMELA CHIRKE.

At this somewhat late point in our story, we must introduce and explain a new character, Mrs. Pamela Chirke.

But who shall say who is a new character, in any story? Mrs. Pamela would have been astonished that in any chronicle of Bonnyborough, to say nothing of its centring at The Knolls, she should not have been introduced and explained long ago.

Mrs. Pamela was a little grasshopper of a woman. She had never been anything, she said herself, but wires and jump. Her name was Spring before she was married; and she had lived with the two successive Mistress Schotts from before the birth of Lyman, whom, as a girl of fourteen, she had "tended," in a bony, bounding, chirrupy way, quite after her own nature and sufficiently acceptable to the boy, until after that of Peace Polly, which she only stayed to see safely over, and the mother provided with a successor to herself, — now and long since become the mainstay of the household, — to fulfill her own promise, of five years' standing, to Jacob Chirke, a comfortable carpenter, and go with him to " Woodiford, Statermaine." Statermaine was where she had originally come from, and Woodiford was in her native county. It was " goin' back to folks; only Bonnyborough folks had got to be so *like* folks that she could n't scurcely tell which was whichest."

Shortly after, she had sent her niece, Rebeccarabby

Pownes, to reinforce the Schott *ménage*, beginning over again the story of the aunt's apprenticeship as " young girl," and fulfilling, as we have seen, the same after mission and destiny, " savin' an' exceptin'," as Rabby was wont to say, " the circumstahnce of Chirke."

At Rebeccarabby's coming, Peace Polly's mother was already in that delicate health which foretokened the quiet slipping away that happened at last, after a few years of the semi-detached struggle which so many American woman know, and which is, perhaps, as fibre after fibre slowly yields, the most exquisite illustration of the sharpness of death.

When Peace Polly was a little maid of seven, Rebeccarabby — strange to say, because the thing never occurred before nor since — " failed some in her health," and had a longing for the " Statermaine," as the only place and means for regaining it.

Whether it were a " circumstahnce," though not the " circumstahnce of Chirke," were hard to say, since it never transpired sufficiently to come with verity into this record; but Aunt Pamely left Woodiford "for a spell," and came and kept Joshua Schott's house again; this also fitting in, for Chirke had got a long job of building in a somewhat distant mill-village, and could only come home " occasional, any way; " and there were no children to leave.

Mrs. Pamela stayed, " off 'n on, the biggest part of a year or two," the current of events favoring. They were a thrifty couple, the Chirkes, and not averse to " earnin' at both ends," even at the cost of some lengthy separations; and Aunt Pamela averred that, " whether or no, it was her dooty, by Joshuay Schott and Rebeccarabby both; and she 'd be willin' to give up consider'ble for either."

It is always well, and one should be grateful for the

beneficent Providence, when the dutiful sacrifice and the compensatory benefit run so evidently on what Serena Wyse might have called parallel lines.

Rebeccarabby recovered; certain individuals in the neighborhood of The Knolls, of whom Aunt Pamely cautiously wrote to her niece under cover of general Bonnyborough news, went West; and Rabby came back again, blithe and resolved; thrilling and whirling through the house in her old way, a bit toned down by time or experience, — she must be either alive or dead, she said, — the very spirit of energy and cleansing, like a wind of March or October, to be taken with all the concomitants of flying chaff and last year's dust, sudden, bewildering bursts and impacts, slambangs and breakages inevitable, whenever matter, that was not the immediate matter in hand, obstructed or checked her powerful way.

It was a sufficiently funny thing to see the two women together, as they were in the days of this summer visit, to which both had looked forward, and which had been hope deferred, season after season; for " Chirke was gitt'n in years, now, an' did n't need ner perpose t' work hard; he only kep' his hand in with neighborly jobs; and he wanted his wife round, — that was nat'ral. They could afford t' take things easy, and t' take 'em t'gether." Aunt " Pamely could n't stay but a week, now she had come. 'T was kinder 's if she was sent, that it happened so 's 't she got started."

I was only going to say that it was funny to see them " visitin'," as Yankee women call a comfortable talk and companionship, every time they sit down, or pursue any little avocation, together. It was not often actual sitting still, with these. Rebeccarabby pealed and swirled tumultuously about, and Aunt Pamely hopped and dodged. When Rabby kept about her " chores," though she rarely permitted help, Mrs. Chirke could not make herself stationary. She took her ball of yarn under her elbow, and with spectacles on nose, and needles clicking, followed and stood round, springing and jerking to make wonderful escapes for herself or get out of Rabby's way, as a broom, or pail, or the sweep of a mop-stick threatened her and called for space.

It was the Wednesday after Aunt Pamely's arrival, and it rained.

A slow, southeasterly rain in August is a forlorn, abnormal sort of thing. It shuts up the dog-day heat, with the added damps that seem but the sweltering of the over-aggravated planet under the torment of Sirius, into the necessarily half-closed house; it thrusts into a sudden imprisonment life and plan that demand the sunshine; it is not a good time of year for household enterprises that at a different season might revel in the opportunity. If the rain has begun after the wash was out, and the dripping "starched things" and the delicate linens have had to be all brought in again, and soused in tubs or hung on horses, the condition is an exasperating one. And this was what had partly happened now. Rebeccarabby had risen by starlight on the Monday, had got out the heavy clothes before breakfast, and ironed them all up out of the way in time to straighten things with cheerful tidiness, and make her tea-cake before her aunt's arrival, leaving the fine articles to do on Tuesday for "company work;" and on the Tuesday the showers had begun which had become the Wednesday's determined pour.

Peace Polly had been left alone. The house had seemed, within the week or more, to have relapsed into its old dullness and solitariness, except as these had been broken by what had so briefly, though emphatically, touched upon it from without. Its own life had "simmered down," as even Rebeccarabby had felt and expressed it, before the announcement of Aunt Pamely's coming had been like chips to the slow fire for her. Now, at least, there was the cheer of " mis'ry likes company " in the kitchen and the kitchen " settin'-room." Up-stairs there was a blank.

Peace Polly could not run up to Serena's ; that is, she hardly felt to care enough for anything to run through the rain, which with a sufficient impetus she might have done. And she was conscious of a shrinking dread lest Pamela Chirke should " step in " with her knitting-work, and offer a " visit " in her own territories, with all the inevitable old-time memories that were sure to be un-wound. Often, indeed, she might greatly have enjoyed them ; to-day the present time seemed quite enough.

There was a place of refuge, which, like the panel-chambers in the old romances, she kept a secret to herself for just such times, and she fled to it this morning.

She was not too far off to know if any sign or move-ment in the house should indicate an actual need or in-terest for her; but if Rebeccarabby or Mrs. Pamela looked for her, it would be concluded, in Rabby's phrase, that she had " cleared out to S'reeny's ; " whereas she was only quite comfortably ensconced, with a book and her rug-work, in the low, narrow recess of a window in a large back press-closet, fenced in by movable shelves full of bedding, that made an alcove of the space, and before whose inward open end she had planted a tall old blind-door, and before that, again, a piece-trunk. It was her own domain, any way ; there would hardly be an errand here for anybody else, and a casual searching glance would not discover her. The window looked north, up field ; there never was any sun there, the summer through, to make it hot ; and through the blind-screen there crept a draught, if wanted, from the high, upper hall.

It happened that this window was just over the north window of the "kitchen settin'-room." Peace Polly had not been settled long before voices, of a pitch and resonance that might easily have risen or penetrated further, came up to her ears.

The door from sitting-room to kitchen was evidently open : Rebeccarabby was rampaging around ; a frequent period, or italic, or exclamation point was made by shove, or clap-to, or energetic setting down ; Aunt Pamely's shrill tones betokened frequent flights and sudden shiftings. Peace Polly listened, amused. There was certainly nothing secret, to be scrupulous about.

"Is n't it holdin' up a leetle mite?" she heard Mrs. Pamela hopefully suggest from directly underneath, taking observation evidently from the north window, away from which the fine rain slightly slanted.

"Donno whuther it 's holdin' up or holdin' daown," shouted Rebeccarabby from a different outlook ; "it jest rains in a straight, uppendickler colume, *this* way !"

Mrs. Chirke's next remark came from some little further distance. The clatter and gyration of a clothes-horse on its stilted legs followed. Rebeccarabby had apparently made onset with her folding-bars full of damp, slapping draperies, and Aunt Pamely had hopped. Doing that, she had come back toward the window again, and Rebeccarabby seemed to have taken breath and followed. There was a sound as of a heavy subsiding and the creak of rockers, proclaiming that the latter was about to indulge in a "between-spell." Mrs. Chirke had alighted noiselessly, but they were evidently settled for a few minutes of "clear comfort," for Rebeccarabby said, with mighty emphasis of content and a forcible outbreathed sigh, "I declare to 't, Aunt Pum, it 's real clever to be visitin' like this, along o' you. I 've ben livin', most o' the time, like a settin' hen in a barril. Thiz no more cump'ny to this house, ornery times, thin thiz to a stopped-up marten-box. 'F I did n't stram round considderble, I should n't scursely know I was here myself. Ben more lively, in a solemn kind o' way, for Peace Polly, I s'pose, latterly; but 't ain't reached round t' me much."

"Well, I donno," said Aunt Pamela. "It's kind of a still fam'ly, to be sure; but yit 'n so, it's a fam'ly. An' a fam'ly 's cump'ny."

"That depends. When us three's alone, 't ain't nothin' o' the sort. We 're jest three individgiwil folks, as fur apart an' sep'rit an' as set to as many pints o' the compass, as three sharp corners to a ten-acre heater-piece. Ev'ry one of us is dretful diff'runt. I can't say t' my soul which is the diff'runtest. Sometimes I think Lyman is, an' then agin seems 's if 't wuz Peace Polly. An' fin'ly I ain't sure but what I be. Prob'ly we all are, only not all in the same pertickler way. It's ben a trial, times past, I tell ye."

"You 've stuffed it out pooty well."

"I ain't never beat," said Rebeccarabby. "I 'd be mortified t' be. Ther wuz a spell when it come kinder hard. But 's soon 's I ree'lized it, I took myself over my knee, an' giv' myself a tutorin'. I says, ' Rebeccarabby Pownes, it 's mind you want. Them thet hez mind ain't lonesome, not ef they wuz on topper-Rarrarat. Cump'ny ain't nuthin', only jest t' give yer mind somethin' t' work on. You jest find yerself! You ken hev mind ef you 're a min' ter!' So I set myself t' see things, an' put myself to 'em. I give myself up t' gravies, one time, an' I guess you could n't stump me on a gravy now, ef ther warn't more 'n a wishbone of a pidgin t' start off on; only gi' me the salt-suller an' the drudgin' box an' a scrap o' pork an' a fryin'-pan. Then agin 't wuz pie-paste, and by the time I 'd got the full upper hand o' that, Lor, 't warn't flakes, I will say, but clear feathers! F'r a long spell 't wuz patchwork; I 've got six quilts an' a silk spread. An' 'long back it 's ben hookin'. That 's the most up-takin' thing of all. I declare t' man, I can't fairly look at a new gownd in church 'thout thinkin' what strips 't would make, an' wishin' I could be a-hookin' of it right straight off. I 've tore up a real decent old Bay-State shawl fer groundin', an' a red flannil petticoat that only wanted bindin' round the bottom an' turnin' hind side afront, afore it got any thinner on the knees. Fact, when you git a-runnin' on one thing, the whole 'arth an' firmi-mint seems t' be jest made raound it en fer it! Say, Aunt Pum! What 's come o' that old undershot blue-an'-gol'-colored Chuzan you use t' hev? The' wuz six brea't's in the day of it, an' ther' warn't no wear-out t' the stuff, I know. Why can't ye look it up, ef yu 'v got it, an' send it along? Mail it; I 'll pay the postidge."

"I 'll see 'bout it, some time, p'raps," said Aunt Pamela. "But tell 'bout Lyman, Rabby. He did n't use t' be so dretful shet up when I wuz here; an' he was a little feller fust, an' then a young feller. I know him, both ways. I knew all his growin' up, an' some things most folks did n't know. Ef he 's sp'ilt, I know jest who did it, an' jest when."

There was a pause. Aunt Pamela changed her knit-ting-needle, and drew out her yarn, with elbows at sharp, high, lively angles, and set her feet on the rung of her chair, bringing up her knees to correspond. It was her attitude of attention and expectation. Where another woman would have settled herself in passive comfort, she was spry.

Peace Polly could not see this; she was leaning intent,

however, toward the low window, as if she would fain
both see and hear.   Peace Polly was straightforward,
with the rectitude of the very earth's axis, that points
from nether to upper star; but she was not literal, nor
squeamish with an arbitrary righteousness. If the com-
pass-needle be true to Polaris, north, it must be true southward, also, though there be no visible named Polaris
there.

Peace Polly felt she had a right to this; it might be
the key to their whole lives. If this woman knew, and
could tell it to this other, who were they, even with their
long, old service, that they should dare to know her
brother better than she?

So she had not a thought of leaving it unlistened; she
leaned, and waited, and held her breath.

"Le' me go an' fetch along some stuff t' strip," said
Rebeccarabby. "I can't never waggle my tongue an'
keep my fingers still." In the noise of her departure and
return, Peace Polly slid from her low seat, crept closer to
the window, and knelt there by the sill.

"Too," said Rebeccarabby, talking with her scissors in
her mouth and her teeth shut, while she shook out and
examined an old woolen table-cover, to see which way the
threads and thins ran, "'t ought t' be you, I sh'd think,
t' *tell.* You seem t' ev got all the nub on 't."

"Tell me how things work now, an' I 'll tell ye what
the nub wuz."

"Well, then, ef yer 'd arst me that any time two munts
ago er more, I sh'd ev said they did n't work at all;
no more 'n 'east athout barm. 'T warn't that, igzackly,
nuther, cos now an' agin the' *would* be a fermint. 'T wuz
more like things thet would n't fay in, ner jine; y'
could n't make a pattun out on 't, ner a hull piec'n, nuther.
Ev'rything wuz jib-jab, an' catty-cornered. Them two

jest settin' ther eyes by one another, but both on 'em with sech a side-squint o' ther own thet they could n't never see it. Lyman hectors, an' Peace Polly snaps; an' then one goes off an' aches over it, an' t'other hides up an' cries. Seems as ef 't wuz jest *because* they had n't only one another, an' they wuz both missin' sunthin' else."

"Lyman missed it, like enough, an' Peace Polly hed n't come to it. Well, go 'long."

"Why don't ye say 'gee'?" asked Rebeccarabby, a little resentfully. "I can't gee over a stun wall; an' thet's about the upcome 'f all I ken tell ye. Guess yer know the rest, es the little boy said t' the school-marm."

"You wuz alwers in a proper pickle fer a story, Rebeccarabby Pownes! Could n't never let one keep."

"*Whut* did Lyman miss?" demanded Rebeccarabby, uncompromisingly, as one standing upon her rights.

"*Whur's* the peck o' pickled peppers Peter Piper picked? *If* a peck" — began Aunt Pamela, mockingly. "Well, then, I 'll tell ye. 'T ain't nothin' t' make fun of; 't wuz pooty sober 'arnest in the time. I wuz here, 'n I know. He wanted S'reeny Wyse. Did n't so much want her, as thought he 'd got her; they growed up together, an' they *growed* together. 'T warn't no queschin o' comin' ter pass; when it stopped, 't wuz like a horse stoppin' at full go, — everybody wuz pitched out."

"*Whut* stopped it?" exploded Rebeccarabby.

"Wy, *she!* No, her mother. *Nerves.* Nerves is at the bottom of ev'rything that gits upsot. The old lady wuz childish, breakin' up; kinder crazy. S'reeny would n't leave her; I don't blame her fer that, but she never giv' Lyman a word t' wait on. Whut fools women ken be! They think a man *can't* wait. I know better, ef he only *is* a man! Jacob waited."

She did not say whether she meant the son of Isaac or her carpenter. It was true of both.

She began again.

"I wuz here, an' I know," she repeated. "I wuz out t' the mow, after hen's eggs, thet blessed afternoon, — day afore the Fourth, — 'leven year ago this very las' come an' gone July, an' I found him there, flat-face on the hay, a-cryin', — the way a man cries, dry an' hard; ef y' don't know how thet is, Lord keep ye f'om ever findin' out. It's turrible! He warn't much more 'n a boy, — whut's five 'r six 'n twenty? But there he wuz, a struck-down man. 'T warn't no losin' of a jack-knife, ner gitt'n cheated out o' marbles, ner his pa a-thrashin' of him; ther' warn't but jest one thing thet could 'a done it, ner but jest one woman. I know that."

"Warn't it sperritooal wrass'lin', may be?" suggested Rebeccarabby.

"To the land, child, no! Wy, he 'd *hed* his expee-r'unce, an' come out all clear an' hopeful, years afore. It wuz the one thing else thet happens to a man, an' it happened to him hard! Pore soul! He hed n't had no other womankind. His mother she died when he wuz twelve, an' Peace Polly she warn't ten, then; an' ye know 's well 's I do it laid on him t' be womankind 'n all, himself, t' Peace Polly, — not jest knowin' how, nuther."

Peace Polly had got enough. Her heart was throbbing up in her throat. Her teeth were set. Her conscience — is conscience all over and through one, like a flame? — was wrapping her in a sudden, live torment.

"My one, one brother!" she gasped. "All these years!"

If she had learned this a little while ago, would she have known it so? Life had grown in her, strangely.

She sank; she crouched down; she crept backward. She flung her head, she buried her face against a thick, soft pile of blankets and coverlets that were filled in upon the lowermost of the tall shelves that shielded her.

Nobody could hear her there. She shrieked little smothered shrieks of pain into the deadening folds. "My brother! My one brother!" she still cried, with a strong, inward cry, though the words were whispered.

She remembered every hard, cross, contemptuous word she had ever said to him. She forgot every tease, every pettiness, she had ever endured from him. Oh, she pitied him so, that he had borne that, all these years, — and she had never known. Then the tears came like rain.

And at last a soft, tired breath. "But I *do* love him," — the thought swept through her like a calm, — "or I could not care about it so!"

"'From all our sins, negligences, and ignorances, good Lord, deliver us!'"

Out of her Prayer-Book, in this hour, she experienced this.

And by and by, as she sat there, there came to her these other words: "Thou, to whom all hearts are open, all desires known, and from whom no secrets are hid, cleanse the thoughts of our hearts" — "Oh, take away all these old and bitter ones, and all the mischief of them!" was her unspoken interruption.

Other sentences linked themselves, brokenly; the book was full of them. She blessed it, — as her thoughts lit up with them like tempest-clouds shot through with sun-gleams, — that it had kept them for her at this need; that so she knew that other souls had needed them.

"Grant unto thy people pardon and peace; that they may serve thee with a quiet mind."

A quiet mind; oh, how she had needed, and failed of, that!

"Absolve thy people from their offenses, that through thy bountiful goodness we may all be delivered from the bands of those sins which by our frailty we have committed."

She went away and looked for those two little prayers; beneath each, in the day's Gospel, she found a resurrection.

"Thy son liveth!"

"He took her by the hand, and the maid arose."

"It is *so* He forgives, and makes good again! Oh, 'in all our troubles let us put our whole trust and confidence in thy mercy!'" she said, in her rejoicing, softened heart.

She bathed her face and smoothed her hair; she took some little work she had to do for Lyman, — some new handkerchiefs to hem, — and went and sat with it by the up-stairs hall-window, waiting his return.

She had left her rug-work in a heap on the floor in the press-closet. It was many days before she had the heart to go back there and gather it up.

When Lyman came, he was walking slowly. She saw him coming along under the ash and maple trees.

His step sounded weary and heavy on the porch. She heard him come in, make a few steps into the hallway, and then the movement ceased.

She rose, — paused and listened, — went gently toward the landing, and leaned upon the baluster. No further word or motion down below. She could not see him as she stood; but he was surely there. Why had he come in like that? she wondered.

Peace Polly slipped noiselessly down the stairway.

Lyman's hat was thrown upon the table; he sat beside it in one of the old harp-backed carved chairs. His head was in his hand; he was tired; his troubles lifted themselves up against him; they do when a man is tired. All this Peace Polly thought with a great surge of tenderness, as she came softly down.

It had not been like other things that disappoint a man, and leave him to endure awhile and then get over it.

This thing had stayed right by. Its denial had been right before his face; it had not changed, or gone to some one else instead of him; when other troubles came, and other thwartings, there it was, always mocking with its nearness, its impossibility. It said relentlessly, "Neither may you have this, that would have comforted you for all."

And even his sister had not known or cared. How could she have known? But, oh, she might have cared! She need not have left him alone with his hard, half life, — her "dull, slow Lyman!"

Her whole heart reached out to her brother, — folded him warm in full, pitying, repentant love.

In a moment she was beside him; her two arms about his neck; her head bent down to him, her cheek coming softly against his.

"Oh, Lyman, I am so sorry — for everything! That I have n't been a better sister to you all the time, — not half knowing you, dear! I 'd be the whole world to you now if I only could!"

It was so true, she hesitated not a thought about saying it. Truth makes its own way to truth. She knew Lyman's heart now, and she was not afraid.

Lyman turned, and held her suddenly in his arms; his strong, good arms that had never held her so before.

"Why, Peace Polly! Little sister! How could *you* know, possibly?"

Polly only cried a little, tenderly.

"Don't worry, Polly," Lyman said, still keeping her close, "nothing really bad can ever happen, you know. I 've meant right, — and I mean right now. I 'll do the best I can, and the Lord will take care of everybody."

Peace Polly pushed herself back a little, lovingly, so that she could see his face.

"Why, Lyman," she cried, between sobs and exultation, "what a beauty of a man you are!" And then she laughed, and then she sobbed outright, upon his shoulder.

She had found her brother; she knew that she wholeloved him now; he was a glory of a man. And Lyman thought the premium of years was well paid in, — yes, and the calamity well befallen at last, — that brought him such equivalent as this.

What matter was it that for the moment they were talking of two different things? Their discovery of each other was the same; explanations of mere present circumstance would come later.

Lyman had had bad final news that day; the builder at East Bend had failed.

Dinner was upon the table; why not? Lyman had come home to dinner. It is a blessed thing, after all, that these needs and customs hold us so to our tracks and hours. We should rush off frantic, all detached from safe and common things, at times, if it were not so.

The two sat down together. The meal was nearly ended when Dr. Fuller came in; he brought also, — not bad news, I will not write it so, — but a tender sadness.

Dr. Blithecome had died.

As they finally left the table, Lyman said quietly to his friend, "I have had a blow to-day, C. P. Hatherton has stopped. It stops me, — partially, and for a time at least."

"Old fellow?" Dr. Fuller exclaimed, turning quickly. He gave one look at Lyman's face. "*Brave* fellow!" he said, and put forth his hand with eager warmth.

Peace Polly started, but her first movement passed unnoticed; she put down her surprise. She saw in an instant how it had been; she said to herself, "Let it remain; what matter? We have each other now, — for everything!"

She slipped round beside Lyman, and stood there, her head inclining gently, tenderly, towards him, as he stood straight and firm. Her hand stole into his. Her eyes, shining, splendid, thanked his friend; her friend, who had all along shown her her brother.

Dr. Fuller looked at them. She had known it before, he supposed, of course. He saw her face, so full, so loving, so radiant, so strong. Not a trace of dismay, even for Lyman; only a holy pride, a steadfast devotion; for herself, no thought. It was a perfect woman's face for a man's trouble.

He left them so. "They do not need me, or any one," he said, and in his own great heart — great enough to bear and to see through trouble, that it was nothing — he was very glad for them.

19

XXX.

QUITTANCE.

RAWSON MORGAN chuckled when the news came in. "That 'll slice him down pretty well. A whole summer's work on his hands, — fancy, too, that nobody 'll take off. May be he won't turn up his nose at my ten thousand now. I can make it fifteen; I know where. I 've alwers held to that sharp old story in the Noo Testameant, and ben beholden to St. Luke for sett'n of it down. Rest on 'em skipped it."

And the unjust steward slapped his mean sides with a grin.

He had a certain decorum for the counting-room, however. He could almost put on the gentleman at times, when it was serving his purpose; if that purpose fell through, or his passions roused, he was intensely, coarsely, furiously, vernacular. Lyman Schott, though he had come to dislike and distrust the man, had never yet seen him with his visor quite thrown up.

"You have heard about the Hathertons?" he said, interrogatively, when the fellow came up-stairs at noontime the next day.

"Yaas; bad business," drawled Morgan. He meant his drawl for regretful reluctance; but if Lyman had scrutinized, he might have detected the chuckle still lurking in his eye. Morgan had his hat in his hand, and tried to keep his regards on that.

The rumor had been in town the day before, — rumor

only. Lyman had had his own immediate and certain information, but he had borne himself as usual at the mill, and the mill people and manager were puzzled. That Lyman left it to come to Morgan by hearsay marked the footing he chose to maintain with the man others looked upon as in his closest interest and confidence. But it was necessary to speak to the foreman of it now; and Morgan knew what he was wanted in the office for.

Even now, Lyman so disliked to open the matter that he was silent for a moment after that first inquiry and answer.

Morgan could not wait.

"S'pose you 'll shet down on them mouldin's an' mullions, for a while?" he said, interrogatively, in his turn.

"Yes; I sent for you to say that."

"How do y' expect to git red on 'em, these dull times?"

"I don't expect; further than to do the right thing, and take what comes."

"Hope 't won't be no serious set-back to you, sir."

No answer.

"Mr. Schott, look here! I 've ben with you for fifteen year an' more. I told ye awhile back I 'd something laid by; now, if you should find yourself in anything of a little tight place, temperairy, — I know it could n't only be temperairy, — just remember, will ye, it 's kindly at your service."

It was a pretty good little speech, if an honest man had made it.

Morgan twisted his hat-rim modestly, as he spoke, shyly offering his small help; but he leered out of his eye-corners all the same.

Lyman did not look round. He felt the unpleasant encroachment of Morgan's nearer pressure to his side, but he kept busy with his papers.

"Thank you, Rawson," he said, quietly. "I should not take that except on the terms that were impossible before, and are impossible now."

The leer darkened into wrath and threatening, but was still held in leash in the corner of the ugly eye.

"Yer mean ter say that yer would n't have me in — on a small share — nohow?" he demanded.

"That 's about it, Morgan; though I did n't put it so."

"You hain't got no sale for them flumdiddlums," — Morgan was rapidly growing dialectic, — "nor yit fer all the extry stock, — *'less 't was to the insurance companies*," he added, in low, slight italics.

Lyman hardly noticed. He was really very busy. "Looks about so," he repeated. He did not want either advice or commiseration from this man.

Morgan still lingered. He drew yet a little nearer. He had two cards in his hand to play; one he must indicate with the greatest caution. He scarcely expected to take the trick with that; still there was a possibility, — everything was possible to the father of temptations and lies; every man had his price, he believed, though it might not always be in money. This was a money question, first; but it touched that which came closer, — Lyman Schott's lifelong pride in his inherited and well-augmented business. Morgan had been watching for such a chance for years; he would not let it go by now for want of trying.

The other card, — well, it would change the character of the game; it would be thoroughly against Lyman that he should play that; a card of revenge, also a play of self-defense in a last emergency; for the present crisis of affairs would prompt a pretty general review and estimate of things, and Rawson Morgan could not afford an over-hauling when he might not be there to shift and count.

"I did n't ask nothin' o' you, Lyman, except leave to help a little. Every little dooes help ; I 've got ten thousand, and I could have the command of five more. 'T was at yer service, as I said. I 'd run most any resk fer you, Lyman." The men had been youths together, working on the wharves and in the mill with Joshua Schott ; and they called each other now and then, when the one wished to be a little kind, and the other insinuating, by their Christian names. "I never supposed ten thousand, nor even fifteen, would fill the bill ; you should have more if I 'd got it. But if you won't have it of me, there 's no more to say."

"No," said Lyman, "there 's no more to say, beyond my thanks. I would n't take your money without doing what you 've always wanted for it. I hope I don't need it ; I certainly don't want any partnership."

Then Morgan showed stealthily a corner of the card he could play, but so as it could be withdrawn with due safety. To know at the instant which he must decide, he keenly watched the sidewise face his employer showed him ; he was ready for the first twitch of a muscle, either way.

He assumed a quite fresh tone. "All right, then ; that matter 's done with. If you change your mind, the money 's there, that 's all. But, speakin' of insurance, I jest meant to ask if you had looked up them old policies lately, an' *how much they was fer ?* "

His enunciation grew slow and careful ; his italics were very soft and slight ; his eye fastened itself like a leech upon Lyman's cheek, temple, brow ; he would rather have that half-face, his own being shielded, than encounter openly the whole.

"There 's the overside wharf, — the' ain't so much stock there now as the' was ; but I alwers said, you know, it was the reskiest place : right in the cove, with them dry pastures overhead each side; there 's so many *grass-fires* these droughty times."

"I 'll take care of the insurance; that is n't in your charge," said Lyman, shortly. He still but half attended to his manager's persistent broaching of impertinent topics; he had some difficult papers to look through; he had purposely sent for Morgan at a time when he might see that he was occupied, and must be brief. His brows knit; Morgan saw that.

"Well, never mind. Thought I 'd mention it. The cove wharf is my look-out you know, chiefly, as to handling. I say, Lyman,"—the card was out between his fingers now; a black ace; it almost dropped;—"ye 've paid a lot o' money to them companies, fust an' last; ef it 's all true they say about bread on the waters, you need n't want much better luck "—

He never finished his sentence. Without one warning change of muscle, Lyman's face squared suddenly round. A back-handed stroke across the miserable, mean, dishonest lips stopped their speech. Lightning, such as no stormy cloud ever sent forth, fell upon him out of Lyman's righteous eyes.

"Get out of my way, *Satan!* " he thundered. " I know you now. You are what I have suspected. You 've been robbing me, all along; and now you think I 'd let you help me rob other people! Quit!' "

He was on his feet; his face was pale; he was awfully angry.

Rawson Morgan cowered; he half turned to go, but he stopped, in a shrunken, dogged defiance, to withdraw his play with a threatening sneer.

"Ye 're all-fired pious an' mealy-mouthed, Lyman Schott! *one side on yer!* Butter would n't melt there, while anybody was lookin'. But t'other, — Lo'd Amighty's own words ain't too big ner too blastin' fer yer! Yer 've jumped too quick, though; shows what 's in yer own mind. '*Looked about so*' to yer, a minute ago. I c'n swear ter that!"

For all reply, Lyman made one slow step toward him, the lightning streaming vivid from his eyes.

The sneak, the bully, the scoundrel, backed then, and got the door between them. Down the dark stairs he went with a muttering roar, into the covering whirl and roar of the machinery.

"By the ——!" and he uttered with blasphemous lips the highest title, name, and attribute to seal his devilish vow, "if I don 't slap that back in your own face, with smart and ache and shame, may I be —— to everlastin' blazes!"

He ground the last words hard between his teeth; for some one brushed lightly past him at the stairway foot.

He went off through the din of the moulding-room, past the men working at their different noisy posts; black, frowning, his eyes determinedly cast down.

"The news is true," the men said. "And it must be bad enough."

But the labor went on; the wheels whirled, and not a hand paused from its duty. Every man there would have worked on for Lyman Schott, till he himself gave word to stop, whether the pay should come or not.

Rawson Morgan walked down between huge piles of lumber to the waterside. He lived beyond the hill, across the river; the stream ran narrow here, between the wharves, and a light little foot-bridge, with a hand-rail, made communication; it was always his way of going to and fro; and the "overside" lumber was, as he had said, his particular charge.

Morgan sat down upon the river-wall below the looming heaps that stood like buildings in great blocks far behind and above him, toward the mill. The cove wharf lay obliquely downwards from these main piles upon the hither bluff. The land opposite rose suddenly from the farther brink, making an amphitheatre-like bend around the pier, that crossed and filled nearly the entire water-space. All these brinks, and the rising upland beyond, were overhung and covered with pasture grass and shrubbery. It would be, as Morgan had suggested, a wild place for a grass-fire.

The opposite wharf looked well stocked; it presented a but slightly broken front of edgewise boards, solid stacks of fine clapboards and shingles, with long-lying parallels of joist timbers at either end. A fair bit of property by itself; only Morgan knew how the body of it was thinned out, beyond what the record of true sales would show.

He sat and regarded it morosely; looking up and down the river at all bearings, holding up his hand once or twice, to feel the way of the wind.

"It's got to happen, anyhow," he mused; "that's decreed. It *would* have ben with a light wind, like this, *down stream from the cove,* ef he had n't ben a blasted pig-head; ef he had n't *struck,* —— ! Now, the wind'll be *up river,* — don't take so much difference in these crooks t' make it so, 's fer 's the mill's concerned, — a leetle south, — the dry-spell wind, that's working round again now, an' that alwers blows up full strength just afore a shift fer rain. It'll last this way fer a week 'r two, like 's not; let it! an' then fer a breeder, — an' between that an' a sea-turn, Mr. Schott, ef things should transpire ' a-ba-out so,' 't was only the way it '*looked*' t' yerself, aforehand. *I* sh'll be up to Hopper's Falls, bein' 's you 're done with me; yer need n't look t' me, less 't was ter testify!"

He sat silent a minute or two longer; then he got up,

put on his hat, that he had been holding in his hands, crowded it down upon his head viciously, and took his way across the bridge and the lumber-pier, and over the hillside, through the dry, wild herbage and shrubbery that showed scarcely a noticeable freshening from the rain of yesterday, after the long scorching of the August sun.

XXXI.

SERENA had come over to The Knolls that morning, as soon after breakfast as she had made sure that Peace Polly was not coming, the very first thing, to her.

Peace Polly had her mind full of her brother; of Serena also. She was in doubt how to meet her friend; whether to go to her or not; what to tell her, — what to ask her, or to refrain from asking. How was she to meet her at all, with this unspoken thing between them?

Serena came over, heart and eyes full; words of eager inquiry on her lips. As soon as she saw Peace Polly's face, she knew, though it was not troubled, or even uncheerful, that there was something in it that had not been there when she saw her last. A certain calm, high cheer sat there, as if enthroned amid all else that some new, deep experience of the days had brought forth. And a dignity of reserve, a kind of waiting judgment, was in the eyes and on the composure of the lips, as she moved to meet her, and gave her first greeting. It was as if they had changed ages suddenly.

"Peace Polly," said the elder woman, looking up to the girl who stood so tall and grave and serene, "the news is true, then? Oh, I am so sorry!" and she kept the one hand Peace Polly had given her in a close hold, and put forth her own other hand to cover it.

Peace Polly felt so stiff, so dumb! her eyes would stay so unmovingly on Serena's face! She did not mean to look so; it was as if something took possession of her, and looked through her, refusing to look otherwise.

"Are you?" she asked, slowly, almost dreamily.

"Why, Peace Polly! what should I be? the old friend of years! — Tell me, how does Lyman take it?"

"Lyman takes it like a strong man; no, he takes it like a child of God!"

"Oh, is it so great a trouble, then?" cried Serena. "Will it mean great changes to him?"

"I do not know about the changes; I do not think he does. Why, Serena, *this* is not great trouble to him; it is worry, it is uncertainty; loss, more or less, — he does not know. It is hard work, disappointment; but not great trouble. I think people cannot have that, really, more than once in all their lives."

"Peace Polly, child, how different you are! What makes you so? What else has happened? What are you thinking of? What are you meaning?"

Then the something in Peace Polly that would look forth from her still eyes took speech, and uttered itself as involuntarily through her lips.

"I am meaning what he has borne all these years, and I never knew. All these years that you have been saying to me, 'Lyman Schott is a good man!' Just that; you have kept saying that, Serena; that was all you had for him. And he — had all for you!"

Every bit of color fled from Serena's face. She dropped Peace Polly's hand out of hers, and slid down into a chair. She looked up, as one suddenly arraigned for an old, long-covered guilt.

"You know *that*, Peace Polly? Did he tell you?" The one question sounded of dismay; the other had in it some strange leap of gladness, or of hope.

"No, indeed; he never said one word. He has just

taken what you laid on him, and borne it. But I know. Oh, Serena, *this*, now, is not the trouble of his life. How could you do it? How could you keep to it, all this time that he has waited? And you only saying of him, always, He is a good man!"

She stood like the woman's accusing angel, — this girl who had been petulant with her brother, who had gone to the other with complaints of little things, who had been vexed to hear her answer always, not understanding her sisterly need or pain, "Lyman Schott is a good man."

"Did you wait for him to be better?"

Peace Polly uttered the question, as she had said all else, as if it were put upon her so to do. A subtle irony accented the slow words. They went straight to Serena Wyse's conscience. She *had* waited for him to be better. What right had she had to claim, to postpone, like that?

But something else came back to her, and she justified herself.

"Peace Polly," she said, as quietly as Peace Polly had spoken to her, "I should not have done it, — that second time, — if it had not been for you. You had just quarreled with him, you wanted to live separate, and he came to me. I could not take him so, in a resentment, and away from you."

Then the reproachful spirit that had possessed and used the young girl left her, deserted her. It went over swiftly, and sat in those other gently remonstrant eyes. Peace Polly's hands, that had clasped each other firmly, fell to her sides. A keen arrow-shaft went through her of perception, of remorse.

"There was a second time?" she cried. "Did I do that, Serena? Am I to blame for that, too? Oh, where is the end of my mistakes? But how could I know?" she began again. "It was years before, and it changed him.   You are to blame for *me*, Serena!   If you did not break his heart you twisted it, you shut it up.   I did not even have my whole brother.   And I did not know!"

Peace Polly sat down in another chair and cried.   Serena got up, then, and came over to her.   "What are we two doing for him now?" she said.   "You are still his sister, and I his friend.   Why don't we strengthen the things that remain?"

And then the two women put their arms around each other, and cried together, as women do when quarrel and forgiveness have both been because of love.

"Do not tell Lyman I have been here, please!" Serena said to Peace Polly, when, after a little embracing and a few self-accusing words and a little comforting each way, she got up to go home.

Peace Polly would not let a tacit promise pass without knowing why.   If they were to strengthen the things that remained, she would keep in mind the first part of that sentence, and "be watchful."

"Why not?" she asked.

"Because I have an errand to him," said Serena, "and I must do it, just as I meant and wanted to do it days ago. I have been thinking; I have been afraid; this is not the first of it, to me; but I did not suppose it would come so soon.   I am his friend, you know, Peace Polly."

Peace Polly felt a little anxious misgiving.   Lyman was so stiff, she thought, in some things.

"Are you sure it is a real sensible errand?" she asked, with a bit of a smile.   "Lyman is so particular with his friends."

"It is something I have wanted of him, and that I want now.   I shall ask him, just the same," Serena said.

XXXII.

SERENA'S ERRAND.

As the creature of darkness, breathing evil breath, went on down the passage from the stair-foot to the big swing-door that opened into the machine-room, a creature of light, all full of sweet pulses of love and peace, glided upward through the gloom, making her own sunbeam as she went.

Serena stood and knocked at Lyman's counting-room door.

"Come in!" The words were half questioning, half repellent, in their utterance. How differently, indeed, those two words can be spoken! How differently our hearts speak them to whatsoever may be knocking there!

Lyman did not think that Rawson Morgan had turned back upon him with any new crawl, or slaver, or sting; but that he was near, and might have done so, put the doubt and half-repulse into his voice. Besides, to our humanity, the receding edge of any sphere that has crossed and touched our own will qualify it in the reception of the next that may approach, however contrasting and amending this may prove.

"It is I. Shall I trouble you?" came the gentle answer, and Serena Wyse was in the opened doorway.

Lyman came down off his high desk-stool. "You, Serena!" he exclaimed, and he hastened to meet her and to put a chair for her.

"Yes, Lyman. I have an errand. I won't keep you long."

Not a word of any news, not a look of any anxiety or asking; simply an errand.

"First," she said, "tell me this. You believe I always say just what I mean, just what is true?"

"I have always had reason to think so," Lyman answered, not without a touch of fine significance.

"Then take every word as I say it now, will you?"

"I'll try; but, Serena, there may be some words — Don't give me any that would be hard to answer!"

She did not stop to invent a meaning for his words that might have troubled or shamed her. She would have known that he would speak none such. She went straight to her purpose.

"My errand had been waiting for a week." She paused, as if to bid him note that as a bit of statement, and receive it on the compact of full reliance. "I have been thinking, wishing, hesitating, — not on my own account, but only how to bring my wish to you. Lyman, I have had some investments come back upon my hands, — some expired bonds. I have been uncertain for a long time what I could do when they fell in. And now they have come, and I have thought I would rather the money should go into some work where I could have a pleasure in it, as you men do, than into a corporation. Don't say anything. Don't stop me. Listen! If it had not been for coming to you — just you — with such a thing," — Serena said this bravely, that he might feel all the more surely that her plain business meaning was true, — "I should have asked you sooner if you could use it; if you would let me put that much into your work here, and how much interest you could pay me? It is fifteen thousand dollars. It has been in trust bonds of a Boston company for as many years.

I mean for fifteen," she added, laughing at herself; but at once resuming, " Now I want it near home."

It was every word true, as she had said. It was a woman's notion, to whom business, while subject to its own laws and limits, is yet a piece and part of the eternal life that men are living. She wanted her money to go somehow into that, where she could see what it was doing, whom it was helping, what it meant and stood for, besides her coupons. And it was also just as true, though she did not feel bound to put it on that ground, that Lyman Schott, under the pressure of his accumulating care and responsibility, was the man whose work she wanted it to help. Perhaps some indistinct idea had come in that he would be more careful, would be less likely to take bold, harassing risk, if her little property were with his own. And without a perhaps she had watched his anxieties, had feared for some burden under which he might be bending too nearly to the giving way; and with a woman's whether or no, which is her final argument, had made up her mind.

Lyman was a very perplexed and astonished man. When a man is astonished and perplexed, it is his ordinary nature to be a little vexed as well.

" Twice in one morning ! " he ejaculated, involuntarily, with wonder and slight impatience. " Serena," collecting himself, " you are good — too good; but " — the slight impatience recurring, in spite of what touched him in her offer — " it is a mistake. I don't want anybody's money."

He might have said something different from that. Was she " anybody " ? Yet she bore that, even, and whatever other misconstruction might be put upon her persistence.

" Lyman," she said, " try to think it is a man-friend instead of me, — a man, who ought to know perfectly well what he was about."

"But it is n't, and you don't. *He* would n't, just at this moment. Have n't you heard, Serena, that the Hathertons have failed?"

"Yes, since I made up my mind; but that has n't altered it, not a particle, either way. I know you, and that you have n't chanced anything that you could n't honestly meet. Only — yes, I was glad that I had it; because I know this much of business, that when a person has a good deal out, even a little may come in at a welcome time. I know there are corners to time; if this would be the least help to you round this one, — but I did n't offer it for help," she ended. "I would like to have it here."

She returned to her first position, and made her stand there, shutting up her lips. She could say just so much, with truth; yet she must be cautious of any unconsidered multiplication of words.

"Won't you do it for me?" was all she added, after a moment's silence.

"I have just refused to do a — no, it was n't a similar, it was precisely a contrary, thing," said Lyman, an odd expression flitting over his face as he corrected himself. "Did n't you meet Rawson Morgan on the stairs?"

"Somebody passed me. Was that Morgan? I did n't see. He was grumbling, Lyman; he was angry. What had you done?"

"I 've sent him off; he 's a scheming rascal. I ought to have sent him off long ago; but I was n't sure. He has been fishing for a partnership this good while; and he thought, now, I was to be bought! — *bought* into a piece of knavery! I don't want any partnerships; I don't want anybody's money risked. I 've always paddled my own canoe, and I 'm not going to take in help now, because rapids are in sight. All the same, I thank you, Serena. I knew, without this, that you were my friend." And he held out a warm, steady hand. "You must n't mind my being plain. I 've no time to chisel my sentences. I 've heavy work to do, and the whole load is left on my shoulders. Yet I 'm relieved he 's gone."

Serena was dumb. He "did not want partnerships." That word silenced her. She knew he did not mean it to; that it was accidental, its touching her; but she had got her refusal, and her remonstrances were at an end. Only she said, as he still held her hand kindly, and she looked up, pure and brave, into his face, —

"If you *were* in the rapids, Lyman, and I could throw you a rope, would n't you let me ?"

"Not that kind of a rope. I tell you, Serena, I would n't involve anybody. If you were my — if you were Peace Polly, I would not use your money so."

He had not called her his sister, as he seemed to have come near to do; or had he begun to say just that ? She was glad he had stopped short of it; something made her hand tremble a little in his, and she withdrew it.

She took up another matter.

"It troubles me that you should have made an enemy just now, and that you should be left alone."

"One is better without an enemy inside the camp, surely," returned Lyman.

"But he 's a snake," said Serena. A woman, since Eve's day, could scarcely say more than that, of contempt or dread.

"I 've had warning," said Lyman. "I 've heard his rattle. I 'm not afraid."

"But he 's off in the grass," said Serena. "You don't know where he is, or how he 'll strike."

"An honest man is not afraid," repeated Lyman. "He 's better off than on."

"Good-by," said Serena, lingeringly. "I 've done my

errand, and I 've failed, for now. But if you ever think differently " —

" I hardly ever do 'think differently,' " said Lyman, smiling. And his eyes had that steadfast look that in some things people read for obstinacy. Serena knew that it meant one truth for everything, all back into all the years; back to where he had first left her so, and on through all the time that afterward he had stayed away. She knew now, — for she never doubted Peace Polly's certainty of something more than she had said ; she had not dared to question her further, but her charge had driven conviction straight home with it, — she knew now the one deep thing, deeper than she had ever seen or understood, that it had been with him, and that he had not "thought differently."

But she knew also that in that unwaveringness of his were decisions not to be reconsidered.

She could only hope to be his friend, — it was all she had left to herself, — but she would be that until she died.

He went with her to see her safely down the dark stairway. In the passage below, he took a little key from his pocket, and opened a side door into the sunshine. Ho would not let her go down through the machine-room, past all those men.

When he reached his office again, he stood thinking a moment before he went back to his desk.

" Two partnerships," he said to himself, with a queer humor : " one that I would n't have, and one that would n't take me. And both, with just those dead weights against them, coming to me to-day with money. Life 's a strange thing, and worlds are mixed. The devils and the angels go up and down together ; no wonder we want the telling of the sure foundation. 'The Lord knoweth them that are his!' and if He knows that, He knows the rest of it, — them that are each other's, and how to sort us out at last.　It's all one!"

And with that, he set his brows, and went back to his books again.

XXXIII.

IN individual life, in families, in communities, in nations, in the church, and in the world, it is undoubtedly and historically true that not only one event brings on another, in natural cause and sequence, and thus that things gather to epochs; but also that quite different and unconnected occurrences come and crowd toward one point, like meteoric showers through which the earth's path passes. Cause and connection are simply in the realm above our cognizance; reason why is in the Thought that no man can search or fathom.

Follow any little human story, however simple, and you will come to such conjunctures; in a made-up story, if stories ever are or can be entirely that, people say it is all in the make-up. Very well; we transcribers will patiently suffer the accrediting that is thrust upon us, and only tell the tales as we feel them told.

Bonnyborough was having enough to talk and to think of in these days; enough that transpired openly, and interested all. Underneath, and quietly alongside and interwoven, a great deal that it did not know was working. It was a mercy to the general sanity that it could not know all. Did you ever think what would become of us if we should be possessed of all, in every detail, that is happening around us? We pick curiously at the presented edges; we guess, and peer, and theorize; and we do not know that if we were obliged to know all we should be possessed indeed by the legion that would drive us wild.

Dr. Blithecome was buried on the Saturday. Everybody went to the funeral; everybody was in tears. A good, faithful, helpful life was ended; a face had vanished that had carried cheer wherever it went; a strength and wisdom had been withdrawn in the safety of which mothers of little children had slept secure that it was close by, sufferers had borne their pain better in the intervals between the encouragements and assuagings of its presence, they who knew they must die had looked forward more bravely to the last dark hour, for the hope that when the Lord should stand by in spirit to receive their souls the good doctor would stand upon the earthly side to minister to the last bodily need and extremity.

There would be a time when Bonnyborough would not be sure whom it had for a doctor; and this is a terrible interregnum to a country folk.

There were three new tin signs in the village, already; these always freckle out quickly enough. There was Dr. Fuller, whom everybody knew the old doctor had chosen and preferred. But here came in the question and the talk; would he stay among them? Along after this trailed the whole fragmentary hearsay from which were to be gathered pros or cons.

Why was he here, away from his home and his wife? Why was his wife off there in Europe? What separated them, and in fact who knew anything about them? Would he come here without his family? Would he bring his family here? Would the family ever consent to be brought? Would it be a comfortable sort of thing, any way, for Bonnyborough people?

Meanwhile, the sick ones, to a patient, following their dear doctor's last wishes and advice, sent for Dr. Fuller.

He was their remedy prescribed. The matter was like to settle itself, provided Dr. Fuller would remain. And so the discussion completed its continued round, and reverted to the first question.

Then, there was Lyman Schott's trouble. Everybody knew that it was a trouble, and everybody wondered, with more or less of sympathy, how far it would go. Necessarily, his history had to be discussed, also. He had buried himself in his mill and his lumber-piles; he had kept himself aloof from everything else, and from almost everybody; how would it be with him if he lost his money, and his business broke down? Had n't he been laying up too much of his treasure on earth? Some of the goody ones wondered that, who had never seemed to have very much treasure themselves to invest anywhere.

Miss Serena did not escape. She was "great" with the Schotts in these days. Everybody knew how much more The Knolls and the Wyse-Place had been neighboring after the old fashion; the latter was pretty much the only house Lyman ever did go to; and though time had been, and a good long time, when it was the special one he stayed away from, people could remember things before that, even. All was resuscitated, now, and re-descanted on; a real good old tale, half forgotten, and well brought up again, has a charm, sometimes, beyond even that of a new, contemporaneous fiction. Bonnyborough could have solved all Lyman's troubles for him, very comfortably, it thought, if only he had not always been such an odd stickleback of a man; and Serena, — well, they had n't made her out; they did n't know, to tell the truth, what she had been, a fool or a wise woman.

And in her turn came up Peace Polly; after her, on the docket, in suggestive association, — though semi-detached in the gossipry of the place since Miss Mallis's diversion and shrewdly sown, untraceable bits of contrary comment, — the new young rector; the Institution, which was to be so soon; the Bishop's visit, following after; the Confirmation, and the candidates.

Peace Polly, once more.   Would n't she be confirmed? She was n't in the class; and why not? Then the young clergyman again, and Rose Howick?? Here were double interrogation-marks, and no satisfactory answer to any-thing.

Bonnyborough had more upon its hands than it could well attend to.

In the midst of all these interests and agitations Peace Polly went quietly to Dr. Farron.

"It is not you I want; it is the rector," she said to Mrs. Dora, who met her eagerly and kindly at the door.

"I 'm glad of it," said the rector's wife; " yet all the same, I 'm glad to see you myself. I know my place; I can give way modestly; but I 'm glad to show you in." And she led her along to the study door, and threw it open. " Sebastian," she said, " here 's Peace, — come to your house and you, without an invocation."

"Wifie!" remonstrated Dr. Farron, rising and turning round. But "Wifie" was gone, and the door was shut. He came forward to Peace Polly, and held out both his hands. "I am very glad to see you, my child," he said. "I knew you would come."

"Then may be you know why," said Peace Polly, let-ting him seat her beside him on the long, deep sofa that filled the alcove of the pleasant garden-window.

"Because the dear Lord has led you," said Dr. Farron. "And because I knew He was bringing you his own way, I have not said a word before."

Peace Polly did not answer that for a minute or two.

"I was going to say," she said then, " that I had come

now, because so many things are happening that I might get interrupted and prevented. But you have explained everything," she added, shyly. "Only we have to say why we think we have done things, you know."

" ' As from ourselves, yet knowing that it is from the Lord.' A very wise man said that, himself led and enlightened," said Dr. Farron. "It is a good word, — a great word, well spoken ; only some have forgotten that it and others have been given before, among the 'all things necessary to our salvation.' Why, do you think," the good man asked, carefully adhering to her own phrase, "you have not come sooner ?·"

"I have not wanted to do anything just by the book," Peace Polly answered, speaking low, yet firmly.

" I think I understand," returned the old rector. " You wish that everything you do shall be very real ? "

"Yes. I almost think that if everything done by the Prayer-Book were done *really* we might not have need of it any more, at all. And if it is *not* " —

She stopped. The rector passed over, for the moment, the last unfinished word, though the drift of their alternative was obvious enough.

" If it were," he said, "it would be the kingdom of heaven realized, and we should be in the Church Triumphant. To that very end we want now that which teaches and leads us continually in the ways of the kingdom. The Prayer-Book is the Church's showing forth of that which shall be, in the King's name, until He come. The children of the Church have the pattern of the things in the heavens, that they may live more and more into them. And every promise is an 'I will, *with the help of God.*' ' Our help is in the Name of the Lord.' "

"But it is so easy to say words, Dr. Farron ! And whole congregations saying them every Sunday ; and the world-congregation, what it is, all the week through, after all ! ”

“Nevertheless, ‘ the Lord *is* in his holy temple ; ’ and his temple is his Word, and his Church, and every separate human heart. He will make a congregation of clean hearts, with the truth in them, at last, Peace ! ‘ In every place incense shall be offered to his name, and a pure offering.’ Did it ever occur to you that his Name is every word by which He has spoken himself, in sign or speech ? And how shall we learn without a preacher ? It must be set forth to us, and we must look to it, and search to know it, and live it out, by little obediences, one by one, until the kingdom comes to us. If we had not the word, how should we ever reproach ourselves for not having that which the word stands for ? ‘ My Word ! ’ ‘ my Name ! ’ they are what He has proclaimed to us, in all his dealing and teaching. ‘ Heaven and earth shall pass away, but my word shall not pass away, in no wise, not in one jot or one tittle, till all be fulfilled.’ ‘ Blessed is the man who cometh in the Name of the Lord ! ’ ”

The good rector spoke that which burned up from his heart ; his face was lighted with it ; his eyes were lifted, like pure flames that sought upward.

Peace Polly was moved ; she was drawn upward also. “ I am glad I came to you,” she said.

“ And you will come for the promise, and the blessing ? ” Dr. Farron asked.

Then Peace Polly spoke to him from out her heart : telling him of her faults, her struggles, her mistakes ; of things that it was her fault now that they were not otherwise for others ; of the poor thing she had made of her life, so far ; of the little, and the spoilt, it was, to bring and make an offering of, — all this not in full, measured sentences, or careful detail of circumstance, but as the minister drew her on and helped her see and show herself, that he might see how to give her the help he was intrusted with.

"It is all so miserable, so frittered into bits, so out of joint," she said. "And how can I tell that it will be any better?"

"You are told how, my child; *you* could not tell. It is when we feel all broken up and wasted, and that we can only bring the bits to God, that He says Come, and He will take us, and mend us, and make us whole again. 'The sacrifices of God are a broken spirit;' 'rend your heart, and turn unto the Lord your God, for He is gracious and merciful, and of great kindness, and repenteth *Him* of the evil.' What is that but the word to come to Him, with the broken and rent of our lives and our selves, as a child to its mother with a torn garment, that it may be made good again, and that new may be given? 'He repenteth *Him;*' He takes the turning and changing upon Himself. And hear what the Lord Jesus Christ says, — 'Blessed are the poor in spirit; for theirs is the kingdom of heaven!' and think, too, that it was his own body that was broken for our bodies, his own life that was poured out for our lives! Was not that 'repenting *Him*'?"

"Broken for our *bodies?*" repeated Peace Polly, inquiringly, as with surprise.

"'That our bodies may be made clean by his body,' — that is what we pray in the Communion service," returned the Doctor. "Is not the body the form of life, the clothing and the circumstance of it, the garment of spirit? Is not that what we have spoiled, and want to have made clean again? Did He not lay aside his heavenly garment, that He might stoop down to wash even our feet?"

"Oh, is all that in those words?" cried Peace Polly, with a great gladness.

"All that, and more. In every word, there is the saving, the enlightening, the whole mystery of the eternal life. They are miracle-doors into the everlasting glory. It seems as if it hardly mattered which were opened to us. And we have them all there, kept and handed down to us through the blessed company that has believed, and has had the sight."

Peace Polly stood up. She felt as if she could not hear any more, just now. She had thought about "experiencing her Prayer-Book." Was this but the beautiful beginning of it? What should the great, the exhaustless fulfillment of it be?

She stood silent. Dr. Farron took her hand within his own, and stood silent also.

"I will come," said Peace Polly, then, softly.

"The Lord bless thee, and keep thee; the Lord lift up his countenance upon thee, and give thee peace!"

As the good clergyman uttered his benediction, the girl felt as if she had received her name in a new baptism.

She smiled, and went away. As she stood upon the doorstep, she made one request. "Don't speak of it, please, Dr. Farron," she said. "Except, if you wish, to Mrs. Farron. I don't want to talk any more, and I don't want other people to talk at all."

"It shall be as you wish," the Doctor told her.

XXXIV.

If Dr. Farron had waited for and expected Peace Polly, he certainly had never, in like manner, waited for or expected the visitor who came to him twenty-four hours later, and was shown in as she had been.

Dr. Fuller was an old friend; he was familiar at the rectory, but he had not been in the habit of seeking Dr. Farron in his study for any especial, private conversation. He seemed rather, in their intercourse, to have avoided opportunity or topic that might have led to personal discussion of the things of Dr. Farron's ministry. The rector knew as little of the physician's inmost mind upon those subjects as it is possible for one friend to know of another. He could only judge by what the other chose to show. There was never slighting, cavil, or irreverence; there was simply silence. When scientific interest, or the sympathies of life, touched that verge where it would seem reserve must lift a little, showing that what had seemed distant was not really separate, but only a more glorious reach in the same direction, the horizon-line fixed itself as if among great mountains, always there, but not to be unveiled by any small comparative approach; waiting, in remote sublimities, until the traveler should be himself among them.

It was not Dr. Fuller's way to declare, or to impose, conclusions; the habit of his mind and search was to show that which led toward them, — it might be very closely;

even so, he would draw back when he had done, and leave others to conclude, or to draw uncertain inference of his own persuasions. Many a help to deep and strong analogy, or immediate mighty indication, had the man of science given to the man of faith, but he left them with him there; of his own faith he said, directly, nothing.

So now, when Dr. Farron put aside the sheets of the sermon he was writing, and came forward with ready welcome, he had no least suspicion of the present errand of the man before him.

But Dr. Fuller was not a person to put off an explanation, or to make many words where he had first made up his mind.

"I have come," he said, "to ask to be enrolled."

"Enrolled! My dear sir! — is it possible you mean in the Church?"

"Possible, and true. I have never done it before."

"And why not?" was the natural inquiry; but Dr. Farron did not put it. He waited for his friend's next word. He was very wise in waiting, this tarrier for the Lord.

"It is not that I have not believed," said Dr. Fuller. "Perhaps it is rather that — so far as I have got — I have believed more than I have always found set for me. I have never wished to take upon me that whose full meaning seemed to me so tremendously more than it was generally accepted for."

Dr. Farron sat still, and thought within himself: "Here are two real souls, with the same thought in them! Do they know, or divine it, of each other, I wonder?"

Instead of saying that, however, he asked Dr. Fuller if he thought the general acceptation would be made the larger or truer for the holding back of such as saw what he saw.

"Not at all," was the other's answer. "I should only be afraid of falling to the general level myself."

"And what is to keep you up, now?"

"The grace of God, I hope," said Dr. Fuller, simply.

"Forgive me; I do not mean to treat you as a boy; but you interest me greatly. Do you mind my questions?"

"I will answer any that I can answer."

"What has persuaded you, now, of this grace of God?"

"I do not know that I am persuaded differently; I will just come and take it, — if I may."

"Surely you may; but if you have known and believed that it was always there?"

Dr. Fuller turned somewhat more squarely to his companion, and lifted up his head, with a full, declaring look in his serious eyes.

"I have believed that it was everywhere," he said; "for every man, as the truth is, — lying open to the search. I have lived for truth, — I have worked in fact; I have found fact but the outshown presentment of something always greater than itself; of a meaning that lay somewhere in a Mind. Science has never made me doubt; that my thought could search for that which was hidden made me continually sure that the thing hidden was a word, from a Thought also. As to the Church, I have never doubted a revelation committed to men; a spiritual order and fellowship into which God must gather men, to be of his household. I know He could not be, and never say to his children, 'I Am.' And I find this self-presentment in the Christ, as I find the separate presentments of his word in the things that He has made. But I have esteemed the order and fellowship in humanity a more wholly spiritual thing than is set forth in any body;

at least, the feeling of this has kept me from the visible church-membership. I have not questioned that the reality was in the Church, but that it was kept there only. I have not been willing to subscribe to an exclusiveness."

Dr. Fuller paused.

"Was it an exclusiveness in the Lord, and in his Twelve, when they only had the Good News in all the earth?" asked Dr. Farron.

"No. I am quite with you in your principle, in your faith and your argument," said Dr. Fuller; "but men — and bodies of men — have made it exclusive."

"That may be, — that has been, and is. It always must be with imperfect creatures. The disciples asked for them to be utterly forbidden who walked not with themselves. But while this may be the danger, the alternative is a greater danger; the disintegration of Christ's body, until each member says to all the others, I have no need of ye! And I think there must be something exclusive, if you call it so, but not conceit of narrowness, which *has* to exclude all but the simple, common, catholic truth. God is One; his household is one. I cannot find any fellowship which maintains that essential unity of faith and promise of all knowledge, save the historic Christian Church. She stands for that in the integrity of its first commission. She is sure, I believe, to shake off — and doubtless the departures have rebuked her into much shaking off of them — the adhering errors, if only she hold fundamentally to that. The Lord planted in her the mustard seed that was to grow into the great tree, in which all thoughts should find room, all searchings rest. And so, a churchman must needs be a churchman, loyal to his household and his inheritance, though he be called for it a mere ecclesiast and dogmatist. Ecclesiast let him be; since 'Ecclesia' is the 'House,' God's Home with his family."

"Ah, yes," said Dr. Fuller, "if the family abide in the house, — if the life is there; if it be not a mere household of *things* which the heirs of it keep in beautiful order, indeed, from their pride and a certain conscience; paying stewards and housekeepers for the duty; but to and from which they only come and go casually, turning the key meanwhiles, and living, practically, elsewhere. No wonder that sort of living has got into the individual homes, since the spirit of it is in the Church!"

"You are severe, but you are true," said Dr. Farron; "yet I ask, as I asked before, — is it any help to the restoration of the family that any brother of it should say, There is no home, and I will none of it? My friend, the moment the Church, or any appreciable portion of it, absolutely embodies and acts forth its every word of faith, there will be no longer a word of skepticism left against it! The life from God in the world, instant, actual, indisputable, will kill utterly the denial or the doubt of it!"

Dr. Fuller only bowed.

"You have seen that, then?" asked Dr. Farron.

Dr. Fuller inclined his head again. "I have seen," he said, "that the Lord will have enlisted soldiers. The guerrilla may be true and brave; he may fight well upon the mountains; none the less the Captain calls his followers by name into his columns, that He may lead them as one man. I will enlist, Dr. Farron."

There were not many more words between them then; the faces of both shone as they looked upon each other, as they rose and took each other by the hand, and moved toward the door.

On the threshold, Dr. Farron recalled what had been said there by Peace Polly and himself.

"Have you spoken of this?" he asked Dr. Fuller.

"To no one; it had better not be talked of."

"Quite so," returned the rector, "but — I think, if I were you, I would speak of it, at home, — to Miss Schott."

Dr. Fuller glanced up, surprised. "And why to her?" he asked, rather quickly.

"To avoid any disturbing consciousness of surprise," answered Dr. Farron. "I think, my dear friend, if you take my advice, you will see that I have been right."

I do not mean to put down the conversation which resulted between Dr. Fuller and Peace Polly. It was but brief; and it would be, in some points, to repeat what each had said separately to Dr. Farron. In saying it to each other, doubtless, two friends, two "real souls, with the same thought in them," could not do other than come wonderfully near. But that nearness would belong to themselves, and to no one else. It would be even more sacred than any tale, or interview, of human love.

XXXV.

LYMAN went to and from the mill with but brief home intervals. He often stayed at evening, until bedtime; until after that which had been his wont, rather, for his bedtimes now became very much postponed. He sometimes asked Peace Polly to put up for him, or to send down, a midday lunch. He had frequently to drive over to East Bend. There were creditors' meetings, and there were interviews with the Company, for which the Hathertons had been contracting and building, and of which they were themselves large shareholders. It was a complicated business, a speculation of a new, fast-growing, manufacturing place, of which the Company, with its factories, was the centre, and for whose increasing population its streets and blocks were rapidly stretching out and going up. The private residences of two of the mill-owners were the edifices for which much of Lyman's fine work had been done. A public hall was also being constructed. It was a big enterprise; one of those too suddenly enlarging ones of which very prudent men are sometimes shy. The Hathertons had stopped, because there was trouble behind them. Manufactures were down, just now; there had come a glut in the market of the particular goods which East Bend furnished.

But all this, in the business explanation, cannot well come into our story.

It was enough that the trouble had come round and

touched Lyman Schott; that its tide had spread and shut him in, where deep water might come overhead with him. He grew paler and thinner, from half-resting nights and anxious, overworked days. Two women watched him, with sorrowful, beseeching eyes. They said to each other, "He ought not to overstrain himself so;" and they knew in their hearts that the overstrain was laid upon him, and that he could not help it now.

All Peace Polly could do was to make home brighter, daintier in homely comfort; to have things in readiness at his hours of coming and going, and in waiting, at careful points of preparation, for his uncertainties. She smiled and talked when he seemed to care for it, and she kept silence when he kept silence.

What Serena Wyse could do just now was absolutely nothing.

Dr. Fuller came and went on his physician's rounds; Peace Polly had to calculate and prepare for him also.

After the one talk they had together, nothing more was said between them of their church interest, or of religious matters at all. But there was an unspoken sympathy, a light of friendliness, in their greetings and good-bys, and in all their commonplace, accidental intercourse. In truth, something had become common between them which forever set aside the commonplace. It was that which is in the Creed, after the Holy Ghost and the Church; which is of the Church, — or the Church of it, in the Life of the Spirit. Peace Polly chanted the words softly to herself, sometimes, as she went, all alone up and down the house.

I said just now that Serena Wyse could do nothing.

Nothing outwardly, I mean: she could think little prayers for Lyman in her heart; that he might be strengthened with strength, kept quiet in confidence,.and be delivered from the power of any adversaries. She put that in, always. The Psalms of David were full of petitions framed to her want in these days. I am afraid the denunciatory ones were not altogether out of her mind at times. She had never felt easy about Rawson Morgan; and she was sure, if he could, he would do Lyman a mischief now. Sometimes, — but no soul would ever know that, — she put on a shawl and bonnet in the late evening, and went down across the road and by an upper meadow path that came out behind the village gardens to the high point of the Mill Lane, whence she could see Lyman's light in the counting-room window. Now and then, of a daytime, she would take a good field-glass that had been her father's, and walk through Lyman's own woods to an opening which gave her view all up and down the river landing and the wharves. She hardly knew what she expected, or feared, to see; she wanted to see that all was as usual, and safe. She believed if there were anything happening, ever, that it would be good for her to know, — that it would help or save her friend that she should know, — time and place and presence would be matched accordingly; she was not afraid of the times when she could not watch; she went as she was moved, and her heart kept guard continually.

Except that cares and fatigues wrote their lines and colors on Lyman's face, as they will do through whatever calmness or cheerfulness, the family at home would not have judged him oppressed. He wore no dejection; he carried no flag at half-mast; his tribulation, no more than his prosperity, was a thing prominent. As he had been busy before, he was hard-worked now; he accepted each as its own necessity; he was simply a strong man bearing that which was laid upon him. He ate his meals, and seasoned them with neither sighs nor frowns; he was easier to please, even, than he had sometimes been when his leisure was easier. So that, often, when talk arose among them, and led off in quite other directions, two of them half forgot for the moment what lay behind, and Lyman, if he remembered, did not remind them.

"Your brother is grand," said Dr. Fuller to Peace Polly; but if he had needed to lend his eyes to her before, to see her brother with, he did not need to do it now. Hers flashed up with a glad, proud gratefulness to him for saying it; with no half surprise of pleasure as they had done sometimes.

Dr. Fuller did not speak of his own plans. He did what had fallen into his hands to do; he went where he was called; how long he meant to remain to do this he did not say. He watched for his mails, and received his letters alertly.

One morning they all sat at the breakfast-table in the pleasant open hall. They used it in this way in the summer mornings, often. Lyman had been down to his mill at daylight, and had returned to take the meal with the others, his real breaking of fast having been a bowl of milk hours earlier.

There were flowers on the table; Rebeccarabby's delicate rolls, — one wondered how the dainty things she did produce could come from under her dynamic handling, — a comb of translucent honey, a fragrant, golden-hearted melon, coffee steaming with Arabian perfume, — these did not hint of distress or pressure, either in time or substance. Peace Polly did not mean they should. She had not been to Lyman to beg him to take her separate portion and put it into the lumber-piles with his; she kept the home as she had kept it, as she knew she could go on keeping it, for him, and troubled him with no questions or demands. Things spoke their comfort for themselves.

If Serena could have done this, she might not, either, have gone to him with her fifteen thousand. So far off the very nearest may be put, until their rightful place opens to them, or they accept it. I think Serena, for her one fault, was being chastened now.

A step scraped on the doorstone. Lyman did not notice, and Dr. Fuller sat with his back that way; Peace Polly turned her head to see.

A messenger from the village telegraph-office, with the yellow, black-lettered envelope in his hand.

"Dr. C. P. Fuller," he announced perfunctorily, like a brakeman calling out a railway station, with no interest whatever for those whose destination it might be, upon whatever errand of joy or pain. "Cable."

The last word was uttered with some importance.

Dr. Fuller got up quickly, went and took it, and signed the book.

He stood in the doorway and read it. When he turned round and came back toward them at the table, his face was radiant.

"No bad news, I imagine," said Lyman, with some pleasant, friendly relief in his tone. One does watch rather breathlessly the opening of a telegram ; and this had come with the urgency of that which must be said instantly from over seas.

"No," returned Dr. Fuller ; and his tone ran lightly. "Mrs. Fuller arrives in Boston by the Cephalonia, about the 5th. I must go down then for a day or two. She sends me a message of extravagant length, in the delight of her new affluence, I suppose. An aunt of hers died lately, — I saw the notice at the time. Odd woman ; has n't communicated with Cecilia, who is her namesake, for years ; now she has left her a handsome property."

"I 'm sure I congratulate you both, very much," said Lyman.

Peace Polly said not a word. A color rose upon her face, as the doctor glanced toward her, with a half-inquiring, curious look. Then he answered Lyman.

"You may," he said. "It lifts one great responsibility from my mind. There will be no anxiety about money now, except for the wise and careful spending of it. I hope that will be guarded, somehow."

It was a singular speech for a man whose wife was the person concerned.

Peace Polly ate her melon mechanically. She put a teaspoonful of salt upon it, instead of sugar. But then some people do eat salt with melons. Perhaps she was trying to take it with the estimate of Dr. Fuller which his words and manner might thrust upon her.

"I think," resumed the gentleman, very slowly, "that it removes *one* doubt, — that it may make it possible that I should remain in Bonnyborough."

Two astonished, mystified faces turned upon him.

He looked from one to the other with a quiet smile. He had not meant any little denouement of his own to be sudden or dramatic; but it had come in just this way, and it would be foolish to make a concealment of it any longer. He would not presume to think of any difference it could make, of any preparation needed.

"I do not believe," said he, "that you have ever understood that Mrs. Fuller is only — my sister-in-law?"

"Not Mrs. C. P. at all?" cried Lyman, astounded.

The color in Peace Polly's face rushed and mounted. Her eyes shone; but she kept them steady, and bore her blushing bravely. What he might think, for a moment, she could not tell; but she could afford to carry all the truth in cheeks and eyes. Her friend was vindicated.

"I am so glad!" she said, earnestly, the shining eyes clear and full on his.

Dr. Fuller came close to her end of the table, and touched the hand to it that held the telegram, leaning down a little toward her.

"Why, Miss Peace?"

She was glad he asked her why.

"Because," she answered, and notwithstanding her straight, steady look her voice thrilled a little, — "I have wondered so much, — at her; and it made you seem" —

"How, Miss Peace?"

In the midst of her sweet gladness and frankness a sudden fun sparkled. It came to her relief. The mystical letters flashed up to her out of the alphabet.

"Such a Confusing Paradox," she said.

That was so like Peace Polly; the old Peace Polly, who had not had so much to stop and think for.

The doctor did not fail of her meaning. He had been used to plays and suggestions upon his impenetrable initials. He threw back his head and laughed like a boy.

Then he leaned forward again.

"I think I grow less confusing, to myself, every day. I will try, soon, to explain things a little more clearly to you."

Lyman got up to go. He stopped a moment to say, quaintly, —

"You've been a shrewd man, doctor. Mrs. Fuller has no doubt been a great comfort to you, here in Bonnyborough!"

"Bonnyborough has jumped to its own conclusions, and has made its own mistakes," said Dr. Fuller, laughing.

It seemed, somehow, as if his very life laughed for him, now.

XXXVI.

I HAD got thus far in my writing of the record of these things that happened up in Bonnyborough, when I read it over to a friend.

"Well!" was the exclamation, "I 'm glad Mrs. Dora did n't have a finger in it this time!"

Now I will just pause exactly here, to say a word in justice to Mrs. Dora. She did n't want to have a finger in it. She was quietly and faithfully waiting to see the finger of Providence in it, as she felt assured it would be, having received, as she honestly confessed to herself, a pretty clear intimation that it had no need or work just now for her own. For myself, I like Mrs. Dora, with all her faults, and I know she was a good woman, who meant exceedingly well. Her temptation was that her wits were bright, her heart was warm, and that little finger of hers of a peculiar cleverness. And cleverness cannot help itching, whether in brain or digits.

What Mrs. Dora saw, or thought she saw, to do, she did it with her might. When she saw that she had better do nothing, she did that with her might also. Which I think was the extreme point, after all, both of her cleverness and strength of mind.

Dr. Fuller went to the rectory with his news. Dr. Farron was from home, so he saw Mrs. Dora again in the delicious cosiness of the vine-curtained balcony, and gave it to her.

Mrs. Dora clapped her hands, first with gladness at that which had befallen, and again with ecstatic sense of the flank move upon Bonnyborough gossip.

"It is exquisite!" she exclaimed. "And don't say a word, now, if you can help it, until there really *is* a Mrs. Fuller, a Mrs. C. P., I mean," she added, linking the letters again, softly, with her old mischief.

"There will have to be some very important words spoken before that," suggested Dr. Fuller, smiling.

"Yes, by the important persons. But think of the loveliness of the course of a human event of which no unimportant or impertinent words are spoken!"

"I do feel delightfully relieved," she said to her husband when she reported to him the conversation. "So out of responsibility in the business! It will be such enjoyment just to be holding my tongue and looking on! And the other matter is taking care of itself beautifully, too; I can see that. Better, indeed, than if I had n't meddled. I think, Sebastian, the Lord did make a little use of me, after all. Rose Howick has been growing twice the woman in these last weeks that she ever bid fair to be before."

"I don't think you are altogether clear of responsibility yet, however," remarked Sebastian, quietly. "I think you have mentioned one duty that will give you quite enough to do."

"Sebastian! I never will say anything to you again!"

The next day, late in the afternoon, Dr. Fuller found Peace Polly sitting in her often-wonted place at the fore door. He drew a chair, and sat down near her.

"I have not much of a story to tell, Miss Peace," he said. "But what there is I think you have a right to hear."

Peace Polly lifted her eyes from her work to his face

with a look of listening and thanks. Then she turned again without a word to her twisting of yarn stitches, and he went on.

"I had a dear brother, — little Tom," he said. tenderly. " He was not much more than three years younger than I, but he was always little Tom to me, — even when he went astray. For the world was too much, in some things, for my little brother, Peace."

He did not notice what he had done until an instant later ; but Peace Polly's face took the color of a rose set suddenly in a sunny light.

" He married hastily, as he did everything. His marriage did not help him as it should have done ; Cecilia is not a bad woman, but she was hardly woman enough for that which she undertook. It was eager young fancy, on both sides. Her friends were bitterly opposed, and we could hardly blame them ; the less, that we were not desirous of the match for Tom, either. By and by Cecilia got discouraged ; then came unhappiness ; she reproached him with all that she had given up. He said he would do all he could for her ; he would take himself away. So he did." Dr. Fuller paused here for a few seconds ; Peace Polly breathed softly, and her needle was held still.

" He went away, to Japan ; we never saw him again. He sent home a little money, and after he died — it was a sudden death — there came a letter he had left, written to me. He asked me to take care of his boys. I have done the best I could. I could not always make other plans and do this too ; I have put this first. It was all I could do for little Tom."

Peace Polly felt slow tears escaping from her eyes. She turned a little aside, and brushed them off.

" After all, it was their mother's right to decide much ;

I could not always use my own full judgment. So, among other things, they have gone to Europe. I would rather have made Americans of them, but they may yet be that. I shall always help when I can. Their mother is rich, now ; she will take her own way, and I think she will be glad to be independent of me. So, Miss Peace, I think I shall stay in Bonnyborough now, and try to make a home here, where my boys may sometimes come. If they do, will you, who are my friend, lend them some of your pleasant influence ? "

Peace Polly's eyes were full, and her face was like that sunlit rose. But she looked up straight to Dr. Fuller, and put up her hand to his.

"If I might," she said. "If there was anything possible to me. I can never repay you in any way what you have done for me, Dr. Fuller! You have been strength and comfort to me."

" Have I ? have I that ? " he said, eagerly. " I would be so glad to be ! " Then that curious smile of his played over his face, and he added, quietly, " I think, perhaps, I have understood you, as you should be understood."

"It is so good to have anybody know ! " said Peace Polly, softly, sedately,

Do you suppose Dr. Fuller is going to say more to this girl, now ? Indeed, he knew a great deal better. It was not many days since she had believed that other woman to be his wife. What could have grown in her toward him in these few days ? He had had all summer, if it had needed that, to grow to know her, and to love her, as he owned to himself that he loved her now. He had too much reverence in his love, too much delicate nobleness in his nature, to ask Peace Polly yet if she had learned to care for him. But the gentle light and color in her face, the glad, low way in which she answered to his friendliness, were very sweet and hopeful to him. He replied to her words with something quite apart from self.

"It is good to *know* that anybody knows," he said. "And we are sure that there is nothing really hidden, but that the great, perfect understanding is all about us and through us. There is a world in us, Miss Peace, that God keeps to himself, except when he calls some few souls, with special errand for us, to receive a glimpse. It is full of life, and growths, and wonders, that are to be developed and revealed. We ourselves know not what we shall be; but He knows that we shall be like Him!"

"I see; oh, how beautiful it is, Dr. Fuller! It is the world of the spiritual microscope!"

"It is always what the microscope reminds me of," he answered.

A few moments after that, he went away. "Do not wait tea for me," he told her. "I must take a ride of three or four miles first."

He left her, and went up through the house to the garden side and the stables. He kept a horse here now, at The Knolls. Peace Polly saw him presently, on the handsome black creature, moving quietly down the shaded drive, and then cantering swiftly up the high road under the maple-trees. She put by her work, and walked down the grass-path to the low gate.

Away out westward, from between tall elms, she could see the sun going down in the great, clear sky. Lyman had said he should be late, and she had already told Rebeccarabby that they would not have tea before seven.

It was the loveliest hour in all the day. It seemed, somehow, the loveliest hour to Peace Polly that she had had in all her life.

There was no cloud anywhere. The sunset light rose

and rose from the horizon in an amber tide. It lifted toward the zenith, where it met the blue and turned it to a pale, clear, wonderful chrysoprase. Then the depths eastward took a purple shadow, an intense, restful calm of coming dusk.

But Peace Polly did not look back into the shadows, however softened. They were of the day that had been. She stood and gazed after the sun, where it had flooded over into a marvelous to-morrow, of which the beauty was swept backward, making the afterlight of to-day.

"It is so still, so wide," she said. "There is such a firmament-full of gladness!"

While she spoke within herself, up out of the very glory burst a living cloud. A motion, a joy, swept skyward, higher and higher, from the very horizon line. As it neared, it resolved into myriad separate forms; it was a swallow-flight, that strange, multitudinous one that happens in the late summer. Surging up and up, there seemed no end to its coming, thousands and thousands pouring from the translucent depths, as if suddenly born there, mounting and separating and gathering again, in crowds, in columns, in streams of glad activity, of most exquisite, graceful motion. The whole expanse was over-traced in swift, intricate curves and lines of beauty.

And life, exulting life, was in it all.

Peace Polly hardly knew, at first, what it told her. She watched it, breathless, for a while; then she turned and went up, slowly, between the rows of lilies by the walk. Scarlet and pure white, they flamed and gleamed beside her. The breath of the sweet day-lilies had hung there all day, and was exhaling still, as the long-fair cups were closing. She took in at every sense some wondrous, gracious word.

She went in through the hall, where the waiting table

stood, set now for tea. She heard Rebeccarabby clattering with waffle-irons in the kitchen. She went up-stairs to her own room, that she might be alone and quiet till the others came. As she sat in the bay-window, half watching, half musing, the sun-colors, the bird-flight, the lilies, wove themselves together in clear, beautiful thought; they wrote out their message within her. She learned it by heart, and later, almost in the words that had first come (but not quite, for things rushed in presently that blotted them into temporary forgetfulness), she wrote it down, as she had written that dream of hers that had come to her — oh, so many weeks — if it could be only weeks — before! Long after, she showed them both to one person only.

And this was how she wrote it : —

FULFILLED.

" He was known of them in the breaking of bread."

Good things had befallen me all through the day :
A blessing of morsels, — small helps by the way ;
Work running on even, and coming out right ;
Bright thoughts with the morning, good words at the night.

So evening was sweet, and as shadows fell deep,
My spirit was turned to the Lord of the sheep.
" Thou leadest ! thou feedest !" in silence I said ;
" And the crumbs from thy hand are the best of the bread.

" We know how Thou blessest and breakest it then ;
Not giving thy life to the children of men
As whole in the loaf, and thou done with us so,
But meed to our need, every step that we go.

" O dear daily bread, and the thought for no more !
The not knowing whence, that is infinite store !
The grand peradventure it is to be poor,
Through sureness of waiting on Him who is sure !

"O lilies and birds !"   In a redolence sweet
  One word of the parable breathed at my feet ;
  And a sign in the depths of the amber-lit west,
  Alive with winged creatures, was saying the rest.

  They rushed up in clouds, like a tempest of life ;
  All heaven was full of the beautiful strife ;
  From the gold to the blue in a rapturous chase,
  They crowded, and crowded, and yet there was space.

  They gathered and parted, they shot and they swept,
  Ever east, where the first early duskiness crept ;
  From heart of the glory to edge of the shade,
  All the way, as they moved, a sweet scripture they made.

  For, swirling and darting, each line of their flight
  Scored a letter of promise across the clear light ;
" In a seeming of emptiness, teeming with good,
  God's forecastless swallows are finding their food !"

22

XXXVII

THE WIND UP RIVER.

Dr. Fuller came back about eight o'clock. Lyman had not yet returned. Peace Polly poured out tea, and helped the waffles and the thin pink slices of cold ham. Dr. Fuller ate ; Peace Polly made believe, and managed a slight repast ; for even in making believe she did things with a kind of inevitable honesty. She hardly knew, however, what she took ; for she was growing anxious about her brother. He had looked so tired, when he went away after his early dinner, and she had so hoped that asking for a late tea hour had meant that he would be punctual then, and not do any afterwork at night.

Serena came over, in her quiet fashion, while they were at table. She just glanced at the two, saw that they were but two, and stopped upon the threshold. She had got what she had come for, and it did not answer to her wish. "How late you are ! " she said.

"Yes," Peace Polly answered. "They both kept me waiting, and Lyman has not come in yet. Sit down." She spoke as if it were quite natural and insignificant ; she looked eagerly at Serena, though, to see how it might seem to her.

"Oh, no," Serena said, treating it as carelessly. "I won't stay to hinder you. When Lyman comes, he'll want to be quiet. I wish he would n't do so, Polly. But I know you can't ever interfere with a man."

And with that old-fashioned, submissive feminine allowance and a disappointed breath, she slipped away again.

Neither of these women would let the other see, when it came to the point, that she thought there could be any excuse for special uneasiness ; each was secretly afraid of the other's corroboration.

Serena had been over in the pasture woods that afternoon ; she had been restless all day ; and she had taken the field-glass with her. She had walked down on the far southerly slope, where the cedars grew, from whose still openings there were such wide, pretty outlooks upon meadow and river and the great, uprising hill that slanted away opposite, a clear mile's walk over the long crown.

She had sat in a shady rock-nook and opened out her glass, that brought all that soft swell of brown and green so clear to sight, making even the little juniper bushes and the clumps of moss and the bracken-patches plain to her. She loved dearly to take her glass for company, though it were only for the delight of it; choosing some sheltered resting-place and drawing all things around her, even the birds and squirrels, that did not dream how near her human eyes were, and that they bent so close toward them at their safe, shy distances, and looked into their very own, and traced the blends and contrasts of their colors in glossy stripe and fluffy wave, and on shining breast and wing-tip.

She had seen something else to-night, just before she turned to come homeward as the shadows fell : something that had as little thought of her overlooking ; as little, indeed, as it had — for I will speak of it as a thing or a creature only, though I shame the birds and squirrels with such classing — of the compassing of the cloud of witnesses above, and of God's watching over all.

She was almost sure she had seen Rawson Morgan walking stealthily along the river-bank on the other side, from one covert of overhanging trees and shrubs to another. There was no path or road that could have brought him down to that point, if he came from overside the hill. It was out of any natural track of communication, and he seemed as if loitering, waiting, rather than moving on with any present purpose. It was very strange, if it were he; but, indeed, how should it be?

Rawson Morgan had gone away, they said, from town.

Was her fancy so distempered by her watchings and apprehensions that she should make out some stranger — some harmless foot-traveler — to be this man of whom she was afraid? And, "too," she said to herself, "that sideways turn and drop of the head to the right, that lift of the left shoulder, with the left-handed push into the pocket, — certainly they were most like Morgan!"

She wished she could have seen his face; but it was turned aside from her, and even with the glass she could hardly have made certain about that. He was too far off upon the left. If he had come up the river round the hill-foot, she wondered she had not noticed him before. He must have come from behind the thick woods that spread off westward, Crickford way.

Whoever it was, after passing across the open space in which she had caught sight of him, he had disappeared behind the alder thicket, and had not emerged again in the next break beyond.

Serena had gone home disquieted; had flitted over, after her own solitary tea, in this anxious way, to Lyman's. She did not know whether she ought to say anything of what she imagined she had seen, or not. She did not wish to make a worry out of nothing; she did not care to let her own worry be so plainly seen.

She went home again, sat half an hour by herself in the

broad back porch that looked down an orchard to the turn of the white road just visible in the gloaming; then she took a shawl and garden hat from their peg in the passage, and sped softly, almost stealthily, through the tree-shadows and over the low wall-steps, into and across the bit of road, and so on by the meadow-path, as she had done so many times before. She did not know why; she never knew why; she was restless. She should feel better about it if she just saw Lyman's light burning steadily in the mill-window, and everything quiet around outside; or, if the light was out, she would know that she had missed him, and that he had gone home by his own short cut the other way. Only a few minutes' walk, and all so quiet!

It was so still she could hear away across the fields the soft rush of the water, and the whir and boom of night-birds that now and then flapped up out of the hedgy hollows.

The crickets sang, the stars shone, the air was sweet and tender. How should there be any harm about in such a peace? Or how could such peace be broken, and any wakeful ear not know?

The kind night, now she was out in it, pacified her nerves. Yes, she had been nervous. Why should not some stranger have walked up from Crickford way? All up the river there was work, — in mills, on farms. There were so many people seeking for it. And Rawson Morgan had gone up north, to Hopper's Falls.

Now the country was not impassable, nor of so vast a stretch, or without rail and roadways, between Hopper's Falls and Crickford, although, through simplicity or secret shrinking, Serena did not consider that.

She would just go to the head of the lane and look. Perhaps she would wait awhile. Surely Lyman would soon leave his counting-room, and go home by the short cut. When the light was out she would go home herself, in hearing of that other field-track all the way.

By and by, she would be so glad to see the candle-signal in the east-corner bedroom, that would tell her he was going to rest, and that all was well for this time. That was how it would be, of course. It always was. Only, she was so foolish.

She never went to rest herself, now, till she had seen that sign.

How she had to steal about to do that which she might have done as open love and duty! How the nearest woman in the world to him — for she knew in her heart she was that, in spite of all — had to hide and forego her claim, and long to say words to the sister, out of her sharing, nay, her transcending anxieties, which, as things were, as she had let them be, it would not be seemly or a thing called for that she should say or feel!

There is no false position so utterly false as that of a supreme affection out of its rightful place.

Serena had one night walked in the lonely, quiet lane till ten o'clock. If any one had met her at any turn, either up or down, she would then have passed by and gone home by the direct or indirect way; but no one came, and so, up and down, keeping between the gardens, where it would not be quite unaccountable that she might be, according to the safe, easy visiting fashion of Bonnyborough women, she went, longer than she had thought, until the great church bell pealed out upon the stillness its ten strokes. Lyman's light still burned. Serena could hardly refrain from going to Peace Polly to say it must not be. Could they not go down together, and beg him to come home?

But Serena was a poor pretender. She knew she could put no face upon it other than that she had been purposely watching. It had been no accident that she had seen the lamp-light away down there in the great, lonely mill.

Peace Polly knew a great deal of her story, true; but all that was in the past. Serena could not show her her very heart so now. She had to go home and bear her worry and her exclusion.

Peace Polly would have been glad to see her that other night. She was waiting up till Lyman came, which he did at nearly eleven. But that evening he had had a good supper at six, and when he had got back hungry there were sweet apples and milk and fresh-baked country brown-bread for him; and he had gone to bed at least refreshed.

But to-night he had missed his tea, and yet he had stayed on and on.

At half past nine, Peace Polly said to Rebeccarabby, "I shall take something to Lyman to eat. Get me some bread and butter, and thin ham, and a bottle of milk, — cream-milk, Rabby."

And so, making a little basket ready, she took a wrap and tied a scarf about her head, and was going forth without even Rabby for an escort. She had put the good woman's offer back. "I should leave you in the lane," she said; "and it is nothing *to* the lane, — or after, either."

She thought that Dr. Fuller had gone out, but before she reached the garden-corner of the road he came beside her. He asked no leave, but quietly took possession of her basket, merely saying, "Which way, Miss Peace? By the street, or by the meadow?"

And Peace, something to her own astonishment, took him as quietly for granted.

"This way, I think," she said; and crossed the road to the little gap in the fence which let them, with a slight twist as through a stileway, into the oblique footpath to the lane.

They walked on silently. Peace Polly was intent upon her errand, and Dr. Fuller had not put his company upon her save to help her through with that.

They were moving at a sharp angle to the river. The wharves were below the shoulder of the sloping ground, and the hill beyond the stream was away at their right; they almost turned from it as they went. When they came out into the lane, and upon the bend, they faced it.

What was it that they suddenly saw, and cried out at with one breath?

A glittering, creeping line along the pasture-side, half-way up.

It flashed, it ran; it sent little shining serpents writhing here and there; it was coming down, and toward them, in a line with, just beyond, the overside landing. And the wind was up the river, warm and strong, toward the mill. Lyman's light burned steadily in the window at this further corner nearest them.

"Go call your brother, Peace! I will rouse up the men."

There were two or three cottages a little off the lane, on the downward slope; they were occupied by some of the saw-men and their families. Dr. Fuller sprang over the wall, and made a straight run for these. Peace Polly hurried on by the path, which was the shortest way to Lyman's private door.

But somebody was there before her.

Somebody else had seen that dazzling, threatening edge of fire. It had not been in vain, at last, that Serena Wyse had followed her restless impulse, and come forth to her reconnoissance.

Already, when the other two had come where she had just been standing, she was down across the team-way that lay, a faint, dull line of dust, parallel with the water, with the mill between. Another track followed the opposite shore. They ended, one at either end of the bridge, a half mile higher, where the town-road crossed.

Serena sprang to the closed door. It was closed, indeed, and bolted.

The light above shone down clear upon the wagon-track, and shot across to lose itself against the dark herbage of the bank.

Serena shook the door. She struck it with all the might of her clenched fists. Why did not Lyman hear?

A terrible dread seized her. Could he be ill, worn out, unconscious; or even fast asleep over his long work? And that line of fire was creeping down!

The rush of the half-head of water, deep down beneath the mill, and past the huge, still wheel, made a dull, continuous sound. From the far-off dam came also the noise of the lessened run, falling, falling, upon the stones below.

Lyman could not hear her. The intermediate doors were shut.

All at once she remembered. She flew to the angle of the building, where the great noon-bell hung from a projecting timber like a hoisting-beam. She clutched, with a spring, at the long loop of rope that dropped from a large staple in the wall through which its end was passed. She pulled it down, and rang — rang — rang.

Lyman's window was flung up; he leaned forth, and saw the outline of a woman's figure with reached-up arms, swinging at the rope. Between the peals, he shouted, —

"Who's there? What is it?" And a pale face showed palely in the streaming light, and some one called out, breathlessly, —

"Fire! on the overside pasture, Lyman; coming down toward the wharf; and the wind is up!"

For all the darkness and the strain, he knew Serena's voice.

"Ring on!" he shouted, for all answer; and the next instant was plunging down the stairs. As he dashed out of the side doorway, with two fagot brooms and a hatchet that he had snatched up, Peace Polly came down with a swoop like a bird, from the bank upon the team-way.

Nobody stopped to be surprised. Serena rang on, until Dr. Fuller and the men appeared, armed in like manner as Lyman, with whatever they could lay hands on that would whip fire, — big brushes, brooms, bushes broken from the hedges; knives and hatchets also; one man had a reaping-hook. These Bonnyborough people knew what a grass-fire was.

Some small boys came, and begged to be allowed to ring the bell. Serena gave it up to them, and followed the others; down between the blocks of plank, and board, and shingle, to the water's edge, to the little bridge across the narrow river-strait.

One by one the men leaped over; then they crowded up the wharf, and upon the hillside. There they scattered, and rushed, at varying points, upon the advancing flame.

Peace Polly and Serena sat down on some low boards nearest.

"How came you here, Peace Polly?" gasped Serena.

"And how came *you?*" Peace Polly gasped the exclamation back.

"I don't know; I was in the lane; I've been afraid," the woman answered the girl, meekly.

"Of this?"

"Of Morgan; I did n't know how. And I've been worried for Lyman." She was getting her breath now, and she said the words without demur, in a sudden assertion, as if she meant, "Why should I not?"

She hastened into another question, though, as if she feared Peace Polly would have answered that.

"Do you think they will get it under? Ah, see that sparkle, rushing right this way! There's a flash right in the edge, Peace Polly!"

"Serena! your skirts! take care!"

Serena doubled her skirts around her; folded and pinned her woolen shawl across them, hastily; ran up the green of the bank from the trodden space about the lumber; tore up the tall, tough sweet-fern bushes; and hurried back to where the tiny quiver of fire had from some wind-swept spark burst out in this close-threatening place.

It was but an instant's work to quench it; as she stepped back over the bare ground toward the boards again, another spark, close to the pile, shone up at her out of the gravel.

She stooped, and picked up a something like a dried, crumbly stem; it broke brittlely in her fingers; there was a creep of fire at the tip.

"What is this, Peace Polly?" she asked, holding it before her.

"That!" cried Polly, — "*that* is a slowmatch, — lighted!"

The women went and searched. They found a fusee trailed along from where the slowmatch had been lying, toward the lumber. Under a projecting end, they traced it to a packed-in heap of pine slips and shavings.

"Morgan!" broke forth Serena. "It was him, then! I saw him, Polly, down in the river-edge, this afternoon, — slinking and waiting. I thought it was, — and so it must have been! He meant the pasture fire should cover it; but he meant to make it sure!"

"If he has been lurking and watching about for this he might know that Lyman was in the mill! Did he mean" — Peace Polly stopped, and shuddered.

"He meant — anything that might happen ; destruction, death, — disgrace ! If *this* fire had worked quickest, or if this trap had been found, — Lyman, only Lyman, was at the mill, or near. Do not people sometimes fire their property for insurance, Polly ? "

Serena's words came thick, with a great pressure behind them of swift conviction and of horror. She had thought, when she passed Morgan on the stairs that day, that she had not understood his muttering, beyond its broken, wrathful growl. It came back upon her memory now, in that strange way that things unheard do make themselves plain after, — clear as if just spoken to her afresh.

"Back in your face — with smart and ache and *shame !* " and then the horrible oath, that perhaps had driven the rest back from her recollection instantly.

The moon, near her last quarter, was rising now in the southeast. Her level light struck upon the smoke-clouds that poured up from the burning hillside. The flare and creep of the fire itself showed lurid underneath. The air was getting full and thick. The two women could not stay any longer where it swirled so in their faces. They went back across the foot-bridge, and down the southerly bank a little way, till the choke of it drifted by them on the south wind, up the stream.

The Little Happigo is a very winding river, and here, for a mile or two, its trend is almost south, although, parallel with the high road between The Knolls and the village, and with the village street itself, for a brief distance back, it comes down almost from east to west. Up at the bridge at the east end of the village is its crossing from the northward. A mile or more below the cove wharf, now threatened by the fire, it bends southeasterly toward the sea.

The thickening crowd of men, with brooms, tree-branches, whatever they could gather and wield, were fighting with the flames. They had to run before them into the driving smother of the smoke, beating it down away from the endangered wharf. All along the advancing, evading line that darted forward everywhere between their repulses they sprang hither and thither, thrashing it, stamping it, conquering it back. Some tore up and cut away the scattered clumps of bushes that might have given it greater force and weight and headway.

Lyman seemed everywhere. He was in his shirt-sleeves; so were other men, but they wore mostly flannel working garments, gray or red; his white arms, uplifted, showed in the growing moonlight, in the reddening glares; they came down swiftly, with strong, unfaltering blows.

"Oh, how tired he will be!" said Peace Polly. Serena said nothing, but her hand that held Peace Polly's in her lap quivered and clutched.

Dr. Fuller had been farther on, where the eastward end of the fire came flanking round. He worked from there, where others presently gathered, down toward Lyman near the wharf-head. Then there were two pairs of strong, white-clad, swinging arms that the women watched silently, with short breath.

There was a thicket of furze and juniper, and a fringe of barberry bushes, near the team-way, right across from the wharf-side, in the face of the wind. Lyman was on one side of it as Dr. Fuller came down upon the other. A smoke and sparkling curled and shot up from the midst of the wild growth. It seemed for a minute or two as if the fire would get past them there, and in spite of all their endeavors sweep over into the light lumber that stood endwise near.

One moment's breathless flagging, and all would have been lost.

And Lyman was fighting more than fire; nobody but himself knew how.

Direct temptation, a clear voice of evil, he could scorn; but underneath growing exhaustion, in the face of fresh threat and terrible overbearing, something that dared not whisper just touched an abeyant consciousness in him, and called it up.

He would do his best, — he had done, he was doing it — but if this got the better now, — he was hard spent —

Dr. Fuller heard suddenly an ·outbreath of strange, husky words, between fierce blows, as he came near the tall, grand figure gathering itself up and swaying in the smoke and shine.

"Lord keep that thought out of me, with all thy might!"

And then Lyman, with a great shout to the men to come this way, fell upon the smouldering shrubbery anew, tore it and scattered it and stamped it, crying out to the first who ran to him, "The lumber, boys! heave it off, if you can; back, toward the river!"

It had not been so very long; the mill-bell was still ringing, men still running up. Only a little later, — but that little interval might have meant all, — the small, old-fashioned country engine came clattering, amid whoops and shouts, down the wagon-road on that side of the river: it was planted at the wharf-side; its hose unrolled, and plunged into the water; in a few moments more a stream played upon the piles of boards; then it left them dripping, and was turned toward the pasture. The fire gave way before its ordained foe.

The crowds of men and boys worked on at the outskirts; the engine held the centre.

An hour later, Lyman Schott thanked God that all was safe.

They begged him to go home and rest; a sufficient force volunteered to keep faithful watch, and the little engine, that had done such good work, waited also.

"If it starts again, — ever so little, to call starting, — some one run and let me know. And two or three of you boys run across now and meet us at the house, to bring down food and drink."

Giving that order, Lyman took his way with the doctor and the women, first around by the mill, that he might close all properly there, then up the lane and by the little meadow-paths over to The Knolls.

He came to Serena's side as they paused at the height of the lane-way and looked back. He knew right well all she had done, but he could not speak of it now. He only drew himself near, and stood, slightly apart from the others, at her side.

Serena said, "You have fought bravely, Lyman; and it all seems safe, and we are thankful. But you must care for your strength now. A man can't work like that without a risk. You struggled for life; some life goes in such a fight."

Lyman passed his hand up across his bared forehead, and shook his hair back in the warm wind. "Life," he repeated; "yes, all that a man hath he will give for his life. And he will give even that for what makes life."

And Serena did not yet know what life he meant. Could he still think of earthly means as making it?

"If it had all gone, and made you poor, it would not have mattered like that," she said.

"If it had all gone, I should have been safe from being poor, Serena. It was nearly all covered. I took out new insurances a month ago."

Now, in a flash, Serena did know.

She could not breathe at first, as she heard that. Was

she to be crushed with the nobleness of this plain, practical, over-thrifty man, whom she had kept out of his joy of life all these years, — sitting in judgment on him?

"Oh, Lyman!" she cried, and stopped an instant, but not because of being heard. She forgot to care for being heard. The others caught the two words, and their tone, and they walked quietly on.

"And I thought you had loved money so!"

"So I have; and so I do love money, Serena; but not as I love God's truth, thank Him! and not as I love you."

Serena trembled from head to foot at the calm, strong words, the words she never had thought to hear again.

"Oh, it shames me that you say that!" she cried, "after all, — and all! How can I feel a right to take it, or to answer?"

"I don't care whether you answer it or not," said Lyman, buoyantly. He had too much delicate knighthood to tell her that she had answered it already. But the fact that she had come to him — that she had thought of and had watched for him — had given him, all through that terrible battle with the fire, the strength of twenty men. It gave him now the brightness of the morning, conquering for the moment all exhaustion of the night.

"You must go home, Lyman. You must be taken care of now."

In those words, that seemed to put him off, she answered him again.

There was a sweet ring of humble triumph in her voice. At least now she could care for him! She took up her right of ministry. None could forbid her now, or make her ashamed.

He went up with her over the wall-steps, through her

own sweet, gloomy orchard. He only left her at her door, and before he turned to take the old garden way across he stood and held her face between his hands, rough and stained, thorn-torn and smoke-scented, — and kissed her on the mouth.

23

XXXVIII

ANOTHER DANGER.

SERENA let him say good-night. She bade him go home and rest. She told him she should look for the light in the northeast corner, to let her know he was in his room.

Lyman went home, and went up-stairs and lit his candle. He did not stop to determine deliberately whether he would make true the sign or not. He would come back as soon as he could; meantime Serena must not sit up watching. Then he went down-stairs to see what was doing for the men.

Rebeccarabby was storming through her territories like a beneficent hurricane. Aunt Pamely, — she was still here, for Chirke's sister, from "Ioway," had come to Woodiford, and the old carpenter had written to his wife to "put on an ell-piece, and go her lengths," — Aunt Pamely, arms akimbo, was hopping and alighting out of Rabby's way, which was all Miss Pownes would give her to do, though she chirped shrilly and stridently, "I could fix that, Rebeccarabby! Gi' me a chance at somethin'! Le' me ketch 'old o' that 'ere pail!" But the pail swung through the air from one of Rabby's mighty hands to the other, and Mrs. Chirke could only put the half-width of the kitchen and the whole of the cooking-stove between herself and her overwhelming niece with a spasmodic bound.

"It 's a goodness-mussy you ha'n't got no call t'

move the stove, — ner the chimbley!" she said, palpitatingly.

Rebeccarabby exploded a hasty rejoinder as she hurtled by again.

"When I'm to work in earnest I can't stop to hand over no helpins to nobody. I should fly to pieces if I did. If folks wants to help me, they must go an' do somethin' diffrunt!"

Peace Polly was gathering together biscuits, crackers, cold meat, pies, doughnuts, cheese; all the contents of a bountiful New England larder. A great preserve-caldron was on the fire, sending up clouds of fragrance from two or three gallons of boiling coffee. Big baskets stood upon the floor; half a dozen boys were waiting to carry them off.

Serena glided in with a tin pail full of fresh eggs, boiled; she had put them on the minute she had reached her kitchen, and had piled up a chip fire under them.

Rebeccarabby was pouring coffee into large, wide-mouthed cans. Serena dropped the eggs rapidly, one by one, right in. "They're clean," she said. "They'll all keep hot together, and the eggs 'll be sure to be hard. I was some in a hurry, for fear the things would be gone. You can tip 'em right out anywhere, when you've emptied the coffee."

Rebeccarabby did not say a word of objection. She knew that nothing from Serena Wyse's hands — not even egg-shells — could be other than "chany-clean an' silver-sweet." She did not speak thanks or approval, either. She had been a little shy of Serena ever since her Aunt Pamely's revelation, but she "was not one," she said, "to upset *all* the mind she had ever made up about a person, because some perticklers had come to her that she had n't heerd on afore. She 'd kinder wait awhile to see 'f they would n't reconcile." "She'd alwers said S'reeny was clean, an' a Christian." These remarks, with others of a similar tenor, she had made and reiterated to Aunt Pamely, in their continued "visitins;" and declared her intention to "hold to 'em in her treatmunt." Aunt Pamely sniffed, and hunched her elbows very aggressively; she had little to say to Miss Wyse. On this occasion she skipped carefully aside from her, and whispered raspingly to herself in a corner, "Anybody'd think 't was *her* fire! The way folks takes upon 'em clear beats me!"

Rebeccarabby acquiesced effectually without words, by emptying a big pitcher of "cream-milk" into the coffee-cans, over eggs and all. It was odd serving: but it is genius which departs from custom in emergencies, and it is cleverness which recognizes and adopts a cleverness. Besides, people always make a point of doing odd things at fires.

Serena tied the bail of her egg-pail to the handle of a basket, and packed therein a wedge of cheese. "That'll save room, and keep it separate. You'll know where 't is," she said. "Too, the tin mugs won't answer for all, and a good many can drink out of the pail."

Aunt Pamely had hit nearer the truth than her satire intended: it *was* Serena's fire, now, and her work; though nobody knew it yet but Lyman, it made her very happy with her bit of help, her hard-boiled eggs and her tin pail. It takes so little to make the sign, when the large reality is there.

Nevertheless, finding Lyman still down-stairs, she had been shy, after that good-night in the doorway; and for that had kept herself the busier in any small way that she could. She had come with her neighborly help, only, as was natural, and as might have been expected by the others. She had not, surely, come to say good-night again!

That made it difficult, even, to withdraw; for she felt Lyman's eyes upon her, with their proud, glad watching, though he let her have what he saw was her way, and keep her demure aloofness. She knew she could not escape him if she moved to go.

But when the baskets were all ready, and the boys took them up and departed, under orders to detail fresh messengers for more; when the big caldron had gone on again, and Rebeccarabby was again ransacking the buttery, she faced her dilemma, and went straight over to where he stood.

"Your light is there, and you are here," she said. "This is women's work; you can be spared. Leave it to us; we can rest up to-morrow."

Lyman looked as if he would have stood there all night, just to let her order him off continually. But as he opened his lips to answer her, he turned suddenly pale; his jaws trembled; shiver after shiver ran quickly over him; he grew giddy.

In the midst of everything, in the beginning of his gladness, the strong man was taken ill.

Serena and Dr. Fuller were on either side of him; both sprang to him; between them they helped him to the big kitchen lounge, and laid him down.

"It was nothing," he told them; but his teeth chattered as he spoke.

Hot water, restoratives, all things that were needed, were right at hand. In a little while, with stimulant nourishment, chafing, soft warm wraps, and Rebeccarabby's perpetual hot footstone from the oven-corner, the rigor was abated. Then Miss Pownes spoke up, lifting her huge ladle in signal of authority.

"You three take care o' him," she said, "an' git him to bed. I'll see to the victuals, ef 't was a ridgimint. I've ben expectin' it, an' now it's come." And she turned back to her caldron with stern self-possession, like a soldier in charge.

There is no need to dwell upon detail. Hot fever flush followed the chill; great pain set in, in head and limbs; strength and nerve had at last been exceeded by their strain; the very reaction of a conflicting happiness after long years of denial and repression had come in with its culminating touch, and the sharply reversed springs, though of goodly, tempered steel, were nigh to break.

Lyman, by the next day, was very ill indeed.

There were two bitterly self-blaming women in the house. For Serena, making no word of explanation, simply took her post there, only going home for meals and for her turn at sleep. They said nothing to each other; they paused not to confess, or to console, or to reassure; each went about with her own heavy heart, but they would not take the minutes from their work, or risk the self-control that was their strength for Lyman's need, to speak a word of their own heaviness or sore repentance.

They had not half known him heretofore, the brother or the lover. A great, true heart, under an unmoved front, a teasing banter, a common routine of money-earning. Was he only to be shown to them to be lifted away out of their life into that to which they might not follow him? Did God say to them, "He was yours a little while; you did not understand him; you rejected him; I know him, and he comes to *Me*"?

Dr. Fuller watched him like a brother. Now was the opportunity for those young men with the new tin signs out, to take whatever they could of the practice they had come for. All but the critical cases were relegated to whomever might serve the call, during those days and nights of brief, sore struggle.

The fever was sharp, was swift. The skill that met it was fine, the sympathy and discernment quick; the devotion of the nursing was absolute; the mercy of God was above all. I will not try to carry you through the suspense, the alternations; the like are known to most of us, sufficiently, in the realities of our own histories. We have enough to bear, in these.

It was in the second week that the turn came: one of those long, exhausted sleeps, in which the spirit seems to be but just kept hovering while the body's life waits undetermined, and then a gentle waking, in utter weakness, but with the soul surely there again, and looking out from within the quiet eyes. Their first look was upon Serena. She had asked to come when he should show signs of rousing, and for fourteen hours, from afternoon to morning, she had not left the house or gone from hearing. She knew that her face, if anything, would call him fully back, and hold him on this side. And so it did.

"It is you, — it is my wife?" he whispered; for all through his bewilderment of sickness he had not lost memory of that. It had rested, a consciousness back of all unconsciousness, his very anchorage with earth.

And Serena stooped and kissed him, and answered, "Yes."

XXXIX.

PEACE POLLY came softly to the door a moment or two later, saw that her own moment had not come, and moved away even more softly.

Gaining so the end of the upper hall, she turned there, swiftly, fled into her own room, hid herself in the deep window-seat behind the straight-falling curtains of white dimity, and cried as she had never known how to cry before.

Gladness, thankfulness, a tempest of tenderness, jealousy, remorse; a meeting and bursting in her heart of brooding clouds that would not be clouds any more, but whose outpour was a stormy torrent; a break of gloom, a rushing forth of sunshine that penetrated her through and through, yet in the midst of whose dazzle there was, between the heaven and earth of her, a weeping like strong javelins of rain. Heaven and earth, and the waters under the earth, were moved and fused. She did not know the why of all the tumult in her, either of joy or pain, or what the stir was of her life's atmosphere with change and blessing close impending, but as yet beyond her conscious intuition.

Her supreme thought was that her brother had come back; that he had gone from her. Her day and opportunity were over. She had wasted them; had lost the sisterhood she might have filled to him, forever. So she cried, and cried, though for all that there was surging in her both a presence and monition of great joy.

This great good — this enlargement and completion — that had come to Lyman, was she not glad, even to a fine anguish, for that? Was not all life suddenly larger for them all? It was only that something had gone by her, as in a darkness, that she had not known until too late; that all these years her brother's waiting had been harder, because she had not seen.

Two great commandments wrote themselves up over against her thought like the writing on Belshazzar's palace wall.

"Thou shalt not kill."

"Thou shalt not steal."

Had she not kept back, and defrauded? Had she not lessened, and deprived, a life?

Ah, the depth of the righteousness of these mighty, terrible laws did indeed exceed all common obedience of scribe and pharisee! She was proving them to their heart, a heart of fire!

And yet, even in the tempest, even through the midst of the fire, she felt a hand that led her with a blessing; she knew the presence of the forgiving and restoring Son of Man.

She could not have borne this very long.

A message came to her. Dr. Fuller stood by the half-opened door.

"Miss Peace," he said gently, "he asks, ' Where is my little sister?' Come!"

And she came forth with all the tears and conflict in her face.

Her friend said nothing; only took her kindly by the hand, and led her round to her brother's room again.

"Pease Porridge, kiss me. I am very happy," Lyman said, in his weak voice.

How different from the old strong speech, — from the provoking "Pease Porridge"!

As she leaned over him, she whispered one word, with her whole heart in it, " Forgive ! "

" Dear little Polly ! " was all Lyman's answer. And then Peace Polly had to hasten away, and outside the door let her tears break forth afresh.

Dr. Fuller followed her. He led her to the other end of the long hall, where a tall, fan-topped window lighted it, opposite another at the north side, that overlooked the broad staircase landing. He put her in a chair, and stood beside her.

" I am glad you have had a good cry," he said. " It is the best ending to the long tension. I should have been afraid for you without it. Now, you must grow calm and happy, and take rest. Those two can almost do without us, now."

Did he guess the chord, and touch it purposely ?

" Oh, that is it ! " she cried, through tremulous lips. " They are like people gone to heaven. The time when Lyman could not do without me is over, — and I left him without any one ! "

" I do not think you did. I think you were both lonely, and you could not help it. We are not bound to see things beyond our horizon. And — Peace — I do not think he would have been where he is now, — I mean in that place in his life where he ought to be, — if it had not been for you."

" I kept him from it, — once, — I know ! " sobbed Peace.

" If you did, it has been given you to bring it to him again. I believe the making-up is always given, where there is a right, loving will to touch, — wherever, therefore, a repentance, or a sorrow for a mistake or failure, can be."

A face was lifted to him in reply that was, in its single,

separate, yet full-fraught way, a type of the face of the world lifted up to Christus Consolator.

The great consoling of his words swept down her self-upbraiding. But she wanted her own special, definite assurance, if he had such for her.

"What have I done?" she asked; and her tone implored him eagerly.

"Serena said," he answered her, "when I had come in, and they had signed or told me something that did not need a sign or telling, and then they had both begun to ask for you, — Serena said, 'It was all Peace Polly, Lyman; if she had not flown at me that morning in your quarrel like a little angry angel, I should never have known; things would never have come different.' I believe she thought I had gone, then; but I think I made very little odds, — as Rabby says."

He went away then, and left her with that balm.

Late in the day, he came up-stairs, and found her in the selfsame spot again. Serena was sitting beside Lyman, and Peace Polly had brought a rug-strip, and sat working where she could feel near, and hear a call. She had given the first place up, and was already taking with joy the second.

The color she had chosen to work with was a tender olive, shaded up with light to almost primrose. Outside the tall, Queen-Anne window, western sunshine shot along through the green leaves, making the same mellow, sober brightness.

Dr. Fuller looked at her an instant, from the stair-head, then walked on, past Lyman's door and his own, and came to her.

"How quiet and beautiful, — how right, — it all is now!" he said.

Peace Polly knew very well that quite one half his meaning was for her. She looked up.

"Yes, it is quiet, and right, and happy," she answered him. "And I think you came here to be comfort to me," she said, in her clear, simple fashion, with eyes full of thankful sweetness lifted up as he thought only those eyes could lift.

Was it possible for him to do otherwise now? He drew a chair close, and sat beside her.

"Do you know, Peace, you have called me by my name?" he asked her.

She could only repeat his words in bewilderment. "By your name?" she said.

"Yes. I will tell you. Somewhere, far back in my Puritan ancestry, a mother, or a father, — a pious woman or a repentant, godly man, — named a firstborn child out of the fortieth chapter of Isaiah. It has been handed down, the quaint, queer inheritance in baptism, until it has come to me. On the way, it may have been a legacy of hope and solace — it may have been meant and provided so by those who had known what the ache and need and answering were with men — to more than one trouble or repentance. I have always felt it a kind of sacred thing. Do you remember those first verses of that chapter?"

Peace did remember them. A few years before, when a wonderful, gracious man, a teacher and revealer of human souls, had been in the country from a home beyond the sea, she had heard him read them in a church. After that, she could never have forgotten their place and number in the Holy Book.

"I know," she replied, as her companion waited. And she repeated, lowly, as he still did not speak, "'Comfort ye, comfort ye my people!' I knew a woman once who was called so," she said.

"There are a few names that are fitted, and have been

used, for man or woman," Dr. Fuller said. "I do not care that every one should know me familiarly by such a word. It is a lovely one for a mother to call her child by, or a wife her husband; but it is not for the crowd. It is long since I have had the one to speak to me; the other I have never had. But I have kept the name for some one."

There was no word — scarcely a breath — to answer him, as he paused.

" You have called me by it twice, — Peace ! "

Not a word, no movement, even yet. Unless the rising and falling of the bosom where the breath that had been caught now came and went were motion.

"Could you call me by it always? Would you let my name be yours, Peace ? "

The odd conceit that came to her suddenly, after a minute's utter silence, was her only refuge; for the rest, there was too much to take on words. It was just like her, and no one else, that she looked up at him with that shy, happy daring, her face all rosy and trembling and laughing in sweet light, and said, half frightened after all, —

" I suppose I should be — Peace-Fuller ! "

She sprang up when she had said it, and would have fled away, but he stood up quickly, also, and put his arms about her, holding her most gently, fast.

"It has been spoken, and it shall be, God helping me!" he said. And so he kept her there, and made her sit again beside him.

" You have not told me the rest of it," she said, when some unspoken emphasis had been laid, she thought sufficiently, upon the word.

" The rest? Oh, it will take my life long to tell you all, I think. The rest of what, Peace ? "

"The name." It was cunning of her that she used the article, and not the pronoun. Or perhaps it was unwitting.

"Can you say that next verse half through?" he asked her.

"'Speak ye comfortably to Jerusalem, and cry unto her that her warfare is accomplished, her iniquity is *pardoned!*'" repeated Peace Polly, slowly. "Yes, you have brought me the whole message," she said, with a quick humbleness.

"My little Peace!" he exclaimed, drawing her close again. "Did you think I meant that?"

"*It* means so; and it is true, and I am glad," said Peace.

"Dear heart, all your iniquity is but the *merest* unequalness, which is the rightful word. And the Pardon always waits."

"I am glad it is in your name," said Peace, again. "Now I know that it has really come to me."

"It hides behind the other; it is not wanted now, it will be seldom wanted, but it will be always there."

"Oh, I want them both!" Peace Polly cried.

"And I," he answered. "We both want them; they are given us together. What is that other verse, about the calling by name?"

Even now he did not tell her these things as from above or beyond, or even as one to whom they were very ready. He but touched her own knowledge or memory of them, and left them to her lips, if they would, to say.

"'Fear not, for I have redeemed thee; I have called thee by thy name; thou art mine.'"

She did not say them with her lips, but they rested, like a gift, in her heart, and her heart had a double meaning for them from that day.

XL

BETROTHALS.

It was in one of those days just after, when Dr. Fuller had gone up to Boston for his deferred meeting with his sister-in-law, — who had been left, while Lyman was so ill, to the greetings and hospitalities of her other dear friends, more multitudinous and more intense, now, to the value of exactly one hundred and fifty thousand dollars, — that Peace Polly had, and received, a morning visitor. People had come, day after day, all along, to inquire, but Rebeccarabby had answered them, tramping with a high-stepping lightness, yet with all the air and motion of the old tremendous tread, through the hall, to interrupt their knocking, and to deliver, like a culverin, the day's report.

Rose Howick had come now, and was admitted.

It did not take the kinship of fellow-feeling to tell Peace Polly that she was happy, and that she had come with news.

Mr. Innesley had been away for his ordination, and had returned. The Institution was just over. The September weeks were speeding, and the Confirmation was close at hand. Dr. Fuller was to be back for that; it would be on the very next approaching Sunday. Peace Polly sat happy, with all her thoughts for company, yet she let Rose come and bring her hers.

"I have something that I do not know how to tell you; but you are the very first," said the young girl to her who felt whole lustres the elder, though they were very nearly of the same years.

"Look this way, Rose!" and Peace Polly touched her finger to the pink, dimpled chin of the half-averted face, and as with a magnet turned it gently round. "I think it tells itself," she said, laughing.

Then Rose laughed too. But the laugh died softly down upon her face, and left a very earnest, wistful look there.

"I do not know how it ever came to be true!" she said. "Richard Inuesley has asked me to be his wife." She spoke his name, and told her tidings, notwithstanding they had told themselves, with a proud, sweet air. She was, indeed, a Rose Enthroned.

"And you will be the rector's lady," said Peace Polly. "I hope you and Mrs. Farron will agree."

"Oh, Mrs. Farron is lovely. She has seen it ever so long, from the very beginning; but she has never looked, or seemed — She is n't like anybody else in Bonnyborough but you and Miss Serena; and she is n't a bit like either of you, either!"

Peace Polly could not quite keep down a smile. But there was reason for it, beyond the good reasons she was witting to, why Mrs. Dora first had not, and then with consistency or carefulness would not, make sign or interference in this thing.

"I thought I was the very first," she said to Rose.

"Oh, yes, that I have told; except, of course, my father and my mother. It was Mr. Innesley" —

"Oh!"

"He said it was quite due to her, for though she has never seemed to see, she has really been so much the means of it; she has had us both with her so much, and he thinks she has wished it, somehow, from the first."

" Oh ! " said Peace Polly, again. It is such a beautiful thing, sometimes, how little people know.

Rose knew more than she thought for, though, and presently it came forth, not quite to her own easement.

" But that is not all I have to say to you, Peace Polly. There was a time when he did not quite know, — when it was all uncertain, I mean, Polly. Mr. Innesley would not ask me until he had told me that he had come very near to asking you, and that you had known him better than he knew himself, and had shown him his mistake. *That* is why I come to you first, Peace Polly ! "

It was surely a great deal better than if Mr. Innesley had come !

But she put away any thought about herself, and certainly any little secret amusement. This was her friends' life-crisis and great joy. It should not want, now, for any certainty, or sympathy, that she could give. Was it indeed, all grateful acknowledgment, or some lingering little wish to read in her a complete assurance, that had sent Rose Howick with her early news ?

" I am so glad you know," she said to her. " It was very right, and like a noble man, for Mr. Innesley to tell you. And I am glad you have told me, because else you might always imagine I was thinking of it as a thing you did not know. He only *liked* me, Rose ; I am sure he loved you, always. How could he help it ? I was not lovable at all. But he liked my thoughts, and my trying to grow higher, and he had, I suppose, a kind of judgment over himself that he was not to do the thing that pleased him, but the thing that was to keep him at his greatest elevation ! As if there was anything but just such dear love as he has for you that would do that ! It is all right, Rose ; any other way, it was all a mistake, and would have been all wrong. And he never really did ask me. It is you who are the ' very first.' "

Rose put her arms around Peace Polly's neck, and kissed her. "There was never anybody just like you," she said.

She did not stay long after that. Peace Polly felt almost ungrateful, after she had gone, that she had let her go without a confidence in return. But they had all agreed here at The Knolls that absolutely nothing should be said.

If Dr. Fuller also felt under a kind of mortgage to Mrs. Dora with his intelligence, he either let it remain on interest a little longer, or Mrs. Dora kept the secret like the great pyramid of Egypt.

All Bonnyborough was under the impression still that Mrs. C. P. Fuller was already on the earth, the wife of his youth; only that she was just now in Europe.

As Lyman got well, they had some of those delicious days together when an invalid is, as such, still off active duty, but capable of every sort of passive enjoyment. Serena talked to him; Peace Polly read to both, while Lyman rested and Serena had her needlework. They went over now, by degrees, all the incidents of the fire. Serena had kept the crumbled slowmatch and the piece of fuse; some boys had found and quarreled over a clasp-knife that turned up between the displaced boards; a workman had come along, and taken it, saying that it was Mr. Morgan's. There was no reason, in other minds, to connect it with the fire; the foreman might have dropped it any day. But they knew, here at The Knolls, that it completed the strong chain of circumstantial proof against the evil-doing man.

Peace Polly had asked Lyman what he would do about it.

"I shall return him the knife some day," Lyman said.

It was all he did do; but the very silence concerning

all else, save that it was picked up between the spruce planks after the fire, was sufficient; the fellow knew well what else might have been discovered, and where the power of disclosure lay; there was not much danger from him hereafter, at least so far as boards and shingles were concerned. It was not very long before he sought and found at a distance such occupation as he could, without reference to his late employer. As regarded that, he knew he had lost his links; that he was off the track. A man without a referable antecedent is worse off even than a man without a country; he is self-detached; in beginning a new account with the world he finds indeed that a man cannot be born, in any earthly sense, when he is old.

Peace Polly wrote Lyman's letters. She had gone, while he was ill, to Mr. Howick, who was a man of business, and president of the Bonnyborough bank: he had, at her request, gone down to the counting-room, and looked a little into Lyman's memoranda; just enough to see what might be immediately pending, and if there were any payments to meet. And Peace Polly had talked over orders with the young fellow who had been next under Morgan, and who now came to the front and head with capacity that matched his opportunity.

There had been one considerable note falling due within a few days of the fire. Lyman was a shareholder and depositor in the Bonnyborough bank, and had at this time — probably in provision for this immediate payment — a large balance there; within a third, indeed, of enough to meet the amount. But Lyman was in the delirium of fever; the bank discounted Peace Polly's note, indorsed by Serena Wyse, for the entire sum, and paid it into the Boston bank where Lyman's lay.

The two women, in the midst of their trouble, made their brave little meddle in business with a certain triumphant sweetness of satisfaction.

When Lyman asked, bewilderedly, between his blinder wanderings, of the day of the month, and tried to talk of something to "take up," and of "going to protest," Peace Polly stooped down to him with a kiss, and told him there was nothing to take up but his gruel, and no protesting to be done; and if he meant that note to Harrimans, Mr. Howick had seen to that, and there would be nothing else but the mill until long after he would be about again; and she and Serena and John Golden could run the mill. They were all partners now, with John for foreman; and John Golden was worth twenty Morgans, with the rascality left out.

The insurance company which had taken the chief risk had written a hearty acknowledgment of his great energy and faithfulness in averting the loss; his name was in the mouths of men with admiration and honor; there would be no trouble about any service or accommodation he might need. And it ended, shortly, in his needing none; it seemed as if all the threatening had but been to work the special good that could only in some such way have come about; for a large contractor wrote to him from a seaboard town for an immediate shipping, by water, of the very class of finishings which they had learned from the Hathertons he had under way.

Lyman's convalescence was almost like the waking of an earth-wearied "pilgrim" on the calm, new shores where, indeed,

> "All things are spring to God's dear, new beginnings."

"I feel," he said to Serena, when they walked down the grass-path to the low gate, together, for the first time, "as if I were twenty-five years old again."

And Serena's smile at him made her look like the twenty that would have corresponded.

Rebeccarabby saw them when they came in. She was

writing that night to Aunt Pamely, who had gone back to Woodiford with very much mollified sentiments toward Serena, and it must be confessed toward Providence itself, for the outcome of things that she had never before been able to "see through."

"You can not get married till your time comes any more than you can die," Rebeccarabby wrote. "I begin to realize now what folks mean when they say it will be all the same a hundred years hence. The Lord takes his time; but it is his own, and He has got lots of it."

Rebeccarabby wrote very exactly; indeed, abbreviations in script were quite beyond her, curious as she was in them in lively speech. She also let punctuation modestly alone, as a thing too high for her, except when she came to an undeniable full stop. But she had been head girl at the "spellin'-matches" down in Statermaine, and Aunt Pamely and all the Woodiford kin were as proud of her letters as the townsmen of a member of Congress may be of his printed speeches.

The Bishop arrived, the Sunday came, and Lyman was able to be driven to church for the confirmation service. He was not quite strong enough to go in time for prayers and sermon; but he would not stay away when Peace Polly was to enter upon this solemn consecration of her life. Even he did not know that any other of his household was to share the ordinance.

Peace Polly and Serena and Dr. Fuller had taken seats together near the entrance of one of the little transepts. Lyman could come in quietly, they had kept room beside them.

Once, Lyman might have regretted that his sister could not go his way into the sheepfold: he had learned better; the four friends, though without many definite words, had come so near each other in some talks that had arisen in that pleasant room of his recovery that he could understand how only they who would climb up without the Shepherd are the trespassers or the unknown of Him ; and that He may indeed open more than one door, though the fold, the true kingdom, is and ever shall be one.

As the beautiful hymn rose with its petition,

"Arm these thy soldiers, mighty Lord,"

and the music swelled to a sweet chorus, and they who were come for the "promise and the blessing" softly left places and moved through the aisles into the chancel, he felt a great thrill, and was conscious of the surprise that stirred in those about him and throughout the assembly, as following eyes expressed, when the tall, noble figure of Dr. Fuller was seen to advance, close behind Peace Polly in her soft white dress, with some fair asters in her bosom ; and the two knelt side by side, among the others, by the rail.

There were very young girls and lads ; there were one or two old persons, men and women ; these two were in the grand fullness, the sweet perfection, of manhood and womanhood. Upon them all were the hands laid, solemn, tender, each in turn ; over each was the prayer prayed,—

"Defend, O Lord, this thy child."

No difference mattered, of age or any other, here, before Him. They were all children, especially in this coming to their Father's house and family. The fair, shining head of Peace, the grand one, lightly time-touched, next her, alike and in succession received the grace ; they bent alike and at once, in the beseeching, for themselves and for each other, of the petition uttered over them, — "that they might daily increase in the Holy Spirit more and more, until they should come into the everlasting kingdom."

The one leading, "in the knowledge and obedience of

the word," the one " fatherly hand to be ever over them,"
the one " mighty protection, for hearts and bodies, both here
and ever," that they might " be preserved both in body
and soul " were invoked for them ; and at last the " blessing of God Almighty, the Father, the Son, and the Holy
Ghost," to "be upon " and "remain with" them "forever."

Lyman and Serena said " Amen," with all their hearts.

As the little lines came down the aisles again, from the
choir-voices and from the standing congregation, from
many of their own, as they stood once more in their places,
came the ringing refrains of the hymn : —

" Onward, Christian soldier,
Marching as to war ;
With the cross of Jesus
Going on before !
Christ the royal master
Leads against the foe ;
Forward into battle
See his banners go.
Onward, Christian soldier,
Marching as to war,
With the cross of Jesus
Going on before ! "

Dr. Fuller sang, in a full, glorious voice, with uplifted
head ; a soldier of the King, — an " enlisted soldier."
Peace, with her sweet tones, kept clear harmony. Many
an eye rested, many an ear bent, upon those two. But
none knew, or could surmise anything, beyond the one
holy purpose of the hour ; and it was well.

To them it was at once consecration and high betrothal.

XLI.

IPOMÆA.

THE summer lingered into late September. The sun slipped easily past the equinox. One day and night of steady, bounteous, fountain-filling rain, and the southwest wind came round again. The grass was green, the foliage of the trees just dashed with rainbows, as if a prism hung quivering somewhere in the sky. The Little Happigo ran blue and full toward the sea.

Serena and Peace Polly were spending busy, happy days. Their lives had been rained full of freshness; the river of their hopes brimmed up and flowed abundant on, beneath a bright present shining, unto a future of fulfillment ocean deep and wide.

There was no reason why either of the marriages should wait, beyond the completion of such pretty industries as women invent and urge for weddings. And in these days those are easily accomplished.

All Peace Polly's side of the house was being brightened to the last dainty touch of order and replenishment. New treasures and old — but the old were the better — were procured or brought forth from safe, unused keeping, and were filling up the rooms. The things that had waited through generations were to appear before a generation that would almost give for them the eyes they looked with, now that they were only purchasable in modern imitations. Peace Polly's housekeeping would be among real, old, lovely things that had a history to them.

For Serena, she would shut up the Wyse-Place through the winter. In the spring, Mr. Mark Thurleigh, artist, author, poet, who had been breaking the tenth commandment for it these five years past, — only he said he saved the letter and some of the spirit by keeping discreetly out of the neighborhood, — might come and hire it.

And all the plans, the talk, the quiet sewing, went on entirely among themselves. It was nothing new for Serena and Peace Polly to be much together. There was no intermeddling or surmise, further than that people said it was a good thing for the girl having Serena Wyse to "kind of half-mother her," — so they expressed chaperonage, and in a far better wording, — " as long as things were as they were ; Dr. Fuller there, and his wife not coming, and nobody but Peace Polly to take the head of the house. Lyman showed his sense in making himself a little more neighborly for the sake of that." One thing covered the other ; the shield was double.

The Bonnyborough chit-chat had been full, even as the brooks were, with the plentiful autumn befallings. It was busy now with the young rector and Rose Howick. One regular wedding in open preparation, with all circumstance, did very well for a stand-by ; for variation, it had enough to guess at about Dr. Fuller and his practice, and his coming into the church, and where his wife was and was going to be, — without once hitting the real mark. There is nothing like having a few extra strings to the bow, — I was tempted to say a few children to throw out to the wolves, — in the way of subjects to furnish to one's neighborhood, for enabling one for a limited time to keep some special subject to one's self.

Some time early in October, Miss Serena meant to have a little tea-party, — the Schotts and Dr. Fuller, Rose Howick and the young rector, the old rector and Mrs. Dora, and her own minister, Mr. Dawney, with his family. She had not made up her mind as to the asking of Miss Mallis. The reason why was that she was not quite sure as to the Christian charity of her motive.

Dr. Fuller came in one afternoon at the west doorway, and went up the west side stairs. A few minutes after, Miss Serena went away home. Peace Polly was left by herself in her own room. She was moving about, singing, as she put away some work she had been doing, bestowing various fine little garnishings in her bureau drawers, and then setting her sewing-table straight to leave it for the night.

Dr. Fuller's door opened, on the opposite side of the hall, and he came and tapped at hers. "Will you come over into your other house, Peace?" he asked her. And as she joined him, with her frank face and charming blush, putting her hand in his, he bent over her with his tender, reverent salute, and said, —

"You don't call me to look, Peace, when you put the pretty things into your new, old rooms. You are as shy as a bird with her nest; but I can't help seeing sometimes as I pass. And now I have taken a little liberty to put something there myself. Don't be frightened," as the head came up inquiringly. "It is nothing rich or overwhelming; you know I don't seek my Peace with gifts, — of the things that perish. Have n't I been good?"

Peace looked down upon the simple band of gold, with its little signet of pure, glistening chalcedony, delicately, wonderfully graven with lettering that only they two knew, and that could never, by any chance, be read by curious, intruding eye without a microscope. She touched it gently, involuntarily, with her finger, and said, "Yes."

"It is only a sweet, growing thing," he told her. "I have been keeping it for weeks, till it should be just ready.

Mrs. Farron helped me with my little plan. It is a plant for open air, but we have trained it for your window. It will blossom, I think, quite on into the winter, for it was started late."

They went into the northwest, sunset room, which at the side projected with a great square bay that also let in the noon-shine. Some straight curtains of a filmy Indian stuff fell from the carven cornice across it to the floor. Through the folds the sky-glow gleamed from the down-sinking sun.

Dr. Fuller parted the fine draperies, and led Peace in. He put her in a low cushioned chair, and seated himself upon the running divan beneath the long-cut windows. The sashes were all pushed up; the mild, sweet air was throbbing through. The delicate curtains swayed softly inward.

Against the southerly corner stood a small *jardinière* of wire-work. A green, oval pan, with handles, fitted into its basket, and was full of garden earth that smelled fresh from watering. A light arched rod bent over it from end to end. From the basket-rim slight lines were carried up and fastened to it. All made a slender, hidden trellis for a vine which grew with large, soft, crowding leaves of cool, pale green, and covered it. Sprays and tendrils swept and curled around it, fringing it airily.

Not a blossom was open, but there were long, folded, twisted buds, convolvulus-like, thrust here and there from among the leafage. Tapering ribs of clear green marked them from stem to tip with their strong curves. Between these showed pure white lines of unbloomed corollas.

The level sunshine lay shimmering upon the green, and coaxed the buds with warmth. The summery air breathed through them with whispered persuasion.

"Now watch! As the sun goes down they open."

They sat together, still, as before some unshown mystery. Was this flower, so closely rolled, to unfold, visibly, before her eyes? Peace wondered.

One bud, a little larger, a little more swollen, than the rest, the fine tip just visibly parted from its singleness into yet finer separating points, and the white seams slightly broadened, fixed her attention. It reached straight toward her on its stem, straight toward the sunshine that seemed like a soft lightning caught upon its point and quivering down its sides.

The bud trembled. Was it all the movement of the gentle air? The needle-slender tips stood yet a little more apart; the green ribs surely stirred reversely to their twistings.

White loops of the corolla-edge showed, like little open nectaries of columbines. They stretched, they made their beautiful curves wider; the green ribs appeared, lance-shaped, with strong, tense, central ridges; they divided the white bell with their five graceful, narrowing lines.

It could be seen that the flower was a bell, — a trumpet, rather; but it was not yet shaken free. The motion swept along the loosening edges; the loops dropped further; they were just barely, lightly, fluted in now at the five seams. By and by the pure, delicate membrane would gain its perfect span. Yes, the flower was opening, slowly, like a dream.

Slowly? By and by? All at once, it sprang, it flashed, it leaped to its absolute beauty. It threw its curving borders back, — its ridge-centres made a pale-green star of exquisite gradual rays, — its glorious white life took on full shape; it leaned suddenly, and looked at Peace, like a face into her own; the little filaments and down-balls of its stamens standing perfect in its soft, amber depth, — bright, fresh dewdrops at the heart, and the rapture of its fragrance pouring forth. Life, splendor, breath, — where there had been but the blind, closed, waiting thing.

Something almost like a pain moved Peace Polly. Something almost like tears came quickly to her eyes.

Dr. Fuller waited until she should speak. While they were silent, another and another flower crept, quivered, stole, as it were, groping, toward its lovely declaration. A few more breathless instants, and three blooms stood forth, stately-sweet with their own shining, in the dimming light.

"It *is* a dream," said Peace Polly, with a hushed voice, " and I have dreamed it all before."

It was the flower of life, she thought, the King of the Country had shown her, when he walked and talked with her by the way.

" I know what it means," she said again. " It is — the words."

" What words? " he asked her. They stood now, hand in hand, fronting the blossomed vine that had revealed itself before them like the bush that burned for Moses.

" God's words; the things that Dr. Farron made me think of, that unfold while you are looking at them, till they flower out suddenly with all their meanings; white with light, sweet-smelling, full of dew."

Her words came like the flower's word; she could not help them.

" After that," said Dr. Fuller, putting his arm about her, " I scarcely dare to say what I have been thinking of. And yet, surely God's highest word is a fair human soul. You have been like that to me, Peace."

" I ! "

" Yes: all folded up at first; something like hard, restraining ridges round you; a sharpness, a closeness, a hiding of yourself. And then, such a sweet, true, gradual revealing; and at last — and for me — the perfect flower of peace!"

"Oh, I am not that! You know I am not, yet! But some time, for both of us — for all of us — it may be like that; suddenly — after all the hindrances — oh, my friend! will it seem like that, do you suppose?"

"'He will perfect that which concerneth us,'" said Dr. Fuller; "you have got the right word, Peace, I do think."

"We shall *wake*, satisfied," said Peace Polly.

The wakened flowers still held up their pure, perfect faces; flowers of the gloaming, — sunset-glories; larger, fairer, more triumphant, than the dear old glory of the morning, even: telling that other word, that the true day is never done; that after all our brightest noon is but a folded waiting; that at the evening time it shall be light, and we shall live.

XLII.

THE DAY OF ALL SAINTS.

THERE is not much more to tell; but I wonder if you are half as loath to part from Peace Polly as I, the teller of her bit of story, am?

Serena had her little tea-party, in the midst of the October glow and brightness. A splendid harvest moon was riding in the sky; crickets were chirping by the old house-hearths, and in the full-stored barns and out in the wide stubble - fields the kindly fruits of the earth were gathering in; the Thanksgiving days were coming, and all the long, beautiful winter for the hearth-side joy. That was what the crickets sang of.

Lyman Schott and Serena Wyse stood side by side, — a mere happening it might appear to those who did not know, — in front of the deep-recessed window, where *we* know they had stood twice before in the seeming determination of their fate.

Peace Polly, Dr. Fuller, Mrs. Dora, Mrs. Dawney, had managed to draw near, and to keep the little group uninvaded. It was half an hour or so after the tea-drinking was over.

Good Mr. Dawney came quietly toward them from the middle of the room.

"My friends," he said; and Mrs. Dawney gave a surreptitious little tap upon the table beside her, as she had been used to do when calling the sewing-circle to order for a report.

Everybody turned.

"We are met together to join this man and this woman in holy matrimony."

He gave time for the astonishment to pass, and for grave decorum to assert itself. And then, with his earnest "Let us pray," the simple service began, went on, was finished.

Lyman and Serena Schott were man and wife.

Bonnyborough had never been so defrauded, so beguiled, before. It shook its head, half in rue and half in wrath.

"We might have known," it said; "another time we *would* know! That could not be done twice." And it shook its head again in forewarned wisdom.

But it was done now; and at The Knolls there was a happy household, going on just as if it had gone on so always. Already the secondary wonder stirred, that it could possibly have been hindered happening before; that —like any other fact accomplished — it should ever have been different or doubtful.

But lightning does strike twice, sometimes, in the same place.

It had been a season of remarkable catastrophes.

All Saints' Day came; still, gorgeous, tender, hazy with sweetness; heaven and earth leaning together as they do not lean even in June. The breath of very quietness for joy was upon the hills; the sureness of the complete year apart from heats or storms was like the rest and sureness of the souls in Paradise. Fulfillment, and remembrance, and repose; calmness of delight; rapture of tranquillity. A marriage of the Indian summer must certainly, like the coming of the Sabbath child, be "bonnie and lucky, and wise and gay."

The little church of St. Matthew's stood with open doors. No one was surprised at that. There was always Service on All Saints'. Very few went in, — not even a Sunday congregation ; that was as usual, also.

Dr. Fuller and Peace Polly walked over together ; Lyman and Serena went down the street a little after ; Dr. Farron and his wife came out from the old rectory as they passed ; the four turned into the cross-street that led by the south transept door. Great Norway spruces shaded the west angle ; their rich, low, spreading branches trailed along the turf ; their spires, like beautiful green rockets, shot above the level of the roof. They were thick with impenetrable shade ; their cones, brown and green, of last year's growth and this, hung like pagoda-bells along the outstretched boughs. The little group disappeared beyond them from all but the few worshipers who were going in.

The Morning Prayers were said ; the Anthems chanted ; the Creed recited ; the lovely Collect for the day repeated in a tender solemnity. " O Almighty God, who hast knit together thine elect in one communion and fellowship, . . . grant us grace so to follow thy blessed saints in all virtuous and godly living, that we may come to those unspeakable joys which Thou hast prepared for those who unfeignedly love Thee ; through Jesus Christ our Lord."

And then was read the vision of the sealed of the living God ; of the great multitude with the white robes and the palms ; of the glory and the thanksgiving. And after that the Gospel of the Beatitudes, saying who are these blessed, that are sealed of the Spirit even in the earth : the poor in spirit, the meek, the sorrowful for all sin and wrong, the hungerers for all righteousness, the merciful, the pure, the peacemakers.

Beautiful, indeed, is the Day of All Saints for a marriage day.

Peace Polly wore a plain, soft, fine white gown; her straw bonnet, tied with white, had white chrysanthemums clustered on it, their sober green leaves just bronzed and crisped with edge of autumn brown; a black silk wrap, lace-fringed and hooded, covered her dress sedately.

After Dr. Farron had finished the short address instead of sermon, whose double text was, "We are come unto the city of the living God," and "Let your conversation be in heaven," instead of pronouncing the benediction, he went back behind the altar rails; some one stepped forward and closed the entrance-bars, while a sweet, low hymn began, sung by the few voices which led as choir that day.

Peace Polly, her outer wrap laid by, disclosing her dress adorned at belt and bosom with white chrysanthemums, the flowers of gold and of the sun, laid her hand within the arm of her brother, while Dr. Fuller gave his to Serena, and the four walked up the aisle into the chancel. Lyman and Serena went to left and right; Peace Polly and Dr. Fuller came side by side between, and knelt there.

When they rose, Dr. Farron began the hallowed words: —

"Dearly beloved, we are gathered here in the sight of God, and in the face of this company, to join together this man and this woman in holy matrimony;" and so went on, to the solemn adjuration to any who could show cause why they might not so be joined, and to the awful charge and requisition to themselves to confess any known impediment as they would answer at the dreadful day of judgment.

Truly no one could have testified to aught; yet that moment was the first assurance to most of the witnessing company that this marriage could be possible.

"Comfort, wilt thou have this woman " —

"Peace, wilt thou have this man " —

The questions were asked and answered.

At the word "Who giveth this woman to be married to this man?" Lyman came and took his sister's hand with a loving pressure, and put it in the minister's to be given away; the holy troth was plighted; the ring was placed; the prayers were said; once more the right hands were joined, and the injunction, "Those whom God hath joined together let no man put asunder," uttered over them. They were declared and pronounced — Comfort and Peace — to be man and wife, in the Thrice Holy Name; and the blessing was spoken above their bowed heads, — the prayer for all grace and benediction; that they might so live together in this life that in the world to come they might have life everlasting.

They went down the aisle and out together; Serena and Lyman followed; they all walked home as they had come.

"Well, we know now what we never knew before," said Miss Mallis, ignoring bravely the chief ignorance, "and that's a comfort! He didn't mean his name should be Common Parlance, did he?"

"It'll be Peace and Comfort now, all the rest of their lives," said Mrs. Farron to Dr. Sebastian, walking home.

"At this very corner, again, Dora!" reminded her husband, laughing.

"So history — and prophecy — repeat themselves," returned the lady, with her most serious dignity.

"Gaining some surer, blesseder step, each time," said

the good Doctor. " Let us hope so, in this history, at least."

" I *know* so ! " asserted Mrs. Dora, positively.

After that, can one add anything ?

Mrs. Dora had the first word in our story, and we will yield her, cordially, the last.

Standard and Popular Library Books

John Adams and Abigail Adams. Familiar Letters of, during the Revolution, 12mo, $2.00.

Oscar Fay Adams. Handbook of English Authors, 16mo, 75 cents; Handbook of American Authors, 16mo, 75 cents.

Louis Agassiz. Methods of Study in Natural History, Illustrated, 16mo, $1.50; Geological Sketches, Series I. and II., each, 16mo, $1.50; A Journey in Brazil, Illustrated, 8vo, $5.00; Life and Letters, edited by his wife, 2 vols. $4.00.

Anne A. Agge and Mary M. Brooks. Marblehead Sketches. 4to, $3.00.

Thomas Bailey Aldrich. Story of a Bad Boy, Illustrated, 12mo, $1.50; Marjorie Daw and Other People, 12mo, $1.50; Prudence Palfrey, 12mo, $1.50; The Queen of Sheba, 12mo, $1.50; The Stillwater Tragedy, 12mo, $1.50; Poems, *Household Edition*, 12mo, $2.00; full gilt, $2.50; The above six vols. 12mo, uniform, $12.00; From Ponkapog to Pesth, 16mo, $1.25; Poems, Complete, Illustrated, 8vo, $5.00; Mercedes, and Later Lyrics, cr. 8vo, $1.25.

Rev. A. V. G. Allen. Continuity of Christian Thought, 12mo, $2.00.

American Commonwealths.
Virginia. By John Esten Cooke.
Oregon. By William Barrows.
Maryland. By Wm. Hand Browne.
Kentucky. By N. S. Shaler.
Michigan. By Hon. T. M. Cooley.
Kansas. By Leverett W. Spring.

(*In Preparation.*)

Pennsylvania   By Hon. Wayne MacVeagh.
California.   By Josiah Royce.
South Carolina.   By Hon. W. H. Trescot.
Connecticut.   By Alexander Johnston.
Tennessee.   By James Phelan.
New York.   By Ellis H. Roberts.
Missouri.   By Lucien Carr.
Massachusetts.   By Brooks Adams.

Each volume, 16mo, $1.25.

American Men of Letters.

Washington Irving.   By Charles Dudley Warner.
Noah Webster.   By Horace E. Scudder.
Henry D. Thoreau.   By Frank B. Sanborn.
George Ripley.   By O. B. Frothingham.
J. Fenimore Cooper.   By Prof. T. R. Lounsbury.
Margaret Fuller Ossoli.   By T. W. Higginson.
Ralph Waldo Emerson.   By Oliver Wendell Holmes.
Edgar Allan Poe.   By George E. Woodberry.
Nathaniel Parker Willis.   By H. A. Beers.

(*In Preparation.*)

Nathaniel Hawthorne.   By James Russell Lowell.
William Cullen Bryant.   By John Bigelow.
Bayard Taylor.   By J. R. G. Hassard.
William Gilmore Simms.   By George W. Cable.
Benjamin Franklin.   By John Bach McMaster.

Each volume, with Portrait, 16mo, $1.25.

American Statesmen.

John Quincy Adams.   By John T. Morse, Jr.
Alexander Hamilton.   By Henry Cabot Lodge.
John C. Calhoun.   By Dr. H. von Holst.
Andrew Jackson.   By Prof. W. G. Sumner.
John Randolph.   By Henry Adams.
James Monroe.   By Pres. D. C. Gilman.
Thomas Jefferson.   By John T. Morse, Jr.
Daniel Webster.   By Henry Cabot Lodge.
Albert Gallatin.   By John Austin Stevens.

James Madison. By Sydney Howard Gay.
John Adams. By John T. Morse, Jr.
John Marshall. By Allan B. Magruder.
Samuel Adams. By J. K. Hosmer.
(*In Preparation.*)
Henry Clay. By Hon. Carl Schurz.
Martin Van Buren. By Hon. Wm. Dorsheimer.
Each volume, 16mo, $1.25.

Martha Babcock Amory. Life of John Singleton Copley, 8vo, $3.00.

Hans Christian Andersen. Complete Works, 10 vols. 12mo, each $1.50. New Edition, 10 vols. 12mo, $10.00. (*Sold only in sets.*)

Francis, Lord Bacon. Works, 15 vols. cr. 8vo, $33.75; *Popular Edition,* with Portraits, 2 vols. cr. 8vo, $5.00; Promus of Formularies and Elegancies, 8vo, $5.00; Life and Times of Bacon, 2 vols. cr. 8vo, $5.00.

L. H. Bailey, Jr. Talks Afield, Illustrated, 16mo, $1.00.

E. D. R. Bianciardi. At Home in Italy, 16mo, $1.25.

William Henry Bishop. The House of a Merchant Prince, a Novel, 12mo, $1.50; Detmold, a Novel, 18mo, $1.25; Choy Susan and other Stories, 16mo, $1.25.

Björnstjerne Björnson. Norwegian Novels, 7 vols. 16mo, each $1.00; New Edition, 3 vols. 12mo, the set, $4.50.

Anne C. Lynch Botta. Handbook of Universal Literature, New Edition, 12mo, $2.00.

British Poets. *Riverside Edition,* cr. 8vo, each $1.75; the set, 68 vols. $100.00.

John Brown, M. D. Spare Hours, 3 vols. 16mo, each $1.50.

Robert Browning. Poems and Dramas, etc., 15 vols. 16mo, $22.00; Complete Works, *New Edition,* 7 vols. cr. 8vo, $12.00; Ferishtah's Fancies, 16mo, $1.00; cr. 8vo, $1.00.

William Cullen Bryant. Translation of Homer, The Iliad, cr. 8vo, $3.00; 2 vols. royal 8vo, $9.00; cr. 8vo, $4.50; The Odyssey, cr. 8vo, $3.00; 2 vols. royal 8vo, $9.00; cr. 8vo, $4.50.

John Burroughs. Works, 6 vols. 16mo, each $1.50.

Thomas Carlyle. Essays, with Portrait and Index, 4 vols. 12mo, $7.50; *Popular Edition*, 2 vols. 12mo, $3.50.

Alice and Phœbe Cary. Poems, *Household Edition*, 12mo, $2.00; the same, 12mo, full gilt, $2.50; *Library Edition*, including Memorial by Mary Clemmer, Portraits and 24 Illustrations, 8vo, $4.00.

Lydia Maria Child. Looking Toward Sunset, 12mo, $2.50; Letters, with Biography by Whittier, 16mo, $1.50.

James Freeman Clarke. Ten Great Religions, Parts I. and II., 8vo, each $3.00; Common Sense in Religion, 12mo, $2.00; Memorial and Biographical Sketches, 12mo, $2.00.

John Esten Cooke. My Lady Pokahontas, 16mo, $1.25.

James Fenimore Cooper. Works, new *Household Edition*, Illustrated, 32 vols. 16mo, each $1.00; the set, $32.00; *Fireside Edition*, Illustrated, 16 vols. 12mo, $20.00.

Charles Egbert Craddock. In the Tennessee Mountains, 16mo, $1.25; Down the Ravine, Illustrated, $1.00; The Prophet of the Great Smoky Mountains, 16mo, $1.25.

T. F. Crane. Italian Popular Tales, 8vo, $2.50.

F. Marion Crawford. To Leeward, 16mo, $1.25; A Roman Singer, 16mo, $1.25; An American Politician, 16mo, $1.25.

M. Creighton. The Papacy during the Reformation, 2 vols. 8vo, $10.00.

Richard H. Dana. To Cuba and Back, 16mo, $1.25; Two Years Before the Mast, 12mo, $1.50.

Thomas De Quincey. Works, 12 vols. 12mo, each $1.50; the set, $18.00.

Madame De Staël. Germany, 12mo, $2.50.

Charles Dickens. Works, *Illustrated Library Edition*, with Dickens Dictionary, 30 vols. 12mo, each $1.50; the set, $45.00; *Globe Edition*, 15 vols. 16mo, each $1.25; the set, $18.75.

J. Lewis Diman. The Theistic Argument, etc., cr. 8vo, $2.00; Orations and Essays, cr. 8vo, $2.50.

Theodore A. Dodge. Patroclus and Penelope, Illustrated, 8vo, $3.00.

Eight Studies of the Lord's Day. 12mo, $1.50.

George Eliot. The Spanish Gypsy, a Poem, 16mo, $1.00.

Ralph Waldo Emerson. Works, *Riverside Edition*, 11 vols. each $1.75; the set, $19.25; *"Little Classic" Edition*, 11 vols. 18mo each, $1.50; Parnassus, *Household Edition*, 12mo, $2.00; *Library Edition*, 8vo, $4.00; Poems, *Household Edition*, Portrait, 12mo, $2.00.

English Dramatists. Vols. 1–3, Marlowe's Works; Vols. 4–11, Middleton's Works; each vol. $3.00; *Large-Paper Edition*, each vol. $4.00.

Edgar Fawcett. A Hopeless Case, 18mo, $1.25; A Gentleman of Leisure, 18mo, $1.00; An Ambitious Woman, 12mo, $1.50.

F. de S. de la Motte Fénelon. Adventures of Telemachus, 12mo, $2.25.

James T. Fields. Yesterdays with Authors, 12mo, $2.00; 8vo, $3.00; Underbrush, 18mo, $1.25; Ballads and other Verses, 16mo, $1.00; The Family Library of British Poetry, royal 8vo, $5.00; Memoirs and Correspondence, 8vo, $2.00.

John Fiske. Myths and Mythmakers, 12mo, $2.00; Outlines of Cosmic Philosophy, 2 vols. 8vo, $6.00; The Unseen World, and other Essays, 12mo, $2.00; Excursions of an Evolutionist, 12mo, $2.00; The Destiny of Man, 16mo, $1.00; The Idea of God, 16mo, $1.00; Darwinism, and Other Essays, New Edition, enlarged, 12mo, $2.00.

Dorsey Gardner. Quatre Bras, Ligney, and Waterloo, 8vo, $5.00.

Gentleman's Magazine Library. 14 vols. 8vo, each $2.50; Roxburg, $3.50; *Large-Paper Edition*, $6.00. I. Manners and Customs. II. Dialect, Proverbs, and Word-Lore. III. Popular Superstitions and Traditions. IV. English Traditions and Foreign Customs. (*Last two styles sold only in sets.*)

John F. Genung. Tennyson's In Memoriam, A Study, cr. 8vo, $1.25.

Johann Wolfgang von Goethe. Faust, Part First, Translated by C. T. Brooks, 16mo, $1.25; Faust, Translated by Bayard Taylor, cr. 8vo, $3.00; 2 vols. royal 8vo, $9.00; 12mo, $4.50; Correspondence with a Child, 12mo, $1.50; Wilhelm Meister, Translated by Carlyle, 2 vols. 12mo, $3.00.

Oliver Goldsmith. The Vicar of Wakefield. *Handy-Volume Edition.* 32mo, $1.25.

Charles George Gordon. Diaries and Letters, 8vo, $2.00.

George Zabriskie Gray. The Children's Crusade, 12mo, $1.50; Husband and Wife, 16mo, $1.00.

Anna Davis Hallowell. James and Lucretia Mott, cr. 8vo, $2.00.

Arthur Sherburne Hardy. But Yet a Woman, 16mo, $1.25.

Bret Harte. Works, 5 vols. cr. 8vo, each $2.00; In the Carquinez Woods, 18mo, $1.00; Flip, and Found at Blazing Star, 18mo, $1.00; On the Frontier, 18mo, $1.00; By Shore and Sedge, 18mo, $1.00; Maruja, 18mo, $1.00; Poems, *Household Edition,* 12mo, $2.00; the same, 12mo, full gilt, $2.50; *Red-Line Edition,* small 4to, $2.50; *Diamond Edition,* $1.00.

Nathaniel Hawthorne. Works, *"Little Classic"* Edition, Illustrated, 25 vols. 18mo, each $1.00; the set $25.00; *New Riverside Edition,* Introductions by G. P. Lathrop, 11 Etchings and Portrait, 12 vols. cr. 8vo, each $2.00; *Wayside Edition,* with Introductions, Etchings, etc., 24 vols. 12mo, $36.00. (*Sold only in sets.*)

John Hay. Pike County Ballads, 12mo, $1.50; Castilian Days, 16mo, $2.00.

Rev. S. E. Herrick. Some Heretics of Yesterday, cr. 8vo, $1.50.

George S. Hillard. Six Months in Italy, 12mo, $2.00.

Oliver Wendell Holmes. Poems, *Household Edition,* 12mo, $2.00; the same, 12mo, full gilt, $2.50; *Illustrated Library Edition,* 8vo, $4.00; *Handy-Volume Edition,* 2 vols. 32mo, $2.50; The Autocrat of the Breakfast-Table, cr. 8vo, $2.00; *Handy-Volume Edition,* 32mo, $1.25; The Professor at the Breakfast-Table, cr. 8vo, $2.00; The Poet at the Breakfast-Table, cr. 8vo, $2.00; Elsie Venner, cr. 8vo, $2.00; The Guardian Angel, cr. 8vo, $2.00; Medical Essays, cr. 8vo, $2.00; Pages from an Old Volume of Life, cr. 8vo, $2.00; John Lothrop Motley, A Memoir, 16mo, $1.50; Illustrated Poems, 8vo, $5.00; A Mortal Antipathy, cr. 8vo.

William D. Howells. Venetian Life, 12mo, $1.50; Italian

Journeys, 12mo, $1.50; Their Wedding Journey, Illustrated, 12mo, $1.50; 18mo, $1.25; Suburban Sketches, Illustrated, 12mo, $1.50; A Chance Acquaintance, Illustrated, 12mo. $1.50; 18mo, $1.25; A Foregone Conclusion, 12mo, $1.50; The Lady of the Aroostook, 12mo, $1.50; The Undiscovered Country, 12mo, $1.50.

Thomas Hughes. Tom Brown's School-Days at Rugby, 16mo, $1.00; Tom Brown at Oxford, 16mo, $1.25; The Manliness of Christ, 16mo, $1.00; paper, 25 cents.

William Morris Hunt. Talks on Art, Series I. and II. 8vo, each $1.00.

Henry James, Jr. A Passionate Pilgrim and other Tales, 12mo, $2.00; Transatlantic Sketches, 12mo, $2.00; Roderick Hudson, 12mo, $2.00; The American, 12mo, $2.00; Watch and Ward, 18mo, $1.25; The Europeans, 12mo, $1.50; Confidence, 12mo, $1.50; The Portrait of a Lady, 12mo, $2.00.

Mrs. Anna Jameson. Writings upon Art Subjects, 10 vols. 18mo, each $1.50.

Sarah Orne Jewett. Deephaven, 18mo, $1.25; Old Friends and New, 18mo, $1.25; Country By-Ways, 18mo, $1.25; Play-Days, Stories for Children, square 16mo, $1.50; The Mate of the Daylight, 18mo, $1.25: A Country Doctor, 16mo, $1.25; A Marsh Island, 16mo, $1.25.

Rossiter Johnson. Little Classics, 18 vols. 18mo, each $1.00; the set, $18.00. 9 vols. square 16mo, $13.50. (*Sold only in sets.*)

Samuel Johnson. Oriental Religions: India, 8vo, $5.00; China, 8vo, $5.00: Persia, 8vo, $5.00; Lectures, Essays, and Sermons, cr. 8vo, $1.75.

Charles C. Jones, Jr. History of Georgia, 2 vols. 8vo, $10.00.

Omar Khayyám. Rubáiyát, *Red-Line Edition*, square 16mo. $1.00; the same, with 56 Illustrations by Vedder, folio, $25.00.

T. Starr King. Christianity and Humanity, with Portrait. 16mo, $2.00; Substance and Show, 16mo, $2.00.

Charles and Mary Lamb. Tales from Shakespeare. *Handy-Volume Edition.* 32mo, $1.25.

Henry Lansdell. Russian Central Asia. 2 vols. $10.00.

Lucy Larcom. Poems, 16mo, $1.25; An Idyl of Work, 16mo, $1.25; Wild Roses of Cape Ann and other Poems, 16mo, $1.25; Breathings of the Better Life, 16mo, $1.25; Poems, *Household Edition*, 12mo, $2.00; the same, 12mo, full gilt, $2.50.

George Parsons Lathrop. A Study of Hawthorne, 18mo, $1.25.

Henry C. Lea. Sacerdotal Celibacy, 8vo, $4.50.

Charles G. Leland. The Gypsies, cr. 8vo, $2.00; Algonquin Legends of New England, cr. 8vo, $2.00.

George Henry Lewes. The Story of Goethe's Life, Portrait, 12mo, $1.50; Problems of Life and Mind, 5 vols. 8vo, $14.00.

J. G. Lockhart. Life of Sir W. Scott, 3 vols. 12mo, $4.50.

Henry Cabot Lodge. Studies in History, cr. 8vo, $1.50.

Henry Wadsworth Longfellow. Poetical Works, *Cambridge Edition*, 4 vols. 12mo, $9.00; Poems, *Octavo Edition*, Portrait and 300 Illustrations, $8.00; *Household Edition*, Portrait, 12mo, $2.00; the same 12mo, full gilt, $2.50; *Red-Line Edition*, Portrait and 12 Illustrations, small 4to, $2.50; *Diamond Edition*, $1.00; *Library Edition*, Portrait and 32 Illustrations, 8vo, $4.00; Christus, *Household Edition*, $2.00; the same, 12mo, full gilt, $2.50; *Diamond Edition*, $1.00; Prose Works, *Cambridge Edition*, 2 vols. 12mo, $4.50; Hyperion, 16mo, $1.50; Kavanagh, 16mo, $1.50; Outre-Mer, 16mo, $1.50; In the Harbor, 16mo, $1.00; Michael Angelo: a Drama, Illustrated, folio, $7.50; Twenty Poems, Illustrated, small 4to, $3.00; Translation of the Divina Commedia of Dante, 1 vol. cr. 8vo, $3.00; 3 vols. royal 8vo, $13.50; cr. 8vo, $6.00; Poets and Poetry of Europe, royal 8vo, $5.00; Poems of Places, 31 vols. each $1.00; the set, $25.00.

James Russell Lowell. Poems, *Red-Line Edition*, Portrait, Illustrated, small 4to, $2.50; *Household Edition*, Portrait, 12mo $2.00; the same, 12mo, full gilt, $2.50; *Library Edition*, Portrait and 32 Illustrations, 8vo, $4.00; *Diamond Edition*, $1.00; Fireside Travels, 12mo, $1.50; Among my Books, Series I. and II. 12mo, each $2.00; My Study Windows, 12mo, $2.00.

Thomas Babington Macaulay. Complete Works, 8 vols. 12mo, $10.00.

Harriet Martineau. Autobiography, New Edition, 2 vols. 12mo, $4.00; Household Education, 18mo, $1.25.

G. W. Melville. In the Lena Delta, Maps and Illustrations, 8vo, $2.50.

Owen Meredith. Poems, *Household Edition*, Illustrated, 12mo, $2.00; the same, 12mo, full gilt, $2.50; *Library Edition*, Portrait and 32 Illustrations, 8vo, $4.00; Lucile, *Red-Line Edition*, 8 Illustrations, small 4to, $2.50; *Diamond Edition*, 8 Illustrations, $1.00.

Olive Thorne Miller. Bird-Ways, 16mo, $1.25.

John Milton. Paradise Lost. *Handy-Volume Edition.* 32mo. $1.25.

S. Weir Mitchell. In War Time, 16mo, $1.25.

J. W. Mollett. Illustrated Dictionary of Words used in Art and Archæology, small 4to, $5.00.

Michael de Montaigne. Complete Works, Portrait, 4 vols. 12mo, $7.50.

William Mountford. Euthanasy, 12mo, $2.00.

T. Mozley. Reminiscences of Oriel College, etc., 2 vols. 16mo. $3.00.

Elisha Mulford. The Nation, 8vo, $2.50; The Republic of God, 8vo, $2.00.

T. T. Munger. On the Threshold, 16mo, $1.00; The Freedom of Faith, 16mo, $1.50; Lamps and Paths, 16mo, $1.00.

J. A. W. Neander. History of the Christian Religion and Church, with Index volume, 6 vols. 8vo, $20.00; Index alone, $3.00.

Joseph Neilson. Memories of Rufus Choate, 8vo, $5.00.

Edmund Noble. The Russian Revolt, 16mo, $1.00.

Charles Eliot Norton. Notes of Travel and Study in Italy, 16mo, $1.25; Translation of Dante's New Life, royal 8vo, $3.00.

G. H. Palmer. Translation of Homer's Odyssey, Books 1–12, 8vo, $2.50.

James Parton. Life of Benjamin Franklin, 2 vols. 8vo, $5.00;

Life of Thomas Jefferson, 8vo, $2.50; Life of Aaron Burr, 2 vols. 8vo, $5.00; Life of Andrew Jackson, 3 vols. 8vo, $7.50; Life of Horace Greeley, 8vo, $2.50; General Butler in New Orleans, 8vo, $2.50; Humorous Poetry of the English Language, 8vo, $2.00; Famous Americans of Recent Times, 8vo, $2.50: Life of Voltaire, 2 vols. 8vo, $6.00; The French Parnassus, 12mo, $2.00; crown 8vo, $3.50; Captains of Industry, 16mo, $1.25.

Blaise Pascal. Thoughts, 12mo, $2.25; Letters, 12mo, $2.25.

Elizabeth Stuart Phelps. The Gates Ajar, 16mo, $1.50; Beyond the Gates, 16mo, $1.25; Men, Women, and Ghosts, 16mo, $1.50; Hedged In, 16mo, $1.50; The Silent Partner, 16mo, $1.50; The Story of Avis, 16mo, $1.50; Sealed Orders, and other Stories, 16mo, $1.50; Friends: A Duet, 16mo, $1.25; Doctor Zay, 16mo, $1.25; Songs of the Silent World, 16mo, gilt top, $1.25; An Old Maid's Paradise, 16mo, paper, .50.

Carl Ploetz. Epitome of Universal History, 12mo, $3.00.

Antonin Lefèvre Pontalis. The Life of John DeWitt, Grand Pensionary of Holland, 2 vols. 8vo, $9.00.

Adelaide A. Procter. Poems, *Diamond Edition*, $1.00; *Red-Line Edition*, small 4to, $2.50.

Sampson Reed. Observations on the Growth of the Mind. New Edition. Portrait. 16mo, $1.00.

C. F. Richardson. Primer of American Literature, 18mo, .30.

Riverside Aldine Series. Each volume, 16mo, $1.00. First edition, $1.50.

1. Marjorie Daw, etc.   By T. B. ALDRICH.
2. My Summer in a Garden.   By C. D. WARNER.
3. Fireside Travels.   By J. R. LOWELL.
4. The Luck of Roaring Camp, etc.   By BRET HARTE.
5, 6. Venetian Life.   2 vols.   By W. D. HOWELLS.
7. Wake Robin.   By JOHN BURROUGHS.
8, 9. The Biglow Papers.   2 vols.   By J. R. LOWELL.

Henry Crabb Robinson. Diary, Reminis., etc. cr. 8vo, $2.50.

John C. Ropes. The First Napoleon, with Maps, cr. 8vo, $2.00.

Josiah Royce. Religious Aspect of Philosophy, 12mo, $2.00.

Edgar Evertson Saltus. Balzac, cr. 8vo, $1.25; The Philosophy of Disenchantment, cr. 8vo, $1.25.

John Godfrey Saxe. Poems, *Red-Line Edition*, Illustrated, small 4to, $2.50; *Diamond Edition*, $1.00; *Household Edition*, 12mo, $2.00; the same, full gilt, 12mo, $2.50.

Sir Walter Scott. Waverley Novels, *Illustrated Library Edition*, 25 vols. 12mo, each $1.00; the set, $25.00; *Globe Edition*, 100 Illustrations, 13 vols. 16mo, $16.25; Tales of a Grandfather, 3 vols. 12mo, $4.50; Poems, *Red-Line Edition*, Illustrated, small 4to, $2.50; *Diamond Edition*, $1.00.

W. H. Seward. Works, 5 vols. 8vo, $15.00; Diplomatic History of the War, 8vo, $3.00.

John Campbell Shairp. Culture and Religion, 16mo, $1.25; Poetic Interpretation of Nature, 16mo, $1.25; Studies in Poetry and Philosophy, 16mo, $1.50; Aspects of Poetry, 16mo, $1.50.

William Shakespeare. Works, edited by R. G. White, *Riverside Edition*, 3 vols. cr. 8vo, $7.50; 6 vols. 8vo, $15.00.

A. P. Sinnett. Esoteric Buddhism, 16mo, $1.25; The Occult World, 16mo, $1.25.

Dr. William Smith. Bible Dictionary, *American Edition*, 4 vols. 8vo, $20.00.

Edmund Clarence Stedman. Poems, *Farringford Edition*, Portrait, 16mo, $2.00; *Household Edition*, Portrait, 12mo, $2.00; full gilt, 12mo, $2.50; Victorian Poets, 12mo, $2.00; Poets of America, 12mo, $2.25. The set, 3 vols., uniform, 12mo, $6.00; Edgar Allan Poe, an Essay, vellum, 18mo, $1.00.

Harriet Beecher Stowe. Novels and Stories, 10 vols. 12mo, uniform, each $1.50; A Dog's Mission, Little Pussy Willow, Queer Little People, illustrated, small 4to, each $1.25; Uncle Tom's Cabin, 100 Illustrations, 8vo, $3.50; *Library Edition*, Illustrated, 12mo, $2.00; *Popular Edition*, 12mo, $1.00.

Jonathan Swift. Works, *Edition de Luxe*, 19 vols. 8vo, the set, $76.00.

T. P. Taswell-Langmead. English Constitutional History. New Edition, revised, 8vo, $7.50.

Bayard Taylor. Poetical Works, *Household Edition*, 12mo, $2.00; full gilt, $2.50; Melodies of Verse, 18mo, vellum, $1.00; Life and Letters, 2 vols. cr. 8vo, $4.00; Dramatic Poems, 12mo,

$2.25; *Household Edition*, 12mo, $2.00; Life and Poetical Works, 6 vols. uniform. Including Life, 2 vols.; Faust, 2 vols.; Poems, 1 vol.; Dramatic Poems, 1 vol. The set, cr. 8vo, $12.00.

Alfred Tennyson. Poems, *Household Edition*, Portrait and Illustrations, 12mo, $2.00; the same, full gilt, 12mo, $2.50; *Illustrated Crown Edition*, 2 vols. 8vo, $5.00; *Library Edition*, Portrait and 60 Illustrations, 8vo, $4.00; *Red-Line Edition*, Portrait and Illustrations, small 4to, $2.50; *Diamond Edition*, $1.00.

Celia Thaxter. Among the Isles of Shoals, 18mo, $1.25; Poems, small 4to, $1.50; Drift-Weed, 18mo, $1.50; Poems for Children, Illustrated, small 4to, $1.50.

Edith M. Thomas. A New Year's Masque and other Poems, 16mo, $1.50.

Joseph P. Thompson. American Comments on European Questions, 8vo, $3.00.

Joseph Thomson. To the Central African Lakes, 2 vols. 12mo, $6.00; Through Masai Land, 8vo, $5.00.

Henry D. Thoreau. Works, 9 vols. 12mo, each $1.50; the set, $13.50.

George Ticknor. History of Spanish Literature, 3 vols. 8vo, $10.00; Life, Letters, and Journals, Portraits, 2 vols. 12mo, $4.00.

Bradford Torrey. Birds in the Bush, 16mo, $1.25.

Sophus Tromholt. Under the Rays of the Aurora Borealis, Illustrated, 2 vols. $7.50.

Charles Dudley Warner. My Summer in a Garden, 16mo, $1.00; *Illustrated Edition*, square 16mo, $1.50; Saunterings, 18mo, $1.25; Back-Log Studies, Illustrated, square 16mo, $1.50; Baddeck, and that Sort of Thing, 18mo, $1.00; My Winter on the Nile, cr. 8vo, $2.00; In the Levant, cr. 8vo, $2.00; Being a Boy, Illustrated, square 16mo, $1.50; In the Wilderness, 18mo, 75 cents; A Roundabout Journey, 12mo, $1.50.

William F. Warren, LL. D. Paradise Found, cr. 8vo, $2.00.

William A. Wheeler. Dictionary of Noted Names of Fiction, 12mo, $2.00.

Edwin P. Whipple. Essays, 6 vols. cr. 8vo, each $1.50.

Richard Grant White. Every-Day English, 12mo, $2.00; Words and their Uses, 12mo, $2.00; England Without and Within, 12mo, $2.00; The Fate of Mansfield Humphreys, 16mo, $1.25; Studies in Shakespeare, 12mo, $1.75.

Mrs. A. D. T. Whitney. Stories, 12 vols. 12mo, each $1.50; Mother Goose for Grown Folks, 12mo, $1.50; Pansies, square 16mo, $1.50; Just How, 16mo, $1.00; Bonnyborough, 12mo, $1.50.

John Greenleaf Whittier. Poems, *Household Edition*, Portrait, 12mo, $2.00; the same, full gilt, 12mo, $2.50; *Cambridge Edition*, Portrait, 3 vols. 12mo, $6.75; *Red-Line Edition*, Portrait, Illustrated, small 4to, $2.50; *Diamond Edition*, $1.00; *Library Edition*, Portrait, 32 Illustrations, 8vo, $4.00; Prose Works, *Cambridge Edition*, 2 vols. 12mo, $4.50; The Bay of Seven Islands, Portrait, 16mo, $1.00; John Woolman's Journal, Introduction by Whittier, $1.50; Child Life in Poetry, selected by Whittier, Illustrated, 12mo, $2.00; Child Life in Prose, 12mo, $2.00; Songs of Three Centuries, selected by Whittier; *Household Edition*, 12mo, $2.00; the same, full gilt, 12mo, $2.50; *Library Edition*, 32 Illustrations, 8vo, $4.00; Text and Verse, 18mo, 75 cents; Poems of Nature, 4to, Illus. $6.00.

Woodrow Wilson. Congressional Government, 16mo, $1.25.

J. A. Wilstach. Translation of Virgil's Works, 2 vols. cr. 8vo, $5.00.

Justin Winsor. Reader's Handbook of American Revolution. 16mo, $1.25.

www.ingramcontent.com/pod-product-compliance
Lightning Source LLC
Chambersburg PA
CBHW020237110726

47898CB00004B/1295